With

Mercy's

Eyes

D. T. Powell

A powerful debut novel, With Mercy's Eyes will open readers' eyes to a new perspective. Compelling, well-written, and gritty, this book will simultaneously challenge its readers and encourage them in their relationship with Christ. Readers who appreciate deep, meaningful fiction will enjoy getting to know the unique and complex characters in this story. Prepare to feel the tug of spiritual growth as the plot unfolds. D. T. Powell is a fresh, much-needed voice in Christian fiction.

- Valerie Howard, Author of the New England Inspirations Series

In With Mercy's Eyes, D. T. Powell addresses a number of challenging subjects, and she treats each one with grace, love, and honesty. There are a number of things in these pages that we wish we could say, if only we could find the right words. D. T. Powell found them, and she shared them with us. Moreover, she shares God's heart. It behooves every Christian to read this book.

- Aubrey Taylor, Author of German-perspective World War Fiction

Handling difficult topics with the right balance of tact and boldness is hard to achieve, but D. T. Powell did so in a way that clearly delivers the truths of the Bible without using its teachings as a justification for judgement or hatred. With Mercy's Eyes is an incredible testament to the righteous character of God. It will encourage you to search the depths of your heart and ask, "Am I truly being His hands and feet? Am I truly viewing others as He views them?" This book will wreck you and leave you with tears in your eyes, but through it, you will learn how to act as His vessel of love and mercy. That is something we need more of in the Christian community.

- Elizabeth Mae Wolfram, Christian Dystopian Author & Publisher

D. T. Powell's profoundly moving contemporary novel, *With Mercy's Eyes,* treads topical and long-neglected spiritual territory with gently confident strides. Readers meet and empathize with a homosexual protagonist experiencing the worst six months of his life; if anything can go wrong, it does. His husband has recently passed away in a car accident, and dire challenges continue piling on him while the narrative approaches a climax surrounding his spiritual fate.

Along this dizzying journey of grief, loss, personal freedom, and faith, Powell poses these crucial questions: Can we overcome religious trauma? Does God care about how Christians treat members of "the World?" Do homosexuals deserve happy endings? Redemption? Love? Lane Harris's tale—weighted by tragedy, pockmarked with pain—beckons faith-based and secular readers to ponder the nature of God's love and His intended design for love between His greatest creations: us... whether romantically, platonically, or otherwise.

- Alyssa Charpentier, Author of *A Maiden's Wish*

Content Warnings

General Content Warnings Include:

Homosexuality, suicide and suicidal thoughts, sexual assault, infant loss, terminal illness, death, domestic violence, depression, mentions of abortion.

These subjects are never taken lightly. Each one is very present in our world today, and far too many people suffer from/because of them. This book portrays individuals who both do and do not hold to a Biblical worldview, and some characters don't handle crises very well.

The purpose of this book is to help Christians better understand how to show love to people living in sexual sin without endorsing lifestyle choices that are contrary to the Word of God.

There is NO sexually explicit content in this book; however, because of the heavy themes and subjects, the author personally recommends this book for readers age 25+.

Chapter-Specific Content Warnings:

Sexual assault (Occurs off-page):
    Chapter 7

Infant death and mentions of infant death (Occur off-page, but results are seen on-page):
    Chapters 28, 42

Attempted suicide and mentions of attempted suicide (Occur on-page):
    Chapters 28, 42, 46, 60, 70, 74, 85, 86, 127

Suicidal thoughts (Occur on-page):
    Chapters 34, 39, 42, 70, 74, 85, 86

Additional reader resources, such as practical tips and discussion questions are included in the back of this book.

1 John 4:10 (KJV)

Herein is love, not that we loved God, but that he loved us, and sent his Son to be the propitiation for our sins.

For two men named John.

The first, God used to teach me how to go to war.

The second, He used to teach me how to live in peace.

God gives strength
for all things in life.

D.T. Powell

1

St. Philip Hospital, Los Angeles, CA
Tuesday, October 2nd

Lane wished he'd been in the car instead of Stephen. It should've been him unconscious in this hospital bed instead of the man he loved. He gripped Stephen's hand under the double blanket as an ER doctor and two nurses rushed in.

"We've got to take him now, or he won't make it," the doctor said.

This wasn't right—wasn't real.

A woman in scrubs motioned Lane away. "Sir, we need to get your information."

He ignored the woman and ran after the staff as they quickly wheeled Stephen out. "Stephen? Stephen, I'm here. You're going to be okay!"

He followed them to the elevator.

They wouldn't let him in.

He cursed and ran for the stairs.

Two floors up, he caught them.

Halfway down the hall, an "Authorized Personnel Only" sign glared from wide doors, which swung open two seconds later.

Lane sprinted to make it through before the doors shut.

"Sir, you can't go back there." A nurse barred his way, separating him from his husband.

The staff took Stephen down the long, white hall. Distance blurred the label on the room they entered.

"Are you all right?" A man in scrubs tapped his shoulder as the partitioning door clicked closed. "There's a waiting room right over there if you need to sit down." He pointed over Lane's shoulder.

Lane's gaze flicked from the indicated room to the doors that separated him and Stephen.

"Mr. Harris?" The woman from before appeared beside him. She carried a tablet and stylus. "I'm sorry to have to ask, but we need to get these intake forms done." She led him to a private alcove.

He numbly answered questions about Stephen's health and produced an insurance card.

When they were through, he pushed into the waiting room and took the seat farthest from the door.

A man in mint-green scrubs entered, holding a bag of personal effects. "Family for Stephen Parker?"

"Y-yeah. Here."

The man approached and set the bag in Lane's waiting hands. "He's in surgery. Someone will be out to talk with you soon."

"Thanks." It was the right word, but it made his tongue curl. There was nothing to be thankful for.

As the man slipped out, Lane opened the bag.

The sharp stink of asphalt and burnt rubber escaped the tattered pieces of his husband's favorite lime-green dress shirt and khakis.

Slivers of glass sneaked into the bag's crimped corners.

Stephen's watch, its face hopelessly broken, settled into the pool of glass. He'd given his husband this watch for Christmas three years ago, when they were still dating. It wasn't the Rolex Stephen's father wore, but he hadn't cared. He'd proudly worn it to work every day.

Lane found Stephen's phone, tangled in the remains of his pants. They hadn't even pulled it out of his pocket.

It had been brand new two weeks ago. Now the once-pristine silver backing was bowed. The screen protector held the phone's face together, but cracks crisscrossed every bit of it. Even if the phone still worked, it was impossible to use.

Cold metal kissed Lane's hand.

Stephen's ring.

He slipped it onto his right ring finger and clasped both hands together so the matching tungsten bands touched.

Six years wasn't enough time.

He shut the bag and kept it close.

As the minutes crawled, he scrolled through album after album of pictures on his phone: their first date, Stephen's sister Stacey's thirtieth birthday party, the night he and Stephen got engaged, their wedding two months ago...

An hour passed. Then two.

A surgeon stepped into the waiting room. "Lane Harris?"

Lane met him a few feet inside the door.

"Let's take a seat over there." The man gestured to an empty set of chairs near the window.

Others quietly shuffled toward the opposite side of the room, pretending not to pay them any attention.

Lane followed, but every step dragged him down, as if sand filled his shoes.

The surgeon took a seat, but Lane hesitated. He knew what those furrowed brows and tight jaw meant. If he sat, the world would end. He paced between a snack machine and the chair to stall reality until he was ready. But he could never be ready.

To his credit, the surgeon waited.

A boy bought pretzels from the vending machine. The bag's sharp crackle seemed to rip away bits of air as breathing grew impossible.

A newscaster droned about politics on the flatscreen mounted on the opposite wall. His voice picked Lane's nerves, stealing snippets of attention, but not enough to eclipse the doctor's presence.

Finally, he sat.

"I'm sorry, Mr. Harris."

Lane knew what came next. Those soul-crushing words—they would drown him. But there was nothing he could do to stop them.

"We did everything we could, but his injuries were too severe. Your husband is dead."

Kennedy Funeral Home, Huntington Park
Saturday, October 6th

Lane sat in the front row as Stephen's mother, extended family, and friends filed out. Only Stacey remained, sobbing on her knees between two lavish flower arrangements. Stephen's father, as expected, was nowhere to be seen.

A cousin put an arm around Stacey and shepherded her out, leaving Lane alone in the cold chapel.

Silence filled every crevice.

Stephen should be standing beside him. Not laying in that casket.

"Mr. Harris, I'm so sorry to interrupt, but the graveside will begin shortly. Your sister-in-law and her family are waiting for you." Kennedy's director seemed comfortable in his black suit and tie, and compassion warmed his eyes.

Lane slipped both hands into his pockets to fight the chapel's cool air. Stephen's wedding band still hugged his right ring finger.

At the graveside, a mutual friend lauded Stephen's character and accomplishments until everyone dabbed their eyes and Stacey wailed.

Guests filed past Lane and Stacey to shake their hands or offer hugs and condolences one more time before leaving. All except Stephen's mother, who bypassed Lane altogether, laid a hand on her son's casket, and left.

Stacey hugged Lane tightly. "I can't take anything else today." She choked each word. Her heels left a trail of holes in the tended grass as she ran to her car and drove away.

Fall leaves rained onto the canopy, and two dozen empty folding chairs topped a roll of Woodstock grass. Behind him, the coffin waited to be lowered.

Lane touched the lid. Filigreed roses textured its edge.

No more late-night talks over coffee and gas station pizza. No more running lines while Stephen did horrible voices for his scene partners. No more burning Thanksgiving casseroles or watching Stacey's cat

Huddles together.

"I don't want to do this without you." Lane sank to his knees. "You're what got me out of bed these past six years. You promised you wouldn't leave me." He hid his face. "You promised."

2

Studio 73-C, Hollywood
Thursday, January 31st

Lane sat in his gray '17 Versa. Rain spattered his windshield.

Tina said this was a good opportunity. Movies based on bestselling books sometimes promised more press, and press meant opportunities to showcase his talent.

He opened his umbrella and tromped through the wet parking lot to the studio. The guy at the security gate had given him good directions. Inside, he took a seat with over thirty men. Some he recognized, but none of them seemed to notice his arrival.

Signs posted on each wall read, "Please email your resume, headshot, and contact information for yourself and your agent to the address at the top of the provided sides."

Lane did as instructed before reviewing the material for three characters Tina had thought he might be interested in auditioning for. The first was the female lead's boyfriend, the second a police chief, and the third a forensics specialist.

Stacey liked the book this movie was based on, Vic Garrison's *Evident*.

Lane had perused a few chapters, and Garrison seemed a good writer.

Apparently millions of others shared that opinion, because *Evident* had landed on the New York Times' Best Seller list for a solid eighteen months after it had released.

One by one, auditioners took their turn and left.

"Next." A woman wearing a headset motioned Lane forward. "Three minutes. Time starts as soon as you walk on screen." The woman shut the door, attention on the tablet in her hand.

Lane took the ten feet to the green screen in three long strides. "Lane Harris," he said to the camera, "auditioning for Grayson Field, Hunter West, or Terrance Fitzpatrick."

He settled into character for the first set of lines, but each word drained an ounce of will, and by the time he finished the last sentence, he slumped, spent.

Lane didn't bother to use his umbrella on the way back to his car.

Marcelle St. Apartments, Huntington Park
Friday, February 1st

Bills scattered the kitchen table. The hospital's logo decorated some of them. Others were from the funeral home, but most were from credit card companies and other places Stephen had owed money.

Despite being heir apparent to a hefty inheritance, Stephen had never wanted his family's money. Something Stephen's father, the famed Ian Parker, hadn't been happy about.

Takeout containers and stray laundry now filled the one-bedroom apartment, which had always been neat under Stephen's care. Dishes overflowed both sink and dishwasher, and Lane couldn't speculate how old the apples on the counter were.

He retreated to the bedroom and shut the door on the mess. Without bothering to move the unfolded laundry at the end of the bed, he pulled musty covers over his head.

His phone, still tucked in his pocket, buzzed.

A text from Tina. Second audition for Evident this afternoon, 4 p.m. Be there.

It was 2:30 already, and getting to the studio in the middle of the day would take at least an hour.

He stretched wrinkles from a semi-clean shirt and dark pants, dressed, and left.

Studio 73-C

Lane pulled into the parking lot at 3:55 and rushed to the door. At least it wasn't raining today. He stopped, took a steadying breath, and stepped inside.

The same woman from yesterday motioned him directly into the recording area.

"Lane Harris?" Two men and two women met him near the green screen. "I'm Jack Gibson, director. This is Russell Menendez, our executive producer, and Ashleigh Donohugh, casting director."

The second woman, visibly pregnant, whispered to Gibson before disappearing into the cast restroom.

"I suppose she'll introduce herself when she gets back." Gibson handed Lane a single paper. "Look this over and start when you're ready."

Lane perused the partial scene—a retirement party for an aging detective. Seemed straightforward. He kept the page in hand.

The pregnant woman returned as he assumed the role of Matt Barnes, one of the party attendees. Each line reminded him of a similar party Stephen had organized for one of their co-workers, before Lane left office work to pursue acting.

"Can you brighten it up? This isn't a funeral," Gibson said halfway through the section.

The pregnant woman tapped Gibson's shoulder and whispered to him again.

"Never mind. Go ahead." Gibson waved him on.

Lane finished the partial scene.

Gibson, Menendez, and Donohugh passed notes, scribbled comments, and offered quiet input. When they finished, Gibson gave the pregnant woman a nod.

She approached Lane and offered him a hand. "Vic. Nice to meet you, Mr. Harris." A gold band hung from a matching chain around her neck.

"Lane, please."

"On behalf of everyone, I'd like to offer you Detective Barnes' role—male lead. We'll talk details with your agent, but if you want the part, it's yours."

"Thank you, Vic. Wait...Vic? As in Vic Garrison?"

"That's me." She smiled, but sadness tinged it. "The minute Jack played your first audition video, I knew I wanted you to be Barnes. They don't let me make a lot of decisions, but I insisted on this one. Ashleigh agreed with me. I saw you in Jim Renfrow's last movie. Glad you came."

"Thank you. I'll talk with Tina the second I get home. I'm sure you'll hear from her tonight."

His agent was nothing if not persistent. She'd be thrilled to hear he'd finally landed a part—and a good one, at that.

Marcelle St. Apartments

The moment after he texted Stacey about his casting, Lane's phone rang.

"You got a part? What movie is it? Tell me, tell me, tell me!"

"Evident."

"As in the Vic Garrison novel? I loved that book! What part did you get?"

"Detective Barnes."

"That's like the best part in the entire story. That's so amazing! We've got to go celebrate. Benny's tomorrow?" Stacey's enthusiasm rushed through the receiver.

He wished he could share it, but all he felt right now was the same empty numbness that had filled him since Stephen's death.

"Sure."

3

Lane kept his script open on his phone, even though he'd memorized today's scenes three or four days before. Never hurt to have a backup ready.

Monica Henderson, playing Hannah Stanton, the other lead, flipped through her lines. "Start at 34."

Lane did as instructed, but his voice died near the end of each sentence as he remembered the last time he'd run lines with Stephen.

Monica performed flawlessly, but her eyes kept darting to a couple guys adjusting lights under Gibson's direction. A handful of other cast members waited to be sent on camera. "If they're going to shoot minor characters this morning, why do we have to be here? I have other things to do, ya know." She huffed. One hand sneaked into a pocket, and her eyes darted to Gibson and the lighting guys again. Her hand came out of her pocket empty. "If anyone asks, I'm in the bathroom." She stalked off.

A few minutes later she returned, stopping less than two feet from

Lane. A faint whiff of something sharp clung to her hair. Makeup must have used too much hairspray.

Gibson still hadn't called them for their first scene.

"What is taking so long?" Monica growled. "I can't stand around in these heels anymore." She shifted her weight to one foot, then the other. "If I ever meet that costume designer again, I'll wring his pimpled neck." She pulled off her shoes and slung them three feet into the corner. One heel pegged a trash can, which thunked onto its side. Balled paper and empty coffee cups spilled across the floor, drawing a scowl from the maintenance guy who'd just finished cleaning up a broken coffee mug.

Lane gave him an apologetic look. "Hazard of the business," he told Monica.

"Easy for you to say. You get a comfy pair of pants and a nice jacket that doesn't itch. Not to mention the shoes. I'd *kill* for those." Monica eyed his tactical boots as she straightened her pencil skirt and button-up. "This shirt must be infested with bedbugs." She clawed her neck, leaving wide, red streaks.

"Get wardrobe to bring another one."

Monica snorted. "Haven't seen them since we got here." She scratched her wrist and cursed.

Lane flagged one of the crew.

The young man hurried over. "Can I help—"

Monica flung the shirt at the kid. "Get it away!" Red splotches covered her arms and neck, and she shivered in her cami. With manicured fingers, she pulled her arms close.

"Here." Lane donated his jacket.

Monica immediately pulled it on but kept scratching until the set medic arrived.

"Are you allergic to any laundry detergents?" The medic took Monica's vitals.

"No. Just make it stop already!"

"Here's an antihistamine, and this should alleviate any discomfort." The medic squeezed hydrocortisone cream on two fingers and spread it over the splotches decorating her forearms and neck.

When he tried to push the borrowed jacket sleeves above her elbows, Monica ripped her arm away. "Leave it," she snapped.

Gibson trotted over. "Everyone okay?"

"Miss Henderson may be allergic to the laundry detergent," said the medic. "Wardrobe should switch varieties."

Gibson sent a quick text—probably to the costume department. "I'm sorry, Henderson. We'll have to start your scenes in a day or two, when those spots fade."

Monica grumbled and stormed away, still scratching.

Lane stood to go.

"Oh, not you. We've got shots we can do without her. Phil, we're doing 67."

A middle-aged man with a small whiteboard gave Gibson a thumbs-up and scrawled the number with a black Expo.

"Let's see if Vic made a good choice with you," said Gibson.

Baker Memorial Park, Huntington Park
Friday, February 8th

Lane walked beside Stacey, who had her cat Huddles on a leash and harness.

"My boss got fired yesterday," she said. "Nobody knows why. Just—poof—gone."

"Henry? He's been there since...I don't know when."

"The way he told it, he helped open the place." Stacey steered Huddles away from a patch of grass he wanted to gnaw.

"I remember him stopping by everyone's cubicles and telling stories. He had some crazy ones," Lane said.

"Like the snowman somebody put in his cubicle—in August? Like, where'd they even get the snow?"

"Yeah. I remember when he told us the whole ordeal about the microwave in the break room exploding," said Lane. "I wonder what he's doing now. He was old enough to retire soon."

"Maybe he's working on cars in his shed or learning to rock climb, or something else cool." Stacey picked up Huddles when the tubby cat sat and refused to walk any farther. "No telling with Henry. Looks like Huddles wants to get home. He hates these early morning walks." She tapped the cat's nose. "But the vet says you need to lose weight, silly kitty." To Lane she said, "See you Sunday?"

"Sunday."

Lane walked back to the parking lot with Stacey and a glowering Huddles.

UR World Fitness, Huntington Park
Sunday, February 10th

Lane and Stacey ran on side-by-side treadmills.

"I'm beating you," she teased.

"You might be faster, but I can do this all day." He tried to match her tone, but the effort fell flat.

"Whatever."

They stopped when Stacey reached five miles—before Lane hit four. Then they headed for the leg area.

Stacey whispered to Lane about other gym members as he did a few reps on one machine. "She's so into that guy at the chin-up bar. She won't quit talking to him."

Lane followed Stacey's clandestine glances. A young woman, no older than twenty, chattered to a man five or six years older than her as he pulled himself up to the bar a few more times than necessary. "Seems mutual."

"Still the hopeless romantic." Stacey knocked his shoulder.

"Hey, people should be happy."

"Yeah, they should." Stacey smiled as the pair left the gym together.

She hadn't smiled much since the accident. Neither had he. How could he be happy when the person who brought him the most joy was gone?

On set
Monday, February 11th

Lane took another bite of chicken. Whoever picked the caterer chose well.

At his table sat three other men and one woman, all cast members.

"Guess who's back?" Monica sang as she slid into the seat beside

Lane and plopped a full plate on the table. "Talk about a boring five days. Stupid allergies."

"I thought you told the medic you weren't allergic," he said.

She stabbed her chicken. "Well, I guess I was wrong." Annoyance edged her tone. "Is the interrogation over?"

"Sorry. I didn't mean to—"

Monica waved him silent. "Whatever. I must've reread that script a hundred times while I was out." Monica cocked a lip in disgust. "I'm surprised there isn't any of that religious garbage in this movie."

"Vic's religious?" Lane found Vic Garrison several tables away, eating with Gibson and Menendez. Vic's plate held a handful of pretzels and half an orange. A little girl—maybe five years old—sat beside Vic as the woman monitored the girl's stack of Goldfish and green apple slices. The child's skin and hair were a few shades darker than her mother's.

"Very." Monica dabbed her lipsticked mouth with a napkin. "You've never read her books?"

Lane shook his head.

"I have." Monica looked exasperated. "The Hannah Stanton set was fine, but after that she dropped off the publishing scene—wrote a strange one-off fantasy novel, then disappeared into the religious market. Nobody heard of her again until this movie. You haven't heard anything about her?" Monica rolled her eyes. "She prays over her food. Who does that anymore?"

"Why does it matter?" Lane said. "If it makes her feel better, let her."

Monica's bitter laugh held thick disdain. "Better watch out. If she finds out about you, you'll be gone quicker than Garrison can cover her pious little face."

Lane quirked a brow.

"She's homophobic," Monica said. "People like her always are. Once she discovers you've been involved with other guys, she'll make Gibson fire you. I guarantee it."

The band on Lane's right hand burned. "My personal life isn't your business. Or anyone else's."

"Just warning you." Monica speared a broccoli floret. "I'd stay away from her."

Everyone else at Lane's table conversed with Monica throughout the rest of the meal.

Lane didn't finish his food.

Religious people—especially Christians—shunned him. If what Monica said was true, and Vic was religious, why had she chosen him? She seemed intelligent, informed. She had to know about him.

Stephen's death had made local news, and Lane's name and face had come up dozens of times during TV spots. Not to mention the ensuing social media frenzy. Stephen's family garnered more attention for Lane than anything else ever had, and their son's death had prompted a flood of posts.

Tina had been invaluable during those horrific weeks just after the accident. She kept her eye on social media, told him which places to avoid, and ensured no one bothered him for interviews. She'd even intercepted paparazzi.

Thankfully, the tabloids had since found other victims.

Vic had to be blind and deaf not to know who he was. If she was as proactive as Monica made her out to be, he'd have to watch his step around her. That, or risk losing the only source of income he'd had in six months. He'd lost too much already. He couldn't lose his livelihood too.

4

Benny's Café

Wednesday, February 13th

Lane stepped up to the counter.

"Mr. Harris." The cashier brightened.

"Hey, Vince. Good to see you back from Michigan."

"Yeah. It's been a minute since I saw ya last."

Lane nodded.

"The usual?"

"No, thanks. One double espresso."

"Comin' up." Vince gave Lane his total.

As Vince made his coffee, Lane paid with his phone.

"Enjoy." Vince handed over the espresso.

"Thanks." Lane sat at a two-person table near the front window.

The bell on the door jingled, and Vic Garrison walked in, holding her daughter's hand. She got in line with half a dozen people. More piled in behind her as the morning rush started in earnest. Her daughter stood quietly, watching people sitting at tables, texting, or talking. The instant she noticed Lane, she grinned and tugged her mother's hand.

Lane ducked, face to the window. Too late.

Vic got coffee and a bagel and approached Lane's table. "I didn't know you came to Benny's. You waiting for someone?"

He wanted to say yes. Maybe she'd leave if he did. "No." The word slipped out.

"All right if we sit with you?"

He could tell her no, but how would it look for him to turn away a pregnant woman and a little kid? Seating was filling up fast this morning. "Sure."

Vic sat and hauled her daughter onto her limited lap. She gave half the bagel to the girl and supplied a juice box from a small backpack.

"I used to come here every morning when I worked downtown—before I started acting." Lane scrolled through his unread emails. Why was she talking to him?

"You're in Mommy's movie." The girl took a small bite of bagel and sipped her juice.

"Yes, I am." The child's simplicity made Lane wish he could wind the clock back a couple decades.

"You're nice," she said.

"Thank you." If she knew he'd wanted to avoid them, she wouldn't have said that. "I'm Lane."

"Like a street?"

Lane smiled despite himself. "Yes."

"Hi, Mr. Lane, I'm Sophie." She wore a serious expression as she brushed bagel crumbs on a napkin and held out her hand for him to shake.

Lane took it, hoping Vic wouldn't ask about Stephen's ring, now prominently displayed. He quickly gave Sophie's hand a gentle shake and pulled away.

"Are we going to Papa and Nana's?" Sophie said to Vic.

"Soon, sweetie." Vic kissed Sophie's head and held her as the girl ate. Vic's coffee sat on the table beside her untouched bagel half.

"How'd shooting go yesterday?" Vic said. "I would have been there, but I had an appointment."

"Fine. Monica's still complaining, Gibson still makes us run every scene five times, and that sticky side door still won't open, but the food's great, and we get paid on time."

"That door hasn't been right since Jack ran a light stand into it a couple months ago. I told him to let the light crew move it, but you know Jack. The door's not really that hard to get open. You just have to push down on the crash bar at just the right angle as you're going out, and make sure to click it shut when you're outside, or it'll stay open."

"I'll have to remember that."

Vic sipped her coffee. "I miss caffeine. Decaf isn't the same."

"I'd never make it without espresso." Lane held up his cup.

"I'm getting used to it, but those first few weeks were rough." She tucked the gold band and chain she always wore into her shirt. "There's a Valentine's party on set tomorrow. If you'd like to bring anyone, you can."

"Thanks, but"—Lane fingered Stephen's ring—"I don't have anyone to take to parties."

Vic hugged Sophie closer. "Well, we unattached few will have to make it through on our own, won't we?" She smiled, but joy's spark didn't light her eyes. "All right, sweetie." She eased Sophie down. "Let's get you to Nana and Papa's." Vic shouldered the backpack and said to Lane, "Good to see you again."

Lane nodded, numb. Last year, he and Stephen spent Valentine's Day with the wedding planner. This year...he'd spend it alone.

5

Marcelle St. Apartments
Wednesday, February 13th

On his laptop at the kitchen table, Lane totaled the balance of every bill he owed. The hospital had given him a payment plan, but the minimum installment would eat too much of his check. He'd have to tell them he wasn't able to pay.

The bigger problem was the credit card debt. Stephen's spending habits hadn't adjusted to his new living situation, so their bills had skyrocketed.

Lane had talked with Stephen about trying for a debt settlement program or something similar that would allow them to get out from under the thousands they owed, but they'd never gotten around to making a decision. Just having those conversations had strained their relationship, so they'd avoided it whenever possible.

Stacey had offered to help, but her budget was tighter than his since she'd broken up with Frank. Lane wouldn't ask her to sacrifice what little she had for his sake.

He shut the laptop.

This apartment had been home for almost six years. Stephen had even added Lane's name to the lease shortly after they started dating.

A selection of Stephen's baseball collectibles decorated the entryway wall. Cards, two gloves, a jersey, and a bat hung in display cases. Spotlights shone on them, catching every detail. Each piece was worth at least two hundred dollars—most more. Not a lot compared to some, but enough to cover a bill, or part of one.

Lane plopped on the couch, remote in hand, but his finger paused over the power button. Stephen's collection seemed to stare at him, as if they had heard him consider selling them. Was that what Stephen would have wanted?

An old argument surfaced—from the day before the accident.

Stephen had told his parents once again that if they couldn't support his marriage, he didn't want their money. With mounting debt, Lane had suggested a compromise: a temporary loan. But Stephen had insisted he wanted nothing to do with bigots.

Lane understood. Taking money, even temporarily, from people who refused to look him in the eye or address him by name was degrading. But the other solution, talking down creditors, was just as humiliating.

If only that hadn't been their last in-depth conversation. He and Stephen had been on good terms the morning afterward. But what he wouldn't give to take back that argument. Maybe Stephen would have been thinking more clearly, have seen the other car coming, gotten out of the way in time.

Lane tossed the remote on the coffee table and retreated to the bedroom. Stephen's side of the bed was empty. Waiting, as if he might come home any moment.

But he couldn't come home. Never again.

11:30 became midnight.

He needed to be on set by 6 a.m. for makeup, and he had to hit the gym before that.

At 12:15 he crawled into bed, beginning his first Valentine's Day alone.

URWorld Fitness
Thursday, February 14th

Lane scanned his membership card at the unmanned desk. A sign propped by the check-in station said, "Cleaning bathrooms. Back in 20."

This early, it was Lane and two guys at the weights. He dropped his duffel in the locker room, stretched, and took a warm-up jog on the treadmill.

The large calendar clock on the opposite wall declared February 14th, 4:21 a.m. He should be at home, with Stephen, not alone at the gym. His husband had come here with him a few times, but he'd never liked it. The last time Lane had tried to bring him, Stephen had chuckled and said, "I'd rather watch baseball than train for it."

If he'd been in better shape, he might have made it out of surgery—not sustained as many injuries in the crash.

No. If anyone was liable, it was the drug addict who'd hit him. The guy had been so high, he hadn't even known the car had stopped.

Before Lane finished his jog, the guys at the weights left.

As he did bench press reps, 250 pounds seemed heavier—a result of deviating from his meal schedule. He had to restabilize his diet.

Done, he showered, tossed his duffel in the trunk, and left.

On set

Lane and Monica stood in front of the green screen and leaned against lime, cloth-covered blocks that would become alley walls in post. They would shoot the rest of the alley scenes later, on site, with stunt guys ready to jump in.

He leaned in for the first kiss the script called for.

The eager spark in Monica's eyes stopped him.

What was he doing?

Lane's gut curdled, and the urge to throw up hammered his throat. He couldn't kiss someone else—not even like this.

Cast and crew members had brought significant others today, and a dozen extra people fought to watch the shoot until Gibson shooed them away. Most circled the refreshment tables, grabbing coffee, doughnuts, or fresh fruit.

"I'm sorry, I need a minute." Lane downed half a bottle of water, trying to flush the bite of stomach acid off his tongue.

"No. I like it," Gibson said. "Builds tension. Good thinking, Harris. That's a keeper."

Monica winked at Lane. Once they were off screen, she whispered, "Wanna sit with me at the party later? I didn't have anyone to bring."

Lane had met Stephen at a work party like the one today. Maybe this would be a good way to remember him, going with another lonely single. The thought of sitting at home alone again tonight was overwhelming. Monica was far from his type, but she already knew that. "Sure."

Monica wore sultry triumph as she gave Lane a peck on the cheek and joined the gawkers at the refreshment tables. A few pointed and whispered, and one college-age girl shot Monica a look of jealousy that could have melted stone.

Stacey quietly entered the studio, breaking up the group of oglers. Lane motioned her over just as Vic returned from a brief conversation with Gibson.

"Who's this?" Vic brightened. "I thought you weren't bringing anyone today."

"Vic, this is Stacey, my sister-in-law. Stacey, meet Vic Garrison."

Stacey's eyes glowed as if she'd just seen the sun for the first time. "Y-you're V-Vic Garrison? This is amazing!" Stacey took Vic's offered hand and, instead of shaking it, held it in awe. "W-when are you due—if that's okay to ask?"

"June 12th, but this one might come sooner than that, I think," Vic said.

Stacey laughed. "That's so great. Good luck with everything." She glanced at Lane. "When he told me I could come meet you, I almost fainted."

Vic smiled. But just like at the coffee shop, something kept it from reaching her eyes. "We can talk over here, away from the crew. Are you staying for the Valentine's Day party a little later?" She slipped her hand free of Stacey's grip and ushered her toward the refreshments.

"No, I have to get back to work. Wish I could stay, though."

"Harris, you're up. We're doing 41," Gibson said.

As Vic talked with Stacey, Lane followed two other cast members on camera.

6

Ten Years Ago

North Kingsville University, Fresno, CA
Wednesday, October 28th

Leigh trudged back to her dorm room. Classes today had been brutal. She had two big assignments due at the start of the week, and she'd started the one for her writing class...yesterday. She'd make the deadline even if she had to write all night. But the physical science project would probably be a couple days late. At least it wasn't a significant part of her grade. She kicked a pebble off the sidewalk. It rocketed into the street with a rhythmic clack.

"Victoria." One of her professors nodded as he passed her.

She disguised a grimace and gave him a vaguely polite nod before he headed for the parking garage. He was the only one who refused to call her by her middle name, and it irked her every time he did it. His other go-to was "Miss Ellis," which was no better.

She passed a group of three guys and two girls. Each carried an open beer, and they all laughed as they took turns telling lewd jokes about classmates. One girl, with deep brown skin, no makeup, and short hair tightly curled atop her head, glanced Leigh's way and gave her an approving grin. Nakasha. She remembered thinking it was a pretty name. Didn't hurt that the other girl was just the right balance of sarcastic and sweet. Or that her wide nose wrinkled just a little when she smiled.

Leigh had never asked another girl out before. Maybe she'd muster the courage one day. But Trev took up way too much time to even think about shopping around.

If only she could go to a party or hang out with friends and unwind. But if she messed this up—failed a class—she'd be the one paying for it. Her bank balance hovered frighteningly near zero, and her part-time job wasn't doing much to help.

A black Nissan Altima pulled alongside Leigh. A booming subwoofer made the entire vehicle vibrate. The passenger window rolled down.

"Get in here, baby girl."

"I'm almost back to my dorm, Trev. I've got a lot of work to do."

"I said, get in." His tone was sharp.

"Fine." Leigh popped the door handle and slipped inside.

Trev floored it before she'd buckled her seatbelt, and they flew through campus at twenty over. They almost ran down two students and one professor, but no protest was loud enough to cut through the booming stereo. Not even Leigh's when Trev ran a light and almost got them rammed by a bus.

"Let me out," she finally shouted in his ear as they passed the McDonald's just off Garland St. "I'm not getting killed because of you!" She fumbled with her seatbelt as they rolled to a stoplight.

Trev locked the doors.

Leigh unlocked hers, but Trev hit the button a second time, and before she could unlock her door again, they were zipping through the light. If she got out now, she'd wind up in the hospital, missing half her skin. "Where are we going?" she demanded over the stereo.

When Trev didn't reply, she reached for the volume knob.

He swatted her hand away and jerked the Altima down a back road. He stopped in front of a house with chipped paint and a screen door with holes the size of Leigh's hand. Only when he turned off the car did the pounding music stop. The doors were still locked.

"What was that about?" Trev yanked his keys from the ignition. "My girl gets to ride with me. Not touch my stereo. And since when is school more important than me?" He grabbed Leigh's arm and yanked her across the console to steal a kiss.

He tasted like beer—and not even the decent stuff.

"Get off me." She shoved him into the driver's side door.

Trev flung his door open and rounded the car, unlocking her door a half second before yanking it open. His hand wrapped her arm as he pulled her out. "You think you can do me like that?" He crushed her against the car. His breath curled around her face, making her want to gag, but his weight was so much she barely caught another breath. "I'm talkin' to you." He stepped back, but kept her pinned with both hands.

She'd worn a long T-shirt today—and most of the past two weeks—to hide the almost-healed bruises on her ribs and stomach. Before that, it had been her legs, arms, back. He'd hit her in the face too. Just once, though.

"Nothing to say, huh?" Trev let go of one shoulder, ready to hit her.

She had just started gaining credibility with her professors. Her short stories and personal essays were outperforming upperclassmen. If Trev put her in the hospital again, she'd miss another few days of class. Not to mention the bills that would rack up.

It was humiliating.

"No," Leigh shouted in his face. "You're not going to knock me around again, Trev. I'm sick of it!" Though one shoulder was still pinned, she used her free hand to slam a fist into the exposed inside of Trev's elbow.

He recoiled, guarded his arm, and prepared a counterstrike. If he got hold of her now, she might as well count on being out the rest of the semester. That wasn't an option.

She rushed Trev. Her fists would do too little damage, but one solid kick to Trev's groin was all it took. He went down in a sad pile and wailed as Leigh gave him two extra kicks to the back and one knock to the jaw—just to make things more even.

Trev's keys lay in a pothole.

Leigh grabbed them.

She never liked this car. The shriek of metal on metal squealed down the street as Leigh dragged Trev's car key along the side of his pristine Altima before hurling the keys into someone's yard.

A prominent sign outside the fence declared, "Beware of Dog," and the snarls of an enthusiastic Doberman echoed behind Leigh as she ran toward the highway and the Kingsville U campus.

7

At the party, Lane stood with Monica and a group of her friends from the crew. The well-lit tent housed everyone comfortably, including the Craft Services crew serving everyone from a line of well-laden tables on the other side of the tent. Monica showered her friends with gossip. Vic sat in a folding chair outside the crowd's buzz, sipping a ginger ale. No one approached her. The din of conversation, people eating, and chairs creaking almost drowned Lane's thoughts. Stephen would have jumped right into a gathering like this. He was always good at talking with strangers, making friends.

As the conversation drifted, Lane wandered toward Vic. She had pulled out that ring again and slipped it on next to her wedding set. She'd never mentioned a husband.

"You're with me tonight." Monica snagged his arm. "Leave Garrison to her dull self." She hauled Lane back to her friends and pulled him into their group for selfies before sneaking a beer out of her purse.

She popped the tab, which instantly summoned Gibson.

"No alcohol or drugs on my set, Henderson. Do I have to get out your contract?" Gibson scowled until Monica tossed the beer—but not before taking one long swig.

"Garrison probably pointed me out." She sneered in Vic's direction. "Wanna get a real drink?" Monica draped an arm around Lane's waist. "This party's dead. I know a great bar a few streets over."

Why not? He needed to relax. "Sounds good."

A few other cast and crew crowded after them.

Grand Ferdinand Apartments, Hollywood

Lane stumbled into Monica's apartment and leaned against the entry wall. Everything canted left—even the ceiling. Three or four drinks shouldn't have done this to him.

Monica's hands roamed his shoulders and back as she jerked him toward her. She was stronger than she looked. Or it could have been the five shots of whiskey and three margaritas she'd had.

He brushed her hands away. His arms were so heavy. "W-wait—"

Monica's lips crushed his. Her fingers found Stephen's ring and tugged it off. The tungsten band clanked to the floor.

Lane wanted to be furious, but even Monica's desecration of something so beloved couldn't jerk him from the haze. She unfastened his button-up and tossed it in the corner by the door. Her fingers tangled in a fistful of T-shirt, and she pulled him further into the dim apartment.

He tried to push her away, but his efforts had no effect as she tugged his undershirt off.

The low light seemed to embolden her, and she grabbed his waist.

He tried again to stop her. His limbs wouldn't cooperate. "No—"

She smothered the protest with another hard kiss as she unfastened his belt.

Friday, February 15th

Every blink stabbed Lane's head like an ice pick.

Something was wrong. This wasn't his ceiling—or his bed.

A light cinnamon scent tinted the flowery comforter, but it couldn't disguise that distinct, lingering musk—evidence that the snippets of memory from earlier were real.

The digital clock on the opposite wall read 1:49 a.m.

Monica still slept on the other side of the bed, bare back and shoulders toward him.

Lane shoveled off the covers, found his clothes, and yanked them on. He staggered into the living room, head pounding. It took too long to reach the front door. He left his button-up in the corner.

In the hall, he pushed past two guys and into the empty elevator. On the way to the ground floor, he opened the Uber app.

8

Lane's head still pounded as he muddled through his lines on screen...for the sixth time.

"No, no, no!" Gibson clasped his hands and leaned forward in the director's chair. "It's not right. Take a break, Harris. Let's set up for 12. Get Henderson over here."

Lane took his chair and moved farther from the lights—and Gibson's too-loud baritone.

Gibson's assistant bustled in. "Monica's still with Makeup."

"When did she get here? Half an hour ago?" Gibson shook his head. "Scratch 12. Set up 24. You," he pointed to another cast member, "get over here." Gibson muttered about irresponsibility until the crew finished setting up the new scene.

By take three, Monica strolled in, hooked Lane's collar, and stole a kiss. Lane turned away, but she didn't let go.

"Don't pretend you didn't want that," Monica said. "Quit sitting by yourself and moping, or you'll turn into Garrison. The world won't wait for you, Laney."

"Don't call me that."

Monica whispered in his ear, "Let's get drinks again soon."

"Henderson, get moving!" Gibson waved Monica to his chair. "You should have been on set three hours ago."

Even after Monica let go of his collar, Lane wanted to vomit.

"Water?" Vic handed him a full bottle, a pack of crackers, and one of Sophie's juice boxes. "I know a hangover when I see one." She snagged Monica's chair and set it beside Lane's. "What happened to your other ring? I thought you had a matching pair." She pointed to his naked right hand.

"Must've left it at home." The cold clank of tungsten on Monica's floor sparked in his memory. It was still in her apartment. The morning's coffee almost came up.

"Hello." Sophie waved up at Lane, yawned, and rubbed her eyes. "I'm tired."

"Me too." Lane rubbed his throbbing forehead.

Vic leaned forward to pick up her daughter, but the chair design made it impossible to navigate around her pregnant belly. Lane hoisted the little girl into his arms, and Vic mouthed "Thank you," as her daughter snuggled into Lane's shoulder and dozed off.

One-handed, Lane opened the water and sipped until half of it was gone, then downed two crackers. His stomach roiled, then settled.

"Ever thought about having kids?" Vic watched Monica's scene as Gibson critiqued every take.

That dream had died with Stephen. Lane's vision blurred.

"I didn't mean to bring up anything upsetting. I'm sorry."

"It's all right. I...drank too much last night, and the lights make my eyes water." He brushed his eyes clear. "I considered kids once, but those days are gone for me."

"You never know."

Vic was right about one thing: life was unpredictable.

Pieces of last night haunted him—the many times he tried to stop Monica, only for his own body to betray him. The awful sense of helplessness lingered. He flexed his free hand, making sure every joint bent on command. At least the room wasn't swimming like it had last night.

Why had he been stupid enough to set his last drink down and turn his back?

Lane held on to Sophie, as if she could salve the raw ache inside him.

9

Ten Years Ago

North Kingsville University, Fresno, CA
Friday, December 18th

Leigh threw the empty Clearblue box across her dorm room, cursing as it landed on her roommate's pastel pink pillowcase. She'd hoped last month's missed period was because of stress. Another line of curses longer than the DMV queue spilled from her.

It was Trev's. No mistake about that.

With all her classwork, she hadn't had time to be with anyone else since they'd broken up, and Trev had always insisted they be exclusive.

She couldn't deal with this right now. Just two days ago, she'd accepted a position with the college paper. Journalism wasn't her passion, but it was a writing job that paid. It might as well have been gold.

She dropped the pregnancy test on the carpet and ground it to pieces under her shoe. The family planning clinic down the street would be open all weekend. She'd go first thing in the morning.

Trev would not upend her life.

Caring Hands Women's Center
Sunday, December 20th

Leigh sat in the lobby, waiting for her name to be called.

She'd come in yesterday, but there weren't any openings for walk-ins until late, and she had a shift at her other job, so she left.

Today there were far fewer women waiting to be seen. One girl looked no older than fifteen, and she bounced one leg the entire time she waited. Another woman was thin-faced and wrinkled. She wore five necklaces, all displaying religious symbols from differing faiths. She leaned into her chair, feet spread, arms crossed, as if being here meant nothing more than waiting on a load of clothes at the laundromat. Her eyes were dull, numb.

"Heidi." When no one got up, the nurse double-checked her tablet. "Sloan. Heidi Sloan?"

The teenager gripped her legs until patches of sweat darkened her jeans.

"Last call for Heidi Sloan." The nurse sighed. She tapped her tablet and skimmed the screen's contents. "Therese."

The wrinkle-faced woman responded immediately, and the nurse ushered her into the back.

The teenager, Heidi, wiped sweaty palms on her pink tee before getting up. Her legs shook, and she looked ready to throw up any second, but she made it outside and didn't come back in.

Did this girl's parents know she was here?

Probably not.

Would they even care?

Leigh imagined her mother's face if she found out about this. Years of sermons pronouncing "abortion is murder" cascaded through her head. But what did a bunch of middle-aged men know? They'd never faced the impossibility of carrying a deadbeat's baby—raising it, paying for medical bills, food, diapers, spending time with it, and having it depend on them for the next two decades, all while having it remind them every day of a man who ruined their life—a man they hated. Wasn't it worth her sanity, her well-being, to get rid of this baby? No, she wouldn't even call it a baby. It was just a fetus—mindless tissue. It was about as alive as the magazines on the table in front of her.

She flipped through an issue of Cosmo.

A woman Leigh's age came out of the patient area. She walked stiffly and kept one hand over her middle. With the other hand, she caught tears on a battered Kleenex.

Why was she crying? She should be relieved. The burden of responsibility was gone. She was free again. Instead, she looked...empty.

Leigh's hands tangled in her lap, and the burn of tears crept up her throat as the other young woman left the clinic.

Was she sure this was what she wanted?

She was only a couple months along. She didn't have to decide this right now. Why rush things? There was plenty of time to make up her mind.

"Leigh." The nurse mispronounced her name.

"I'm not a flower necklace," Leigh snapped before marching out of the clinic.

10

Lane was first in line when Benny's opened at 6:30.

Ten minutes later, Stacey arrived. Makeup, hair, clothes, shoes—everything was perfect, except for the deep frown. She sat across from him at his two-person corner table.

Lane wrapped his hands around Benny's cheapest cup of coffee.

"Sorry if I woke you with my text last night," she said.

"No problem. What's wrong?"

Stacey's jaw hardened. "I'm telling them I want a raise. They owe me. I work my butt off for them, and what do I get? Two bucks an hour more than the newbies."

"What happened? It used to be a great place to work."

Stacey dabbed angry tears with a napkin. "They replaced Henry with this Gunther guy and hired a new HR lead—Louis. I caught Louis in the break room with Hayley last week. And they weren't exactly talking, if you know what I mean. So guess who gets to lead the team for our Orlando conference this time?"

"Go to corporate."

"I did. They told me it was an internal issue and to take it up with my manager. Gunther's no better! He told Iris, our front-desk lady, that she needed to find another Botox guy. She's fifty-two and the nicest person I know. There's nothing wrong with how she looks. A few wrinkles never hurt anybody. Who says something so insensitive?"

Stacey recounted two dozen more offenses as Lane rationed his coffee.

"I don't know if I can stand it much longer." She drained the last of her latte. "What should I do?"

"It's your life. You need to do whatever's best for you. Take control."

Stacey nodded. "I'll try. Thanks for listening."

"Any time."

As they left, she side-hugged him.

Lane jumped at her touch. The sensation of Monica's hands on him—her nails scraping his skin—roared back. He wanted to push Stacey away.

"Didn't mean to startle you." She let him go. "You okay?"

"Yeah. Just...was thinking about something else." The thought of seeing Monica on Monday filled him with equal parts rage and dread.

"You miss Stephen. I do too... He'd have known how to fix this."

Lane walked Stacey to her car in silence. If Stephen were here, none of this would have happened.

Marcelle St. Apartments

Lane opened the door to his landlady's quiet knock.

"Everything okay? Usually, you've paid last month's rent before now," Mrs. Olsen said.

"I'm sorry. With Stephen's..." Lane couldn't say it. Not again. He'd thought and said it far too often these past four months.

"It's all right, dear." Mrs. Olsen patted his shoulder.

He fought not to swat away the unexpected touch.

"You and Stephen always were my best tenants. I can afford a month or two of letting things slide a little." She covered a harsh cough with her sweater.

"Thank you. I'll get the money as soon as I can." He hated this. Having to subsist on the charity of others.

"No worries." She shuffled toward the elevator.

Lane shut the door and sank onto the couch.

Four months.

It seemed like the accident had happened yesterday.

And now there was Monica. He should have watched his drink more carefully. At her apartment, he should have made her stop, or just left.

How could he have let her do that to him?

Rape—a word he never imagined using, especially about himself. Should he report her? It was his word against hers. By now, any evidence was long gone. She'd have made sure of that. Who would believe a woman assaulted a man twice her size? They would say he'd wanted it. Alcohol and roofies clouded most of the memory, but they didn't hide the truth still etched on his mind and body.

Tracks from Monica's nails traced his back and both thighs, and her warmth still burned his chest and stomach. Her smell invaded his nose, stuck to the roof of his mouth like old grime.

His naked right hand stared at him. He wanted to demand Monica give him his ring. But if he went to her apartment and she was home...he wasn't sure how he'd react.

Nausea rooted him to the couch.

Mrs. Olsen's visit was another sore spot. He and Stephen had never been late with rent. Ever. He had to get the money.

He opened the laptop, and before he could talk himself out of it, he listed Stephen's prized baseball bat, signed by Hector Espino—record holder for most career home runs in the minor leagues. He set the auction to run for three days.

Sunday, February 17th

With no work responsibilities or family to visit, Sunday mornings had always been peaceful. But it was already 8:30, and Lane hadn't eaten breakfast yet. Bits of what happened with Monica kept coming back at unexpected moments, and not even the drone of the TV could cover them.

The scrape of nails on skin. The reek of alcohol and sweat. The taste of lime and salt.

He retreated to the bedroom. From the closet, he pulled Stephen's favorite sweater, a white turtleneck. With such mild winters, he hadn't worn it often. Mostly to Christmas parties.

Lane buried his face in it. Traces of his husband's cologne still clung to the cable knitting, but not even the familiar spiced citrus took away the lingering scent of that night with Monica. He was afraid nothing could.

11

On set

Monday, February 18th

Lane stayed near the coffee dispenser while Monica was on camera with two other actors, who were playing pranks on a fellow detective. At least the schedule kept him away from her for now. They weren't supposed to shoot another scene together until after lunch.

Every time she looked at him with that poisonous smile, he wanted to grab her by the mouth and squeeze until the same horror he'd felt last week bloomed in her eyes. Until she knew what it meant to no longer be in control.

"Everything all right?" Vic grabbed a cup of decaf and dumped in enough creamer to turn it the color of weak hot chocolate.

"Yeah." He took a long sip of his third cup of coffee. "Just tired."

"Well, I understand that. Enjoy your coffee." Vic returned to where she'd left Sophie, near Gibson.

The little girl covered giggles as the actors duct-taped an office chair to the faux ceiling and covered their colleague's desk with peanut butter.

Lane imagined the suspended chair falling just as Monica walked under it.

Tuesday, February 19th

Two hours into shooting, Lane stepped off camera and his phone buzzed. Stacey's name popped onto the screen, so he picked up.

"Lane? I need help. I think...I think I just got fired." Fear edged her voice.

"Where are you?"

"Work. The lobby." Her quick breaths and tight voice said she was on the verge of a panic attack.

"I'll be there as soon as I can. Will you be all right if I hang up?"

"I don't know."

"I'll call you back as soon as I'm in the car."

"Okay."

Lane approached Gibson. "I have to leave. I'll be back as soon as I—"

"Hold on, Harris. This isn't a hotel. You don't get to check out whenever—"

"Family emergency." Lane didn't wait for the director's reply before hurrying out.

The Normandy Building, Huntington Park

Lane rushed into the lobby, phone pressed to his ear. "Where are you?"

"By the vending machines."

Across the lobby, Stacey's bright yellow blouse flashed. She was crammed into the corner beside a glass-faced snack machine that housed chips, pretzels, and a variety of candy bars. A few gray chairs lay scattered in the wide room, and recessed bulbs provided non-intrusive lighting.

"I see you."

Men and women passed him as he beelined for Stacey. Soft, slate-gray carpet muffled his steps.

When he reached her, tears poured down her cheeks. She rifled through her purse. "I know I have tissues somewhere." Her voice caught near the end of her sentence.

Lane stopped her rummaging with a gentle hand and methodically searched the purse until it produced a travel pack of Kleenex.

"Thanks." Stacy covered her smearing mascara and blotched foundation. Her sobs quieted into occasional sniffs.

He pulled a chair over and sat in front of her. "What happened?"

Stacey let out a stuttered breath. "Gunther found out about me complaining to corporate. He got way too close and then said he'd let it go if I convinced him I was sorry." She shuddered. "I told him very clearly to go somewhere a whole lot hotter than Death Valley. He—he told me to get out. I grabbed my purse and ran."

If he was sure he wouldn't get arrested, Lane would have headed for Gunther's office that second and knocked a little respect into the roach of a man. But Stacey needed him. "You stay right here. I'll get my car—"

"No. I don't want to be here another minute." Stacey swiped her eyes once more before standing straight, shoulders back. "I deserve better than this." She shouldered her purse. "Will you walk me to my car? I'll be driving home myself. I'm not coming back."

Lane put his chair back where it belonged.

They left the lobby, eliciting multiple stares.

12

Lane met Stacey at 4:30 a.m.

The only other person here was Chuck, half asleep at the check-in desk.

"I'm not in the mood for running this morning." She stretched on one of the mats set off to the side of the weight machines. "I need to hit something."

He pictured Monica's smug face. "I could use some time with a punching bag too."

An hour later, Lane stepped out of the shower and threw on clothes. He grabbed his nearly empty duffel.

A few minutes passed before Stacey came out of the women's locker room, hair still damp. "Thanks for...being there yesterday." The confidence she'd showcased walking out of the Normandy Building the day before had vanished. "I can't believe I'm not going into the office anymore." Tears sheened her eyes. "I was there for eight years. Eight whole years of my life. Gone. It's surreal."

Lane walked beside her as they headed for the parking lot. "Life changes so fast." He said it in a thick whisper as Stephen's face came to mind.

"Yeah. Yeah, it does," Stacey replied.

Marcelle St. Apartments
Thursday, February 21st

A text from Tina.

Check Lakeisha Anderson. Now.

Lane turned on the TV.

Jim Renfrow sat in the guest's seat as Lakeisha tossed perfectly styled hair over one shoulder. "You had Lane Harris in your last movie."

Renfrow nodded. "Great guy to work with."

"We see that." Lakeisha nodded to several pictures on a big screen behind her and Renfrow.

They were all...of him. And Monica. From the night she assaulted him. The most revealing shots were censored, but just enough to make them acceptable for TV.

"The audience might remember last fall when Stephen Parker—heir apparent to the Parker estate—died tragically, leaving behind grieving husband, Lane Harris. But these pictures make it look like he's already moving on—and with a woman." Lakeisha gave the in-studio audience a conspiratorial look before turning back to Renfrow. "What's your opinion of Harris' recent exploits?" She emphasized the last word, and the audience tittered.

"What he does outside the studio is his business. Any publicity is good publicity. What he did wasn't illegal. Nothing wrong with him having some fun outside work. Publicizing these wouldn't have been my choice, but that's between him and Monica Henderson."

"So you're saying you wouldn't have at least talked to him about it?"

"As long as it didn't interfere with his work, no. It's not my business."

Lane turned off the TV.

On set
Friday, February 22ⁿᵈ

Lane stepped inside.

The crew set up another scene.

As he passed the refreshment tables, two sound guys nodded to him and kept eating.

"Hey, Laney." Monica's manicured hand curled around his arm.

He jerked out of her grip. "I said, don't call me that."

"Don't get salty."

Lane put three feet between them before he could do something he'd regret. "And don't touch me again."

"That's no way to treat your girlfriend." She wagged a finger at him.

"Girlfriend?" Just saying the word was enough to make his neck burn. Now the TV spot last night made more sense. She was using him to get publicity. "I don't want anything to do with you."

"Oh, don't be like that." She reached for his arm again.

He grabbed her wrist. Red nail polish. Just like she'd worn that night.

"Save the drama for the cameras. Gibson wants to do that big scene today—where Hannah declares her love for Detective Barnes."

Lane's coffee crept up his throat. He would have to kiss Monica.

It had been eight days, and still the memory of her stale breath and unrelenting mouth made him want to wrap his fist in her hair and yank.

He let go of her wrist before he acted on the urge.

She walked away as if nothing had happened and snagged a bagel and hot latte.

Lane gagged on the lingering scent of her overdone perfume. She'd been wearing the same one for several weeks. He scrambled to the men's room and made it to a stall. No one came in while he deposited his stomach in the toilet.

Cold water from the faucet soothed his eyes and face and rinsed the acid from his mouth.

He left only to discover someone retching in the adjoining women's room.

Vic came out, face red, hand over her stomach. She sagged against the wall.

"You okay?"

"Good as I can be, I suppose." She smiled, but no spark reached her eyes. "Killer nausea."

"I didn't think morning sickness was common after the first few months." Lane offered her his arm.

She took it. "I thought kids weren't in your plans."

"They were once." Lane guided Vic to a set of chairs. "My...partner and I..." He waited for her to react. She didn't. "We wanted to adopt, but it was never the right time. Then he—" That day at the hospital came crashing in on him.

Vic eased into one chair, and Lane took the other. She laid a gentle hand on his arm, and he tensed but didn't withdraw.

Knowing filled Vic's eyes. "Sometimes life gets tougher than we think we can handle." She pulled a room-temperature ginger ale from her bag under the chair. "Thanks for your help."

He wanted to say "you're welcome," but the words stuck in his throat. He nodded instead.

13

Nine Years Ago

Valley View OB/GYN, West Park, CA
Saturday, March 6th

The ultrasound wand was cold against Leigh's skin.

"There it is." The nurse pointed to the screen. "Two legs, two arms, and a strong heartbeat." She adjusted the wand. "Oh, and look at that little button nose."

Leigh wanted to tell the nurse to shut up. The woman's bubbly conversation had been incessant since Leigh had left the waiting room, and she wanted it to stop. She hadn't come here because she wanted to hear cutesy sentiments about a baby—fetus—she wasn't even sure she'd keep. "So I'm fine?"

"Oh yeah. You're exactly where you should be."

Leigh pushed the ultrasound wand away. "That's all I wanted to know."

"You don't want to know the sex?"

"No." Leigh jerked her top down to cover the baby bump. Gel still coated her middle, and it stuck to the inside of her shirt as she shifted off the table.

"Want it to be a surprise." The nurse nodded. "I get it. My sister did the same thing."

"Will you be quiet for one second already?"

The nurse dropped into a stunned pause before silently wiping off the equipment and putting it back where it belonged. "You're good to go," she finally said. "Door's down the hall to the left." She didn't meet Leigh's eyes.

Without another word to the nurse, Leigh left the OB's office and headed for the bus stop two blocks down the street. By the time she reached the covered benches, the sky was clouding over. It would rain later. Probably.

She sat. Her backpack sagged beside her.

Ten more minutes before the bus stopped here again. Cars whizzed past, heading to jobs, homes, families. They all had people who cared about them, would worry if they never arrived at their destination.

What did she have?

Just her writing classes. And a roommate who was out with her boyfriend all the time and didn't even sleep in their dorm room most nights.

Two voicemails and five missed calls said her mother had tried to call earlier, but Leigh wasn't in the mood for another awkward conversation. Lately, their sporadic talks consisted mostly of a few stuttered sentences interspersed with long stretches of silence. She hadn't mentioned the pregnancy, and as far as she knew, her mother was still none the wiser.

She'd go back to Caring Hands after class Monday. She didn't have a shift that evening, and her article for the paper wasn't due until Wednesday. It was almost done anyway.

A flutter tickled her middle.

Not again. She wouldn't lose her nerve to end this a fourth time.

Another flutter.

No. It had to be done. She had no place in her life for a baby.

Two more flutters, in quick succession, made her breath catch.

This wasn't nerves.

Her hand covered the sensation just in time to feel her baby kick.

Her...baby...

The bus pulled up to the stop, and the doors kicked open.

"Gettin' on?" said the man at the wheel.

Leigh's vision clouded as tears poured down her face. She tried to tell the man she just needed a moment. Then, she'd be aboard. But when she said nothing, the driver shrugged and pulled away.

She buried her face in her backpack.

There would be no more trips to Caring Hands.

14

Lane stepped into camera view. Two feet away stood Monica.

He didn't want to do this.

"You can't kiss her from there." Gibson waved Lane closer. "Go on. We don't have all day."

Monica crossed the distance between them before he could avoid her. She grabbed his hand and pressed close.

He fought not to shove her off him. He had to do this. Last time he'd avoided kissing her, but that wouldn't work again.

Gibson's stare made everything worse.

"Just one little kiss," Monica whispered. "It's not even real."

Bile scratched the back of his throat. The memory of her mouth crushing his left a new gouge.

Monica moved first. She pulled him in—like last time. He could take control, get free of her. Without drugs inhibiting him, he'd overpower her in a moment.

But then he'd have to do this scene one more time, and he couldn't stomach that.

Lane masked his revulsion. The need to break contact flooded every inch of him. He held it back, pushing away the stench of Monica's perfume and that odd burning rubber scent that lingered in her hair again today.

Then it was over.

"Great stuff, Henderson—Harris. Let's get 9 set up." Gibson snagged coffee and a doughnut.

At least he wouldn't have to endure another four takes.

Once out of the crew's way, Lane stopped Monica. "I want my ring back."

"What ring?" Her false innocence made his teeth grind.

"The one you took off," he said, anger barely hidden.

"Oh, that. Not sure where it is."

Lane clenched his jaw so hard it ached.

"I'll let you know if I find it." Monica turned her back and headed for a stack of fresh muffins.

The rest of the day crawled by.

"Meet here at 5 a.m. Monday. We're heading to Franklin Park to shoot," said Gibson before everyone left. "Don't be late." He glared at Monica and Lane. "We're bound to have enough delays as is. This crew isn't waiting because you lot can't pour your coffee on time. If anyone has allergies they haven't disclosed, do it now. We don't need another incident like a couple weeks ago." He pointedly eyed Monica again.

Two cast members trotted to the medics.

"Good night." Gibson disappeared into his office in the back as Lane left and got into his car.

At the stop sign outside the studio complex, Lane adjusted his rearview mirror. The gate guard was squirreled away in his booth, phone to his ear, eyes darting to and from Lane's car.

A break in traffic.

Lane took it.

15

Lane set his protein powder and a bag of apples on the conveyor.

Magazines lined the top of the register, spanning from him to the cashier.

"Fifty-two easy recipes for weight loss."

"Holiday flavors now!"

"Texas oil tycoon turns environmental activist."

"Transform your desk into a Zen garden."

"Billionaire turned archeologist finds ancient pottery in Boston."

"Gibson film leads dating?"

The most revealing of Monica's pictures plastered a tabloid cover. This one showed both of them. It had been censored, but still left little to the imagination.

The man behind Lane stared at his phone, and the woman ahead of him unwrapped gum.

Lane flipped the tabloid over. He reached the front of the line, and no one said anything to him about the magazine.

"I love these apples!" said the cashier as she passed the fruit over the scanner.

Lane nodded. "Yeah. They're great."

"Would you like a bag?"

"No. Thanks." He held his phone to the pin pad and tried to think of anything other than that vile picture.

Franklin Park, Hollywood
Monday, February 25th

Lane finished a scene with two minor characters and gave Monica a wide berth as she and the stunt crew passed. Ordinarily he would have stayed to watch the scene, but being around Monica any longer than necessary made him sick.

He headed for the path running parallel to their shooting location.

Saplings, spaced six feet apart, lined the trail. Kids, adults, and pets stayed clear of the film crew and their designated area.

He passed a taco stand.

"Hey, you wanna try one of these?" The kid running the stand, probably no older than nineteen, waved a fish taco at Lane. "Half off."

Lane backtracked. "No. Thanks."

"Hey, aren't you that guy from those pictures?" The kid grabbed his phone and held it up to compare Lane's face with Monica's photos. "Sweet. On the house, bro." He set the taco in a paper wrapper and handed the whole thing to Lane.

"Really, I don't need—"

"Was it great?" The kid's attention shifted to Monica as she scaled a tree, but only after complaining twice about chipped nails. "Bet it was."

To be polite, Lane accepted the taco. While the boy was still staring at Monica, he slipped away and donated the unsolicited food to one of the film crew, who ate it in three enthusiastic bites.

Monica's scene ended, and as soon as she was off camera, Makeup swarmed her, pulling leaves out of her hair and touching up blush and lipstick.

"Rumor is Garrison's hooking up with one of the producers, and that's why she's gone all the time," Monica said to the woman brushing a tangle from her hair. "Talk about pathetic."

"She's pregnant. Isn't she at doctor appointments?" said another of the makeup crew.

Monica laughed. "You believe that? Who needs that many appointments?"

"Somebody with a high-risk pregnancy," Lane said before thinking better of it.

"You're no fun, Laney." Monica picked a fingernail clean.

"I told you not to call me that."

"Whatever." Monica brushed away the makeup crew and strutted back on camera for her next scene.

One of the women who'd touched up Monica didn't retreat with the rest. "I hate working with her. Get on her bad side, and she is so spiteful. She roughed up one guy pretty bad last year—put him in the hospital for a week. She claimed he was threatening her. Bet she didn't pull it off by herself, though. No way she wrestled a guy twice her size and won."

Unless she'd drugged him too. But Lane opted to say, "You've been on crew for another of her movies?"

"Two." The woman groaned. "And they were crazy. Three or four of the more well-off actors in both casts got robbed. Police never figured out who did it. One guy lost everything—house, bank accounts, car, even a dusty coin collection. Wherever Monica Henderson goes, trouble follows. Hopefully this time there won't be any extra drama."

She must not watch talk shows or read tabloids.

He changed subjects. "You wouldn't know anybody looking for weekend help?"

"There's a place not far from the studio. Simmer. Caters mostly to people like us. Been there a couple times with my girlfriend. Seems nice. They put up a 'Now Hiring' sign last week."

"I'll stop by. Thanks."

Gibson waved at Lane and the makeup woman. "You two chatterboxes done? We've got work to do."

16

Lane slipped into the bar just as it opened. Half a dozen customers trickled in. Most ordered early dinner from the wait staff.

"Never seen you here before." The bartender leaned on the counter. His brown Stetson cocked slightly left, and his gray handlebar mustache twitched.

"Never been here." Lane approached the bar.

"What'll it be?"

"I'm not here to drink. I'd like to speak with the manager about the part-time job opening."

"I'll pretend you didn't say that first bit."

"I'm driving."

"Fair. So why should you get this job?"

"You're the manager."

"For eight years. Me and the owner built this place from a drownin' start-up." The bartender rolled one mustache tip and studied Lane. "You look familiar."

"Two movie castings, plus four TV appearances."

"An actor. That's a plus. Why work here? No one to go home to?"

"My...husband died four months ago. The gig I have won't cover the bills."

"All right. A pretty face can't hurt. I'll see you Saturday, two hours before opening time. Most of my regulars are gonna like you. Watch 'em, though. They get rowdy." He extended a hand. "Lester Williams."

"Lane Harris."

"Good to know ya. Business casual for Saturday."

"Be back then." Lane gave Lester a nod and left.

On set
Thursday, February 28th

Other cast members' cars dotted the small studio parking lot. Everyone was already here. Monica's white Jag, even Vic's minivan sat at the end of the row—still idling. She must have just arrived. Lane would be late if he didn't hurry.

Inside, Makeup and Wardrobe fussed over him for twenty minutes.

"Anyone seen Garrison?" Gibson said.

"Her van's in the parking lot." Lane unbuttoned his sleeves, turning them up. "Hasn't she come in yet?"

Vic's bag wasn't by her chair. Something was wrong.

He hurried out of the studio, one sleeve half-rolled.

The van still idled in its spot, and Vic slumped against the door.

Lane got in through the unlocked passenger door. "Vic?" He tapped her arm. "Victoria?" He held one hand two inches from her face. Shallow breathing—and slow pulse.

She was so still.

Stephen had looked far too much like this when the paramedics had pulled him out of his car. Blood had covered his chest and dripped from a gash on his forehead.

Help had come too late then.

Not this time. Lane called 9-1-1 as the rest of the studio spilled into the parking lot. When EMS arrived, they turned the vehicle off and eased Vic from the van. Within a minute, she was conscious.

"Thank you," she said to the paramedics. "I'm all right now."

"Ma'am, we need to get you to Jenkins Rawling—"

"I'm Dr. Gordon's patient."

The paramedics helped Vic sit up, took her vitals a second time, and didn't mention the hospital again.

"It's been a long few weeks. Sorry to bother you." With the paramedics' help, Vic leaned against her van.

"No problem. Don't overexert yourself." EMS took Vic's information, packed into the ambulance, and left.

Gibson marched over. "Go home, Garrison. Better yet, Harris will drive you."

"I could use the rest." She trudged to the passenger door, and Lane helped her in.

Down the street from the studio, they stopped at a light.

"You look awful." Lane adjusted the vents to give her more AC.

"Thanks." Vic chuckled.

"Not what I meant."

"I'll be okay, but you look spooked."

"Difficult memories."

"I'm sorry. Thanks for taking me home. You didn't have to. I could have called a ride."

"No reason to leave your van," Lane said.

Vic directed Lane down the highway and through a few neighborhoods. He pulled into the driveway in front of a modest suburban house. A kids' swing set occupied the front yard, and a pink tricycle sat on the porch.

Lane opened Vic's door and followed her up the front steps. "Can anyone stay with you for a few hours?"

"My neighbor, Ann. I texted her on the way here. She'll be over soon."

"Where's Sophie?"

"With my parents."

"Good. Get some rest." Lane sat on the porch in a chair beside the tricycle until Ann arrived.

Minutes later, his Uber pulled up. He craned to watch Vic's front door until the driver turned onto a side street, headed back to the studio.

17

Simmer Lounge

Saturday, March 2ⁿᵈ

Eleven o'clock passed, and Lane still hadn't gotten used to the bar's table assignment system. Or ordering. Every few minutes, his tablet blipped to let him know he'd done something incorrectly. He hadn't been this inept since middle school.

"Can you cover for a sec?" Alisha held up her phone. "Babysitter's calling."

"Sure." Lane tapped the waitress' section on the seating map. Only two occupied tables. One had just arrived.

Alisha slipped out a side door.

Lane approached table four. "What can I get you tonight?"

Both women stared at him as if he were a museum exhibit.

"You must be new." The older woman sipped a glass of water.

"First night." Lane opened the ordering software.

"You're Lane Harris. This is you." The younger woman held out her phone. Another of Monica's photos, this one at the top of an article on a Hollywood gossip site. "What's it like dating Monica?"

"I'm not—" He swallowed an angry retort. This wasn't the place for a shouting match. "I hear the sirloin's good here." Lane dismissed an error message and opened the menu. "We have a special on ribeye."

The women whispered and covered grins.

"New York strip. Rare." The younger woman gave Lane a sultry smirk.

"Same."

"Soup or salad?"

Both ordered salads.

Another error message glared at him. "I'll relay your order to the kitchen." He forced an even pace. Once out of sight, he scribbled the order on a notepad and delivered it by hand.

Alisha found him as he left the kitchen. "Thanks."

Lane gladly relinquished responsibility for the two women, and a new message popped onto his tablet screen. He headed for Lester at the bar. "What's this thing doing?" He held up the device.

Lester chuckled, tapped a few buttons, and the error message disappeared.

"What did you do?"

"Told it ta be quiet and listen."

"I need more time with this software."

"You'll get it. I think the developer took some shortcuts, but it works well enough for us. Takes a minute to get the hang of, though." Lester tipped his hat to a man as he left. "Already had three or four people askin' about you."

"Is that good?"

Lester laughed again. "They don't pay attention to the wait staff much, but you make 'em take notice. Guess six-four and good-natured goes a long way. Couple of the waitresses whisper and giggle about ya like they're twelve. Tried to tell 'em you were very unlikely to be interested, but they're still optimistic. What movies you say you were in?"

A woman staggered through the door. Her eyes were red, hair plastered to one cheek. She shuffled to the bar and sat in front of Lester. "Gimme a shot a tequila." Every word slurred—some so much Lane barely understood.

"Honey, I think you've had enough for tonight. I'll call you a cab." Lester finished cleaning a glass and went for his cell phone.

"I don't want a cab." She smacked the bar with an open hand. "I want tequila!"

"No can do. Come back tomorrow."

The woman cursed. "Get me my tequila!"

"You'd best get on home."

Customers moved to the opposite end of the bar. Some slipped into the restrooms.

"You faggots won't serve a straight girl? Is that it? What's wrong with you?" She whipped out her phone and snapped pictures of everyone—including Lane and Lester. "This is going online."

"Barry," Lester called into the back of the bar. "Got a live one for ya."

A man, big as any wrestler, stood beside the woman. "I suggest you leave."

At the sight of Barry, she backpedaled to the door. "Fine, but I'm so posting this." She waved her phone at everyone and almost dropped it. One more step from Barry pushed her outside.

"Thanks." Lester waved to the bouncer.

"No trouble." He retreated to his hideout, a hallway in the back corner.

"That happen often?"

"Once in a while," Lester said. "Frank and Marty's probably kicked her out, so she came here. As for the colorful dialogue, we get our share. They'll say what they wanna say, but when they bother my customers, that's where I draw the line. Some people hate anyone different from themselves."

"It's been eighteen years, and my parents still won't speak to me," Lane said.

Lester picked up another shot glass to clean. "Got a brother and sister. Neither one ever calls. Don't even know I've got the bar. Lost my partner to AIDS four years back. Been a long few years."

"Maybe tonight's excitement is over."

Lester laughed.

Marcelle St. Apartments
Sunday, March 3rd

Lane stepped off the elevator at 3 a.m. His keys jangled as he unlocked the door and tossed them on the kitchen table. With a flick, he made sure the front door was locked.

Too tired to eat, he changed and flopped into bed.

But sleep wouldn't come.

When he'd mentioned his partner to Vic the other day, she hadn't commented. Maybe morning sickness had distracted her; she hadn't caught what he'd said. Would she remember their conversation? Realize he was what people like her labeled deviant? He knew what would happen if she did. Either she'd belittle and degrade him like the drunk at Simmer tonight, or she'd look at him with disgust. She would certainly never let him near her daughter again.

Hopefully she wouldn't get him fired. He couldn't afford that. She wouldn't be the first religious person to shun him, though.

The first time he'd dared date another guy was in college. Somehow, his father found out.

"No son of mine is going to date boys!" When he recalled that moment, the words still rang in his head, and he remembered how his gut had dropped into his shoes.

That was the summer his father had kicked him out.

His mother had cried, but hadn't stepped in.

Did they know about his acting career? His, albeit few, successes?

Or were they still pretending he didn't exist?

18

Nine Years Ago

North Kingsville University, Fresno
Wednesday, May 26ᵗʰ

Leigh dropped her backpack on her bed.

Her roommate had moved out two weeks ago, as had most students. Only a few remained for on-campus summer sessions. She wouldn't have bothered with extra classes, but going home right now didn't seem a good idea. There was no way her parents would welcome her back into their house, and none of her friends had any extra room. A surprise scholarship for promising young writers had been the final piece that had convinced her to stay on campus.

The maternity top she wore was sickeningly cute, with orange kittens parading across the hem and a large pawprint right over her middle. She'd picked it up at the local thrift store last week, and it was the only thing clean. Flagging energy last night had ensured she didn't finish the laundry.

She sank onto her bed just as a text came through. Nakasha.

Hibachi tonight? My place?

After the day she'd had, that sounded wonderful.

Can I stay over?

Like I'm gonna say no. You wanna eat early?

5 okay?

Perfect.

Leigh stuffed socks and underwear into her backpack along with her beat-up laptop.

River Ridge Apartments

The smell of grilled beef and vegetables lingered long after dinner as Leigh and Nakasha lounged on the couch, catching the news and then two Primetime shows. They weren't Leigh's favorite, but Nakasha liked them, and being with her was more important than what was on the TV.

Nakasha's arm draped across Leigh's shoulders, pulling her into a safe embrace as they finished an episode of a first-responder show. The clock ticked toward 8.

Leigh yawned.

"Windin' down?" Nakasha planted a kiss on Leigh's forehead.

"I'll fall asleep right here if I don't move soon."

"And would that be so bad?" Nakasha's next kiss met Leigh's lips.

"Other than waking up with a killer neck ache, I guess it wouldn't."

Nakasha turned off the TV. "You don't need anything else to worry about, so I suppose we'd better not sleep here." She headed for the single bedroom.

Leigh followed.

Leigh pulled one last box out of the moving truck. "You're sure about this?"

"Sure about my girlfriend living with me?" said Nakasha. "Do I look unsure to you?" She raised a sassy brow.

"It's just...with the baby and everything..." Leigh scooped up her son's carrier. He was asleep for now, but he could wake up any second.

"That baby is just as welcome here as you are." Nakasha held the door open so Leigh could step inside without putting down box or baby.

"Thanks, Kash. That means...a lot."

"I got the crib set up in the bedroom."

"You didn't have to do that. I could have—"

"You've got enough on your plate," Nakasha said. "Let me do some of the work, okay? You're not in this alone anymore."

Leigh set her last box of things on the kitchen table before giving Nakasha a grateful hug. "You're too good to me."

"No, girl. You deserve the world, and don't you let anybody tell you different."

19

Lane finished a scene with Monica and two detectives.

A crew member dropped a mic boom as Monica left camera view. She whirled to look and tripped on a knot of cables.

"Ow!" She collapsed onto the hard floor and cradled her ankle.

Medics hurried over as Monica muttered curses.

"Sprained." One medic wrapped the ankle and spouted instructions. "Rest it for two weeks."

Gibson dashed over. "Two weeks?"

"If you don't want her limping around set," said the medic.

Gibson scrolled through something on his phone and grimaced. "Get home, Henderson. We finished most of your scene work for today. The rest will have to wait. At this rate, Harris will be done weeks before you."

That sounded good to Lane.

"You can drive, but be careful," the medic said to Monica as he helped her into a wheelchair and pushed her out.

The day's remaining schedule shifted to work around Monica's absence.

"Harris, I want to talk to you." Gibson called Lane over as the cast left for the day.

He met Gibson near the door as the crew straightened up, turned out the lights, and left. One guy, part of the lighting crew maybe, stayed behind. He looked familiar, but Lane couldn't quite place him.

"Don't know what this is about and don't want to." Gibson held up a picture of Lane at Simmer. Had to be one of the drunk customer's pictures. "You seem to have a sordid relationship with the media as of late. Your private life isn't my business, but if you let it keep you from your responsibilities here, then it will become my business."

"I understand."

"Good." Gibson gathered his things and followed the crew outside.

The straggler hung back, examining a light.

Lane trudged out. The door locked behind him.

He sat in his Versa and checked voicemail. Two messages from St. Phillip and one from Kennedy. He deleted them. Just the thought of talking with billing departments was draining. They could wait a little longer to hear from him.

When the parking lot emptied, Lane started the car. He turned on the first inning of a baseball game and drove until it ended.

Marcelle St. Apartments

Soft sobs greeted Lane when he got home. "Stacey? Are you okay?"

His sister-in-law crumpled a Kleenex and tossed it into the trash can beside the couch. Huddles meowed from his carrier. Tears streamed down Stacey's cheeks. "I got evicted."

"What?" Lane set his keys and wallet in the tray by the door and sat beside Stacey.

She pulled her dark pink sweater tighter and curled both feet under her. "I couldn't make rent the past three months. Getting fired two weeks ago didn't help. And Gunther and Louis bad-mouthed me to every investment firm in Southern California. No one will hire me."

Huddles' meows became desperate yowling. Stacey must have been here for several hours before he got home.

"Where's all your stuff? Your car?"

She looked away. "I sold my car last week. That's everything I brought from Frank's when I moved out." Stacey nodded to two fuchsia suitcases. "I called Dad."

Lane bit back a rude comment at the mention of Ian Parker.

"He said he knew I'd never make it in the corporate world and then hung up."

"Stace, you should have said something. I'd have helped—"

"No." Stacey wiped her running nose. "You've got enough going on with all those credit card debts, and bills from Stephen's—" She covered her mouth to stifle a sob. "I can't believe Dad is so heartless. He didn't even send flowers to the funeral. He could have bought Kennedy's without blinking, but he won't do anything for either of us since you and Stephen got married." Angry tears stained her cheeks. "Aunt Sherry will let me stay with her, but she lives in Bakersfield. Can

Huddles and I sleep on your couch tonight? We'll be on a bus tomorrow."

"Whatever you need."

"Thanks." Stacey smiled through her tears. She picked up the framed 4x6 on the side table. "You two were great together. I miss him so much." She touched her brother's picture lovingly.

"Me too," Lane whispered.

"Sometimes I think I hear him downstairs, making omelets, or those awful fried egg and banana sandwiches." She took a shuddering breath. "But he's never there." She opened the pet carrier and buried her face in Huddles' gray tabby fur.

The cat squirmed, more than ready to be free. Lane understood the feeling.

"I'd do anything to spend another day with him," he said.

"I want life to be uncomplicated again." Stacey let Huddles go, and the cat ran a few frantic circles around the living room before curling up in her lap. "Just for a day or two."

Lane nodded. "I'd like that too."

But that kind of peace was impossible.

Merrill Avenue Bus Station, Huntington Park
Tuesday, March 5th

Lane stood with Stacey outside the bus station as they waited for the 5:30 to Bakersfield to start boarding. Sunrise was still forty-five minutes away, and both of them wore light jackets, zipped closed.

"You're sure you won't stay?" he said.

"I can't impose on you." She offered a sad smile. "Aunt Sherry was so excited when I phoned last night. She hasn't had anyone to talk to except her birds since Uncle Ronnie died. It'll be good to get out of here—see someplace new. Maybe hear some stories about Mom again. Before she met Dad."

"Bus 61229 to Bakersfield, now boarding." The announcement played overhead.

As her bus prepared to leave, Stacey hugged Lane. "Tell me when this movie premieres, and I'll come back to celebrate."

"All right."

"Goodbye, Lane. And thanks." Stacey stowed her luggage but kept Huddles' covered carrier in hand.

She waved as the bus pulled away.

Stacey had been the only person still here who considered him family, and now, she'd left him too. He'd never had to face a world where everyone who cared about him was gone. He wasn't sure he wanted to.

20

Marcelle St. Apartments
Friday, March 8th

A knock interrupted Lane mid-bite. He set his dinner on the coffee table.

Must be the landlady. He would have to apologize again for not getting her the rest of his previous month's rent yet. So far, he hadn't had any luck selling Stephen's collectibles.

He opened the door. "Monica?"

"Hey, Laney—"

"Don't call me that." He moved to lock her out.

Just before the door closed, she sneaked a hand into the gap between it and the doorframe. "Is this how you treat a lady?" She gave him a disapproving look. "Here's your shirt." The folded button-up he'd left at her apartment two-and-a-half weeks ago dangled from her long, bloodred fingernails.

He didn't take it.

"Nice collection." She admired Stephen's baseball memorabilia, displayed near the door. "Aren't you going to invite me in?"

Lane stayed in Monica's way. "You're supposed to be at home resting your ankle."

"Had to get out of my apartment. Couldn't stand staring at the walls anymore, and there's nothing fun on TV."

"Ever tried reading a book?" He didn't disguise the edge in his voice.

Monica laughed. "You can be so old-school."

"Why are you here? You didn't drive across town just to bring back a shirt."

"I can't visit my boyfriend?"

"I think you've visited enough."

Monica huffed. "This random woman shared my pictures of you online. Tagged some old lady who's supposedly your mother. Talk about someone who's disappointed." Monica shook her head. "No wonder you never talk about her. She's such a—"

"Don't you dare finish that sentence," he said.

Monica rolled her eyes. "You're welcome for the free publicity, by the way. No one's mentioned poor, sad Lane Harris on a talk show for months. That accident last year was the best thing to happen to you, Laney. Before that, no one even knew your pathetic little name. You were just the billionaire kid's plus one. He was no prize to look at either. How much did he pay you to—"

"Leave." Lane pointed to the elevator. "Now."

She dropped his shirt in the doorway and gave him a sultry smirk.

How he wanted to drag her to the front door of the complex and throw her out, watch her trip down the entryway steps. Maybe fall a few times on her way down. She wasn't supposed to have the entry code. One of the neighbors must have let her in.

"I told you to go."

Monica complied this time, but not without one more self-satisfied grin.

He wanted nothing more than to rip it off her face.

As soon as she let go of the door, Lane slammed and locked it. He sank onto the couch. In the silence, once his anger boiled down, the horror of what Monica had said grew unchecked.

His mother had seen Monica's pictures.

She hadn't called after the funeral. Not even sent a sympathy card. Now she was talking with someone online about him.

Stephen's empty spot on the couch cut into him. Another constant reminder of his husband's absence.

No one would leave him to his grief. When he tried to forget, he ended up losing pieces of himself to people like Monica, who didn't care for anyone except themselves.

"I'm sorry, Stephen..." He laid a hand on the empty cushion. "I wish you were here."

He hadn't cried since the funeral, but now his eyes burned. The fake flowers from Kennedy still sat in the corner atop a tiny table. A thin film of dust covered them.

"I wish I could start over."

21

Baker Memorial Park

Saturday, March 9ᵗʰ

Lane jogged his usual route. On the way back to his car, near the playground, a parade of thirty runners forced him off the trail. As he waited for them to pass, he discovered Vic sitting on a bench beside the play area, a thick paperback in hand.

He turned, hoping she wouldn't notice him.

"Lane? How's shooting going?" She'd caught him.

Maybe talking with her for a minute would be all right. She didn't seem upset with him.

"Monica's out for a couple weeks—sprained ankle." Just saying the woman's name made him tense. "What're you reading?"

Vic stuck a finger between the pages of the worn paperback. She smiled at the book and held it up.

Lane couldn't pronounce the title, but Vic's name adorned the front and much-folded spine. "You wrote this?"

"Years ago." She smoothed the cover lovingly.

"I heard you'd written a fantasy novel."

"This is it. Though how much of it is fantasy, you'd have to decide for yourself." She held the book close. "I wrote this just before reconciling with my parents."

"I can't picture you as an estranged daughter."

Vic snorted. "Oh, I was. And it was quite the reunion when I finally came home."

Monica's words from the night before about his mother came back. "I don't think my family and I will be on speaking terms anytime soon."

"I'm sorry to hear that. But don't discount them just yet." Vic closed the book. "Here. Keep it."

"I couldn't."

"I've got a hardback at home, and a box of paperbacks."

"I don't have much reading time."

"It's all right."

At Vic's polite insistence, he accepted the book.

"I read it every year. Sophie's too young to understand most of it yet, but she will one day." Vic checked the time. "I won't keep you any longer. Sorry to have held you up."

"I was just heading to my car anyway. Are you feeling better?"

"Some. I'll be back at the studio Monday. Enjoy your weekend."

"All right. Thanks for the book." Lane jogged to the parking lot and got in his car.

Marcelle St. Apartments

Lane set Vic's book on the coffee table beside his current read, careful not to bend the old book's faded cover or well-used pages. He tossed together fruit salad and toasted a whole-grain bagel. What Monica had said yesterday about his mother played on repeat in his head.

As he went to his mother's social media page, his gut flipped. Her picture looked older than he remembered. He hadn't spoken to her in eighteen years. Her hair was silver, and wrinkles rimmed her eyes and mouth.

He scrolled until he found the dreaded Valentine's Day pictures someone had publicly shared. Ignoring the temptation to read the comments, he skimmed past the post.

Recipes filled most of his mother's feed. Looked like she still liked to cook and bake. After several minutes of scrolling, Lane found an odd message from one of his mother's friends: "We're so sorry, Esther. Let us know if you need anything."

More comments and similar messages followed it until Lane found a link.

An obituary.

George Matthew Harris, dead at 81. Survived by his wife, Esther Elaine Harris, and one son, Lane Thomas Harris.

Reconciliation was no longer an option.

22

Marcelle St. Apartments
Sunday, March 10th

Simmer closed at 2 a.m.

Lane stepped off the elevator at 2:58.

His apartment door stood half open.

Lane rushed in.

Stephen's collectibles were gone from the entryway wall and kitchen table. The TV stand was bare. In the bedroom, Stephen's college ring and gold chain were missing. So were his suits, Lane's three-year-old laptop, and anything else of value—even the envelope of emergency cash tucked into an old cookbook in the kitchen.

His neighbor knocked on the open door. "They got you too, huh? I was at work when my security app notified me. Got here, and everything was gone. Deadbeat—stealing from honest people. I called the police a few minutes ago. Looks like they hit four other apartments on this floor. No clue how they got in or why nobody saw them."

"Y-your security system doesn't contact the police?"

"Nah. My ferret kept setting it off. Didn't wanna spam-call the police every day, so I turned that feature off."

Vic's book still sat on the coffee table next to his half-read thriller, undisturbed. But what remained of his life with Stephen lay strewn across the floor like shredded trash. Even the 4x6 on the side table had been knocked over and lay on the floor, its frame broken.

"Tough luck, man. Sorry about your stuff. Maybe the cops will find it."

Lane stepped outside, sat beside the door, and waited for the police while his neighbor chattered to the other victims.

Could nothing go right for him?

An hour later, a young officer jotted notes in a small book. "And you didn't see anyone suspicious when you entered the building earlier?"

Lane shook his head.

"When did you get home?"

"Around 3."

"Working late?"

"I have a job in Hollywood. Place closes around 2 or 2:30."

"Know of anybody who'd want to steal from you?"

"No."

"How about neighbors? Anybody get in a fight recently?"

"Just Janet and Riley in 322, but they fight all the time."

"Anybody new on the floor?"

"Not that I know of. Can I get back in my apartment?"

"Not tonight. Sorry. Looks like forensics is gonna be going through yours and everybody else's units until noon. Might wanna find another place to sleep."

"Why the investigation?"

"Fits the MO of a thief we've been tracking since last June. Couldn't get a lead on them for a while before that. Thanks for your cooperation. We'll call if we have any more questions—or if you can come back."

Lane trudged to the elevator.

24/7 Motel, Huntington Park

He tossed his shoes toward the door and sank onto the bed. His socks, he left on. Fresh sheets and pillows hid beneath a worn comforter, and the lampshade wore an aged yellow cast.

Lane set his phone on the bedside table but kept his keys and wallet in his pockets. Even though he'd partially charged his phone on the way here, the battery hovered at twenty-five percent. He switched on battery saver mode.

He'd checked the door three times to make sure it was locked, but when he reached for the lamp, somebody tramped past his door, stopped, then went on. Surely no one would break into a cheap motel this late. Not even the crickets were awake.

But he'd thought his apartment was safe too.

All he'd brought were the clothes he was wearing and the contents of his pockets. There wasn't anything here worth stealing, unless someone wanted his three-year-old phone or a nearly empty wallet.

But just the thought of losing something else made his chest ache. He'd already lost the people he cared about most. Everything of value, except his car, was gone. He couldn't even sleep in his own bed tonight.

Was what he had left worth fighting for?

He finally clicked the lamp off.

23

Lane walked into the studio, so tired he barely cleared the door.

"Harris, this isn't a sleepover!" Gibson pointed one of the makeup crew toward Lane. "Fix that."

While a woman worked to hide the bags under Lane's eyes, Gibson gathered everyone. "We're still behind schedule. We should be a third done with shooting. We're not. With Henderson out, we're using a double in scenes where she's in the background. Let's get going, people. We won't finish on time by standing around."

Lane managed one scene without falling over, then grabbed the biggest cup of coffee available. It wasn't Benny's, but it would work.

As he finished his cup, Vic walked in with Sophie.

Lane sat in his chair and waited for Gibson's next summons while several minor characters did two scenes with Monica's body double.

Sophie tapped Lane's knee. "Are you sad because you're sleepy? I get sad when I'm sleepy."

The sudden news of his father's death and the break-in had stolen much of his sleep this past week. Not that he'd slept well at all since Stephen's death. "Yeah."

"If you need a day off, I can talk to Jack." Vic sat beside him. "He seems a bear, but he's more of a crispy marshmallow."

"Thanks, but I need to keep coming to work." If he missed another day, he wasn't sure he'd come back.

"All right." Vic tucked her purse and Sophie's bag under the chair. She kept stealing glances at him, almost as if she knew what had happened. Maybe she did. He hadn't checked local headlines this morning.

Lane got up. "Can you tell Gibson I'm taking a walk? I'll be back."

"Okay," Vic said.

Sophie waved as he left.

Studio 73-C

Rain sprinkled the sidewalk and dampened Lane's hair. His umbrella was still in his apartment—his jacket too. He took the sidewalk toward the next studio. A few saplings held boughs overhead long enough to offer respite from the rain, but he passed through each narrow refuge far too quickly.

The rain thickened.

Soon his hair clung to his scalp, and his clothes hung like sad paper bags.

He walked for ten or twenty minutes before turning around. He hadn't made it halfway back when Vic appeared, umbrella in hand, raincoat hood up.

"Jack's getting anxious, so I came to find you. Maybe help you stay dry." She offered him the umbrella.

He waved it off. "Thanks, but I think I'm beyond help."

Vic walked with him back to the studio and held part of the umbrella over him anyway. He kept expecting her to mention Stephen or start into some declaration of judgment.

But she never did.

She didn't say a word, didn't ask why he looked so haggard lately or pry into his personal life. So why did he have the strange feeling she knew everything about him?

24

Marcelle St. Apartments

Monday, March 11ᵗʰ

Ten long hours and a dozen cups of coffee later, Lane arrived home. The police had locked the door.

Inside was a mess. Fingerprinting dust covered the apartment like a thin layer of snow.

He kept keys, wallet, and phone in his pockets as he cleaned everything. Fatigue wanted him to sleep, but he couldn't until he'd fixed this.

With no TV or DVR to watch baseball games, he listened to one on his phone. At least the thieves hadn't taken the internet router. He started cleaning in the bathroom, worked through the kitchen and bedroom, and tackled the living room last.

When he found something of Stephen's, he examined it before setting the item reverently in its place. The thieves had left scant few of his husband's belongings. Even the coat beside the door was gone.

The entryway walls were bare, but he had nothing else to hang.

His collection of suspense and thriller novels sat untouched on their shelf by the empty TV stand. Little consolation.

As he finished righting the living room, the game—prerecorded—took a break. He sat on the couch, and a cloud of fingerprinting dust made him cough. He'd forgotten to vacuum, but was too tired to do it now.

Vic's book lay on the coffee table, the one thing spared from a film of dust. Lane was never one for fantasy—all the buff heroes, breath-taking heroines, creatures, and places that didn't exist. But this book seemed different.

"How much of it is fantasy, you'd have to decide for yourself." That's what Vic had said.

He smoothed the cover. It felt like any other paperback. The spine was so wrinkled and broken it was hard to read, but Vic's name and the book's title—which he still couldn't pronounce—were mostly visible.

Lane opened to the foreword. "No matter how far we've gone, God is there with us. Psalm 139."

He shook his head and closed the book. If there was a God, He had a skewed sense of justice. Why let someone good, like Stephen, die when people like Monica and the thief who'd violated his home lived any way they wanted—hurt who they pleased—and didn't suffer consequences?

He returned to the baseball game in time to catch the rest.

Before he went to bed, he turned on all the lights, checked the front door twice, and locked himself inside the bedroom.

25

Marcelle St. Apartments
Tuesday, March 12th

Lane's apartment was bare. He couldn't afford to replace the TV. He might be able to get a cheap one, but why? All he did was watch baseball, which he could do on his phone. Having a game on made it feel like Stephen was still there, probably grabbing something in the kitchen, or touching up his unruly hair in the bathroom after a day at the office.

All the lights were still on—even the hood light over the stove.

Back rent still loomed. He'd only paid a paltry $350 so far. Next month's rent would be due in a couple weeks too. Then there was his car payment. And Kennedy and St. Phillip would hound him again soon. He was dreading telling them he couldn't pay. The credit card companies had already tried to get ahold of him a few times this month.

He started to listen to another game, but thoughts of his father drowned out the announcers. He hadn't even gotten the opportunity to attend the funeral. Not that he wanted to, with all those stuffy churchgoers wedged into the same room. Seeing his father's friends after eighteen years with their disapproving stares wasn't a priority. But he had been curious.

With the game still playing in the corner of his phone screen, he found his mother's comment on Monica's photo and followed the obituary link again.

They had recorded the service.

He paused the game and played the video.

It was like he'd thought. Everyone sat in ordered rows in their suits, ties, dresses, and heels. They all looked the same—stoic expressions, stiff posture, and zero genuineness.

That was what irked him most about his parents and their friends. Nobody cared about anyone else. The goal was to impress one another—and supposedly God.

The service droned for an hour. Soloists sang two songs, and the congregation joined in a cookie-cutter rendition of "Amazing Grace."

After a too-long sermon, which Lane skipped through, the preacher dismissed everyone. They left his mother at the front alone, crying. Not even the preacher said anything to her as he ushered her from the building.

Lane returned to his baseball game.

How could all of them be so fake? Why stay in a religion that offered the compassion of a cardboard box?

Once he'd shouted in his father's face, "You're just as fake as your friends."

More memories of his childhood bubbled up as he let the baseball game drone.

Were all Christians the same? Did they all watch, waiting to condemn? How did they live like that?

An email from Stacey arrived.

Hey Lane,

Aunt Sherry's thrilled to have company at home, and Huddles loves chasing her birds.

Got a new job this week. Started today. Doesn't pay as well as my old one, but I can get enough hours to make up the difference. They're actually letting me work full time!

I'm thinking about talking with a lawyer about everything that happened when I got fired. Do you think I'd have a chance against them? The women there need to know they don't have to put up with being harassed.

Hope you're doing okay. Still waiting to hear about that movie premiere.

Love,

Stacey

The lawsuit was a good idea. And she seemed happy. He wished he could see a future where he was too.

Lane closed his email and focused on the game.

26

A customer hurled insults at Lane. He staved off the urge to shout back.

"You're too stupid to do anything other than food service. I've been waiting fifteen minutes for a table. It's just me. How hard is it to find space for one person? No wonder you couldn't find work anyplace else. I'm never coming here again, and I'm telling everyone I know not to come here either. What kind of idiot can't even seat people?"

"I apologize for the wait, sir. It's a busy night. We'll have a table cleared for you in a moment."

"Oh, no. I wanna talk to your manager."

Lane swallowed a sigh and ushered the man to Lester, who was standing behind the bar, watching.

"I'm the manager. What seems to be the trouble?" Lester replaced two clean shot glasses.

"This guy with pasta for brains can't find me a table. I've been waiting thirty minutes—"

"Have a seat with me here at the bar." Lester held up a bottle of good whiskey. "Care for a shot? On the house."

The man's eyes lit up. "Sure." He took the seat in front of Lester and accepted a filled glass.

Lester flagged the nearest waitress. "Alisha, will you take a special order for me?"

She quickly sent the order to the kitchen.

"There ya go. Food won't be ten minutes. Where're you from? Around Hollywood?" Lester nudged another shot toward the man and kept the customer busy while Lane sneaked back to the host desk.

Hours later, when everyone but Lane, Lester, and the cleaning staff were gone, Lane joined Lester at the bar. "How did you do that?"

"Lots of experience with ornery critters. Don't worry about it. He was being unreasonable. Usually just takes a little redirection to get 'em quiet. But occasionally you'll get a smart one. Then there's no redirectin'. You just gotta take the hit."

"Thanks."

"No problem."

27

Lane arrived five seconds after Monica. She smirked at him and let the door close in his face.

He followed her into the studio, trying to keep at least a six-foot buffer, but the instant they entered the studio, Monica was at his side, her arm snaked around his.

Too many nights without good sleep had caught up to him, and any semblance of civility vanished. "Get away from me." He grabbed her hand and forced it free of his upper arm. "I told you not to—"

Monica shrank away from him, feigning tears. "But you said you wanted to tell everyone about us." She grabbed a tissue from her purse and covered her face. "I thought you loved me!" The desperate wail in her voice might have drawn sympathy from some of the onlookers, but all it did for him was make his teeth grind.

Gibson came out of his office, phone in hand. "All right, people. Henderson's back early with doctor approval, but we've still got doubles for anything more than light walking. Harris, you and Henderson are up. Once Makeup gets done with you, it's scene 8."

Monica dabbed wet eyes. Gibson paid her no mind. The cast and crew who'd witnessed the outburst shifted nervously and kept from meeting Lane's gaze.

He endured the prescribed scene and hurried off camera so Monica could do her next segment without him.

No Vic today. She must have had a doctor's appointment.

Hours later, when everyone headed home, Monica pulled Lane off the sidewalk just outside the studio. As the rest of the cast and crew filed past, she pressed against him, smiling sweetly. That odd burnt smell clung to her again.

"I forgive you for this morning," she said loudly enough for everyone on the sidewalk and near the parking lot to hear. "I know how hard it's been for you the past few months."

"Stop the games." He matched her volume before grabbing her by the shoulders and forcing her away. "I have no interest in being anywhere near you, and you know it."

Several onlookers pretended not to listen as they unlocked their cars and took longer than necessary to get in.

"Calm down." Monica covered his hand with hers.

He jerked it away. "Leave me alone, or I'll—"

One of the lighting guys who always seemed to hang around was taking a video on his phone. Others had stopped to stare.

Lane didn't finish his threat, even though the words burned on his tongue and Monica deserved every one of them.

"Don't you talk to me that way." Monica crossed her arms and leaned toward him. "I'm trying to be supportive." As if she'd just realized people might be watching, she turned around. "It's okay, everybody. He's still getting over…" She pasted on a solemn expression. "The accident last year."

Now she'd dared to drag Stephen into this.

His fist closed, but as much as he wanted to crack her jaw for what she'd said, he knew it would only cast him in an even worse light.

Murmurs of sympathy preceded closing car doors and the rev of engines. Cars filtered out of the lot one by one, leaving Lane and Monica alone in front of the empty studio.

"Don't ever bring up my husband again." Lane took a step toward Monica, forcing her to the edge of the sidewalk.

She huffed. "If you want this to stop, I'll need a little incentive." She unlocked her phone and shoved it in his face. "I think this would be a reasonably compelling amount."

The figure on her screen was more than his bank account had ever held.

"I'm not giving you anything."

"Fine." Monica shoved her phone into a pocket. "Then I guess our relationship is still on. Good luck convincing everyone it isn't." She smirked. "Those pictures I released last month were just the beginning."

She slinked away in her red heels and white jeans. Instead of the Jaguar today, she slipped into a beige Suburban. The look of disgusted rage on her face when she shut the door could have incinerated ice.

28

Nine Years Ago

River Ridge Apartments, Fresno
Thursday, December 2nd

This week had been one whirlwind after another. Two big writing projects due, a review at work, and Nakasha had just started doing twelves, so she could be home more often to help with the baby.

Leigh told her supervisor she wouldn't be coming in tonight.

When she hung up the phone, she barely had the energy to check on her son before flopping into bed six feet away. He'd be five months old in a couple weeks. He was holding his head steady now, but he hadn't sat up yet.

She didn't want to miss even one milestone, but right now, sleep mattered more than anything else.

When Leigh woke, moonlight filtered in through cracked blinds. Nakasha always left them open just enough, so neither of them had to turn on a light if they had to check on the baby.

Her phone said it was a little after midnight.

A text from Nakasha: Went straight to work. Be home around 3.

She sent a thumbs up emoji.

Her stomach growled. She hadn't eaten in...over thirteen hours?

She rubbed her eyes clear. Her son lay on his back in his crib. His blanket covered him from waist to toe. He should have woken up by now, even if it was only for a diaper change.

Leigh went to the crib. "Tim." She gently rubbed his chest. "Tim?" She shook him by the shoulder.

His head rocked with the motion, but he didn't open his eyes.

His chest wasn't moving.

"No. No. Tim?" She scooped him out of the crib and held him against her shoulder. "Wake up, baby. Please, wake up," she sobbed.

He would be okay if she gave him CPR. She'd taken an infant CPR class a few months ago. That had to work.

She kicked stray clothes into the corner and shoved the crib two feet toward the wall before laying her son on the thin carpet. With two fingers she compressed his tiny chest, then paused to give a rescue breath. Each round of compressions was more frantic.

But Tim's heart still refused to beat.

Even in the dark, the blue tinge on his lips was unmissable.

She should have called EMS the second she suspected something was wrong. She should have been awake. Aware.

This was her fault.

Her baby was dead, and it was all her fault.

She leaned over Tim's little body. Her wail stabbed through the walls, and within half a minute, two neighbors pounded the door.

"Is everything all right?" one shouted.

"I've got 9-1-1 on the phone right now," called the other.

It was no use.

She got up, left Tim, staggered through the apartment. When she flung open the door, both neighbors hovered within three feet of her. Leigh shoved past them, knocking one against the wall. She stumbled past the stairs and out into the parking lot.

She had to get out of here.

Go somewhere. Away.

She headed toward campus.

North Kingsville University
Friday, December 3rd

Leigh stepped into the shower stall, grateful NKU had added locking shower doors over the summer.

Her bare feet bled from walking all the way from River Ridge.

A group of sorority girls laughed as they passed the stall. All they had to worry about was breaking a nail while opening beer bottles. They didn't have to go home to an empty crib—a dead baby.

She turned on the water and adjusted the warmth until the stream neared a scald. Her shirt and jeans were soaked within minutes, and a thin trail of blood from her battered, bare feet seeped into the drain. The pain was almost a mercy, but it did too little to dull the all-consuming grief ripping open her heart.

She'd already cried all her tears on the way here. Only numb emptiness remained.

Hot water pounded her face and chest. She turned her back to the spray long enough to wipe her face clear.

Her phone and wallet were still at the apartment. The only things in her pockets were two soaked dollar bills—and her work-issued box cutter. The blade was dull to keep employees from accidentally cutting themselves. But it might be sharp enough to slice skin if she leaned into it.

She tested the blade with a finger pad. Barely a line of irritated flesh.

When she'd lived in the dorms, a girl had cut her wrists during the night and bled out in the shower. No one had found her until morning.

Leigh pressed the blade to her forearm and put every ounce of heartbreak and agony behind the slice, leaving a bloody trail.

Tim—her son—her little boy—was dead.

She gouged another mark, this one straight across her wrist.

She hadn't done enough to save him. She was stupid, horrible, an awful mother.

A third slice across the same wrist.

EMS could have done something—brought him back. If only she'd called them in time.

She switched arms, cutting with sharp, quick strokes as she screamed at the box cutter to end her nightmare.

Leigh slid to the floor of the shower stall. The plastic-handled blade clacked beside her as water washed an increasing amount of red down the drain.

29

Marcelle St. Apartments

Thursday, March 21st

Lane checked the mail when he returned from his morning run at the gym. It was before 4 a.m. when he left. Now it was almost 5.

In the elevator, he sorted ads and bills.

When he reached his apartment, an envelope stuck to his door. He took it inside with the mail and tossed everything, except the envelope, on the table.

An eviction notice.

This couldn't be right.

An hour later, when he was sure Mrs. Olsen would be up, Lane took the notice to her first-floor apartment.

A middle-aged man answered the door. A Rolex knockoff dangled on his thick wrist, and heavy cigar smoke wafted into the hall. "What?"

"Is Mrs. Olsen home?"

"No. Had to move her to a home couple days ago. I'm her son. Whadda you want?"

"I live in 316." Lane held up the eviction notice. "I've been having some...financial trouble. Your mother gave me two months to pay back my rent—"

"She gave you an extension, huh? You got proof?"

"No. But—"

"Then be out by the 31st." The man blew a cloud of smoke in Lane's face and tapped the smoldering butt of his cigarette into a potted plant just outside his door.

"Your mother—"

"She doesn't run this building anymore. I do. Better get packing." He shut and locked the door.

Lane dropped the notice. It hit the faux-wood vinyl with a faint clack.

The pungent odor of tobacco clouded his face. He coughed to clear his nose and throat. One smoldering leaf on the plant in the corner crinkled until it fell from the stem, dead. A faint line of smoke trailed toward the ceiling.

Maybe the sprinklers would come on and soak the hall. It would serve this idiot right.

Lane wondered if the last sprinkler on either end of the corridor was defective, like on his floor. He'd mentioned it to the landlady, but no one had ever come to fix them.

He scooped up the folded paper, returned to his apartment, grabbed a throw pillow, and hurled it across the room. It sailed into the kitchen and scattered the bills littering the table. Several papers fell and skittered across the floor.

If Stephen were still here, he wouldn't have gotten behind on rent, wouldn't be carrying their debts alone or facing the impossibility of finding somewhere else to live on his nonexistent budget.

There wasn't much left to pack. Those thieves had seen to that.

And where would he go? Stacey was in Bakersfield. He didn't have money for another hotel—even a cheap one—and living in his car would only get him fined or jailed for a night.

He couldn't even hire a lawyer to buy time.

30

Simmer Lounge
Saturday, March 23rd

Lane ran between waiting tables and seating guests. Alisha and Barb both had sick kids tonight. That left him, Miguel, and Rhonda, with Lester to cover the bar.

"I'll have the short rib, veggie mac and cheese, and a salad—but hold the tomatoes. And a decaf coffee." A woman with a purple bob fingered two of the dozen rings on her hand as she recited her order.

"And you?" Lane turned to the woman's girlfriend, who could have been a center for the WNBA.

"Sirloin and two loaded potatoes. And we'll take a bottle of red wine."

Lane sent the order to the kitchen. "Can I get you some water or anything else to drink while you wait for your food?"

"Nah. Thanks."

Lane excused himself to seat a group of four guests.

Miguel took their orders as Lane sneaked out back to breathe. Water from the recently used hydrant, which was perched on the elevated street behind the bar, leaked into the alley. Even though it was 11:30

p.m., the customers kept coming. Usually, the dinner rush ended around 9 or 10. The evening's stress made his hands shake.

His phone buzzed. A text.

As he pulled it from his pocket, his fingers slipped and the phone crunched on the pavement. He quickly picked it up, then hissed an expletive. A spiderweb of cracks snaked across the screen and distorted a text from Monica.

You'll like what I have planned for next week.

Lane closed the message and shoved the phone in his pocket. A sliver of loose glass sliced his finger.

Whatever Monica was up to, he wanted no part of it. If what she'd said a few days ago was true, there was no knowing how much false information she had ready to make public. She'd already proven she had contacts in various media outlets, both on screen and in print.

But there had to be a way to stop her.

He wanted to block her number and be done with her, but if he did that, she'd just harass him in person instead. At least this way, he had written proof of their conversations.

The back alley tightened around him like coffin walls. He had to get out—away from here—from everything.

The dumpster's reek tempted him to vomit. Lane hurried inside in time to fend off a wave of nausea. In the men's room, he splashed cold water on his face.

His stomach settled, but his thoughts still scrambled for a way out of Monica's trap.

Fix It Up Cell Phone Repair, Huntington Park
Sunday, March 24th

Lane handed his phone to the tech at the front desk.

The young man tapped the register keyboard. "We can fix it for $98, but you've gotta factory reset it before we can work on it."

"Ninety-eight dollars? But the sign says fifty." Lane pointed to the large cling ad on the window.

"It's in the fine print. That's only for phones purchased through partner suppliers. You bought this phone at an outside retailer. Sorry, but it's gonna be ninety-eight bucks plus tax."

"Can I at least sign something so I don't have to reset the phone?"

"No can do, bro. Can't have anybody goin' around saying we're not secure or we're selling customer data."

Lane took the phone back and held it. If he reset it, he would lose the only pictures he had of him and Stephen from the few months they'd been married. His cloud storage had filled up ages ago, and his only backup copies had been on his stolen laptop. Stephen had some too, but since he never used backups, those had been destroyed in the accident. "Thanks, but...I think I'll wait."

Lane put the phone away and retreated to his car.

His cut finger throbbed under its Band-Aid.

The second he sat, another text arrived. Monica. Again.

Just a selfie this time. Poorly lit. She held what could have been a spoon, but it was more of a silver smudge. Lots of people crowded around.

One more text popped on screen. A string of colorful language preceded a brief, nonsensical paragraph.

He set the phone in the passenger's seat and ignored it the whole ride home.

31

Marcelle St. Apartments
Sunday, March 24th

Lane sat on the couch in front of the empty TV stand. A handful of social media notices cluttered his cracked phone screen. Had his mother said anything about him online after her comment on Monica's photo? He checked her page, avoiding the edges of broken glass on his phone.

The first fifty posts on his mother's feed were about him, dated from February 25th through this morning. Each one expressed disgust, disappointment, or anger about Lane. Most were reactions to Monica's pictures.

"Should have known this would happen," one woman commented.

"That boy always seemed off when I taught him in Sunday School."

One of his father's friends wrote, "You and George tried so hard to raise him right. Sorry it didn't work out."

He scrolled to the last post.

A woman his mother's age or a few years older said, "What a shame. He was such a nice boy."

An additional two hundred and seventeen comments hung from the original post. Each one oozed self-righteousness.

His mother hadn't replied.

Dozens of condolences for his father's death followed the posts about Lane. Each one sounded worse than a lazy greeting card message. Some seemed to care, but most probably posted because their friends had.

If they didn't mean it, why say it? No one had forced them.

He skimmed the wall of insincere comments. After that, miscellaneous Bible verses, inspirational quotes, and more recipes his mother liked cluttered a short section.

On impulse, he started a new private message. *Saw Dad's funeral.*

He hit send before he could talk himself out of it.

For two hours, he stared at the unread status until his eyes itched and spots dotted his vision. What would she say? Anything? Did he even want to hear from her?

The status changed to read.

Please don't message me.

Each word gashed deeper than the last. His own mother didn't want to talk to him.

Lane set his phone on the coffee table beside Vic's book.

In the shower, scalding water rinsed away yesterday's dirt and sweat, but his mother's message—and the hundreds of comments from her friends—clung to him.

32

Marcelle St. Apartments
Monday, March 25th

He stepped off the elevator.

More eviction notices decorated apartment doors on his floor.

Several neighbors loitered in the hall, complaining and shaking their papers in the air. But no one noticed Lane. They were too busy with their own problems.

Wednesday, March 27th

It was 6:45 when Lane got home.

Monica had played the supportive—if irritating—girlfriend again yesterday and today. But she hadn't mentioned his husband again.

As he ate dinner, the last few minutes of a baseball game droned from his phone. Stephen would have liked this one. The last inning stretched. It came down to a single pitch, bases loaded, two outs, two strikes.

The wind-up.

The pitch.

A strike, just catching the inside corner.

Lane almost expected Stephen's excited whoop. But the game ended, and silence closed around him.

Grief sat in his chest.

Almost six months since the accident, and it still didn't seem real.

Maybe it never would.

33

Careful to maintain adequate distance between himself and Monica, Lane kept pace with others in the cast as Gibson and the rest of the team wove through the zoo toward their first shooting location. Half a dozen security personnel surrounded them, blocking the onlookers, who waved and smiled. Some cast members returned waves.

Monica reveled in the attention, blowing kisses, posing for candids, and oozing fake charm.

Luckily, no one in their group had enough popularity to warrant mobs, but two dozen fans tailed them to their spot and watched from a respectful distance. Gibson and the film crew didn't seem to care as long as observers stayed out of the shot.

The makeup crew gave Lane and Monica touch-ups before shooting began.

Nearby, at the lion enclosure, stood Vic, Sophie, and an older couple. Sophie pressed her face to the transparent walls surrounding the habitat and watched the aging lions with fascination. Vic smiled at her daughter.

The couple standing with Vic...her parents? Could be. Vic shared the man's features and the woman's smile and short stature. Sophie had that same smile. It spoke of something...wholesome.

Gibson snapped his fingers twice. "Harris, this isn't naptime."

Lane continued his scene with Monica, counting down the seconds until he could blend back into the crowd of cast members. Every time Monica brushed him, Lane tensed, ready to shove her away or bolt. Shadows of his involuntary night with her were still all too real.

He caught a whiff of her perfume and fought a gag. He remembered that same scent choking him as the drug-induced haze pulled him under.

"Harris, get your head in the game," Gibson barked from off camera.

Lane delivered a few lines, but he couldn't shake away the paralyzing sense of helplessness still lingering.

Vic sat beside her mother on a nearby bench. The older woman seemed concerned as she talked with Vic, but they were too far away to be overheard. Whatever the problem, Vic didn't seem troubled by it, and she shared a hug with her mom.

Her father and mother switched places.

Sophie's attention was still glued to the lions as one grandparent and then the other stood nearby.

"Get closer to Henderson. She doesn't bite." Gibson shooed Lane six inches nearer Monica, who flashed a clandestine leer.

It took three more takes to make Gibson happy.

Vic left afterward with her daughter and parents, probably to get breakfast. It was edging toward 9:30.

Everyone moved to another section of the zoo for one of Monica's solo scenes. The woman in Makeup who'd expressed her distaste for

Monica sipped a bottled water. She tossed the empty container into a can marked for recycling.

"Thanks for that job tip a few weeks ago," Lane said as he let her adjust his hair.

"No problem. Glad to help." She pulled a stray leaf off his jacket and tossed it away. "Got a couple more victims." She tipped her head toward two extras with smeared makeup. "Good luck."

They ran two more scenes with Monica and various minor characters.

Vic returned with her family just as Gibson waved another cast member on camera, and Monica came off and headed for Lane. But Sophie reached him first. The little girl finished an oatmeal cookie and brushed the crumbs from her hand before tucking it into Lane's. She smiled up at him.

Did this kid ever do anything that wasn't cute?

Vic and her parents stayed ten or twelve feet back—close enough to hear. "Isn't that the man from—"

"Yes, Mom. And you know better than to believe gossip rags."

So Vic did know about him.

And yet she was defending him, even to her own mother.

Why?

34

Nine Years Ago

West Grey Springs Hospital, Fresno
Friday, December 3rd

Bandages covered Leigh's arms halfway to her elbows. A nurse checked her vitals.

"What am I doing here?" She sat up slowly.

The nurse gave her a taut smile. "You had an...accident." She pointed to Leigh's wrists.

"No, I didn't," she bit back. "I did this on purpose." She scratched up one corner of a bandage and ripped it off. As she tried to remove the second one, the nurse grabbed her hand and forced it into a soft restraint.

Leigh snatched a cup off the bedside table and flung it at the nurse before she could shackle her other hand. The cup clunked into the woman's forehead and bounced across the floor, leaving a trail of water droplets.

"Stay away from me!" Leigh hurled a string of obscenities as she unstrapped her naked wrist.

The nurse retreated. "Darien, I need you," she called down the hall.

An orderly, slightly shorter than the nurse but built like a lumberjack, hurried into the room. "Let's all just stay calm." He approached slowly.

Scabs, welts, and stitched cuts covered Leigh's arm. She could yank out the stitches. Maybe she'd do more damage that way.

The orderly was almost to her.

Leigh hooked stubbed fingernails under four stitches. "Stay back, or I'll pull."

The man stopped advancing. "I know you're upset. It's okay—"

"Nothing is okay," Leigh cried. "My baby is dead. And it's my fault!" The last sentence escaped as a wail.

Nakasha dashed into the room. "You're awake." She shoved past the nurse and orderly. Her shoe knocked the loose cup into a corner. She pulled the room's single chair to Leigh's bed and gripped her hand, dislodging it from the stitches. "I was so worried." Though her dark skin hid the redness around her eyes, it did nothing to disguise the puffy rings, or the shadows carved along her nose and across her cheeks. "When I came home and found you gone, EMS there, and...Tim..." Her face twisted in grief, and ugly tears streamed down her cheeks and matted stray curls. "Then I went looking for you and found you bleeding out." She held Leigh's hand to her chest. She shook as she sobbed. "I thought I was going to lose you and him in the same night. You can't just leave me, baby girl. I need you!"

Leigh ripped her hand out of Nakasha's grip. "I can't do it, okay? It's too much." She scraped up the corner of her other bandage and ripped it off.

"Leave that alone." Nakasha reached across Leigh to stop her, but she pushed her away.

The orderly closed the distance to the bed in three long strides, but when he tried to get hold of Leigh's arm, she raked her nails across his cheek.

"Get—away!" She grabbed a decorative flower arrangement from the table and cracked it over the man's head before swatting Nakasha with it too. "I don't want to see you again," she growled. "You couldn't just leave me be—let me do one of the few things I've ever really wanted."

"You don't mean that." Nakasha shrank away from her.

"Yeah, I do."

"You really want to die?" Nakasha clasped tear-damp hands. "How...how can you actually want that?"

Leigh hurled the fake flowers at Nakasha, and the plastic vase hit her arm. "Tonight I lost everything, and the one person who claimed to love me wouldn't...just. Let. Me. Die! Go away! Get out!"

Nakasha grabbed her purse and ran from the room. The look of hurt and betrayal etched into her pinched brows, tear-filled eyes, and downturned lips.

The orderly grabbed Leigh and restrained her.

"I hate you," she called after Nakasha. "I hate you all."

35

Los Angeles Zoo
Thursday, March 28th

The group stopped for lunch and headed to one of the restaurants inside the zoo. Lane followed Gibson and a few of the crew. Food in hand, he found a table in the corner.

Two other cast members sat with Gibson and the day's tag-along producer, some well-to-do who'd never seen a film shoot in his life. He was nice enough, but crew members had spent the morning making sure he wasn't in the way.

Monica ate with her fans among the tech crew, including two guys he felt like he should remember. They were both a bit taller than him with dark hair. The way one of them slouched sparked a memory. The guy from the guard shack in front of the studio complex.

"I'll cover ours, Jack," said Vic from in front of the register.

"We got it, Garrison. Don't worry about it. Easier to have it all on one bill."

"All right." Vic smiled at the gruff director and took hers and Sophie's food. Her parents followed, carrying their own meals.

Sophie scurried over to Lane and climbed into the chair beside him. "Hi."

"Hey."

Vic set their food on the table and wrangled a booster seat for Sophie. Vic's mom hauled the little girl into the elevated chair so she could reach her chicken nuggets and mixed fruit.

"These are so good!" Sophie offered Lane a red apple slice.

He took it—partly to appease her, and partly because he agreed.

"My daughter says you're quite a talented actor." Vic's mom held out a hand. "Gabby Ellis. Nice to meet you."

Lane shook her hand.

Vic's dad sat opposite Lane. "Bert." He nodded to Lane. "How different is it, being in a detective movie as opposed to science fiction?"

"A lot less makeup."

The Ellises and Vic laughed.

After an awkward pause while Bert Ellis prayed over the family's meal, they talked about Lane's past film and TV roles most of the hour as everyone ate.

When they finished talking about him, Lane said to Vic, "Any more books planned?"

Gabby looked away, and Bert turned his attention to the last few bites of his burger, but Vic's smile didn't fade.

"Not for a few months." She patted her rounding middle. "After that, I suppose I'll find out."

"Time to get back to it, folks." Gibson tossed his trash and waved everyone out of the packed eatery.

"Dad, can you take Sophie around the zoo some more? Mom and I are going to sit awhile."

"Sure, honey." Bert returned the booster seat, took Sophie from his wife, and helped the little girl throw away her trash.

"Thanks for the company," Lane said.

"You're welcome," said Gabby. "It was great to talk with you."

Marcelle St. Apartments

Lane sluffed off his shoes at the foot of the bed. A long day of shooting, plus too many nights with little to no sleep, were quickly catching up with him. Ten years ago, he could have gone on a few hours of sleep per night indefinitely. Not anymore.

He stepped to the bed, and something crinkled under one foot: an old bank statement. He dropped to the floor and used the flashlight on his phone to peer under the bed. More papers lay strewn across the carpet.

The break-in.

He had to check everything. The thief must have found his document stash—social security card, birth certificate, passport...bank account information.

But oddly enough, the only papers disturbed were bank documents. Nothing else was out of place.

After four attempts, he punched in his online banking password. Dozens of small purchases ate chunks of his check every day, beginning Sunday night. Fraud detection hadn't caught them because the amounts were low, and almost every purchase was from places in the area or sites he frequented.

Lane fumbled for his bank card and called the number on the back.

36

Simmer Lounge
Friday, March 29ᵗʰ

Lane checked one more time to make sure his new debit card was still in his wallet. The customer service rep had said he might not want to get his hopes up for a quick refund.

Lester met him at the door. "Thanks for coming in. Thought you might be working on your movie, but figured I'd come look. Since Barb's out with the flu, I'm gonna need somebody else to host tonight. I can't keep running back and forth from the bar, and everyone else is already too busy waiting tables. I'd bring Barry out, but he hates talking with customers."

"I can always use the extra work."

"Be prepared. It's a big night. Never know what might happen."

After a second day of filming at the zoo, the bar smelled wonderful. Lester's maintenance crew kept it spotless.

Lane grabbed a tablet and took the host desk.

Three hours later, a group of four college guys arrived. Lane seated them near the kitchen door.

"Hey, you're the dude from *Lakeisha Anderson* last month. I knew I recognized you." One of the group pointed to Lane's magnetic name badge.

His hand itched to throw the tag away.

"Thought you weren't into women. Guess you are now," another of the guys snorted.

Alisha caught Lane's eye and came to take the group's orders while he hurried out the back door before he knocked out one, or all four, of those idiots.

He squatted outside. Deep breaths only made him nauseous as the stench of old trash erupted from the dumpster.

Five minutes later, Lester opened the door. "I kicked 'em out. Said if they couldn't be civil with my staff, I didn't need their money."

"You didn't have to do that."

"My bar, my rules. You ever need anything, you say so."

Lane laced his fingers and propped both elbows on his knees.

"What is it? I know that look. Something's eating you worse than those four morons."

"I got evicted."

The rush of a car passing on the next street filled the alley.

"I have to be out in two days, and...I don't have anywhere to go."

"Why don't you get a hotel?"

"Can't afford it. You've been more than generous with my pay, and my other job is fine, but...there are some debts I can't put off."

"What about financing? A loan?"

"Don't qualify. Credit's too bad, and my card's maxed out."

"It's not much, but we've got a room here at the bar. You'd have to use the customer bathrooms and cook in the kitchen, but it's better than a back alley or a shelter. Bring your stuff on over after work, or tomorrow. Let's get inside." Lester waved the dumpster's stench away from his nose. "I left Eve to watch the bar. She can't mix a margarita to save her life." He started for the open door.

"Lester?"

The bar owner stopped.

"Thanks."

"No problem."

37

Marcelle St. Apartments
Saturday, March 30th

Lane packed a box and markered "kitchen" across its side. Since he didn't have a TV or other electronics, his stack of belongings wouldn't impress anyone.

He opened another box. Should he take pots and pans?

Simmer's kitchen had everything he needed to cook, and he wouldn't be able to get another place soon. Too many bills. He couldn't afford to replace anything he didn't have to.

Silverware, utensils, and kitchen gadgets filled another box.

The magnets and notes on the fridge...Stephen's old shopping list, written in his signature messy print. Lane had told him to keep a list on his phone, but Stephen had always handwritten his and tagged it to the refrigerator with a magnet.

Lane reverently placed every piece of paper from the fridge into a thick envelope and tucked it inside the box.

Even now, something of Stephen's remained in every room—his keys sat on the table by the door, shoes under the bed, razor in the bathroom, pictures in the living room.

Lane targeted the bedroom next. Stephen's clothes—minus the ones the thief took—still filled half the bedroom closet.

He packed his clothes into one garment bag and two duffels. Stephen's, he carefully folded and placed in boxes. When he found Stephen's favorite shirt, he stopped. The thing's hem was worn through in several spots. He'd told Stephen to toss this thing ages ago.

It still smelled like him. Printer paper, cappuccino, and his spiced citrus cologne.

He closed his eyes and took a long, slow whiff of the battered, dark green tee. It smelled of friendship, comfort, home. Would it still smell like Stephen after a couple months buried in a cardboard box?

When he finally put the shirt away, it was dotted with a handful of damp patches.

Lane boxed board games, books, and knick-knacks from the living room.

They'd had their third date in this apartment, met with the wedding planner so often they'd bought her a mug to keep here. Half their honeymoon had taken place here, playing games, watching movies and baseball games, reading books together—even though Stephen preferred TV to books.

This was his home.

And he had to leave it.

"You should be here to help me through this," he whispered into the empty apartment.

He wanted to fight the eviction—push back, make his landlord regret ever sending that notice. Better yet, march down to the idiot's apartment and knock every last insolent word out of him. But no matter how satisfying that might be, all it would do was make his life more complicated.

Lane placed the contents of the coffee table in one last box and taped it shut. He ferried three boxes at a time to his car, careful to lock the apartment door every time he left.

Others' things littered the halls and foyer.

His and Stephen's remaining possessions filled the trunk and two-thirds of the backseat.

Evicted tenants loaded moving vans, cars, trucks.

All the apartments came furnished, and several disgruntled neighbors stowed tables, chairs, dressers, and couches in their vehicles. If Lane had the room, he'd have done the same. His Versa might fit a dining room chair, but he didn't feel like lugging it into the elevator and stuffing it in the back, not even out of spite. Something about further violating the space he and Stephen had shared for so long didn't feel right. Besides, he wanted to see out the back window.

He set the last box of Stephen's things behind the passenger's seat and drove away from the only home he'd known for the past six years.

Simmer Lounge

Lester handed Lane two keys. "Might need these. Big one's the front door. Small one's for your room."

"Thanks for letting me stay here."

"It's all yours until you can find someplace else, or you get back on your feet. I'll help ya unload." Lester carried some of Lane's boxes into the bar's small living space.

Inside was a 19" TV, recliner, fridge and freezer, bed, floor lamp, and one tiny table.

All the furniture—except the TV—was older than Lane, but Lester had maintained it well. The chair and bed weren't plagued by that odd musty mothball smell Lane recalled from visiting grandparents as a kid. The tabletop was free of scratches too. Scraggly, rust-colored carpet covered the floor. A rolling garment rack huddled by the far wall and served as a closet.

"I'll see you in a few hours. Feel free to snag any fresh stuff you want from the kitchen. We've always got too much." Lester shut the door.

Lane unpacked necessities, plus a few things to make the room homier. He took out two pictures and the contents of his coffee table, then arranged them around the TV and beside the bed.

Along with the unframed pictures of him and Stephen sat a book of photographs from Oregon—one of Stephen's acquisitions from their trip there two years ago—and Vic's book, still unread.

His stomach grumbled at him for skipping breakfast, but at least he was free to graze off the kitchen's produce until he could make a grocery run. He made it to the kitchen before the staff arrived and grabbed two red apples. Since he still had a month left on his annual gym membership, he could shower there in the mornings after workouts too. A laundromat down the street would work for washing clothes.

After Lane unpacked, he sat in the recliner, tilted it back, and fell asleep. An hour and a half later he woke, just in time to change and get ready for his shift. He was stiff, but he'd be all right once he got moving.

At least he didn't have to drive here from the apartment. If anyone arrived early and saw his car, they'd assume he came in early too. He would have to move the Versa around back during the week so no one knew he was staying here.

He locked the room and helped Lester set up the bar for the night.

38

Simmer Lounge

Sunday, March 31ˢᵗ

The bed sagged on one side and creaked every time Lane moved, making sleep impossible. Just after 4 a.m., he switched to the recliner. Dark blinds covered the little window above the bed, and bars crossed it from the inside, making even open blinds result in little light.

When Lane rose, it was afternoon. He took yesterday morning's chicken and vegetables from the fridge and reheated them in the kitchen. Lester had picked up more fresh fruit, so Lane took an apple. Food in hand, he flipped on the TV in his room and found a baseball game—the first he'd watched since the break-in.

Four innings came and went, and Lane reached for the DVR to catch the rest of the game while he worked his shift.

No DVR.

He would have to check the results online later.

The night's business buzzed. Customers flooded in and out until closing.

Lane returned to his room. Alone.

A notice on his phone: a text from Stacey. *Hey. How's everything in*

Hollywood?

He couldn't tell her the truth. That he'd lost his apartment, was at odds with his co-star, and hated going to the set.

He sat in the recliner in silence and leaned it all the way back. What he wouldn't give to sleep in his own bed again.

Another text from Stacey.

Dad might not want to talk to me, but his lawyers were happy to. They're going to help me build a case against the company that fired me. They're confident enough that they agreed to take a portion of whatever I get instead of charging me up front.

Good for her. He was glad she was standing up for herself. Now he had to find a way to take control of his own life.

39

Nine Years Ago

2785 Wanderer's Way, Los Angeles

Friday, December 17th

Leigh's wrists ached.

She'd been home for one week. Her mom and dad hadn't said much. Dad was at work most days anyway, and Mom had a part-time job at the florist two blocks away.

The clock in the living room ticked, never missing one beat. They never used the fireplace. She wasn't sure why her parents hadn't bricked it up years ago. Tim's ashes sat in the urn atop the mantel, in full view from where she sat on the couch, knees to chest, feet tucked under a blanket.

The clock's constant *tick, tick, tick* exacerbated her headache. She'd already downed the three ibuprofen her mother laid out for her. The rest was hidden somewhere, along with the Tylenol and any other medications she might OD on. Even the Benadryl was gone. She'd looked.

Silverware and knives were also in an undisclosed location. All garden tools were locked in the shed out back, and her parents didn't own bolt cutters.

There were plenty of other methods to end her misery, but none she felt like using. At least not yet.

"Shut up already!" Leigh hurled a throw pillow, and the clock smashed onto the carpet, where it finally went silent. She retrieved the pillow and tossed it back onto the couch.

The plastic shards were sharp. She picked up the largest piece.

The front door opened.

"Sweetie, what happened?"

Leigh dropped the shard.

"Are you okay? Did anything hit you?" Her mom kicked stray pieces into a pile. "I'll pick this up." She dropped her purse by the door and grabbed the broom from the pantry. Within minutes, every piece of the broken clock was cleaned up, tied in a bag, and deposited in the trash can by the street.

"Are you hungry?" Her mom guided her into the kitchen. "What would you like?"

"Nothing." Leigh shuffled out of reach. "I'll be in my room."

Her mom didn't follow.

40

Lane grabbed coffee and dumped in creamer.

Monica rounded the coffee dispenser. "What's the matter? Didn't get enough sleep last night?" She said it loudly and gave him a suggestive grin before snatching an orange from a bowl of fresh fruit.

He gripped his coffee until the Styrofoam crinkled. Thankfully, it didn't buckle. He didn't need a burned hand on top of everything else.

Even the thought of other people looking at him and Monica as a couple stoked rage. He wanted to wring the woman's neck, rip that smirk of victory off her too-red lips. He wanted to shout in Monica's face that the very thought of her touching him made him both angry and sick.

Instead, he uttered a string of expletives.

"What did you just say to me?" Monica's voice shrilled with anger.

Gibson, who had been talking with today's visiting producer, stalked over to Lane. "I don't know what your problem is, Harris, but you'd better be glad Garrison isn't here. She's got enough going on without having to listen to the one person she hand-picked go off."

Cast and crew stared at them.

Monica stood out of Gibson's line of sight, hands on hips, poisonous smile in place.

But Lane wouldn't let her win. Not this time. He pushed past Gibson and stared Monica down. "Everything you say is a lie. I am not and never have been in any sort of relationship with you."

"Then what do you call those photos everyone saw a couple weeks ago?" Monica challenged.

"One-sided."

Monica's face went blank for half a second. Then she burst into tears. "Why can't you just be happy for us? Stop denying that you love me!" She shoved past him and ran to the women's room, mascara tracing black trails down her cheeks.

A hundred disapproving eyes fixed on Lane. The lights hummed, and there wasn't enough air. He'd tried to loosen Monica's hold, only to wind up more thoroughly tangled in her web.

"All right. Show's over. Everyone back to work." Gibson corralled the group away from the coffee dispenser. "You." He pointed to one of the makeup crew. "Go touch up Henderson." He faced Lane. "And you. Keep your personal drama off my set. Am. I. Clear?"

More argument would only make this worse.

41

Lane stood alone while Monica, her makeup again flawless, shot another scene.

One of the boom operators, a guy in his mid-forties with a goatee, finished a doughnut. "Wish I'd had the guts to get with her." He nodded to Monica.

"I didn't—" He curled a fist so tightly his joints ached. "We. Are not. Together."

The crewman crumpled a napkin to rid his fingers of powdered sugar. "I get it. You'd rather keep it under the table for a while." He stepped closer. "Just between you and me, though, that ship sailed a while ago."

Vic walked into the studio. Her eyes were tired, but she smiled. Gibson pulled her aside and talked with her quietly while Monica did three more takes. After each one, Gibson growled adjustments, then kept talking with Vic.

Vic whispered to Gibson, patted his shoulder, and took a chair. The chain and ring she always wore slipped from her collar. She snagged it and tucked it back into her shirt.

"Her husband died in an accident late last year," said the boom guy.

Lane's bare right hand itched. He knew what that was like. "She never mentions him."

"Nah. She's pretty quiet. I wouldn't have known about it if I hadn't seen the newspaper article right after it'd happened. Yeah, I know. Nobody reads newspapers anymore." The man tossed his used napkin and headed back to his post. He switched out with another of the boom crew as Lighting, Makeup, and the prop guys swarmed to set up for another scene.

Lane took the chair next to Vic. Partly because he found her company calming and partly to ward off Monica, who tended to avoid Vic.

"Hey," she said. "Get to read any of *Hahnen'En* yet?"

So that was how it was pronounced. Less complicated than he'd thought. The word had a curious rhythm to it, almost like a horse's gait, just missing the fourth beat. "Not yet. Had a lot going on the past couple weeks."

"Me too."

"Sophie's not with you today?"

"Usually, she goes with her grandparents on my appointment days. Doctors' offices aren't the best places for kids. She's always great when I have to take her, though. I'm glad God gave me such a little ray of sunshine. What'd I miss here? Everyone seems tense—even Jack. He stopped me at the door and said I should go home." She laughed quietly.

"Just a...misunderstanding."

Vic nodded. "Can you believe we've only got six weeks of shooting left? Seems like we just started."

"Yeah. Seems like it." He wanted to say it had felt more like an eternity, and every day he had to spend with Monica made the horror of it seem never-ending.

Simmer Lounge

Customers clamored outside Lane's room, keeping him awake past midnight.

The recliner had acclimated to his shape, but sleeping in it was still challenging. Discomfort and noise from customers and staff jerked him from the verge of sleep at least ten times.

At 1:15 a.m., he gave up. He inclined the chair and clicked on the TV. Too bright.

He clicked it off.

Lane turned on the lamp in the corner. On the bedside table lay Vic's book. All his other books were still in boxes, and reading an e-book on his broken phone would be more hazardous than relaxing. Even if her book bored him, maybe it would lull him to sleep.

He skipped the foreword and went straight to Chapter 1.

42

Eight Years Ago

2785 Wanderer's Way, Los Angeles
Thursday, August 18th

Leigh stared at the email in her inbox, not believing what she'd just read.

An agent wanted her manuscript. After four months of nonstop queries and little to no response, someone wanted her book.

She shut her laptop and stared at the mantel in disbelief. Some writers worked for years trying to get their books published, but she somehow had a "yes" in less than six months. At least one thing had gone right in her wreck of a life.

Tim's urn still sat there, the lone decoration atop the otherwise bare mantel. No one talked about it, but her mother kept it dusted, at least. Seeing the urn always dredged up hatred and bitterness, and until now, she'd always regretted failing to take her own life that night she found Tim's still little body. She still wished she'd succeeded, but maybe the sentiment wasn't quite as strong now.

She opened her laptop again, just to make sure she hadn't imagined the agent acceptance email.

Nope. It was still there.

She closed the computer again and held it close as she hurried to her room to draft a response.

Seven years ago

Monday, May 14th

Leigh hurled a sneaker across the room, and it smacked the bedroom wall loudly enough to summon her mom to her door.

"Everything all right?"

"No, Mom. Everything *isn't* all right," Leigh snapped. "My son is dead. The advance on my book isn't nearly enough to let me finish my degree, and now I can't even get this stupid edit done!" She let out a frustrated yell and hurled the matching shoe across the room to join its partner.

"Victoria Leigh Ellis, we don't throw things in this house."

Leigh cursed. "I'll throw whatever I want." To reinforce this statement, she slung a hardback toward the room's single window. It missed the glass and left a dent in the drywall. "Get out of my room. I can't think with you here." She kicked the door shut. Her mom stood outside her door for a full minute before heading down the hall. The hiss of sink water and the clang of pots said she'd retreated to the kitchen.

Almost a year and a half she'd spent in this house. Would her parents never learn to leave her alone? The only thing keeping her here was a never-growing bank balance. No matter how much she saved, she never managed to have enough to move out.

She hated being here. But she hated the idea of living on the street just a little bit more.

Hopefully, her first royalty check would be decent enough to give back her freedom.

Tuesday, June 12th

Leigh clicked send, and her adjusted manuscript was off to her editor. If they asked her to change anything else, she'd scream.

Wednesday, November 7th

She'd barely slept these past five months. It had been almost two years since Tim's death. No matter what she did, she couldn't get that horrible night out of her mind. His closed eyes, cool skin, blue lips. Her baby boy. Gone before he'd even turned one. He'd be three this year— just coming out of toddlerhood and getting ready for pre-K.

Leigh's fingers flew over her laptop keyboard as she clacked out the last chapter of book three in the series she'd contracted with her publisher. No matter how fast she wrote, how much she edited and re-edited, she couldn't outpace the choking sense of loss that threatened to smother her. Not for a single minute.

"Time to go." Her mom's voice filtered through her door.

Leigh's expression soured even more. She'd forgotten. Sunday, she'd spent tapping out five chapters, so she hadn't gone with her parents to church. Now she was forced to go with them tonight, since it was her only opportunity to fulfill her one-service-a-week agreement for living in her parents' house rent-free. She hated it. Just not enough to pay the exorbitant rates a SoCal apartment would demand from her bank account. Royalties were decent, but they only covered so much, and she never knew what they'd be from month to month.

Grudgingly, she shut her laptop and grabbed a sweater. The church people could get over her torn jeans and old tee.

"Ready?" her mom said when Leigh stepped into the hallway.

"Yeah," was all Leigh said as she brushed past her mom and headed for the RAV-4 parked in the driveway.

New Bethany Baptist Church, Los Angeles

Leigh flipped through a battered hymnal as the new pastor, Silas Hendrick, spoke from the small podium he'd pulled into the middle of the aisle. People sat in the sections directly to either side of him. It was a smaller crowd than usual, not that she was going to complain about that. Fewer people to pepper her with questions.

"God's plan involves work," said Hendrick as he flipped to another page near the front of his Bible. "But even God rested on the seventh day of Creation. It's important we take time to rest and remember the One who gives us strength to work in the first place."

Leigh fanned a section of hymnal pages, and the resulting breeze scattered the unruly strands of hair hanging around her face. She'd thrown her hair into a scrunchie this morning, but hadn't bothered brushing or untangling it since. She'd been too busy writing.

A wave of fatigue hit her as she shoved the hymnal into the rack on the back of the pew in front of her. Maybe Hendrick was right on this one. She could definitely use some down time.

She sneaked a glance around the auditorium.

There was no way she was getting real rest here, in the middle of all these people—half of whom had known her since they'd moved here ten years ago. The other half regarded her as a curiosity, and even tonight, she'd caught some of them staring.

She pulled out her phone—one luxury she'd worked into her limited budget, since the only other option was a junky flip phone. A glance from her mother. Leigh ignored it. The deal was she had to be here, not that she had to pay attention.

She scrolled through travel sites, looking for the cheapest getaway she could find.

43

On set

Tuesday, April 2nd

Lane, Monica, and four extras stood where instructed as the crew finished setting up scene 42. In it, Monica's character worked with Lane and others to uncover the killer's identity. He wanted to take two long steps away from her, but she clung to his arm for the entire scene. When it ended, he was first to escape.

Keeping such late hours the past few nights threatened to catch up with him, and it was only 11 a.m. He poured black coffee—still hot. No creamer.

A few feet away, Vic dropped six crackers in a paper cup—probably for Sophie, who sat nearby watching the production staff. She set the cup on the table and leaned forward like she was about to be sick. Her knees buckled, and she grabbed for the table edge but missed. Her eyes rolled back, and she slumped toward the floor.

Lane dropped his coffee. It sloshed over the cup lip and splashed the table, leaving a brown puddle. He caught Vic and eased her to the floor, keeping her knees up.

She woke seconds later.

"You okay?" He discreetly sent one of the wardrobe guys for the set medic.

"Thanks." Vic's voice was weak as she brushed stray hair over one ear.

The medic came and took her vitals. "Does anything hurt? Did you hit your head?"

"No. I'm fine. Mr. Harris caught me before I did any damage." Vic dusted off her dress, and Lane and the medic helped her stand—slowly. "I'm okay. Really." Vic waved the medic back to his post.

"Do you faint often?" Lane said.

"Sometimes. BP gets too low. My doctor says it's temporary."

Sophie, seemingly unaware of the seriousness of what had just happened, took Vic's hand. "Mommy, can I have a juice?"

"Sure, sweetie." Vic returned to her chair and dug out a juice box for Sophie.

The little girl returned to Lane and looked up at him as he wiped spilled coffee from the table and got a second cup.

"Hi." Sophie waved.

"Hi."

"You're sad." She nudged her empty juice box into the trash can. "I'm sad too sometimes, because my daddy went to Heaven. He's with Jesus now. Mommy says we'll go see him one day."

"I'm sorry about your daddy."

Sophie took Lane's hand and smiled. "It's okay. Mommy gets happy when she talks about seeing Daddy again. I wanna see him too, but Mommy says it's gonna be a long time before I can. Do you know people in Heaven?"

Over the years, Lane's father had been outraged at his choices. His mother had grieved but kept silent. Not once had his father asked him why he'd never had much interest in women, or what made him decide to marry Stephen. Instead, he railed at Lane, threatened to disown him. He hadn't listened, hadn't paid attention, hadn't reserved judgment. He had shoved his conclusions in Lane's face and had refused to back down. From what Lane knew of Heaven—if such a place existed—that wasn't how it was supposed to be.

"I don't think so," he said.

"Oh." Sophie laid a thoughtful finger over her lips. "Well, that's okay. I know lots of people. You can come with me when you get there."

"Thanks, Sophie, but I don't think..." Should he destroy her version of the world? She wasn't even in first grade. "I don't think I'll be going with you."

"Don't worry, Mr. Lane. Mommy will be there before us. She can be your friend until I get there."

She thought he had meant he would end up in Heaven before she arrived. He didn't have the heart to correct her. "Who do you know in Heaven?"

Sophie released his hand and started counting on her fingers. "Daddy, Gram-gram, Poppi, Uncle Fred, Cousin Danny, my friend Terri, Mommy's friend Allie, Pastor Joe, my big brother Tim..."

Death had touched her far too many times. "That's a lot of people."

"Mommy says there are lots of people in Heaven we don't know yet. I wanna meet them all!" She grinned.

"What if Heaven isn't...real?"

Sophie's eyes twinkled, and she stifled a giggle with her small hands. "That's silly, Mr. Lane. Jesus has to take people who love Him somewhere when they can't live here anymore. Mommy says when we love Jesus, He makes sure we don't die for always. He can do lots of things. He can make it rain or snow, and make people well, and give people jobs, and—"

Oh, for simpler times.

"Mommy knows a lot about Jesus. You should talk to her."

"Thanks for telling me."

"You're welcome." Sophie darted back to Vic for a handful of Goldfish.

44

Lane sat, waiting for Gibson to call him back on camera.

Beside Gibson sat Sophie, watching him work. Gibson didn't seem to mind. The little girl was quiet and didn't disturb him or the crew. Lane remembered how rambunctious he'd been at that age and wondered what Vic had done to instill such a sense of respect for others in her daughter.

Vic snagged pretzels and cheese cubes and plopped them into a new Dixie cup.

"My grandmother would say you eat like a bird," Lane said as Vic passed him.

She pulled her chair beside him and sat. "Hazard of my condition, I suppose."

"No more fainting?"

"Just earlier. Nothing else since last time, in the parking lot." She crunched a pretzel.

Vic took a hair tie from her bag and poised to loop her hair into a ponytail, but the elastic band escaped her grip and flopped on the floor.

She reached to pick it up, and the ring she wore around her neck escaped her collar.

She still couldn't reach the hair tie, so Lane got it for her.

"Thanks."

"I've heard a story or two about that." He pointed to the gold band.

Vic smiled through unshed tears. "This belonged to Gavin—my husband."

At least rumors had gotten something right about Vic.

"He died in December, just before I found out I was pregnant." Instead of putting the ring away, she took off the chain and slipped the gold band onto her finger. It was too big and even with the chain still attached, it left a gap between her skin and the metal. "He didn't want anything ornate—said plain suited him better." She took the ring off and let it rest in an open palm. The chain coiled around the band like a golden scarf. "Where's your other ring? Leave it at home again?"

Lane rubbed his empty right ring finger. "I think I lost it."

"Oh. I'm so sorry. I'd cry if I lost this." She put the chain back around her neck. "It was a well-made ring, yours. I've never seen another like it, except that matching one you have."

"I—we...had them made."

"It's hard to lose someone, especially the person you considered your other half."

So she did know about him and Stephen. He expected her to end the conversation, change the subject, take her chair and move across the studio.

"Nights are the roughest." The bags under her eyes seemed more pronounced. Vic covered a cough with one arm before she went on.

"It's like the silence wants to remind you of everything you can't tell them—everything you can't experience again. You want to hold them tight, tell them about the day's frustrations—how you almost forgot your keys or ordered the wrong coffee. But...you can't."

"Yeah..." The word was almost too thick to say.

"That's when I remember how wonderful it will be to be reunited with him at Jesus' feet—when my time here is over. Do you know what that's like?"

He could lie—tell her he understood completely, but something told him she already knew the truth. "I...no. I don't."

Vic nodded. "It's a wonderful thing, Lane—knowing goodbye here on Earth won't last forever. Do you believe in life after death?"

"Not sure." Here it was, the long-awaited salvation from damnation pitch.

"I wasn't either. Once." She patted his arm.

Lane started at the unexpected touch, but didn't pull away.

No pitch. No elaboration. How could someone like her believe the same things his parents did?

Vic finished her pretzels and cheese in silence, and even though a tear ran down her cheek every few minutes, she smiled.

Lane kept to himself during lunch. Lamb with roasted vegetables and garlic butter filled his plate. He picked at it. Though his stomach rumbled, he didn't feel like eating.

Vic sat with Gibson, Sophie, and four production staff. She had lost weight since February. A little too much. Shadows hung beneath her collarbone. Just months ago, her cheeks still had a bit of roundness to them. Now, they were almost flat.

Sophie waved at Lane from her chair. He nodded to her, but he chose to eat the rest of his food alone. People glanced at him occasionally, though most ignored him, for which he was grateful.

Vic had said she was going to be reunited with the man she loved.

He wished with every last piece of himself that he could experience that reunion too.

45

Quik Fuel Convenience Store, Hollywood
Tuesday, April 2nd

Lane pulled up beside the gas pumps. His gauge hovered over E.

When he swiped his card to pay, an error message sent him inside. The line at the register was seven people deep, and it took fifteen minutes to reach the cashier.

"Can I get $30 on 3?" Lane inserted his new bank card into the slot at the base of the pin pad.

"I'm sorry. Could you try again?" The cashier tapped the pin pad. "Sometimes these things don't like chips."

Lane pulled out his card and slipped it back into the reader.

Declined.

"Looks like it's not going to take your card. I'm really sorry. Do you have another one? Or cash?"

Lane flipped through his wallet. This was the only card he had. His credit card was still maxed out, and two crinkled dollar bills were all that was left of his cash. He slipped them onto the counter. At least that would get him back to the bar. He'd used this same card all week. It should have worked.

A quiet voice behind him said, "Add it to mine. Fill-up on 5."

Vic slipped into the narrow space between him and a keychain display and stuck her card in the reader so discreetly he didn't even see her do it. The people in line behind him didn't seem to have noticed either.

Before Lane could protest, the register accepted her payment.

"Hi." Sophie held her mother's hand and waved up at Lane.

He smiled at the little girl as all three of them walked to their vehicles.

Vic got Sophie into her car seat and covered a cough with her arm. "Gas fumes get me every time." She turned on the autofill and leaned against the van.

Lane stood at the pump opposite Vic's. "You didn't have to do that."

"I know. You heading home?"

"Yeah. You?"

Vic nodded. "My parents are cooking dinner tonight at my house. My mom loves to cook for people. She would have done the cast and crew meals, but Jack told her he'd already contracted with a catering company." Vic set the pump handle in its cradle. "See you tomorrow."

Lane nodded. "Yeah. Tomorrow..."

Simmer Lounge

Lane checked his bank balance.

There should have been plenty for gas and his upcoming car payment, plus some groceries and a few other things. His latest statement read the usual, a grocery store down the street, gas stations in Hollywood and Huntington Park...and a large check he hadn't written.

The signature on the check wasn't anywhere near his handwriting.

Lane dialed Fraud Prevention. "A check I didn't write posted to my account this morning."

"No problem, Mr. Harris. The charges will be reversed, but it can take up to five business days."

"Can it go through any faster?"

"It could, but it usually takes at least five days. I apologize for the inconvenience."

"Can I close this account and open a new one? I've had multiple fraud problems."

"Sure. We can do that for you, but we'll need you to go to one of our branches during regular business hours."

"And what're those?"

"Nine to six. Saturdays nine to one."

Yet another delay he couldn't afford.

"Thanks."

Lane plopped into the chair, phone in his lap.

46

Seven Years Ago

Clear Creek Resort, Cabin 25, Rio Nido, CA
Friday, November 16th

Leigh set her single bag of luggage on the porch's top step.

The door creaked open, and a distinctly musty scent filtered out the door. The listing online said this cabin hadn't been used in a while and was in an unpopular location—something about an abundance of pigeons—thus the discounted rate. But the smell wasn't bad enough for her to care, and there wasn't a bird in sight. She pushed inside and shut the door behind her.

As soon as she'd set her bag on the single bed, she opened all the windows. Her laptop, she perched on a bedside table. Not that she intended to write during this trip. She'd brought the laptop more for comfort than anything. Every time she started not to take it with her, a sense of sadness washed over her. As if not having it would somehow be unbearable.

She laughed bitterly.

At least her parents had let her make the seven-hour drive alone. They weren't as worried about her killing herself, or else they'd have forbidden her. Not that they could really stop her if she truly wanted to try again.

Memories of that nightmare stay at the hospital two years ago flashed to mind. She *had* wanted to kill herself—to end this nightmare of guilt and pain and regret—but no matter what she'd done, someone had kept stopping her, whether it was Nakasha, the orderlies, EMS, or her parents. They'd all kept her from doing the one thing she'd most single-mindedly craved at that point in her life.

Now all she wanted to do was rest.

The bathroom was decent. Clean, simple. Just a tub, though. No shower.

She drew hot water and soaked until her fingers wrinkled, and the worst of the tension in her back and shoulders eased. Once she'd thrown on clean clothes and wrapped wet hair in a towel, she headed back to the bedroom. The musty smell still lingered, but it was thinning.

Maybe she'd go for a walk while she waited for the cabin to air out.

Saturday, November 17th

She should have known better than to rent a cabin with no Wi-Fi.

There was an Ethernet port on the wall beside the bed, but she hadn't brought a cable with her, and the guest services building didn't have one to loan her.

She kicked the nightstand, sending the lamp tumbling to the floor. Thankfully it didn't break when it hit the hardwood.

Leigh scooped it back into place with a low curse. She searched the nightstand's single drawer again for an Ethernet cable. No success. She was stuck out here in the middle of redwood country with no internet, no cell service, and nothing to do besides stare at nature and read magazines.

Her phone buzzed, and she snatched it up. Maybe she'd get service for a while before it dropped again.

A text from her mom: Praying for you. Love you.

She dismissed the text and tried to open a web browser, but even search engine home pages got stuck loading.

She tossed her phone onto her bed with an irritated groan.

Might as well finish unpacking. Her deposit was non-refundable, and she wasn't going to waste hard-earned money.

She dumped shirts and jeans into one dresser drawer, socks and underwear into another. When she reached for the sunhat her mother had shoved into her bag seconds before Leigh had zipped it shut, she found something hiding underneath it.

The Bible her parents had given her when she was ten. Her name was embossed in silver on the light blue cover.

She almost left it in the bag. She hadn't touched this Bible in years. Even when she was younger, she hadn't brought it with her to church. After all, her parents always had theirs with them, so why drag another copy to church if she wasn't going to use it?

She flipped open the front cover and fanned through the thick book. The pages were still pristine, a testament to how little she'd handled it.

But when she came to the middle of the Bible, the pages popped open, revealing a note tucked inside.

God loves you, whether you run to Hell or fly to the middle of the ocean.

Leigh read it twice. The words rang familiar, as if she'd read something similar before, but she wasn't quite sure where. Knowing her mom, it was probably something from the Bible. She stuck the note back in place and put the Bible into the dresser's empty bottom drawer.

Another walk.

That was what she needed.

Leigh headed outside, slipping on the sunhat before she stepped onto the porch.

47

Outside Lane's room, customers chattered until closing.

He couldn't sleep.

He considered turning on a game, but lately, they didn't keep his attention. Stephen's continued absence hammered into him every time he turned one on.

Abandoning the remote to the top of the TV, he picked up Vic's book and opened to where he'd stopped last time. The story was interesting so far, well-paced like a good thriller, but it didn't hold the same haunting quality many of his favorites maintained.

He read until Lester left at 3:15.

On set

Lane walked into the studio, on time, but groggy. He'd skipped the gym in lieu of sleep.

Scenes from Vic's book gave rise to odd dreams he was still shaking away. His hand itched for a sword pommel, and his feet seemed cold in cheap sneakers instead of high boots.

Vivid dreams weren't for him. Too real.

A notice near the refreshment tables sat in place of food: "Running late. Lunch at 2:30."

He hadn't had time to grab breakfast. Or coffee. But he could survive until 2:30.

"Harris, you're up." Gibson shooed Lane on camera.

Monica flounced on set before Lane reached his red-tape X. She tried to steal a kiss, but he turned in time to keep her lips from touching his. Instead, they landed firmly on his cheek.

Spearmint almost covered the reek of her breath. She'd forgotten her perfume today, but that same chemical smell lingered in her wake.

A woman from Makeup handed him a wipe. It came away with traces of wine-red lipstick, and he scrubbed his face to banish the lingering itch.

They ran the scene Gibson's standard five times.

"That's a keeper. But we're still behind schedule, so pick it up, everybody." Gibson rushed actors on camera while the crew prepped for the next scene.

Monica waited until they were off camera to trap Lane. She ran her hands up his chest.

"Leave me alone, or I swear, I'll walk off this set, and I won't come back."

Monica glowered. "Don't be like that."

"Then stop harassing me." He grabbed her wrists and pulled her hands away.

"Hello, Monica." Vic walked up, bag over one shoulder, Sophie holding one hand. "How's the morning been?"

Monica smiled, but her eyes flashed when she looked at Vic. "Great, Ms. Garrison. Thank you so much for all the work you've done. This wouldn't be possible without you." Condescension hid behind every word.

A wasp chose that instant to land on Monica's shoulder. She screamed and flailed, cursing at the insect until it buzzed away. With a huff, she straightened her blouse and stalked off.

"Hi." Sophie waved at Lane.

"Hey."

"That lady isn't nice." Sophie watched Monica as she reached for Lane's hand.

He expected Vic to scold her daughter for such bluntness. Instead, she released her hold on Sophie. "She would love to sit with you," she told Lane, "if that's all right. I have to take a call in a few minutes. If I'd known my doctor was going to rope me into this, I'd have taken her to my parents', but—"

"It's no problem."

"Thank you." She set her bag down just as her phone buzzed. "There she is. I'll be back in as soon as I can." Vic left the studio via the sticky exit door.

Lane set Sophie in the chair beside Vic's and took the only remaining seat.

"Daycare's that way." Monica pointed to a non-descript door in the corner as she passed them, headed for the ladies' room.

If Sophie understood Monica's jab, she gave no sign. She took a container of apple slices—yellow this time—from Vic's bag. She popped the lid. "Wanna share?"

"But I don't have anything to give you."

Sophie's tiny giggle bubbled up. "I don't care. Jesus wants me to share." She handed him a juice box.

Vic returned half an hour later, having left the problematic side exit door cracked just enough to get back inside. She seemed more tired than usual.

"Everything okay?"

"Just have a few extra appointments." Vic picked up Sophie with great effort and set the little girl on one knee. "Looks like you're going to see Papa and Nana a lot the next two weeks."

"But what about Mr. Lane?" Sophie closed the empty Tupperware box.

Vic kissed her daughter's head and hugged her.

"I'm sure your grandparents would love spending time with you," Lane offered. "I'll be okay."

Sophie agreed. But not immediately.

48

Lane had just finished his third cup of post-lunch coffee when Gibson signaled the next shot. "Harris, Henderson. Hope you both read the choreographer's notes about your practice sessions. We're shooting 53."

They weren't supposed to do 53 until Friday, and he'd been dreading it. This was a hand-to-hand combat scene where his character turned out to be in on the crime they were investigating. Monica was the only one there to stop him, and she had to stall him until backup arrived. They were supposed to have this big revelatory conversation during the brawl, so a shoot-out wasn't an option. Plus, Gibson wanted something flashier than a gunfight.

Lane wasn't sure how realistic that was, but film didn't always need realism. The only good thing was he wouldn't have to spend the next two days on edge about doing this scene.

He downed the last of his coffee and reviewed notes while the crew set up.

"Henderson, you sure you don't want your double doing this?" Gibson said.

Monica's cold smile made Lane regret lunch. "And miss a chance to dance with my co-star?"

"Fine. Harris?" The look on Gibson's face said Lane had better not abdicate to the stunt crew.

"All good." At least he didn't have to worry about her trying to kiss him during this.

They took their places.

The instant Phil signaled action, Monica lunged.

Lane dodged, tried to get in a shot at her, but she knocked his prop Baretta down stage and blocked his escape. "You're not taking me in." The edge in his voice wasn't entirely fabricated.

He threw a punch the way the choreographer had shown him, stopping just short of actually making contact, then following through inches from Monica's face. If he'd actually hit her, she'd be on the floor.

She put up an arm to deflect. "It doesn't have to be this way." She parried his second hit. "You can give yourself up."

His bitter laugh filled the set. "And let the great Hannah Stanton claim another victory? Haven't you taken enough?" He sneered for good measure.

"You said you loved me." She circled him. Her low heels clicked on the studio floor, and she was closing the distance between them. This wasn't in the choreography. The script called for her to keep her distance.

"I've said a lot of things." He matched steps with her, maintaining a four-foot buffer.

Monica was supposed to cry.

Instead, she attacked.

A year of agility training for a previous role kept him out of her reach, but with each strike, she came closer to landing a blow.

Gibson should have cut by now. Restarted the scene.

Her fist sailed toward his jaw. He blocked with a forearm. Unlike him, she wasn't pulling punches. There was enough power behind the blow to make his arm sting.

"All those people you hurt." She threw another punch.

He sidestepped.

"You're finally getting justice."

"I—I'm sorry for hurting you." Saying it felt so wrong. She was the one who'd violated him. Were this a real fight, he'd have overpowered her long before now.

"Save it," she snapped as two more detectives ran on camera, pistols drawn, to end the scene.

"That's a keeper," Gibson called. "Good use of those notes, Henderson."

Monica strutted off camera, looking far too pleased with herself.

Vic left around 5 p.m., but shooting ran until 7:30.

Once Gibson called it a day, the cast and crew packed up and left within twenty minutes.

Lane sat alone in the studio, which was dark except for emergency exits and a slip of light peaking under Gibson's office door.

A muted phone conversation leaked from the other room. Lane's chair scraped as he got up.

No shift at the bar tonight, but no money for gas to take a drive. The tank Vic paid for yesterday would last him, as long as he walked to get groceries and didn't take side trips.

Outside, a cool breeze swept leaves across the sidewalk as streetlights flickered on, obscuring what few stars broke through the city's dense nightlife.

Time crawled as he drove to Simmer, and traffic seemed five times as thick. The parking lot was full when he arrived, so he pulled around back, beside the dumpster. He rolled up his car windows and locked the doors before stealing in through the back.

Diners clogged every table and packed the bar.

Lester served never-ending drinks, cleaning glasses as they came back only to refill them immediately and pass them to another patron.

"There you are!" Eve tossed his name tag to him.

He barely caught it.

"It's crazier than summer at Disneyland. We're skipping breaks tonight. Alisha's got the desk, but she's having to run between it and her tables. Can you cover until Rhonda gets here? Barb's still on vacation, and Miguel's out with a migraine."

Lane grabbed his tablet.

Simmer Lounge
Thursday, April 4th

Dead on his feet, Lane plunked into the recliner and sluffed off his shoes—keys, wallet, and phone still in his pockets. He leaned the chair back and dozed.

At 4:30, the tap of rain woke him. Water streamed down the wall from the window, covering the floor around the bed.

Not rain.

Fire hydrant.

Lane vaulted from the chair and dragged everything away from the wall before dialing the fire department, then Lester.

"This is the second time in six months," Lester grumbled when he arrived. "Just replaced the seal around the window. Must not be the problem. Gonna have to get a whole new window. And drywall and carpet. Thanks for saving what you could. I'd hate to think what would've happened if it had gotten into the bar."

An hour later, Lane finished mopping the carpet with kitchen towels.

The hydrant was off now, but paint already bubbled from the wet drywall, and the carpet squished.

His pictures with Stephen lay in a crumpled, soaking pile. The only item on the bedside table to survive was Vic's book, which sat on the far edge, completely dry.

Lane set the book in the recliner in case of another incident.

He laid the soaked photos to the side. They'd be badly wrinkled once they dried, but hopefully they'd still be intact.

He hated to, but he had to leave for the studio. Making Gibson even more irate with him wasn't a good way to start the day.

On set

Monica held her nose. "You reek."

He wanted to return the sentiment. "Water problems."

"Harris, this isn't a plumbers' convention. Get to Wardrobe." Gibson shooed him away.

When Lane returned, sans the odor, Monica stayed three feet from him.

He didn't complain.

49

Seven Years Ago

Clear Creek Resort, Cabin 25, Rio Nido, CA
Tuesday, November 20th

Leigh reread three issues of *Gardening USA* for the fourth time as she lay on the couch in the cabin's small living area. She flopped the third issue back onto the coffee table and heaved a loud sigh. She couldn't do this anymore. She needed something to *do*. Walks were nice, but after the tenth one in three days, she was ready to strangle the next bird that chirped at her.

She rolled off the couch and went back into the bedroom. Maybe rearranging her clothes would help pass time. She pulled all three drawers out of the dresser and dumped the contents onto the bed. Her clothes tumbled out, but when she dumped the bottom drawer, her old Bible thumped on top of the pile of clothes.

She pushed it aside, ready to refold and rearrange her clothes, but every time she put something away, her eyes shifted back to the Bible and its light blue cover. She'd loved that color as a girl, even though she couldn't really remember why.

After another three shirts and two pairs of jeans were safely tucked away in the dresser, Leigh sat on the bed and picked up the Bible.

She flipped it open.

Title page stuff, a foreword by some publishing house, a page for the Bible's owner to write their name, and some other stuff she didn't pay much attention to. Finally, she reached the first page of actual text and, after a few minutes, she sank into reading the opening lines of the first section, Genesis.

It wasn't as if there was anything else to do.

She read the first chapter, its familiar words rolling over her as memories from childhood Sunday School lessons came back.

Before she realized, it was dark, and she had to turn on the bedside lamp to keep reading.

50

Vic made no appearance that day.

The crew packed up at 6 and scavenged the remaining snacks on their way out.

Lane got in his Versa but didn't turn it on until after sunset. Crickets joined rushing traffic in an offbeat ensemble. Despite the need to conserve fuel, instead of taking the highway, Lane skirted down back roads and through quiet neighborhoods where everyone was eating dinner or watching Primetime TV.

This had been his life.

Once.

He wasn't sure it ever would be again.

Simmer Lounge

Lane made it inside without being noticed.

The stench of wet carpet punched him when he reached his room. He was about to close the door when Lester came down the hall and grabbed a broom from the adjacent closet.

"Sorry about the stink. Nobody can replace the carpet until tomorrow. Window guy's gonna be here at 7 too. Thanks again. I'd hate to think what would have happened with no one here."

"Have a fan I can borrow once the bar closes?"

Lester tapped the broom closet. "There's one in here."

Two hours later, Lane surrendered to the suffocating stench and cracked the door.

Heedless of his need for sleep, customers chattered and laughed. Barry hung out near the front of the hall, ready in case of trouble.

Lane had unplugged the TV and moved it by the door, same with the lamp. The bare lightbulb hanging from the ceiling glared, but it was better than nothing.

Tucked into the recliner, between the seat and one arm, was Vic's book. Since sleep wasn't an option, he flipped to his bookmark.

He'd left the hero running, a price on his head.

A crash and a muffled yelp.

3:50 a.m.

The box fan whirred, covering the recliner's squeak as Lane rose and sneaked to the door. He was surprised the noise had carried over the roar of the fan.

A shadow passed the narrow hall leading to Lane's room. Too thin to be Lester. Too tall to be maintenance.

Lights were out.

Armed with a Swiffer mop, he hugged the wall outside his room.

The shadow cleared the hall, heading toward the bar. Lane followed, mop ready. The intruder stooped behind the bar.

And came up the instant Lane swung.

A bone-rattling shriek stopped the mop head an instant before it made contact. "Lane!"

"Alisha?"

"What are you doing here?" both said at once.

Lane fished for a lie. "Lester didn't want to leave the place empty tonight—in case something else happened before the repair guys got here in the morning."

"That explains the car around back." Alisha shouldered her purse. "I forgot this. Had to come back."

"How'd you get in?"

"Lester lent me a key a few months ago." She jangled a chain attached to a fluffy pink poof. A car key, a house key, and a key to the bar clanked together. "I always keep this in my pocket instead of my purse. Good thing too. You working tomorrow?"

His eyes drooped at the thought of another long day. "Yeah."

"Okay. Good night."

Lane saw her to the door and waited until her beat-up Corolla rolled out of the parking lot.

On the way to his room, he righted a stool. From under the bar, a seam of light leaked from the extra mini fridge where Lester kept the safe. He nudged it shut.

51

Lane ran the landfill scene a seventh time. The lights beat down on him. Sweat beaded his collar, and damp patches hugged his waistband and underarms. He was about to jettison the jacket.

"Still not right. Come in on the left again," Gibson said.

Wild bangs clung to Lane's forehead as he drew a prop Beretta 92 and, for the eighth time, raced two steps left of a line of red X's.

"One more. I want to feel it, Harris. None of this indifferent garbage. This guy you're after turned on you. He's going to murder you slowly—said so to your face. Give us that rage and desperation." Gibson stood outside camera view and waved Lane to the starting spot.

Phil signaled the cameras into action.

Instead of keeping his focus on the scene they were shooting, Lane thought back to the open fridge from last night.

Sometimes Lester forgot to lock the safe. Lane had found it ajar more than once and had had to close it. On good nights, bills stuffed the cash box until Lester deposited them the next morning. Not the most secure setup, but Lester never seemed to mind.

Lane sprinted to the halfway point, where he ducked behind green foam—a dumpster stand-in.

Lester always counted the night's earnings before he left, but he wasn't always right.

The studio lights shed their harsh glare over Lane.

The bar was doing well. Lester might not miss a few hundred.

A rivulet of sweat crawled down Lane's arm. He needed that money.

He threw his jacket in a pile and drew from his shoulder holster. Sweat beaded under his nose. He swiped it away before popping his head and gun over the would-be dumpster and aimed at a target hung on the other side of the studio.

"Cut! There it is." Gibson clapped. "Perfect touch ditching the jacket. Maybe Garrison was right about you."

Lane retrieved his jacket, but didn't put it on as he walked off scene, out of the smothering warmth of the lights.

Simmer Lounge

The dinner crowd descended en masse, but at least Barb was back now.

A mixed group of six took the table Lane cleared. One of the two women gave him a lurid smile, the glint of recognition on her face. She whispered to the guy next to her and slipped out her phone. "You must be the one everyone's talking about. How long you been here?"

He'd thought people were finally forgetting February's incident. "Couple months. May I take your order?"

"Just a sec." She leaned in. "Can I get a selfie?"

The camera's click made him want to grab the phone and kick it across the bar.

"My friends are going to freak." She posted the picture.

After closing, Lester relined the trash can behind the bar. Maintenance was on vacation until next week. "Roughest night we've had in a while. But we made it. Didn't even have to kick anyone out."

"Helped having Barry hang around the front." Lane rounded the bar.

The mini fridge was open a crack.

"Window's replaced. Guy gave me a money-back guarantee if it happens again. Sorry about the smell last night."

"The fan helped."

"Still. Thanks for looking out for the place. Don't think I'd have had it in me to stay." Lester gathered two other filled trash bags. "Back in a minute."

The row of shaded lights above the bar cast harsh shadows. Not quite as extreme as the lights on set, but enough to make Lane squint.

The back door creaked open, and Lester's jaunt to the dumpster seemed eternal.

With one shoe, he eased open the fridge. The full cash box still sat inside, uncounted.

The dumpster lid thwacked open.

A couple hundred bucks would tide him over until the bank fixed those fraudulent charges. Then he'd pay it back.

Lane took the spare key from under the box and opened it.

52

Terrace Arch Bank, Huntington Park
Saturday, April 6th

Lane sat across from the accounts manager, a guy probably in his early thirties. His eyes jumped from Lane to a desktop monitor. The crooked name badge pinned to his shirt read "Murphy."

"Lots of purchases." Murphy scrolled through a long list of transactions. His glasses mirrored every jump of the screen. "You didn't make any of these?" He turned the monitor so Lane could see.

Not that he needed to. He'd combed through all of it again this morning. "Only the two from Chastain Grocery. The others are from places I've never been."

"They're all local." Murphy pulled down his glasses and squinted at the screen. He tapped his keyboard. "Let's get this old account frozen and start a new one. If you have a bank card or checks, shred them. Minimum starting balance is one hundred dollars."

Lane eased five battered twenties from his wallet. He hesitated just a moment before letting Murphy take them.

Simmer Lounge

Lane parked his Versa by the dumpster at 11:13 a.m. Simmer didn't open until 2. Before he got out, he checked his messages. Another one from Stacey, only a few hours old.

Everything's set with the lawyers. We're going forward with a wrongful termination lawsuit, and we're gonna try for harassment too. Thanks for having my back.

Huddles is loving Bakersfield, even keeps up with me on walks now.

Hope everything's good with you.

Lane tapped Reply but only managed one sentence before erasing it. He hoped Stacey's suit got those idiots she'd worked for fired. For what they'd done to her and who knew how many others, they deserved to be humiliated.

His keys clacked against the knob as he unlocked the back entrance. When he passed the vacant bar, the remaining hundred in his wallet screamed to be returned to the cash box.

His room's fridge was empty except for a few bottles of water and two apples from the kitchen. Tomorrow he needed to make a grocery run.

Returning the money wasn't an option yet.

Lane came out of the men's room as Alisha arrived, just after 1:30.

"You're early again." She stowed her purse behind the bar, right where she'd left it the night before last.

"Avoiding traffic." Lane snapped his nametag in place and grabbed his tablet.

"Didn't see your car out front."

He'd forgotten to move it. "Parked in the back. In case it's busy."

"One more ding in my fender's not going to make much difference." Alisha grabbed her tag and tablet as Miguel, Rhonda, and Eve walked in.

Barb was last to arrive. She adjusted her glasses and tucked a gray curl into place. "Parking lot's filling up. Somebody posted another picture of Mr. Harris here."

The girl from last night.

"Sorry."

Barb chuckled. "My wallet's not complaining."

"Mine either," Alisha said. "Tips have never been this good. I can actually get my kid a real birthday present."

"You're the best thing to happen to this place in a long time," said Miguel. "Lester won't tell you, but we were going under a few months back—'bout to close."

Alisha hugged her tablet. "Don't know why you took this job, but our customer count's quadrupled in the past month."

"Just making ends meet," Lane said.

"That's hard to believe," said Alisha. "I've seen both your movies— that sci-fi one, and a murder mystery, right? And weren't you in a TV show a couple times?"

"Years ago on the TV appearances, and Renfrow's callback was a shock."

"Shouldn't have been. You're good."

The lifted bills in his pocket kept him from agreeing.

A text from Tina. Don't know what you did this time, but you're back on Lakeisha Anderson. Something about you and Monica Henderson again.

"Sorry. Gotta take this." To Tina he sent, *Will watch later.*

Lester opened the doors at exactly 4 p.m.

Barb kept order, but several customers, mostly women, snapped pictures while they waited. Lane kept to the back of the dining area to avoid the self-appointed paparazzi.

After shift, Lane opened a video app and caught snippets of the show Tina texted him about.

Lakeisha, with her perfect hair, manicured nails, and fashion perfect outfit, sat beneath studio lights. "Viewers will recall, back in February, we discussed Lane Harris, co-star of the forthcoming suspense movie, *Evident.* This morning, we received an anonymous source stating Harris and his co-star, Monica Henderson have been spending more time together lately. In fact, rumor is they're an item now. We reached out to director Jack Gibson for his input."

Horror kept Lane from closing the video.

Lakeisha primly crossed her knees. "Unfortunately, he declined our invitation. So let's take a look at this social media post from Monica herself."

A text block, accompanied by a photo, appeared on a large wall screen.

He didn't recognize the picture, but he did remember the bar. This was from the night Monica had assaulted him.

Lakiesha read the post aloud: "So happy we're making it official." She gave the audience a conspiratorial glance. "Looks like we have confirmation Harris isn't so averse to the ladies after all."

Lane stopped the video and closed the app.

53

Simmer Lounge
Sunday, April 7th

Lane replaced the TV and lamp atop new, brown carpet, an improvement over rust shag.

Nothing on but paid programming and a documentary on koalas.

He stowed forty dollars of groceries in the fridge and sat in the recliner.

At 1 p.m., Monica called. He let voicemail take it.

"Did you like our TV spot last night?"

Lane deleted the message.

Customers lined up around the building. New faces, the vast majority of them clearly not the bar's usual clientele.

Barry had to keep count in order to comply with maximum occupancy fire regulations.

Phone cameras flickered everywhere as Lane did his best to ignore shouted questions.

"Is it true? Are you and Monica really together?" said one woman after Lane took her order.

A hot answer scalded his tongue, but he wasn't about to say anything here. Last time he'd tried to reveal the truth, no one had believed him. Besides, this wasn't the time or place.

He refilled the customer's water and moved on.

Across the dining area, two college guys whooped from their table. Alisha obscured their view of Lane. "This isn't a show. People are trying to enjoy their evening."

"Us too," snarked one guy. "Get outta the way. We wanna talk to the guy who landed the hottest girl in Hollywood."

Alisha glared at them, and they quieted, but never stopped chattering about Lane and Monica.

Around 9, the crowd livened, and Lane escaped to the men's room.

"You're Lane Harris." A guy in his early thirties washed and dried his hands. "My sixteen-year-old sister won't quit talking about you. If this place allowed kids, she'd be here in half a second."

Lane gave a curt nod.

The stranger stopped, one foot out the door. "Probably too much to ask if you're keeping your options open?"

Lane retreated to the unoccupied handicap stall and locked it. He just wanted to be left alone. Blue walls smothered him, and cold seeped into his shoes from the tile floor.

Footsteps hammered outside, coming closer.

Someone jangled the door handle. "Anybody in here?"

"Yeah." Lane managed a strangled croak.

"Hurry up."

Two more sets of shoes jumbled into the restroom. "I saw him come in here." The rowdy diners from earlier yanked open the empty adjacent stall before jostling the handicap door.

"Hey, somebody's in there," said the guy who'd first tried the door.

"Got him," said one of the kids. "Hiding from fans."

Lane grabbed the plunger as the two guys wrestled the door. If they got in, they'd get a face full of rancid rubber.

"Just crawl under," said one.

"No way I'm getting these pants dirty," said the other.

Lester barreled in. "Get outta here. Go on. Git!"

Lane replaced the plunger and leaned against the back wall, head down.

A couple of stupid kids didn't bother him. He just wished the world would stop believing Monica without question. Last time he'd tried to take control of this outrageous narrative she'd spun, he'd failed. He wouldn't fail again. If Monica tried anything else, he'd make it explicitly clear he wanted nothing to do with her.

54

Simmer Lounge

Sunday, April 7th

Lester herded everyone out of the men's room before standing in front of the stall door. "You okay?"

Lane gave a vague "Yeah."

"Take the rest of the night off. With pay."

"But it's crazy out there."

"We'll be okay without you for one Sunday night. I see those shadows under your eyes. According to security footage, you don't sleep much. Lots of trips up and down the hall in the middle of the night."

Lane forgot to breathe as he waited for Lester to mention the stolen money.

"Get some rest." Lester left him alone in the men's room.

With the help of Miguel's borrowed hooded jacket, Lane sneaked past the filled bar and made it to his room.

He collapsed into the recliner.

Another text. This one from one of his credit cards, about the overdue balance.

With less than sixty dollars in his new account, he couldn't afford to pay them. He still needed to get with St. Philip's debt forgiveness department and try to talk the funeral home down to something he might be able to pay.

He rubbed throbbing eyes.

Later.

He would deal with money troubles later.

55

Seven Years Ago

Clear Creek Resort, Cabin 25, Rio Nido
Friday, November 23rd

Leigh flipped another page, and her mom's note dropped out of the Bible again. It landed face down on the bedspread, but Leigh shoved it aside as she kept reading. This section resembled poetry—or songs, maybe, but there was no music.

She hadn't appreciated it as a girl, but reading it now, she saw the elegance of phrasing in it, the beauty of the words themselves. Even if she didn't put much stock in what it said, at least it wasn't too boring a read. She had skipped some of the earlier sections, though. Too many names and rules.

Orange and gold filtered through the bedroom window. Sunset already.

Leigh closed the Bible, using her mom's note as a bookmark.

She sat up, stretched her legs. She hadn't taken a walk since the beginning of the week, and she'd been reading nonstop the past few days. It would be good to get in some exercise before going to bed, or else she wouldn't sleep tonight.

Leigh started to toss the Bible onto the bed, like she'd done every other night this week, but somehow that seemed wrong. She carefully set it on her pillow instead.

Most birds were settling in for the evening by now, as the last rays of sunlight filtered through thick boughs. No one was out here. Apparently this wasn't a very popular destination. Not that Leigh was surprised. This wasn't exactly a five-star resort.

She stepped over a dead branch that had fallen across the walking trail. Ahead, a squirrel skittered into the trees.

This place might not be a tourist trap, but it was beautiful. A wild rose poked out of the dirt beside the path, and deep pink petals spilled free of several opening buds. A small waterfall lay a half mile down to the right, and it wasn't far to an abandoned gazebo that must have been something to see when it had been maintained.

She stopped to take in the scenery. Trees, endless fallen leaves, sticks, and grass. It was the perfect setting for one of those fantasy action novels she sometimes glanced through at the local used bookstore back in L.A.

Her fingers itched. Not having written for nearly a week was making her a little spastic. Yesterday she'd opened her laptop, stared at the folder containing the three books in her mystery suspense series, and been overcome with the desire to start something new. But the moment she opened a blank document, all thoughts of what she might write vanished. No amount of trying had been able to push any words onto the page, so she'd closed the document, shut the laptop, and returned to reading. This wasn't a trip focused on writing anyway. She was here to relax, rest, take some time away from it all.

She sighed.

Almost 8:30. She'd better head back before it got dark. All she needed was to get lost and have to be rescued.

Sunday, November 25th

No matter how many times she shut the lid on her laptop without having written anything, she kept coming back to that blank document. It stared at her in expectation, waiting for her to fill it with life—with a story.

She let her hands fall onto the keyboard. There wasn't really anything to write about. Her detective set was done and off with her editor. She wouldn't need to work on it again for several months. In the meantime, she might find something else to write about, but she might not. There was no reason to try, for the moment.

Nothing out here spoke to her.

She pushed the old Bible aside and set her laptop on crossed legs. The blinking cursor stared at her, begging, pleading to move across the blank page—but she had nothing to say. At least, nothing she wanted to think about.

She clasped her hands. Looked out the window.

Morning rays of light shimmered through the trees, casting beautiful shadows and creating lovely patterns. She envisioned a castle with tall spires and a garden filled with roses and lilies of all colors. In that garden stood a lovely young woman, clearly of royal blood, skin dark and smooth, ringleted hair so black the sun left a cobalt halo around her face. Too bad such a scene only existed in the realm of imagination.

But maybe imagination was as good a place as any to find peace.

She turned her attention back to the laptop screen and started typing.

56

On set

Monday, April 8ᵗʰ

The moment Lane stepped into the studio, Monica threw her arms around his neck and kissed him. He grabbed her by the shoulders and pushed her off.

"Later, Laney." She extended one finger, leaving an irritated scratch as her nail grazed his arm.

The lingering sensation of her lips burned. He swiped his mouth with one sleeve to banish the lingering dampness and any traces of lipstick. His resolve from the night before came back. He wouldn't put up with this anymore.

Monica had stopped to get coffee. Her white blouse and jeans reflected nothing of the horror she'd inflicted on him two months ago, or the harassment he'd endured from her since.

She had tortured him long enough.

"I'm not doing this anymore." His voice was hard, angry.

Everyone went quiet.

Heads turned, including Monica's.

"I have told you over and over to leave me alone." In two strides, he'd closed the gap between them. "I don't know what you hope to accomplish with this charade, but I'm ending it. Right now."

Monica didn't even set down her coffee. "We've talked about this. You deserve to be happy. Dating a woman is nothing to be ashamed of." She reached for his arm again.

He batted her hand away, anger rising. She was trying to cast him as inept and confused, which only stoked his rage. He was anything but confused when it came to Monica. "We. Are. Not. Together!"

Everyone stared at him, including Gibson, who had just come out of his office on the other side of the studio.

But Lane didn't care anymore. "You've done nothing but make my life miserable since the day I met you."

Monica turned on fake tears. "Are you—breaking up with me?" She sniffled between words.

That was what broke him. The false pain. She had inflicted worlds of hurt on him, and she had the nerve to pretend this was anything other than a game for her.

His fist impacted Monica's face.

She staggered backward, wearing a look of complete—and very real—shock. Her eyes watered, and a bruise was already creeping across her cheek.

Gibson stormed over. "That's it. Get off my set, Harris. You're gone."

Without a word, Lane left via the front entrance and went to his car, where he sat for fifteen minutes with the windows down.

As his anger dissipated, satisfaction and horror filled him. He'd finally given Monica a small taste of what she'd done to him. He didn't regret it even a little. She'd press charges; he was sure of it. But that wasn't a problem for today.

The reality of losing his paycheck from the studio was the true problem. This put him in even worse shape than he already was. He needed to find a solution. But first, he had to get out of here.

Simmer Lounge

As Lane parked beside the dumpster, he got a text.

Tina.

What on earth possessed you to deck your co-star?!! Call me. NOW!

He wasn't in the mood to talk, so he shoved his phone in his pocket and locked his car. This early, no one was around, not even Lester.

Lane unlocked the back door. The scratch on his arm, from Monica's nail, itched.

He'd thought it through on the way back to the bar. With Simmer as his only income stream now, he'd have to keep slipping funds from the cash box. At least until he found another gig, or something that would let him get by. Then he'd gradually replace the borrowed money.

Lester had mentioned security cameras the other night. In the kitchen, above the grill and to the right, Lane found one. A second stared from the opposite corner.

On the way to his room, he discovered ten other cameras, some obvious, others camouflaged. Likely he'd missed a few exceptionally well-disguised ones too. The camera above the bar faced the dining area to give a complete view of the establishment. Another watched the hall as Lane trudged to his room.

Meager light filtered in from the window.

He didn't turn on the overhead bulb.

Tina's text sat in his messages. If he didn't reply and left it unread, she might assume he hadn't seen it yet. If she called, he'd let it go to voicemail.

Lester arrived an hour before the bar opened.

Lane met him at the broom closet. "Need another hand tonight?"

"Thought you'd still be on set."

"Got done early today. Director's making...revisions."

Lester's phone buzzed. "Eve's not going to make it tonight. You can take her spot if ya like. Barry will be around if you need him."

As Lane helped Lester clean up after closing, he sneaked glances at the camera above the bar and the mini fridge hiding the safe.

His last check from *Evident* would be a fraction of the usual. A few hundred dollars would help get him through the next week since his car payment was due Thursday. He might get extra shifts, but he couldn't count on that.

"I'll get the trash." Lane grabbed the can in the corner, followed by the one behind the bar. As he tied off the bag, he let his hand slip, and half the contents scattered beside the mini fridge.

He positioned himself between the camera and the concealed safe.

As he picked up a wet napkin with one hand, his other strayed toward the cash box.

"Need help?" Lester rounded the bar.

Lane jerked his hand back. "I've got it. These off-brand trash bags." He threw the last piece of garbage into the bag, along with his chances of extra cash tonight.

57

Simmer Lounge

Tuesday, April 9th

Water tapped Lane's window an hour after the bar closed.

No leaks this time.

In the morning, he had three missed calls, all from Tina. By 11 a.m., she'd left four more voicemails. Each one sounded more frustrated than the last.

Lester knocked on Lane's door. "Early out today too?"

"You could say that." Lane put his phone away.

"Miguel's boyfriend's birthday's today, so he won't be in tonight. I forgot to put it on the schedule. You want another shift?"

A second chance at the safe. Maybe he could snag enough to make his car payment and pay a little of his credit card debt this time. "Sure."

"Think you can help me clean up the back before we open? Just found out that hydrant leaked again last night, and it's a lake back there. Got into the dining area too. Gonna hafta mop. I hope the fire department gets this thing fixed before it floods the whole bar."

Lane's stomach grumbled.

"Grab something to eat real quick, and then meet me out back."

After a cheap meal bar—which Lane vowed never to buy again—he slogged through the pond at the back of the dining area, fenced by soaked towels.

"Drain never worked right." The hydrant on the cross street above still burbled. With a long-handled squeegee, Lester swept water toward a grate. No fire department yet. "At least that window's fixed. It do okay?"

"Yeah. Fine." Lane grabbed the mop bucket and swabbed water from the hardwood. No black patches yet, but if they waited too long to get this moisture up, the floor would be ruined.

"Surprised you didn't see this comin' in from the studio this morning. Still parking your car 'round back, I see." Lester nodded to Lane's Versa. "Might wanna check it. Windows are down. Don't usually have problems with thieves, but never hurts to be sure."

The windows.

He'd been distracted by texts yesterday—forgotten to roll the windows up.

Lane rushed to his car. The interior was soaked. Standing water in the floorboards reached above the door lip, and when Lane opened the driver's side, it splashed out.

"Not a good sound." Lester rounded the passenger's side and poked his head through the open window. "Must've happened after you got back from the studio this morning. Got a wet/dry vac you can use. Couple fans oughta do most of the rest, but you'll need three or four boxes of baking soda to keep away the mold. Probably need a proper cleaning to get it back to the way it was."

Lester went inside and returned with a red, rolling six-gallon bucket, hose ready. "Sooner you get to it, the better." He handed Lane the vacuum.

"What about the bar?"

"You got the hard part. I can do the rest."

Lane swallowed guilt as he vacuumed the bulk of the water in fifteen minutes and spent the next hour detailing cracks and crevices. Lester hadn't thought twice about helping him. Ever. And here he was planning to steal from the man. Again.

Not steal. Borrow. He promised himself he would repay Lester.

It was 1:40 now. Not enough time to set up fans or grab baking soda before shift. Barely time to clean up and change. Lane rolled up his windows and hauled the vacuum inside.

Five more missed calls from Tina.

58

Simmer Lounge
Tuesday, April 9th

Another batch of customers stared at Lane as he took orders from newly seated diners.

"What a creep," a young woman from a nearby table said, not quietly enough. Her girlfriend agreed. "Talk about a good reminder of why I stay away from men. They think they're entitled to everything, and when something doesn't go their way, they get violent."

A woman old enough to be Lane's grandmother glowered at him. "Aren't there any other wait staff?"

Alisha balanced a water pitcher and a tray of food. Eve hurried from the kitchen with two orders while Barb seated people, and Rhonda watched the bar while Lester took a restroom break.

"I'm sorry, no. Is there a prob—"

"You oughta be ashamed of yourself. Won't leave a woman alone, then beat on her."

Monica.

She must have publicized what happened yesterday. That explained Tina's persistence.

"You think because you're a man, you have the right to do whatever you want. Maybe you could get away with that in my day, but times have changed. You're no better than a stalker, or a rapist." She left her seat, came within six inches of Lane, and glared up at him. "I hope you get exactly what you deserve."

Lane itched to shove her away, and the muscles in his arm clenched. She had no idea what she was saying.

"I'm shocked you had the nerve to go out in public today." She repeatedly jabbed a finger into his chest.

He ached to grab her hand and twist until her wrist cracked. "Excuse me." He kept his tone painfully even and stepped out of reach.

She lunged for his arm.

He dodged.

"Don't you walk away from me." She swore as she grabbed for him again. "It's men like you who make the world a trash heap for everyone else."

His collar was too tight, but he didn't unbutton it. Glass crashed near the bar, and Lane jumped.

In his instant of distraction, the customer seized him by the shoulders and shook.

The world convulsed, and Lane clawed the woman's hands away. "Get off me!" He struck blindly.

The woman screamed and let go, hand to one red cheek as she spouted more curses.

Spots danced in the room, and Lane couldn't get a full breath. He stumbled back as heat washed over him.

"Time to leave." Barry inserted himself between Lane and the woman.

She threw a punch at Barry, and he didn't bother to avoid it. Her fist thunked into his solid chest.

"I said it's time to go." Barry herded her out of the dining area.

"Having that pig work here is shameful!" She shook a finger at Lane. "I'm telling everyone I know." Barry ensured she found the door.

Alisha touched his shoulder. He jerked away. "You okay?" she said.

A blistering headache overtook him. "No," he whispered. "I have to go. I'm sorry." He wove through shocked diners and bar occupants.

When he reached his room, he locked himself in and slid to the floor.

Yesterday's incident at the studio mixed with what happened minutes ago. The satisfying smack of his fist against Monica's smug face morphed into the horrifying desperation that had filled him tonight as he'd fended off the angry woman. She was so sure he was the one to blame.

Flashes of the night with Monica hammered him until he wanted to scream.

He had a refilled bottle of prescription sleeping pills left over from the months after Stephen's funeral. When he found it buried in the contents of his old bathroom, he downed three pills and collapsed into the recliner.

59

Simmer Lounge
Wednesday, April 10ᵗʰ

Grogginess weighed Lane's eyes and refused to be rubbed away. His arm still itched from Monica's scratch two days ago, and a bruise had formed on his chest where the woman from last night had jabbed him.

He staggered to the door.

Voices. 4:12 p.m.

The bar was open.

He couldn't go out there. Not after last night. People would gawk as if he were an exhibit, and he couldn't do that right now.

His car payment was due tomorrow. But the past month's tips might cover what he lacked, and he hadn't counted last night's meager haul yet. Lane emptied his tip stash—forty-nine dollars short.

He should have deposited the cash yesterday, but with the leaky hydrant, time hadn't permitted, and it was too late to go out this afternoon. In the morning, he'd run to the bank.

The last hundred in his wallet would cover the difference between what he owed and was in his account, but only for the car payment.

The phone bill was due next week. He would drop the health plan. Cut expenses and pick it up again when things were better.

If they ever got better.

Outside, two customers laughed as they passed the hall.

Lane grabbed a bottled water from the fridge, downed another meal bar fast enough to avoid the taste of sugary cardboard, and turned on the TV. Lester's limited channels included two soap opera re-runs, a game show, a historical romance series, and several news stations.

Lane turned it off and sat.

Vic's book, tucked between the recliner arm and seat, popped free. The slightly skewed cover drew him to open to where he'd left off.

This was the strangest fantasy he'd ever encountered. It was heartfelt, uncontrived. Hahnen'En, the main character, was a self-sufficient man making his living doing impossible quests, some of which shocked Lane. He admired the man's accomplishments, but because of Hahnen'En's pride, a rival quester had manipulated him into killing the king's niece, earning Hahnen'En a death penalty.

11 p.m. came, and Lane didn't want to close the book, but he had to get to the bank early, so he tucked it away and leaned back in the recliner. He downed one sleeping pill and set his alarm.

Thursday, April 11th

Lane gagged when he opened his car door. The stink of mold made his eyes water, and he grabbed a kitchen towel to sit on instead of the damp driver's seat. Some of the moisture leaked through anyway.

He'd have to stop on the way home and grab baking soda if his wallet allowed.

With all four windows down and the air on full blast, he made it out of the parking lot.

Terrace Arch Bank

The teller took Lane's deposit slip.

"How soon will this post?"

"Should only be a few hours for a cash deposit." The woman tucked the bills into her drawer and handed him a receipt.

"Thanks."

Stop an' Shop Discount, Huntington Park

At the front of the store, two customers rummaged through a 25¢ bin of expired candy as Lane searched for the baking section.

A lone cashier dusted a battery display as he guarded the register.

In the back corner, Lane found a dozen squished boxes of baking soda at a bargain 10¢ apiece. He grabbed five and, before leaving the parking lot, strategically placed each box inside his car.

Simmer Lounge

Lane checked and rechecked his account, waiting for the money to clear.

Between each refresh of his online banking app, he checked Monica's social media posts. Sure enough, there it was at the top of her page: a picture of her with red eyes, smeared mascara, and a huge bruise on her face. The caption expounded how Lane had violently attacked her after a blowup on set.

There wasn't anything he could do or say to convince anyone she was making up most of it. He hated being railed at by strangers, but what made him truly angry was her claiming they'd ever been romantically involved. The single intimate moment they'd shared had been forced, as was every other instance of physical contact since that night. Just the thought of her made him sick.

He closed Monica's page and refreshed his bank app. Finally, the pending status beside his deposit disappeared. He made his car payment just before Lester knocked.

"Got another shift for ya."

"Sure you want me out there?"

Lester chuckled. "I've had my share of bad customers. One reason I keep Barry on the payroll. He hasn't had this much fun in years. If you're willing to work, I'm willing to have you. Besides, I don't put too much stock in gossip."

"So you don't believe I punched my so-called girlfriend?" The word left a sour taste.

"Not my place to judge. If there's anything I've learned about people over the years, it's that they do things for a reason. Whatever truly happened with you and that woman isn't my business, but I know you well enough to say you didn't just up and decide to hit her without cause."

Lester's faith in him was encouraging, but it also added to Lane's guilt.

"What about the customers?"

"Lot can happen in a day. People forget—find someone new to torment. Talk shows will talk about someone else pretty soon too."

Lane could use the money—and another chance at the safe. The thought bit into his conscience. Here he was taking advantage of the one person who had just given him the benefit of the doubt.

But there wasn't another choice right now.

"I'll take it."

60

Seven Years Ago

Clear Creek Resort, Cabin 25, Rio Nido, CA
Wednesday, November 28th

Leigh stared at the fifty pages of story she'd hammered out since Sunday. It wasn't anything like her suspense set. It wasn't even a genre she usually wrote—or read for that matter. High fantasy wasn't her thing, never had been. But this story, this piece of herself felt most at home in a fantasy world, so she didn't question it.

Her main character became more interesting the longer she spent with him. Something about the man drew her to him in a way no other character had. He was sworn to his king's service, and he did his job so well the king considered giving him a title and the lands to go with it. But that was all superficial. Underneath that noble, loyal exterior burned a rage she completely understood. Writing him brought back the all-consuming anger she'd felt upon waking in the hospital that night she'd tried to kill herself. No matter what she or her character did, that anger remained, simmering just under the surface. They couldn't get rid of it, couldn't fight it. They were helpless. It would remain, persist until it consumed them.

She forged ahead, taking her character into an encounter she already had a bad feeling about even before the worst happened. He murdered the king's niece—and not entirely without knowing what he was doing.

Suddenly her character was thrown into panic, and he fled before the king or his guards could catch him.

Leigh shut her laptop and laid a hand atop it. "I know how you feel." She set the computer on the bed and got up to get something to eat out of the small kitchen. "It just never stops dogging you." She poured a glass of water and drank it before slathering peanut butter on a slice of bread and folding it into a half-sandwich. She went back into the bedroom, intending to continue the scene she was in the middle of, but a wave of fatigue hit her and she pushed the computer aside, reaching instead for the Bible she'd almost finished reading.

She flipped to where she'd left her mother's note last time.

This final third of the book was different from the rest. Instead of a bunch of stories, it was mostly personal letters written to groups or individuals. She didn't understand most of the contents, but she browsed it anyway. Nothing else to read—unless she wanted to memorize more gardening magazines.

61

A few minutes after midnight, he went out back for a quick break. Only the rush of traffic and an insect serenade awaited him instead of the bustle of customers and bar patrons. The waste management company had emptied the dumpster yesterday, so the pungent cloud wasn't as thick.

The back door squealed open again.

Alisha leaned against the wall beside him. "Not too bad tonight."

He was glad he'd remembered to move his car out front before the other wait staff had arrived. "Not so far. Never know, though. Could change."

Alisha chuckled. "Like that birthday party last week? Those execs must've sung every song on the radio by the time Lester and Barry kicked everyone out."

"My sister-in-law's cat sings better. None of those guys were on-key."

"Don't remind my poor ears. Wait. Sister-in-law?" She sagged a little.

Lane displayed his ring.

She flushed. "I don't really follow a lot of Hollywood stuff. You never mention anyone, so I thought—I'm an idiot." She headed inside.

"No, you're not."

She stopped, hand on the doorknob.

"He's...gone." Aside from the veiled reference he'd made to Vic, this was the first time he'd recounted Stephen's death out loud. "Guy was high—hit him head-on when he was going in to work. He never made it out of surgery." He expected to choke, lose composure. But emptiness consumed him instead.

"I am so sorry. I can't imagine—" Alisha covered her mouth with both hands as she teared up.

"It happened last October."

"Only six months ago?" Alisha dabbed her eyes on one shoulder.

"Seems longer. And shorter."

Lane started as Alisha hugged him.

"Sorry!" She backed off.

"It's all right."

"How did you go back to acting so soon?"

"My agent, Tina. She's annoyingly persistent sometimes, but she's usually right. And she put up with me sitting out for three months after...the accident."

"She sounds great."

"She is. Tina's the one who found the audition for *Evident.*" Though, right now, he wished he'd never stepped foot on set. And that he didn't need to apologize to Tina for not taking her calls over the last day or so.

"I can't wait to see the movie when it comes out. Who're you bringing to the premiere?"

She said she didn't follow Hollywood news. She must not know he'd been fired.

"Haven't gotten that far."

"As soon as I have the chance to see it, I'm going to. I can tell people I know one of the co-stars."

Miguel poked his head out. "Incoming batch of late-nighters."

"Be there in a sec," Lane said.

Everyone left just after 3.

Lane changed the corner trash can and set the tied-off bag at the end of the bar. The fridge was shut tonight. He wrestled the full bag from the can behind the bar, but before he could pretend to drop it, Lester held out a hand.

"I'll take it out. Good to get some air after a long night in."

Lane handed over the closed bag. When Lester reached the dining area, Lane wiped sweaty palms on his pants. The instant the back door squeaked open, he kneeled, back to the camera, and pretended to examine an outlet under the bar.

With one hand, he eased open the door enough to snag the spare key and pop the safe. Uncounted bills piled to one side where Lester had stashed them when there were too many to fit in the registers.

Lane sneaked a small stack into his front pocket, locked the safe, and shut the fridge.

The transgression took less than a minute.

62

Simmer Lounge
Friday, April 12th

Once Lester left for the night, Lane retrieved deodorant, shampoo, a box of wet wipes, and a kitchen towel and retreated to the men's room.

Two days without washing his hair had made his scalp itch.

Since his gym membership had expired, he'd had no place to get a shower and limited resources to imitate one. He'd sprayed down with air freshener before and twice during shift to avoid customers noting any lingering body odor. Alisha must have been nose-blind not to have noticed.

He took off shirt and T-shirt and worked off-brand shampoo into his hair. When he rinsed, lukewarm water ran down his chest in thin trails. Only weeks ago, he'd have walked outside like this. Sans the soap.

Not now.

The consequences of flagging diet and lack of proper exercise stared at him. Instead of the screen-ready frame he'd maintained for years, he resembled an overworked and underfed delivery man. Lester wasn't kidding about the bags under his eyes either.

This might make for interesting tabloid headlines, and at least it would be less invasive than what they'd already published about him.

He ruffled his hair dry before taking off the stink of the past two days.

In the morning his car still smelled, but not as badly with the baking soda boxes spread through the cab and back seat. He still rolled the windows down and turned up the air. More gas, but covering the stink of damp was worth it.

Lane deposited a stack of stolen bills as soon as the bank opened. That would cover his phone bill, personal items, and gas when he needed to fill up again.

As he drove back to the bar, his conversation with Alisha last night hammered him. Gibson hadn't announced his replacement yet. Not unusual. Recasting could take a couple weeks, which would infuriate the cranky director. Maybe by now, they'd onboarded more sponsors to cover the costs.

What would Vic say when she found out he was gone? He didn't know why she'd insisted on casting him. His previous work wasn't that impressive.

Blue lights.

Lane pulled over.

The officer came to the driver's side window. "Sir, do you realize you ran that light?"

He hadn't even seen it. "No. I'm sorry. Got a lot going on. Guess I was distracted."

"License and registration, please."

He complied.

The officer examined them before heading to his cruiser.

Lane rested his forehead on top of the steering wheel. This was the last thing he needed. Another expense.

The officer returned within a few minutes. "Gonna have to issue a ticket." He handed Lane a slip. "Got a couple speeding tickets already this year. Better be more careful. Court appearance info's at the bottom."

He signed the ticket.

The officer handed over a copy, returned to his car, and left.

Lane read the slip and cursed. If he paid, this would wipe out half of his deposit. He'd have to contact them ahead of time and disclose his financial state. They might consider reducing the fine.

Simmer Lounge

Several customers snapped pictures of Lane as he waited tables, but no one accosted him.

Alisha offered a hesitant smile every time she passed him to deliver orders. He wanted to return the sentiment, but a neutral front was all he dredged up.

The weekend crowd piled in at their usual hour, making the night pass quickly.

Saturday, April 13th

Lane tossed three trash bags in the dumpster after closing.

Lester stopped him when he went back inside. "Got a minute?"

"What's up?"

"I think somebody's shorting a till."

Lane wanted to lock himself in the broom closet.

"I checked footage of both registers the last couple nights, but can't spot anything wrong."

Heat piled in his throat. "It's been a long week. Someone might've miscounted."

"Not this much."

"Could be stuck in a drawer."

"Checked that."

"Not sure then."

"I'll keep looking into it. Could be I'm the one miscounting." Lester rubbed his arm.

"You okay?"

"Just tired. Served a lotta drinks. Like you said, long week. See you tomorrow."

Lane stood in the dining area until Lester left the parking lot.

63

Silence pinned Lane in the recliner, but he couldn't sleep.

Traffic rushed by outside, and headlights peeped in through the window.

He'd tried watching late night TV, but he could only stomach so much brain-numbing content. One inning of an online baseball game faded to white noise as he slogged through a lake of junk email until he'd spent his last ounce of fortitude.

A new text from Stacey sat unread.

Every conflict from the past few days culminated in a thought-numbing haze. Sleeping pills rattled inside the translucent brown prescription bottle as Lane shook one tablet out and downed it without water.

The haze slowly melted into bearable silence.

Lane cleaned the front windows, swept, and Swiffered before Lester arrived.

Small penance for what he'd done.

"Place looks great," said Lester an hour before opening. "Gotta put down new nonslip mats behind the bar. Old ones have enough holes to strain vegetables. Wanna help?"

"Sure." Lane unloaded a large shipping box from Lester's trunk. It was harder to lift than it should have been. "You can ship this stuff here instead of hauling it from your house."

"What if they deliver while you're on set?"

He realized his near slip. Lester didn't keep up with Hollywood gossip or social media. He didn't know Lane wasn't on *Evident* anymore. "Right. Never mind."

As they tossed the second old mat into the dumpster, Lester grimaced.

"Everything okay?"

"Yeah," Lester grunted. "Think I pulled something." He held his left arm tight. "Haven't felt this old in a long t—time." He wheezed and collapsed against the dumpster. Sweat sheened his face and neck.

"Lester?" Lane kneeled on the hot concrete. "Can you hear me?"

Lester nodded. "Heart—" He gasped for breath.

Lane called 9-1-1.

The ambulance arrived seven minutes later.

One EMT stopped Lane from getting in the back with her and Lester. "We're taking him to Jenkins Rawling. You his son?"

"Employee."

"Gonna do without him tonight, then. It's good you called so fast." She hopped inside and shut the door.

Lane rushed into the bar and taped a note to the door before heading to the hospital, careful to mind the speed limit. License suspension would only add to his problems.

Jenkins Rawling Memorial Hospital, Los Angeles

The reek of sanitized floors, latex, and alcohol wipes accosted Lane the instant he entered the ER. Anxious relatives huddled in groups. People stumbled or dashed in, begging to be seen as the receptionist kept order.

Stephen's accident was like this.

He hadn't spent time in the ER waiting room then. But St. Philip's ER had similar chairs and the same brand of TVs mounted in opposite corners.

"Please sign in here, and someone will see you as soon as possible." The nurse nudged a clipboard under a half-sheet of plexiglass.

"I'm here about a heart-attack patient who just arrived. Lester Williams?"

"You family?"

"Uh...yeah."

The nurse lowered her voice. "I'm not supposed to tell you this. But if it was my family, I'd want to know too. He's stable. It's still touch and go, though. Don't know much more. He can't see anyone, doctor's orders. Probably not going to allow visitors until tomorrow at the earliest."

She hadn't said it, but Lane read the truth in her face. He might see Lester tomorrow, if he lived that long.

"Thanks." Lane sat in a corner chair beneath a TV.

Channel 12's news anchor droned about weather and local politics.

At least here, personal crises occupied everyone. Not a single person snapped a picture of him. He wasn't even sure any of them knew who he was. A relief.

64

Jenkins Rawling Memorial Hospital
Saturday, April 13th

11 p.m.

Lane still sat alone in the waiting room.

No news.

People filed in and out of the ER in various states of disarray. All ignored him.

No one at the bar had his number, so he hadn't expected them to text him, but having at least one other person show up at the hospital seemed decent. Lester had no family—at least none who would speak to him. Lane understood that.

His phone buzzed.

He expected anything except the notice hanging at the top of the screen: a private message on his social media account—from his mother.

At least it's a woman this time.

Lane left it unread.

Sunday, April 14th

Lane approached reception around 1 a.m. "Any updates on Lester Williams?"

"Not yet." The nurse offered what she probably assumed was a reassuring smile, but the flicker of dread in her eyes said she wasn't optimistic. "You should get home. Get some sleep. If you want to leave a contact number, I can call you if anything changes."

He scribbled his cell number.

Simmer Lounge

A few cars swung into the parking lot, but left soon afterward.

Lane paced his room until closing time. No calls. Whoever had arrived first must have taken down his note. Presumably, they'd notified everyone else.

He hadn't eaten since this morning, but he couldn't bring himself to eat anything. Not right now. Any second, he expected the dreaded call. But each circuit of the room yielded nothing except another view of his meager possessions and sparse furniture.

If Lester didn't make it, Lane would have nowhere to go.

He could stay at the bar as long as power and water were on, but after that...

Another notification. His phone bill was due tomorrow.

With a frustrated groan, he paid it—before he forgot—leaving his bank balance a fifth poorer. The traffic ticket slip, still in his pocket, crinkled as he shoved his phone in with it.

Dirty clothes littered the unused bed.

A laundry run would give him something to do.

Spin Cycle 24-hr Coin Laundry, Hollywood

Lane loaded everything into the washer, not bothering to sort. The provided tropical detergent reminded him of cheap cologne, but it was free.

No one else was in the establishment except one employee, jamming to whatever played on his AirPods. The young man didn't even look up as Lane started the washer.

Simmer Lounge

His clothes were still warm when he dumped them on the bed and started folding. Silence buzzed in his ears as the harsh overhead bulb glared down on him. Still no call from the hospital.

Since he had no dresser, he stacked clothes in sorted piles atop the bed. He hadn't bothered hanging anything in the rolling garment rack. He hadn't expected to still be living here.

Before sunrise, he flopped into the recliner to doze.

A nightmare took Lane sometime before dawn. Every detail of that horrible day Stephen died assaulted him without mercy.

So much blood. It covered his hands, his clothes—his face. A pool of crimson on the concrete bathed his shoes and soaked through to his skin.

Stephen lay twisted on the pavement, thrown from the vehicle. EMTs and the man who'd hit Stephen were nowhere to be seen.

This wasn't how it happened.

He fumbled for his phone. He didn't have it.

"Help me," Lane called to passersby. "Someone call 9-1-1!"

No one listened. They passed without a glance. It was as if he didn't exist.

Stephen's eyes glazed, dulled, emptied.

Lane shook Stephen. "Don't leave me. You said you never would!"

But Stephen failed to rouse.

65

Simmer Lounge

Sunday, April 14th

Lane called to check on getting his fine reduced. "Sunday," he muttered as he hung up without speaking to anyone.

He grabbed a water and an apple from his room's small fridge. Nothing on TV, but he let it drone while he ate. He tossed the empty bottle and gnawed core in the garbage and trekked to the men's room to wash his hands.

Cold water splashed his face and neck as he wiped off dried sweat from last night's horrors. His hair was oily again, and he needed a proper shower—badly. It was a wonder the ER nurse hadn't thought him homeless.

He wiped down again and generously applied deodorant.

The silence in his room threatened to smother him.

He fished for the TV remote, which had fallen between the recliner arm and seat, but instead of cold plastic, his fingers brushed the soft, well-read edges of pages.

Vic's book.

The folded Post-it he'd used as a bookmark was ripped on the edges and askew between pages. He flipped to where he'd left off. Hahnen'En was about to be caught by a mercenary hired by the king, but he had one last desperate gamble to evade capture.

Lane woke with Vic's book laying open on his chest. He wasn't sure when he'd fallen asleep.

Strange dreams lingered. Vivid instances of what he'd read hung in his memory, but he felt as if he'd lived them. He'd run so hard his legs ached, and he couldn't breathe. But dogs had found his trail, and he'd had to keep up his pace or risk being dragged to prison for murder. He'd held his sword, and the weight of it still clung to him.

He scratched itching hands.

Still no calls or texts about Lester.

Jenkins Rawling Memorial Hospital

Lane checked with the reception desk. "Is Lester Williams in a room yet? I left a contact number, but no one's called."

The woman checked her computer. "CCU. No visitors." She must have noticed something in his face and offered an apologetic look. "Sorry. He's not doing well. Maybe you can see him when he's a bit better."

Simmer Lounge

Instead of bowing to the temptation to check Monica's social media page again, Lane searched for news on *Evident*. He found an article on a gossip site about Gibson looking for a new cast member—one about the film's onboarding a big, politically conservative company as a sponsor—and one discussing personal relationships among cast members. He stopped reading the last one after seeing his name at the top of the second paragraph.

He wondered what Vic was doing. She'd been off set for almost two weeks—assuming she hadn't come back during his absence.

A quick internet search yielded little. Rumors about her pregnancy being a cover-up for terminal illness, more rumors about illicit trips out of the country with Gibson or other production staff. It all read like a bad soap opera.

He picked up Vic's book and got back to reading.

66

Simmer Lounge

Monday, April 15th

Lane couldn't stand the constant itch of his scalp anymore.

He found the nearest public shower—thirty minutes away.

Los Angeles Public Showers and Restrooms, Facility #2205

Kept shrubs and trees circled the building and dotted the half-full parking lot as vending machines dispensed junk food and drinks to truck drivers and transients.

Lane grabbed a waterproof bag of clothes from his trunk.

He had to wait, but took the first available stall.

Hot water. It rushed over him like a flood, and for ten minutes he stood unmoving beneath the stream. His bag hung from a hook inside the stall, and he dug out soap and shampoo. Wet wipes and sink water couldn't match this.

The guy in the next stall wailed a pop song, and two others joined him.

Lane hated this song.

He pocketed his valuables and tossed his bag in the trunk.

A man several years older than Lane approached. His clothes fit, but smelled in need of a good launder. "Help a fellow out?" He pointed to a rusty junk-heap car at the end of the parking lot. No one was in the vehicle. "Outta gas. Need a few bucks."

"Sorry. I don't carry cash." Lane went for the driver's side door.

The man followed him. "Just a five, man. Please? Gotta get home for my grandma's birthday. Might be the last one I get with her."

"I said I don't carry cash. I'm really sorry, but I have to go."

"Wait." The man squinted. "I know you. You're that actor—the one from *Lakeisha Anderson*. Real piece of work, you are, just like the rest of 'em." The man spit on the concrete. "No actor I've ever heard of don't carry a few bucks. What're you doing here anyway? Dodging paparazzi?"

His phone buzzed.

The hospital.

"I can't help you." He picked up as he slipped into the driver's seat and locked the doors.

"Lane Harris?" A woman's voice.

His stomach dropped. He knew that tone. "Yes."

"You were the only contact number we had. Lester Williams was moved to ICU a few hours ago, but he's now in a coma."

"Thanks for letting me know." He gripped the steering wheel.

The man outside tapped his window with a stick. An insult accompanied each tap.

"I'm sorry. We'll contact you with any further news." The woman hung up.

Lane rolled down the window enough to growl, "Get away from my car."

The man threw vulgar gestures at him as he left the parking lot.

Simmer Lounge

Lane hung a sign on the front door. "Closed until further notice."

In his room, he dialed the number for the traffic call center and, after a run through the auto-attendant, reached customer service. "I need to see about getting my fine reduced."

"Let me transfer you."

Hold music played in a thirty-second loop.

"Court Collections. This is Chris."

"I have a fine I need to get reduced—or put on a payment plan."

"Can you prove paying the full amount would constitute financial hardship?"

"Someone robbed my apartment a couple months ago and stole my bank information. I have a police report."

"Go ahead and give me that."

After Lane gave Chris the information, the collections employee put him on hold.

Lane circled the recliner. The carpet Lester had put in was thinner than before, and his shoes scuffed with every step.

"Mr. Harris? Your fine is reduced by half, and we'll mail you a payment schedule. What is your current address?"

Lane paused. He didn't know the bar's address. "Just a second." He found the information online and gave it to Chris.

"We'll send that out today."

"Does this mean I don't have to come to court?"

"That's correct."

One less thing to worry about. "Great."

At least something was going right today.

67

Seven Years Ago

Clear Creek Resort, Cabin 25, Rio Nido, CA
Friday, November 30th

Leigh sat cross-legged on the wooden floor of the cabin's tiny bedroom, back against the bedframe and ancient box springs. Her laptop cord stretched over the bed and plugged into the outlet beneath the window. Today was the last day she was supposed to be here. Checkout was at 11:30, and it was already 10.

Her fingers flew over the keyboard. This scene was too intense to stop now. Her main character was still on the run, but one persistent bounty hunter and his dogs were right behind him. Ahead loomed mountains far too high to cross on foot without supplies. A dark wood and a wide lake hemmed him in on either side. He'd hoped to lose his pursuer in the wood, but a band of gloam wolves had kept him from entering.

He sprinted through the thickening trees. If he could put enough distance between himself and the dogs, he could find a place to lay a false trail and then double back.

Leigh saw everything vividly in her mind's eye. Baying hounds were nearly audible. The scent of dead leaves, towering pines, and humid air flooded over her. There was no escape from justice. It would find him, and he would pay the price for what he'd done.

A knock at the cabin door made Leigh jump. Her laptop slipped, tipping sideways. She grabbed it before it touched the floor.

"Yes?" she called, hiding most of her irritation at being interrupted.

"You asked for a courtesy call an hour before check-out," said a middle-aged woman, her voice muffled by the still-closed cabin door.

"Thank you." She wanted to tell the woman to shut up and go away.

To Leigh's relief, the woman's footsteps on the low porch signaled she was leaving.

Leigh dove back into her scene with undimmed energy. Her main character—who she had yet to name—tried to break the hunter's dogs off his trail by crossing a skunk. Despite the pungent odor, the dogs stayed on him.

The chase went on until Leigh and her character knew the same panic. Would this pursuit never end? Her hands ached. Her knees were stiff, and every muscle in her legs tensed with the anxiety of what was happening.

"Just get away already!" She stopped typing long enough to smack the floor in frustration. The sharp slap echoed through the room and made her palm sting.

But the pause was no more than a moment.

Like Leigh, her character was getting tired. He couldn't keep this up much longer. He was already past spent, and still the dogs harried him. There was nowhere else to go.

When he passed a thick stand of oaks, he leaped for a low-hanging branch and used it to climb the wide trunk. He scaled the oak until there were no more branches large enough to support his weight.

Below him, the dogs stopped.

His heart sank.

He couldn't run anymore. He was so tired he might fall out of the tree.

The hunter sounded his horn twice, three times. The lead hound bayed and surged ahead. His long strides carried him toward the mountains, and all the other dogs followed. Not long afterward, the hunter rode past. His chestnut gelding hadn't yet broken a sweat.

When the hunter's hoofbeats faded, he let out a disbelieving breath and scrambled out of the tree. He couldn't believe his luck.

Leigh sagged in relief as her character made for the eastern border. If he crossed over into the neighboring kingdom, he'd be safe. It was only a two-hour walk. He'd reach his destination before sunset.

She followed her character through a thicket and over a stream. He was so tired now. All he wanted to do was find a safe place to curl up and rest, but with the hunter still out there, rest was not something he could afford. Not yet.

He dragged weary feet through dead leaves and snarled thorns, scraping his worn boots and snagging his trouser legs.

The sun sank until the sky was a deep orange with streaks of purple clouds, and the harsh light of evening was almost gone. He broke through the trees and into a narrow clearing—and that was when the bay of hunting hounds speared the air.

Somehow, they'd found him.

Despite fatigue, he broke into a dead run, crossing the clearing in seconds and breaking through a line of shrubs. He leaped over a fallen oak tree, nearly stumbled, righted himself, and ran on.

The wind changed, bringing the thick, musty scent of wet dog. They'd been with him since the stream, at the very least. Probably longer.

He silently cursed. Calling the dogs off the tree he'd been in was a ploy, and he'd fallen for it. They would run him out like a scared deer, and there was nothing he could do about it.

Leigh's fingers paused over the keyboard. This couldn't be the end of the story. If her character was caught, he'd be hauled to prison and then executed. The lump in her throat said she wasn't ready for that. She couldn't just let him die. Even though he'd purposefully killed someone else, sentencing him to death felt harsh, unloving. And far too much like something her parents' church friends would do.

She wouldn't—couldn't—let him die.

Another sharp rap on the door.

"What?" Leigh snapped.

"Fifteen minutes until check-out," came the muffled answer. It was the same woman who'd come by last time. "Do you need help with luggage?"

She gritted her teeth before a harsh "go away" escaped. "No. I'm fine." She failed to disguise the edge in her voice.

"Would...you like to extend your stay? We'd be happy to give you a reduced rate."

Leigh's fingers twitched atop her keyboard. "Yeah. Yeah, a couple days would be good."

"I'll take care of it." The woman's heavy footsteps clumped down the porch steps, and Leigh was finally alone again.

68

Lane pulled out of the parking lot. Two bags of groceries sat on top of a towel in the passenger seat.

A quarter of the way back to Simmer, his phone rang. He quickly answered.

"Mr. Harris? This is Rachelle from Jenkins Rawling."

Lane's stomach leaped into his throat. The musty odor lingering inside the car didn't help.

"We did everything we could. I'm so sorry, but Mr. Williams...passed away an hour ago."

He hit the brakes hard and skidded to a red light.

"Mr. Harris?"

"Yeah. Yeah...I'm still here."

"As next of kin—"

"We're not related."

"Oh my. There seems to have been some misunderstanding then. I apologize. We'll get in touch with his family." She hung up.

The traffic light flicked green, but Lane sat at the intersection in numb silence until the truck behind him blared its horn. He eased through the light and kept right, his speedometer hovering well below the speed limit. Cars zoomed around him as people rushed to work or classes.

He could never repay the money he'd taken from the safe now.

Simmer Lounge

The back door to the bar clicked shut behind Lane. He didn't turn on any lights.

The sign he'd hung earlier lay on the floor. Cheap tape. He rehung it.

Sunlight broke in through the little window in his room, and he left the overhead light off. It was too harsh anyway.

He stared at the vacant TV screen, hands folded, elbows on his knees. He wanted—needed—to do something. But heavy emptiness shackled him in place. This wasn't right—wasn't fair. Lester had only ever been good to him. And he'd stolen from the man.

But that was only out of necessity. He'd have paid Lester back. Still, now he owed a debt impossible to repay.

Likely a funeral home would have to arrange Lester's memorial services. Did he have a will? The bar might pass to someone who'd reopen it. Or maybe not. Lester's resources might be liquidated to pay debts, if he had any.

Lane stuck both bags of food in the refrigerator. He would sort them later.

The silent walls crept closer with every horrible second. Good people didn't deserve to die alone. But Lester had.

And Stephen.

Something Vic had said to him on set came back. *"Do you believe in life after death, Mr. Harris?"*

His parents believed in life after death, but he'd never put much stock in it. Existing beyond this world didn't make sense. What was there to do? To be? What was the point? His father would have said people went to either Heaven or Hell. In Hell, they experienced eternal fire and pain. In Heaven, they supposedly spent eternity with God. Lane wasn't sure there was a difference. If God existed, He cared nothing for Lane. He'd already spent far too much time with people who didn't care.

It made much more sense that life after death was fabricated to make people feel better. Live. Die. That was it. All that lay beyond was a great void—peaceful nothing. There, he wouldn't even know he'd existed— wouldn't be aware of anything. No pain, no loneliness, no fear, no problems. And no uncaring deity to be subservient to.

Face in his hands, he absorbed the silence.

Nothingness seemed better than this useless struggle. There, he would never have another worry again. He sagged in the recliner.

Vic's book poked his leg.

He left it closed.

69

Simmer Lounge
Tuesday, April 16ᵗʰ

Lane lay in the recliner all morning. At 2 p.m., he kicked off both shoes, but didn't bother to change clothes. As evening faded to twilight, darkness folded over him. Eyes shut, he waited for sleep.

Lane's dreams returned, throwing him into scenes from Vic's book.

He batted tree limbs from his face. Baying hounds galloped at his heels, the hunter right behind them on a black horse.

"Surrender now or face the king's chains!"

Lane kept running.

A dog launched at him, caught one boot in its jaws. He tried to shake the animal off, but more descended on him, and soon he sprawled in dry leaves, covered with nipping, growling hounds.

"I told you to stop," said the hunter when he caught the dogs. "It's time you paid for your crimes." The mounted man loomed over Lane and the gathered hounds. Where the man's face should have been hung a yawning void. "Off," he commanded the dogs.

They obeyed but stood in an unbroken circle, blocking all escape.

The hunter dismounted, bound Lane's hands behind his back, and remounted his horse. "Home."

The dogs herded Lane through the trees until sunset. Walls surrounding a great keep rose high as they approached.

"Your place, scum. To think we once extolled you as a hero." The hunter spit in his face. "Get going, or we'll not make the keep before nightfall."

Instead of leaves, pebbles and packed ground crunched beneath his boots as they neared the keep. A twelve-foot portcullis raised and then clamped shut upon their entry. The dogs remained in a circle around Lane as the faceless hunter escorted him to a guarded iron door.

The hunter dismounted and tied his reins to a post. "The traitor, Prison Master," he said as he shoved Lane into the keeping of a man armed with a short sword and two daggers. The hunter held out his hand.

"I don't keep bounty money out here. You'll have to come inside." The prison master took Lane's arm and led him in. The hunter followed. Glowing orbs, embedded in rows along the stone walls, provided more light than expected.

Before the prison master took Lane any further, he unlocked a metal box and withdrew a brown bag tagged with Lane's name. The bounty inside gave a hefty jangle. "Here you are." He released it into the faceless hunter's eager hands.

"Pleasure doing business." The hunter left.

When the iron door shut behind Lane, a whoosh of fresh air rushed through the room. It might be the last he'd ever taste.

The prison master kept Lane bound as he ushered him to a winding staircase that plunged into a deep pit. Down, down they circled until he thought his vision would permanently swirl. Along the way, they passed landings for other floors, each containing rows of cells. Several were empty, but the majority housed prisoners.

Men, women, even children, wailed and pleaded for release as the prison master passed. He ignored them all.

At the bottom of the stairs sat a single cell.

"This prison houses only traitors to the crown," said the prison master as he untied Lane, "and this cell is for those who have trespassed most egregiously." He shoved him in. The key clicked in the lock, but to Lane, it rang like a thunderclap. "You die when the hounds bay fourth watch. You do not deserve the courtesy of waiting until dawn."

The prison master ascended the stairs without a backward glance.

Here, the same glowing orbs as above lit the pit, but there were far fewer, and shadows obscured most of the cell. A worn bed sat in the corner.

Lane's fingers curled around cold, steel bars. His only companions were his fellow prisoners and their wails for mercy.

70

3:16 a.m.

Lane roused. A splitting headache worsened as he sat up too fast.

Cold seeped into both palms. He rubbed them together to banish the chill, but it lingered. Didn't matter anyway.

He trudged to the men's room and didn't bother turning on the light.

Tina hadn't contacted him since the incident with Monica. She had to know he was off *Evident*. Unless she was trying to fight the decision.

But it was pointless. Gibson had made his verdict clear, and there would be no changing it.

Back in his room, Lane returned to the recliner. The blank ceiling stared at him. Outside, sparse traffic whooshed past, one car every few minutes, a truck, another car. He couldn't stand the silence, but noise was even more unbearable.

He shut his eyes.

Lester's face.

He'd trusted Lane, given him a place to stay when he had nowhere to go. And how had Lane repaid him? By stealing.

He didn't defend his actions this time.

Crushing guilt took him.

This was all his fault.

He'd walked into Monica's trap. He'd allowed his new landlord to throw him out like trash. He'd taken advantage of Lester's trust. If not for him, Tina wouldn't be inconvenienced. Gibson wouldn't be struggling to find another actor.

Stephen wouldn't be dead. Neither would Lester.

Outside, another car passed.

What was nothingness like? Was it deeper, more peaceful than silence? Had to be.

He needed to know.

Lane reached for the bottle of sleeping pills. He popped the top, poured all twenty-five remaining into one cold palm.

The white pills were smooth. Each rounded edge skimmed his fingertips.

So easy.

He would fade away into eternal silence.

Peace.

Quiet.

He poised to toss the first five in his mouth.

His phone rang—he didn't need to answer it. No one important called him anymore.

It went to voicemail.

He held the pills over open lips.

His phone rang again.

Persistent, whoever they were.

Didn't matter.

Two pills dropped down Lane's throat.

Second call.

Voicemail.

He swallowed three more sleeping pills and chased them with the other twenty.

Thirty minutes later, Lane lay in the recliner, waiting. Traffic still rushed past, but sparser now.

His phone rang a third time.

Outside, another car passed, slower than the rest, as if looking for something. He couldn't even slip into peace without running into problems. If he didn't answer the phone, whoever it was might stop calling.

Minutes later, a muffled banging from outside accompanied a fourth call.

Lane didn't recognize the number. Probably a misdial.

He answered. "Hello?"

"Mr. Harris—Lane?"

Vic?

"I'm outside the bar. Are you all right?"

"Why?"

"Your sister-in-law called me in a panic an hour ago, said she called your landlord and found out you weren't at your apartment. You haven't answered calls, texts, or messages in weeks, but your number hasn't been disconnected. You haven't told her where you are or what's happened, have you?"

"I'm fine. Stacey worries sometimes."

"Can I come in?"

Hopefully he'd be gone by the time Vic realized something was wrong. If he left her outside, she would persist.

He had to get her to leave.

There was no reason for her to be all the way out here in the middle of the night. Nobody left home at 3 in the morning to pay a visit to a stranger—and how had Vic known where to find him? He hadn't told her he was working here.

Didn't matter now. He made the trip to the door.

There stood Vic. She was thinner than last time he'd seen her. The maternity dress hung worse than his own clothes, and like him, deep shadows hovered under her eyes. Worry etched her face.

He unlocked the front door, and she slipped inside.

"I called all the cast members until I found one with your number. Brittany in makeup said you took a job here a while ago."

He tried to turn away from her.

She caught his shoulder.

Despite thickening grogginess from the sleeping pills, he jumped at the touch.

"You're not fine."

His eyes drooped. "Just tired." Fog encroached on his vision. "Gotta get to sleep." He escaped her hold, took three steps toward his room.

Time was up.

71

Seven Years Ago

Clear Creek Resort, Cabin 25, Rio Nido, CA
Friday, November 30th

Leigh stared hard at the laptop screen. The chase scene she'd just written glared back, daring her to find a way out of this impossible situation. She'd tried ten times to find a way to get her character out of this mess, but every time she'd tried, she'd just made things worse.

With a sigh of exasperation, she shut her laptop and tossed it onto the bed.

At least now she had two or three more days to sort it out.

Saturday, December 1st

Those stupid pigeons were back.

"Will you shut up, already?"

Leigh hurled the nearest pillow at the bedroom window to stop the irritating cooing. The red, velvet square hit its target with a loud thump. Outside, pigeons scattered in a flutter of wings.

She flopped face-first onto the bed, which smelled of pine needles and cheap laundry soap. After a frustrated groan, she pounded the bed with loose fists. Why couldn't she figure out how to get out of the corner she'd written her character into?

Her closed laptop sat on the bedside table. She reached for it, intending to try one more time. But when she touched the chipped, silver lid, the urge to leave it closed was too much.

Instead, she pushed off the bed and went outside.

Since it was the weekend, a few more people were staying here, enjoying the mild California winter. Thankfully, her nearest neighbor wasn't too close. Screaming kids and barking dogs weren't exactly inspirational.

She slipped her hands into the pockets of her old jeans and started to take the same trail she'd walked thirty times in the past couple weeks. Before she reached the trailhead, a deer path she'd never noticed branched right. Maybe a change of scenery would help her work through how to get her character un-stuck.

She took the deer trail.

Half an hour later, she stopped at the top of a rise.

Below stretched the river that ran alongside the other trail. She'd never seen it from this perspective. The deep blue of the river blended with the greens and browns of trees and undergrowth. A raccoon dipped his paws in the water before scurrying off with a half-eaten plum, freshly cleaned, probably snatched from someone's lunch. Just upriver, a fox peered from behind a bush only to vanish a moment later. Blackbirds and scrub jays squawked overhead. At least there weren't any pigeons with them.

After a careful inspection for fire ants, Leigh sat atop the rise. The late morning sun was pleasantly warm, but not enough to make her take off her light jacket. She couldn't remember where she'd gotten this jacket. Probably something her mom had picked up at a yard sale ages ago.

A white-tailed buck passed through the trees on the other side of the river. He bent to crop a mouthful of grass, but noticed her and stopped.

Leigh tipped her head to one side. "You look like a Brian."

The buck flicked his tail and went back to his grass, obviously deciding she wasn't dangerous.

"If only it was that easy to name everything." She tossed a stick down the hill. It bounced once and rolled to a stop a few yards short of the riverbank.

Maybe that was her problem with the scene she couldn't work through. She needed a name for her character. But traditional ones wouldn't work for him. She had to give him something unique.

She grabbed another stick and scrawled a large *A* in a patch of dirt. Deciding there were already too many *A* names in the world, she smudged the letter out with her shoe. *B* through *G* didn't spark any ideas either, but when she got to *H*, she stopped. Happily, she kept the *H* and started back through the alphabet, matching vowels until she decided an *A* would pair well with such a noble letter as *H*.

Leigh waded through letter after letter, adding consonants, vowels, and even an apostrophe, whenever they felt right.

Finally, the completed name lay at her feet.

"Hahnen'En," she tested. Saying the name breathed life into her.

She knew how to take the next step in her story.

Leigh leaped to her feet, startling a few squirrels. In fifteen minutes, she was back inside her cabin, laptop open.

72

Jenkins Rawling Memorial Hospital, Room 217
Wednesday, April 17ᵗʰ

Soft, blue light replaced steady darkness.

Lane lay on his back, but he wasn't at the bar. And, to his chagrin, he wasn't dead.

"You're awake." Vic sat in a chair beside Lane's bed. "EMTs found the empty bottle of sleeping pills in your room in the back, so they gave you something to counteract the sedatives."

She knew about him living at the bar.

Lane averted his eyes and pulled the hospital blanket up to his chin, trying to hide. Cold still infused his hands.

The blinds on the window opposite Vic were open. Dawn crept over the sky.

"Shouldn't you be at home?" He didn't look at her.

"I'm where I need to be."

Lane's fingers curled in the sheet. "Why did you stop me?"

Vic's gentle touch lighted on his shoulder.

The wall of palm trees hedging the parking lot below swayed as sunlight burst through them—so bright Lane had to look away. "I'm off *Evident*. You don't owe me anything."

Vic didn't budge.

"Why are you here?" He turned on his side, away from Vic, but the brilliant sunrise threatened to blind him again. "Stacey's message aside, what possessed you to come to a vacant bar at 3:30 in the morning to find a stranger?"

Vic's chair scraped the floor, and she rounded the bed, standing between him and the blinding sun. "God put you on my mind, Lane Harris." With significant effort, she kneeled by the bed. "And He wouldn't let me sleep until I found you." She took the hand that had slipped from beneath the blanket. The warmth of her thin hands muted the persistent chill in his fingers. "You might not value your life, but God does."

Lane pulled away. "God—if He exists—doesn't care about me."

He sat up too fast. The room swirled momentarily.

She didn't understand—never would.

"Besides that, what do you know about my life? You have a successful career, a family who actually cares about you, a house to go back to when you leave here. You don't have to worry about how to pay for next week's groceries or where you'll get your next shower. You have it all. Why couldn't you just let me go? Let me find peace?" He smacked the bed with a fist.

Vic offered upturned wrists. Long-healed, white scars latticed both.

Lane's gaze fastened on the foot of the bed. "Please leave," he whispered hoarsely.

Vic struggled to her feet. She fished something from her purse and set it on the bedside table. Without a word, she shuffled out.

Vic's footsteps echoed in his ears long after she disappeared.

Her scars haunted him. They must have been from an accident.

No way someone like Vic had ever tried...

An admission of something so heinous as attempted suicide by someone claiming their God would appall his parents.

Good thing they weren't here.

A nurse came to check on him. "This your favorite book?"

On the table sat the worn paperback copy of *Hahnen'En* he'd tucked into the recliner at the bar. Vic had brought it back to him.

73

Jenkins Rawling Memorial Hospital, Room 217
Wednesday, April 17th

When the nurse left, Lane reached for the book. In addition to his ragged Post-it note, a slim, metal bookmark jutted from between the pages. On his Post-it was written "1 John 4:9-21."

Childhood memories of Sunday school told him this was a Bible reference, but he hadn't cracked one of those in over two decades and didn't intend to do so now.

He shut the book.

A nurse brought breakfast around 8:15, and Lane grimaced at the mushy oatmeal and slice of limp, whole-grain toast. He wasn't hungry.

"When can I leave?"

The nurse consulted his chart on a tablet. "We'll have you with us until Saturday."

"Three days? But—"

"We want to be sure you won't have a repeat...episode. Can I get you anything else?"

"Got something for this headache?"

"That's a side effect of the flumazenil. I'll get you some ibuprofen."

Lane clasped chilled hands. Naked fingers. "Where's my ring? And my wallet and phone?"

"Locked up."

"Can I have them back?"

"Yes, but if they get misplaced, we're not responsible for—"

"Just give them back." He didn't want to deal with this now.

The nurse tapped something into her tablet. "Security will be up with your things in a few hours."

After a lunch offering of questionable meatloaf, soggy carrots, and green Jell-O, a security officer trotted in, sealed valuables bag in hand. He didn't open it until he stood at Lane's bedside. He withdrew every item as he listed it. "One smartphone, black case, screen cracked. One ring, tungsten, no visible damage. One wallet, brown leather, worn edges, frayed at the top. Contents include driver's license, gym membership card, one American Express credit card, one Visa debit card, one insurance card, one wallet-sized picture, and two store-specific rewards cards. No cash." He set Lane's clothes in a neat stack on the bedside table. "Sign here, please."

The man presented a handheld device and stylus.

The instant the security guy disappeared, Lane slipped on his ring. He'd have to keep the nurse from seeing it, or she'd make him take it off again.

He clicked on the in-room TV. Options included golf, news, classic reruns, a movie he hated, and two daytime talk shows.

He glanced at Vic's book.

And settled on golf.

When the game ended, smoothing wrinkles in his blanket and sheets proved more entertaining than channel surfing.

Dinner consisted of roasted turkey smothered in gravy, mashed potatoes, broccoli, and another helping of Jell-O, blue this time.

He ate the Jell-O.

News droned until he turned off the TV just after dark.

His phone buzzed. Stacey.

Vic said you're in the hospital! I knew something was wrong. Which hospital did they take you to? Are you okay?? Answer me, you bull-headed idiot!

He wished for another bottle of sleeping pills. Nothing was okay. Never would be until he escaped this waking nightmare.

His phone rang. Stacey again.

He let it go to voicemail.

74

Lane kept his ring hidden from the night nurse, who seemed overloaded watching her patients in addition to an absent co-worker's.

He tested the strength of the blanket and sheets. They wouldn't hold his weight, but that didn't matter. Nothing to tie them to. Staff hadn't left him with so much as a plastic butter knife.

Shame.

The bathroom unlocked from the outside, so he couldn't barricade himself in.

Two doses of minimum strength ibuprofen—for his headache—were the only drugs they'd allowed him.

He had his clothes, wallet. He could file the credit card into a razor. Why not make use of his maxed-out AmEx? The side table's edge might work as a sharpener. He scraped the card a full minute with no results.

The bed rail proved inadequate too. Nothing else in the room seemed a decent candidate.

The night nurse walked in. "Doing okay in here?"

Lane slipped the AmEx and his ring under the pillow. "Yeah."

She briefly appraised him. "All right. Try to get some sleep."

When she left, Lane withdrew the card and—

His ring.

He waited until the nurse's footsteps faded before running the credit card edge over the ring's matte black surface until it was sharp enough to cut his finger when he tested it. The nurse returned every two hours. He would wait until after her next visit.

Instead of using the hospital Wi-Fi, he switched to data on his cell. Just in case.

Twelve missed calls from Stacey today, and she'd probably try again tomorrow.

Only 14 percent battery left. That would be plenty.

He searched for a decent diagram of wrist arteries.

Thursday, April 18th

Minutes past 2 a.m., the nurse returned.

Lane pretended to sleep until she left. Leaving the light off, he felt for the faint beat of one radial artery and matched the sharpened card to it. Just one calculated cut to each wrist.

Vic's scars had been frantic, scattered, as if she'd slashed multiple times in hopes of better results.

What might have prompted such desperation? Every time they'd met, she'd offered him a smile. It might have been dulled by exhaustion, but it had been real. Even when he'd woken in this horrible place yesterday, she hadn't harbored disdain for him. She'd sympathized.

Why?

His grip on the card relaxed. He slipped it back inside his wallet and picked up his phone.

5 percent battery.

In the browser search bar, he entered "Vic Garrison suicide." Two pages of results.

He scrolled quickly as his battery dipped to 3 percent.

The last result on page two: "Popular crime author shares personal crisis."

He tapped the link, and his phone died.

75

Jenkins Rawling Memorial Hospital, Room 217
Thursday, April 18th

He wanted to yell at the phone and hurl it out the window, but that would mean losing its contents. Instead, he set it on the bedside table, next to Vic's book. When his fingers brushed the barely legible binding, each rough ridge brought back the sight of Vic's scars.

He picked up the book and turned on the light above his bed.

The old Post-it still wrapped the new bookmark, but he had no way of looking up the reference Vic had written on it now, even if he wanted to. He set the gifted metal bookmark on the desk.

This book had given him the strangest dreams. None of his thrillers had ever resulted in those, not even the most enthralling. Usually, nightmares involving Stephen's death invaded his sleep. Lester's face would probably haunt him in the coming months too. He remembered having the nightmares, but didn't recall any details mere hours afterward.

Pieces of the dreams Vic's book prompted...lingered.

The one about the prison stayed with him the most stubbornly. Cold from cell bars gripped his fingers and kept his hands under the blanket, even though he knew it was all in his head. In the silence, if he concentrated, the voices of hunting dogs still rang far off, as if they were after him, determined to drag him away.

Not that it mattered. Those moments weren't real.

He needed to find out more about Vic—why she hadn't condemned him as so many others would have. Enduring the rest of his stay at Jenkins Rawling seemed a bearable price.

He opened to the last page he'd read.

Just before shift change, the nurse returned, carrying a folded piece of paper. "A woman left this. Asked if we could get it to you." She handed Lane the paper and left, probably eager to get home after a long shift.

The page was a sheet of thick construction paper, light blue. On one side, in wobbly letters, was "Mr. Lane." Inside, strokes of green, blue, and red crayon depicted someone standing outside a hospital. Across the top, in a child's scribble, was, "Get well soon."

Sophie's name sat in the corner.

He wanted to smile, but he wasn't ready for that yet. He folded the paper and tucked it under his dead phone before resuming reading.

This book was thicker than his usual fare, spanning over six hundred pages. When he'd started it, he wondered how anyone could employ a story that long without losing reader interest. He didn't wonder anymore.

If Vic's other books were this good, he understood what got her on the bestseller list.

With talent like this, why try to end her own life?

He wished again for his charger.

76

Jenkins Rawling Memorial Hospital, Room 217
Thursday, April 18th

By dinnertime, Lane's only visitors had been nurses.

With his phone dead, he didn't know if anyone had tried to contact him. But at least he'd paid his phone bill, so he'd have service when he finally got to charge it again.

Between reading sessions, he turned on the TV, catching the last few minutes of a game show, ads for a weight loss program, and an evening talk show, but nothing kept him from Vic's book for more than an hour.

Once he finished half his dinner—more turkey and vegetables—and downed red Jell-O, he clicked off the TV and returned to *Hahnen'En* until well after 10 p.m.

"Good book?" said the night nurse when she came in to check on him.

Lane tucked his left hand under the blanket to hide his ring. "Yeah."

"What is it?"

He held up the open paperback so she could see the cover.

"Hey, isn't that the same author who wrote the Hannah Stanton books? I loved those!"

Lane nodded.

"If I had a chance to meet the guy who wrote them..." She set a fresh blanket at the foot of the bed. "Done with your food?"

"Yeah. And Vic's a woman."

The nurse almost dropped the food tray. "Vic Garrison doesn't do in-person events, and the author bio in every book is so vague. There isn't even a picture. How would you know?"

"I've met her. She's the one who—who saved my life. She was here when they admitted me."

The nurse seemed torn between laughter and blubbering disbelief. "That was not Vic Garrison."

"It was."

The nurse's excitement flagged. "Maybe she'll come back before you leave Saturday. Otherwise, I won't be able to meet her."

"You never know."

The nurse offered an unconvincing smile. "I'll be by later."

More of the same dreams, these just as real as the others.

The hunter dragged him to prison again, and he lay in the dark, empty cell. At least it was dry.

Guards brought water once before the chilling howl of dogs signaled the night's first watch. This deep in the earth, no windows told him how far across the sky the moon had traveled, and though weariness assaulted him, he didn't give in.

If this was his last night to live, he wouldn't fritter it away on sleep.

The second watch came and went as Lane contemplated how he would die. So many options: sword, gallows, arrows, exposure, clubs, animals. All held their own special brand of horror. But perhaps it would be mercifully quick, a swift slice across the throat, or blade through the eye.

The faraway creak of an iron door opening above him sent the entire prison into a cacophony of pleading as the prison master descended the stairs with another captive.

Lane expected them to stop at every landing they passed, but they circled down to his cell.

The prison master's face was hard, and he said nothing as he ushered an unbound prisoner into the cell before locking it again. The prison master didn't leave immediately, choosing instead to gaze at the newcomer in the light of the sparse, wall-mounted orbs of light until the dogs bayed third watch.

When the keeper started up the stairs, the stranger faced Lane.

He didn't recognize this man, but something about him compelled Lane to find out who he was.

"Oren." The stranger offered a hand.

Lane took it.

77

Jenkins Rawling Memorial Hospital, Room 217
Friday, April 19th

Lane started awake. His fingers weren't cold anymore. Instead, the sense of Oren's hand gripping his lingered.

2:48 a.m.

The nurse walked in, unscheduled. "Everything okay? Your chart says you talk in your sleep, but I wanted to make sure."

"Fine," Lane mumbled.

"Okay. Sorry to wake you."

Vic's book stared at him from the bedside table. He laid a hand atop it, as if touching the worn paperback might erase the odd sensation from his dream.

It didn't.

An hour and a half before breakfast, the night nurse hurried in. "Someone's here to see you."

Alisha stepped into the room.

"Have a good visit." The nurse left, probably to finish her shift and head home.

"Hey." Alisha sat beside Lane's bed. "Didn't know how to contact you since you never gave me your number."

"Phone's dead anyway." Lane tapped the broken screen.

"What happened? You made a couple tabloids yesterday. They said you were here at Jenkins Rawling, but no one knows why."

Hopefully she'd believe whatever he told her. "Was cleaning up the bar, fell off a ladder and lost consciousness. Called 9-1-1 just in case. Guess I fell harder than I thought. Got a bad concussion. They're keeping me until Saturday."

"Ouch. I'm sorry. Horrible about Lester too. He was such a nice man." Tears welled in her eyes. "I haven't found another job yet. Most places want me to work days, but I can't do that and take care of my son. It's good you have another job to fall back on."

"Yeah." If only that were true.

Alisha's eyes strayed to Sophie's card. "Who gave you this?"

"A...friend's daughter."

"Aw. That was sweet."

"She's a good kid."

Alisha pointed to *Hahnen'En*. "I didn't know Vic Garrison wrote anything except Hannah Stanton."

"This is different. But good."

"I'll check to see if my library has it." Alisha glanced at her cell. "Gotta go. My neighbor's watching my son, and she has to get to work soon. Here." She scribbled her number on half an index card and tucked it under his phone. "Oh! Almost forgot." She took a paper from her purse. "Lester's memorial's Sunday afternoon, if you're okay to be up and around by then. I'm sure he'd be glad if you came."

"Thanks." Lane took the paper but didn't look at it.

"Bye. Feel better."

When Alisha was gone, he tucked the paper beneath Sophie's card. Going to Lester's funeral was the last thing he wanted to do. He couldn't claim to be the man's friend. Not after what he'd done.

But if he didn't go, his co-workers might notice. Alisha definitely would.

He eased out the slip of paper. 3 p.m. visitation. Funeral at 3:30.

Kennedy Funeral Home, Huntington Park.

78

Jenkins Rawling Memorial Hospital, Room 217
Friday, April 19th

Memories from Stephen's funeral flooded back. Stacey's tears—his grief—Stephen's mother weeping over the closed casket.

He wondered if Kennedy had changed since he'd been there last October. Probably not. Places like that stayed mostly the same. After all, the clientele didn't care. They might change flower arrangements with the seasons, but everything would be in the same place.

At least the staff wouldn't recognize him. Not now.

He mirrored his face in the broken phone screen. The only improvement was he'd gotten some sleep. None of the nurses had commented on his name. They must have thought it a coincidence, if they recognized him at all.

He couldn't say he was a big name. Stephen was more well-known than he'd ever been. *Evident* might have put him on the map, but that wasn't happening anymore.

He rubbed two fingers between his eyes to stave off a headache before pushing the call button.

A nurse came a few minutes later.

"Can I get headache meds?"

"Sure. One second." She ducked outside and returned with a paper cup containing two ibuprofen and a second cup half-filled with water. "Anything else?"

"No. Thanks." Lane took the pills.

After twenty minutes, the headache dulled.

Lunch came and went.

The paper with Lester's funeral information peeked from under Sophie's card. He picked up the handmade card and wondered if Vic had helped write it. Probably, but that didn't lessen the meaning. The funeral announcement fluttered toward the floor. He caught it and replaced Sophie's card on the table.

Visitation, he would skip. He could come a few minutes late to the funeral without anyone noticing and leave immediately after.

There was enough money in his account to Uber to Simmer. Hopefully, no one had vandalized his car while he'd been here.

The nurse came in to take his empty food tray.

He put Lester's funeral announcement away.

79

Jenkins Rawling Memorial Hospital, Room 217
Friday, April 19th

Lane picked up the battered notecard containing Alisha's number. He hadn't added a new contact in months. To keep from losing the scrap, he tucked it into his phone case.

His hand wandered back to Vic's book.

Unlike his bizarre dreams, the storyline hadn't progressed past Hahnen'En running from multiple hunters. He'd done everything possible to hide from them, even up to secluding himself in the mountains.

The hunters had still found him.

He set the Post-it wrapped bookmark aside and returned to the story.

Dinner came, but he was too invested in the book to stop reading.

He stabbed crunchy carrots and cooling slices of turkey with a plastic fork until he'd emptied his plate. Blue Jell-O again tonight. He downed it in three mouthfuls.

When the nurse came to take the emptied tray, he barely noticed.

Saturday, April 20th

More dreams, these mismatched moments, some a result of his reading and others snippets of his life, but they built on one another. Stephen was there, and Monica. Vic appeared, followed by his parents and even Gibson.

Just like his earlier dream, the sequence ended with Oren's outstretched hand. But before Lane could take it, a touch on his shoulder roused him.

"Sorry to wake you," the night nurse whispered, "but you seemed agitated."

He blinked away thick sleep. "I'm fine," he murmured.

"You sure? The past two nights you didn't talk much, but now, every time I come in, you're going on about something."

"I'm fine," he managed again before dropping back to sleep.

By then, the dreams had gone.

Before breakfast, he changed into regular clothes. It was nice to wear pants again.

He'd thought to Uber back to the bar, but with his phone dead, he had no way of calling anyone to get him.

There was a metro station half a mile away. He didn't have cash, so he'd have to get a TAP card. A few dollars he didn't want to spend, but it was less expensive than cab fare and faster than walking.

He pocketed his dead phone before carefully folding Sophie's card and Lester's funeral announcement to fit beside his wallet in another pocket. *Hahnen'En*, he tucked under one arm.

Ten steps from the hospital's front entrance, he stopped.

Standing just outside was Vic, hand in hand with Sophie. The little girl pointed to a flowerbed filled with day lilies. They hadn't bloomed yet—probably wouldn't for a month or two. Vic patted her rounded middle, and Sophie laid a hand beside her mother's, only to jerk back, laugh, and bounce in childlike joy.

Lane hadn't realized Vic's OB was here. Jenkins Rawling was known for their cardiology and oncology departments, not obstetrics. He considered taking another exit, but this was the fastest way to the metro, and after spending three days in bed, he didn't have the energy to spare. He slipped out the glass door, hoping Vic—and Sophie— wouldn't notice him.

He made it as far as a stone bench five feet from the door.

"Lane. Good to see you again," Vic said.

He could pretend not to have heard, but she wouldn't fall for that. He faced her only for Sophie to trap his legs in a hug.

"Mr. Lane! I got to feel my baby brother. Mommy says he's moving lots today, and I'm gonna get to meet him soon."

Vic had said once she was due in June. That was only two months away.

"Hi, Sophie." He hesitantly laid a hand on her head.

"Did you get my card? Mommy helped me spell things. I can write my letters, but Mommy says I won't learn to read until next year. I wanna read all Mommy's books."

"I got it. It was very nice. Thank you."

"Mommy said you weren't feeling good, so I wanted you to feel better. Are you better now, Mr. Lane?"

"Some."

"That's good." She pressed a cheek to his pant leg.

"May we offer you a ride?" Vic said.

Was that allowed for a Christian? Driving someone to an—albeit closed—gay bar? "You don't have to do that."

"I know," Vic said. "Van's this way." She pointed to the patient parking garage.

Sophie took his hand. "I'll walk with you."

Lane followed Vic.

80

He stood between Vic and Sophie on the elevator ride to the second floor. A short hike to the van left Vic coughing when they reached the vehicle.

"You all right?" Lane opened the driver's side door for her.

She sat and sipped from a bottled water snagged from a cup holder. The coughing eased. "I'm okay."

He started to help Sophie into her car seat, but she was heavier than he remembered. Symptom of going off his diet and exercise routine. But, to his relief, she climbed into place on her own and buckled in.

When Lane was in the passenger's seat, Vic tapped the 12V outlet behind a vacant cup holder. "Feel free to use the phone charger. I think mine uses the same cord as yours."

He plugged in his cell as Vic backed up the minivan and circled out of the garage. When he powered the phone up and the home screen flicked on, notifications poured in. Texts, emails, missed calls, app notifications, weather, news stories, everything from the past three days.

He ignored his email, glanced at calls, dismissed apps and news, and opened texts. Another five from Stacey, on top of the dozens of missed calls. Tina had tried getting ahold of him at least three times a day too.

The most recent message from Stacey read, Please talk to me. I'm crazy scared right now. I need to know what's going on!

Desperation filled her words, so he tapped back, Sorry to worry you. Phone's been dead. Concussion. I'm okay. Out of the hospital.

The instant reply read, *Thank God!*

He sent Tina a copy of his text to Stacey. She'd read it within sixty seconds. Her reply: *Good. Glad to hear it. Still working on the Evident fiasco.*

He opened his browser. An article from some Christian pseudo-news site was up. Must have been an ad he'd accidentally tapped before the phone died. He almost closed it, but his finger stopped short of the *X*. This was the article about Vic.

Lane hid the screen—not that he needed to. Vic's eyes were on the road and traffic, not him.

Near the top of the article was a picture of Vic, standing with a man he assumed was Gavin, her husband. His dark hair and medium-brown complexion contrasted with Vic's light-brown hair and pale skin. She held a newborn Sophie.

The way Vic looked at Gavin with strong, contented love...Lane had to stop staring at the photo.

He secreted a few sentences at a time until he reached the section he was looking for.

"Vic Garrison attempted suicide after her five-month-old son's death from Sudden Infant Death Syndrome. Her roommate and then-girlfriend, Nakasha Matthews, called EMTs when she found Garrison, both wrists cut, in a shower stall on the campus of North Kingsville University near Fresno. Of the incident, Garrison said, 'I didn't want to live without my son. Every day was new torture. I blamed myself, even though I couldn't have saved him.'"

This article had to be fake.

Lane sneaked a glance at Vic. She didn't seem to notice as she smiled at two pedestrians ambling through a crosswalk. He saved the link to finish later.

Simmer Lounge

Lane stepped out of the minivan. "Thanks. Like I said, you didn't have to bring me all the way out here."

"No trouble," said Vic through the rolled-down window. "It's on the way home."

"Bye, Mr. Lane." Sophie waved. "See you later."

Lane gave her a brief wave back.

"You have my number. If ever things take a...turn...again, please call."

"All right."

Vic left the parking lot.

Lane pulled up the article again and read the entire thing. The piece ended with a quote from Vic: "Through unique circumstances, I realized only God could rescue someone as broken as me. And He did."

Those last three words struck Lane. Vic spoke and acted as if God were a dear friend. Someone who cared about her, made her life better. But how was that possible? Did God—if He existed—help some people and not others?

Lane walked around behind the bar. He wondered what had led to Vic's conclusions about God.

He tried the kitchen door.

Locked.

His keys were still inside Simmer.

He cursed.

81

Seven Years Ago

Clear Creek Resort, Cabin 25, Rio Nido, CA
Saturday, December 1st

Naming her main character had helped tremendously. Now, instead of writing about an anonymous stranger, Leigh could think of him as a person. As she hammered out a solution to Hahnen'En's predicament, something nagged her.

She pushed it away. It was probably just her brain telling her she'd left the peanut butter out again or forgotten to wash her hair.

When three o'clock rolled around, Leigh was ready for a snack and a nap. She'd sent a character from the neighboring country to rescue Hahnen'En and take him safely over the border. He would be okay. The king and his oh-so-righteous judgments couldn't reach her Hahnen'En now.

So why did this not feel right?

Ignoring the sense, she went into the kitchen and ate another peanut butter sandwich.

Sunday, December 2nd

Everything was wrong.

Leigh highlighted Hahnen'En's entire escape, and with one frustrated tap, deleted it. Why had she ignored that little voice in her head that said she was making a mistake?

Sitting on the bed, head in her hands, she rocked, angry with herself for trying to force the story to do what she wanted. She'd learned a long time ago it never worked. But she'd wanted so much for Hahnen'En to be free. Everything in her screamed for him to be all right, but she knew in her heart he would have to face judgment for his actions.

Tears pricked her eyes, but she refused to wipe them away. Bitterly, she started typing again.

Hahnen'En was soon in the bounty hunter's custody and headed toward the keep reserved for prisoners.

82

Simmer Lounge
Saturday, April 20th

Lane hurled more curses at Simmer's back door as he tugged and yanked, but it wouldn't open. He'd left his keys inside the bar the night the EMTs came. One of them must have locked the door before everyone left.

The only other person who had a key was Lester...

And Alisha! He dug her number out of the back of his phone case and dialed.

"Hello?"

"Alisha. It's Lane."

"Oh, hey! You got your phone back on."

"A...friend let me use their car charger. You don't still have a key to the bar, do you?"

"Yup." Keys jangled in the background.

"You wouldn't be able to swing by here?"

"I have a job interview near there in an hour. I'll finish getting ready and come by before that. Why do you need to get into the bar?"

"Left my keys inside the day I got my concussion."

"Okay. Give me forty-five minutes, and I'll be there."

"Thanks."

"No problem. See you in a few."

While he waited for Alisha, Lane circled the building.

His Versa, unbothered, still sat near the dumpster—mercifully empty. The spare room window was intact, as were all other windows and doors. At least no one had broken in while he was away.

Instead of waiting out front, he returned to the back door and sat, careful to avoid the slick spot beside the dumpster.

Lane's phone buzzed.

"Where are you?" Alisha.

"Around back. Be there in a second." He rounded the building to meet her at the front door.

She turned the key and opened the door. "There ya go."

"Thanks. I'll lock up when I leave." He stepped inside.

Alisha stood out front, taking deep breaths.

Instead of heading back to his room, he stood in the half-open glass door. "Everything all right?"

"Just nervous. This is the first job interview I've had since Lester hired me five years ago. That's a long time to be out of the game."

"You'll do great." He offered a reassuring smile.

"I needed that." She gripped her keys tightly. "Still nervous, but I'll make it."

"Where's the interview?"

"Frank and Marty's down the street. Not as nice as Simmer, but the hours are right. My son turns seven in two weeks. Can't sit still, and hates vegetables, but he loves cars and building things. I got him into an after-school group that lets him tinker as much as he wants. He made a little robot from a kit a few weeks ago. Won't stop playing with it."

Lane leaned against the doorframe.

"I'm rambling. Sorry. Nerves."

"No reason to apologize. But you might be late for your interview if you don't get going."

"Right."

"Hope it goes well for you."

"I'll text you." She hopped in her Corolla and turned left, heading for Frank and Marty's.

When she was out of sight, Lane locked the front door from inside and returned to his room. He clicked the light. At least the power was on. Hopefully, they wouldn't cut it off right away when the bill went unpaid middle of next month.

Clean laundry still sat in piles on the unused bed. The TV was off, and Lane's boxed possessions piled in one corner. The recliner leaned back, just like he'd left it. His keys lay on the bed, beside his clothes. Only one thing was missing. The empty sleeping pill bottle.

His phone buzzed. Stacey.

He picked up.

"Lane Thomas Harris, you'd better never do that to me again!" Stacey's anger was a mask that quickly crumbled as she broke down in tears. "I—I really thought you were dead." She sobbed. "I can't lose you too. Not after Stephen."

"I'm sorry for worrying you." When he'd taken those pills, he'd been caught up in his own desire to escape. He hadn't thought what it might do to Stacey. "Everything's okay now."

It wasn't. But she didn't need to know that.

"How'd you get to the hospital?" Stacey said.

"Vic found me."

"I owe her a huge hug. Who knows what would've happened if nobody came to your apartment. It probably would've taken a couple days for the movie director to know for sure something was wrong, and by then you could have been—" She melted into tears again.

"Hey. It's okay. You don't have to worry about me." Partially true. The urge to step into oblivion had eased. The last thing he wanted to do was cause Stacey more pain. "Tell me what's going on with you. Last I heard, you were making headway on that lawsuit."

Stacey sniffed several times, and a muffled fumbling said she was using a tissue. "Yeah. Good progress there. The lawyers are talking with the company's legal team. I keep hearing the word 'settlement' getting tossed around, but nothing's official yet."

"That's great, Stace. I'm glad it's working out." He yawned. "I'm worn out. Can we talk more later?"

Stacey seemed reticent. "Promise? No more dodging calls?"

"Sure."

"Okay then. Later." She hung up.

He plopped into the recliner, *Hahnen'En* still under his arm. He wanted to go to sleep. Though he'd spent three days in bed, he felt like he'd just climbed four hundred flights of stairs.

Instead of nodding off, he took out his phone and opened the article about Vic again. *Hahnen'En* in one hand, phone in the other, he puzzled over the connection.

Vic's face when she talked about this book reminded him of the days he spent with his friends as a kid. They'd chatter about soccer and football and action figures. A sense of childlike joy had filled the air then. Maybe that was what Vic had felt when she'd read this book.

It was an engaging story so far, but that was all. No life-changing epiphanies. Just a story.

But he opened the book again anyway.

83

Only when Lane's phone buzzed at 9:38 p.m. did he put *Hahnen'En* away.

Text from...Monica?

I'll tell everyone we were never together.

For half a second, he couldn't believe what he'd read.

Then came the second text: *For a price.*

This again. Even if he wanted to pay her, he couldn't. Not that he would ever consider giving Monica a red cent. She'd already taken enough from him. He refused to let her have more.

He left the message unread.

A third text arrived. He dismissed it without reading.

Only two and a half hours until Sunday. He'd bet Vic would be at church in the morning.

These days, even Hollywood was thick with churches and religious centers of every stripe. He hadn't been to church since before his parents had kicked him out. Not that he wanted to go back now. He couldn't bear the thought of walking into another church. All the looks, the frowns, the people who pretended not to notice him, the parents hurrying their kids away.

His parents' church had been large, with vaulted ceilings, stained glass, and chandeliers that made his vision hazy. Four or five hundred people attended on a good day, though only half of them returned for evening services, and even fewer frequented the mid-week gatherings. Unfortunately, his parents had dragged him to every single service— including special meetings with preachers fond of yelling, pulpit pounding, and pacing.

He'd hated every second.

As sleep settled over him, he wondered if Vic's church was like his parents'. It might be, but so far, Vic had proven more than surprising. Maybe he would ask her about her church sometime. Only out of curiosity.

Sunday, April 21st

Lane clicked through channels. A televangelist waved dramatic hands as he prayed. Another touted the benefits of sending him donations, and a third insisted God would bless anyone who had enough faith.

He found a golf game and left it on while he rescued something from the kitchen fridge and ate in the recliner.

Stacey had called earlier, and he'd listened for half an hour as she told him all about Bakersfield, Huddles, Aunt Sherry, and her new job. Last night he hadn't bothered to get out of his clothes, so he changed after his call with Stacey.

Sophie's card and Lester's funeral paper crinkled in one pants pocket.

He took out both. Sophie's card he propped atop the TV stand. Lester's funeral announcement, he reread. He knew where Kennedy Funeral Home was.

Too well.

A thirty-minute drive from here in decent traffic. He'd have to leave in a few hours if he was going to make it.

At least he'd showered at the hospital. He applied a healthy layer of deodorant, brushed his teeth, and combed his unruly hair until he appeared respectful.

Since he'd forgotten last night, he put his phone on to charge.

While he waited for the hours to tick by, he picked up Vic's book. The note Vic wrote on his Post-it stared at him. His phone was on. He could look up the Bible reference Vic had left him.

But now wasn't a good time.

He set the book down and finished the golf game instead.

84

Kennedy Funeral Home
Sunday, April 21st

He sneaked in the back as the service started on time.

The officiant at the front recounted how everyone in attendance loved and would miss Lester. If only he knew the truth of what Lane had done to this man who'd only ever helped him. The amount of money he'd taken wasn't as devastating as the betrayal itself. Just being here made his stomach clench.

If the people here knew what he'd done, they'd hate him.

According to Lester, the man's family had acted for years as if he were dead, so it didn't surprise him the only people filling the relatives' section at the front were bar employees. Lane's clean shirt and good jeans suddenly felt out of place, but it was the best he had that still fit. Even Barry was here, in a suit. Beside him sat Eve and her daughter, then Rhonda, Miguel and his boyfriend, Barb, and Alisha and her son. Alisha kept glancing over her shoulder until she spotted him.

He gave her a discreet wave. She looked relieved to see him, but returned sober attention to the front.

Ushers stood at the back. Lane didn't recognize any of them, and none seemed to remember him. Small mercy.

The details of the room smothered him: eggshell white walls, oak pews padded in deep green, one missing doorstop, and the glaring emergency exit sign at the front left of the room. One corner of the carpet on the platform's second step begged to be righted, and the flower arrangement at the front was off center by two inches—exactly as it had been six months ago. The stiff aroma of cologne, perfume, and too many flowers clogged the room.

He itched to fix every flaw—to change something. Or at least take away the dull ache of being here again.

Stephen's funeral had been held in this same room.

Recessed LED bulbs gave light, though the third one from the front on the left was still out. The same nondescript books filled with readings, religious and otherwise, dotted racks hung on the backs of pews—only half of which contained guests.

The officiant surrendered the floor to a former co-worker of Lester's. Lane didn't recognize him. Could have been someone who worked at Simmer before Lane's arrival. "Lester told me once to live like there was no tomorrow. I followed that advice. Can't say I've always been happy, but it's been an interesting road, and maybe that's the best anyone can expect. Better to live life than run from it because we're afraid to take risks. Rest in peace, Lester. I'm gonna miss you." The man struggled against tears as he left the front. Others, including several bar employees, shared memories of Lester. Barry recounted a few of the most interesting nights at the bar. Alisha almost lost composure when she told how Lester hired her when no one else would. "He was a great person." She choked.

As the service closed, pallbearers took Lester's casket out before the officiant dismissed everyone.

The little-used glass door leading to an auxiliary parking lot promised the easiest escape.

Lane hurried to the door, slipping out of his pew as Barry and Eve passed.

"Lane!" Alisha hurried to him. "Hey. Sorry I didn't text you yesterday. Interview was amazing. They said I could start tonight."

"That's great." He shuffled one step toward the door.

A boy studied the public water fountain as he pushed the button multiple times, watching water stream from the spout down the drain. The kid crouched to peer under the fountain.

Alisha waved the boy to her side. "This is Grayson." She ruffed his straight blond mop.

"Hi." The boy looked up at Lane in curiosity. "Are you my mom's boyfriend?"

Alisha's cheeks reddened. "No, sweetie, this is my friend from work. Remember?"

Lane would have laughed under different circumstances. Instead, he crouched to be at eye-level with Grayson. "You have a great mom, but like she said, we're just friends."

"Oh." Grayson seemed disappointed. "Okay. You can change your mind if you want."

Lane forced a smile. Now wasn't the time to say getting involved with a woman was about as likely as a skyscraper growing wings.

Especially after what Monica had done to him. He had no romantic interest in anyone and didn't know if he ever would again. His stomach twisted at the thought of another relationship. "I'll keep that in mind."

"Come on, we need to get to the graveside." Alisha tugged her son toward the exit. Pink still tinged her cheeks as she said to Lane, "Are you going?"

So many memories from Stephen's funeral. "Sorry. Too close to home."

"Okay. You look tired. Get some rest." She patted his arm. "See you."

As Alisha ushered Grayson after the departing guests, Lane hurried from the building before the past drowned him.

85

Simmer Lounge

Sunday, April 21ˢᵗ

When he got back to the bar, Lane refreshed the note on the door.

He didn't know what would become of the place, but he wouldn't be able to stay here forever, and with no job and no income, he was stuck.

Instead of returning to his room, he grabbed the Swiffer mop.

An hour later, he sat on the lone stool behind the bar.

Rows of alcohol, stowed in mirrored cabinets, stood in pristine order. Lester had kept the bar meticulous. He found what he needed without even looking most of the time.

Lane selected a bottle of Vanilla Smirnoff. He'd never been much for vodka, but Stephen drank it sometimes, so he knew enough to avoid the really cheap stuff.

The crushed ice bin beneath the bar was half full, and Lane scooped a healthy amount into a glass before pouring.

He jammed a straw into the ice mound. Stephen hated using straws, said they made everything taste like plastic. They weren't supposed to serve plastic straws anymore. This one must have been left over from last year.

Several texts sat in his messages unopened. Most were from debt collectors. There was no point in reading them. He knew what they said. He owed money he couldn't pay.

During the years he'd lived with Stephen, he'd gone from working in a cubicle, spending every day wishing he were on a set, to awaiting Tina's every call or text. Now he would give most anything to have his old office job back.

He sipped the cooled vodka.

Outside, traffic zipped past like any other day.

If memory served, the evening church crowd would head to services in an hour or two, then rush home afterward to put kids to bed or get ready for work in the morning. Sunday nights were for ball games and dinner dates, not poorly lit gatherings with semi-strangers.

He finished his glass and poured another.

This would be the last one for today; then he'd haunt online job boards while Sunday evening TV provided background.

He punched the thick straw through wads of ice and wondered when the rent was due for this place.

Several slow sips emptied the glass again.

One more.

Eight drinks later, Lane got up.

He kept one hand on the bar as the world tilted. Looking for jobs tonight would ruin the weekend. Too bad Monica wasn't around. He could tell her what he really thought of her. She had texted him, after all.

He pulled out his phone and called her.

"Decided to take my offer?" Monica said as soon as she picked up.

"You think I would ever give you anything after you drugged and assaulted me?" He let fly a string of alcohol-freed curses, telling her just how much he despised everything about her.

"I don't have to listen to this. Call me when you've seen reason." She threw a handful of choice words before hanging up.

Lane swore at the phone. Only weeks ago, no one would leave him alone. Now, nobody would listen to him.

Alisha.

He dialed her cell. Voicemail.

Lane rambled until the message timed out.

He emptied his pockets onto the bar. In his wallet, he found the razored credit card. Its edge left a bloody slice on one finger pad.

It would be so easy.

No one would call EMS this time.

He could imagine the headlines: "Actor found dead in abandoned bar." "Former *Evident* co-star commits suicide." At least someone might pay attention to those.

He found the pulse in one wrist and pressed the sharp edge to his skin until it stung.

86

The card bit his wrist as he eased the sharpened plastic in a shallow, horizontal swipe. Blood oozed from the cut, but it wasn't deep enough. He repositioned the card for another slice. As he prepared for the second attempt, the memory of Vic's scars cut into him, deeper than the self-inflicted wound on his wrist.

His phone screen swam, but he scrolled through call history until he found an unlabeled number from several days ago.

Vic picked up after two rings. In the background, someone played a piano, and people sang. Her muffled voice said, "Be right back."

The music faded but didn't vanish. She'd probably gone into another room.

"Lane, is everything okay?"

"I want this to be over," he said.

"Are you drunk?"

"Maybe...doesn't matter. I wanna know why you didn't go through with ending it before. How'd you not try again?"

The piano music swelled in the background again, and Vic

whispered, "Mom, can you take Sophie tonight? Yeah. Okay. Thanks." To Lane, she said, "Do not hang up the phone. I'm coming over there."

"You don't have to do that."

"Yes, I do. What's in your other hand?"

"Credit card. It's pretty sharp."

"Okay. Put that away. Have you taken anything in the past couple hours? Sleeping pills? Pain meds?"

"No."

"What did you drink?"

"Vodka."

"How much?"

"Few shots. Don't remember how many."

"Is the bottle close by?"

"Nah. Other end of the bar."

"Can you walk?"

"Suppose so."

"Get to a table and sit."

Lane rounded the bar. The instant he let go, he reeled and almost fell until he adjusted for the tipping landscape. "Chairs are nice here. Could sit in them for hours."

"That's great. What else is around you?" The slam of two car doors echoed in the background.

"Couple plants, lots of tables, trash can in the corner."

"Anything on? TV, radio?"

"No. Left the lights off when I came in earlier too."

"Where did you go?"

"Funeral. Lester's."

"I'm so sorry. Did you know him well?"

"He owned the bar." Blood from the cut on Lane's wrist left a damp red line on his shirt sleeve. "He was a good person. What's fair about good people dying?"

"Things happen that don't make sense to us. We can't control everything. That's not our place. But we can control how we respond."

"Read the article about your son."

"I loved him very much." Tears rose in her voice. "But God's timing was different than mine. I'll see him again one day."

"You're so sure about that, just like when you mentioned your husband on set a couple months ago. I don't get it. Nobody can prove life after death exists."

"God can."

"No, He can't!"

"Have you ever heard of Lazarus?"

The name registered, but he didn't remember why. "I think."

"He was one of Jesus' close friends, but he died. When Jesus came back to town four days after Lazarus' death, He raised Lazarus from the dead. After that, Lazarus wasn't afraid of death anymore."

"The Bible? That's your proof?"

"It is."

"That's made up. No one comes back from death."

"Jesus did. And He brought Lazarus back too."

Lane smacked the empty table. "Those are just stories!"

"No, they're not."

"How do you know?"

"Because Jesus changed me, Lane Harris. He's the reason I'm talking to you right now. He's the reason I'm alive, and the reason I'm not hanging up this phone. He's my Friend. Has been for seven years. If you want to tell me I've been friends with an imaginary person all that time or that someone who doesn't exist changed me, go ahead." This was the first time Vic had been so animated.

He wanted to find a retort, but nothing came. "It's...been a long time since I heard about Lazarus. Suppose...I could stand to hear it again."

87

Simmer Lounge
Sunday, April 21st

By the time Vic's car pulled into Simmer's parking lot, Vic had recounted the entire incident between Jesus and Lazarus, including the disbelief—and hostility—of the religious leaders upon hearing the news of Lazarus' resurrection.

He understood the skepticism. After all, who would believe someone raised another person from the dead? It was crazy.

When Vic stepped inside, mercifully leaving the lights off, Lane was still holding his phone. If she hadn't been pregnant, he'd have mistaken her for a fencepost.

Out in the van sat her father, Bert, behind the wheel. He turned off the vehicle and stayed in the driver's seat.

Aided by the flashlight on her phone, Vic made it to Lane's table. "What happened?" She lightly touched his bloodied sleeve.

"Cut myself."

She scrounged behind the bar until she found a first aid kit. Barehanded, she cleaned the cut.

Lane laughed bitterly. "Not wearing gloves? I might be carrying some horrible disease."

"I don't believe that for a second. Besides, you'd have told me if I needed gloves." She wrapped gauze around his wrist. "That should keep it from getting infected, but you'll have to check it every day." She looked around the bar. "Does this place have a coffeemaker?"

"Kitchen." Lane angled a thumb over his shoulder.

Vic disappeared and reemerged a few minutes later. "Coffee's on. Ready in twenty. You're drinking it black."

"I don't like black coffee. Tastes like tires."

"Tonight, you do. It won't make you sober, but it'll help clear your head." She eased on the bar lights and fished his wallet off the counter. "Why's there blood on—" She stopped. "How'd you file down this card?"

Lane held up his left hand and, with a smirk, tapped his ring.

"You did this today?" She held up the sharpened card.

"Nope. Couple days ago. At the hospital."

"Why didn't you use it?"

Lane pointed to her wrists. "Had to find out what happened."

Vic sat across from Lane. "You read the article about me losing my son. Did you read the whole thing?"

Lane nodded, but each bob sent a wave of nausea through him, the vodka's retribution.

"Then you know pieces of my past."

"Not really. Article was pretty vague." The urge to vomit grew. He shoved back his chair. It toppled and skittered toward the door.

Vic tucked under his arm and shepherded him to the men's room, where he hugged a toilet for fifteen minutes. Between his heaves, Vic vomited into a sink.

When Lane trudged from the stall to rinse his face, Vic looked worse than him. She'd worn makeup to camouflage pale skin and sunken eyes, but most of it now smeared a paper towel.

The coffee maker beeped in the kitchen.

"I'll get it." He staggered for the door, but only made it past one of the three sinks before stopping.

"No, I'll get it." Vic passed him, making it three steps past the paper towel dispenser before leaning against the wall, coughing into one shoulder. When the hacking subsided, Vic took two deep breaths and offered him a hand.

He took it, and they made it to the kitchen after five more stops along the way.

Vic found the biggest cup in the kitchen and filled it.

Lane's first sip elicited a gag of disgust. "What did you do to this?"

"Secret. Used to help curb hangovers." Vic snagged a napkin and coughed into it. "I wasn't always who I am now."

"So who were you?"

Vic's eyes lit, and a little color returned to her face. "If you really want to know, I'll tell you."

"I need something to distract me from this palette-buster." He tapped the steaming cup.

Vic found a chair and sat before she began.

88

Simmer Lounge
Sunday, April 21ˢᵗ

As Lane downed the last sip of his first cup of coffee, caffeine's buzz made him want to pace. The vodka's haze had thinned, but his vision wouldn't cooperate, so he remained beside Vic's chair, elbows propped on the counter.

"I know what cast and crew said about me." Vic propped both hands atop her pregnant belly and chuckled. "Funny how rumors are. Some claim I report every misdeed on set. Others say I have dark secrets of my own, which is why I'm gone so often." She didn't seem upset, only tired. "I would never want to be responsible for what everyone else does. Trust me, I've done enough myself. I might have grown up in church, but though I pretended to be a Christian, God wasn't part of my life, and I didn't want Him to be.

"I finished high school a year early. Instead of going straight to college like my parents wanted, I got a minimum-wage job and ran away from home, hopping from one friend's house to another until I turned eighteen. First drink, first high, first sex—all in the same week. I was so proud of myself for tasting the forbidden. And I liked it."

Even with alcohol still fuzzing his mind, Lane couldn't imagine Vic with anything stronger than coffee in hand—much less drugs.

"I had loved writing for years and wanted an MFA so, to start, I found a good undergrad program at North Kingsville U." The story Vic told over the next half hour was almost unbelievable. A deadbeat boyfriend who hit her, got her pregnant, then disappeared; a romance with another woman; her son's death; the night she'd tried to take her own life. "I didn't even finish the semester after that. When they let me out of the hospital, I had my baby cremated, got my stuff, and went home to my parents' house. When I pulled into the driveway, my mom ran out and hugged me the second I got out of the car."

Lane gripped his coffee so hard his fingers ached. "They let you come back? After all that?"

"Yes, but there were conditions for my staying there—church services, no dating, no drinking or drugs, find a job. I needed to save for a place of my own, so I agreed. It was hard to get used to. I hated all the rules and the suffocating church people, but I had tried things my way, and all I had to show for it was a tiny urn of ashes, a broken heart, and scars—inside and out—that will never fully heal in this life. My wrists still give me trouble sometimes—soft tissue damage." She covered another cough. "Just one more reason to look forward to the life ahead."

"That was when you started writing novels? After you left college?"

"Yes. But my move back home wasn't the end of my troubles. Losing Tim plunged me into a downward spiral of bitterness and anger. I wrote and published my first novel the year after I moved home, but that following year, the anger became overwhelming. I hated everyone and everything.

"Mom and Dad tried to help me, but I pushed them away. I attended the required one church service a week, but other than that, I stayed in my room when I was at the house. That was when I wrote the rest of Hannah Stanton—though I originally published it under my maiden name.

"I finished the other two books in the series at blistering speed. The publisher and my agent were thrilled at the quick progress. But all the rage and the nonstop work burned me out, so I spent some time alone in a cabin out in redwood country. In the silence, my anger consumed me...until Hahnen'En."

Lane stopped, cup halfway to his mouth. "The book?"

Vic shook her head. "The man."

89

Simmer Lounge

Sunday, April 21st

Something in Vic's eyes kept Lane from dismissing her odd words, but he had to ask. "You met a fictional character?"

"In a way. Haven't you ever crossed paths with someone who changed your life?"

Monica came to mind. But so did Stephen. And Vic. "Yes."

"Well, so have I, and Hahnen'En is one of those people. There are those who rush into our lives like speeding trucks, and others who walk in with barely a whisper. But no matter how they arrive, the people God uses to change us leave evidence of their presence, and some never truly leave us, no matter how many years pass without our seeing them. I consider Hahnen'En an old friend." She laid a hand over her heart. "Have you ever been so full of bitterness you thought it might drown you?"

Lane nodded. He'd been there after Stephen's funeral.

"When you're in it, it's a bizarre mix of bliss and agony. You want to get rid of it, but some twisted part of you refuses to let go. When I was writing *Hahnen'En*, that's where I was—stuck between wanting to escape my bitterness and longing to let it consume me. I hated my life, but I was no longer willing to end it." Vic sipped her water. "Hahnen'En was dealing with the same regret and despair as I was. We both came to a place so dark we thought we'd never leave it. For me, that moment came the night my son died. For Hahnen'En, it was—"

"The prison." His dreams came back. The vodka blurred them, but they were clear enough.

She nodded. "It was inescapable. Hahnen'En's crimes demanded he pay for them, and the king's hunters saw to it he would." Tears in her eyes again. "But then came Oren."

His hands remembered the man's touch from those dreams. He flexed itching fingers.

"You've read that section."

He nodded.

Vic's face held a knowing smile. "Oren was like no one Hahnen'En had met. He'd committed no crime, yet he was to die. But as Hahnen'En's hour of execution neared, he had to find out why Oren stood condemned when he was blameless."

Lane remembered the men's conversation, but only pieces of it. He must have read it just before falling asleep.

Vic's eyes seemed brighter, less blighted by whatever ailed her as she recounted the story.

90

Seven Years Ago

Clear Creek Resort, Cabin 25, Rio Nido, CA
Sunday, December 2nd

Leigh held back tears as Hahnen'En was thrown into the lowest, darkest cell in the prison, forced to wait there, resigned to his fate.

Her fingers hovered over the keys, unsure what to do. She couldn't bear to watch him die. She'd sooner leave the story unfinished. What was wrong with her? She'd never let herself care so much about any of the characters she'd written before. They'd been the most convenient means to an end. Sure, readers had liked them, but Leigh herself had never felt much for them outside of vague appreciation.

Slowly, painfully, she let the story go where it needed to. Each key tap stung as the hour of Hahnen'En's execution neared. There would be no stay of punishment.

Tears tracked Leigh's cheeks, but she kept typing.

By the time the faraway clank of an opened door preceded footsteps on the stairs, both Leigh and Hahnen'En had given up all hope. It was too early for the execution, but she supposed the king's men had no qualms about foregoing a few courtesies when it came to those waiting for their sentences to be carried out.

But instead of one man coming to retrieve Hahnen'En, there were two. One was the warden, the same man who'd thrown him into this cell hours ago. The other was a stranger. He wore fine clothes, and an empty scabbard hung from his belt. From the lack of dirt on his face and hands, he couldn't have been brought here the same way Hahnen'En had.

Once the warden was gone, the stranger turned to him. "You're Hahnen'En." The man held out his hand. "Oren."

Hahnen'En eyed the newcomer with suspicion. It was no secret who he was. By now, his name was probably on every wall in the kingdom and in every mercenary's pocket. Which only made this man's seeming cordiality all the more suspect.

Oren patiently waited for Hahnen'En to accept his greeting.

"Are you also sentenced to death?" Hahnen'En kept a wary eye on the other man.

"Yes. And no."

After a long silence, the other man added, "I'm not here to harm you."

"How do I know that?"

Oren lowered his hand. "If I were, would I have come unarmed?" He indicated his empty scabbard.

Hahnen'En kept his distance. "You could be hiding a blade almost anywhere."

"Then search me."

It could be a trick to get him close—make an easy kill. But if this Oren wanted to kill him, why take the trouble to come all the way down here, to the lowest level of the prison? Why not just wait for the king's men to carry out the execution?

But despite Oren's offer, Hahnen'En didn't come any closer. "You must have a very good reason to be here."

"I do," Oren said. "I know what you've done. And I've come to pay your debt to my father."

"Why?"

"Long have I watched your struggle. Long have I waited for you to come to your senses and return to my father's keeping, but you would not—until the hounds caught you."

"I don't need anyone else to pay my debts."

"This is a debt you cannot repay. Even offering your own life could never right the wrong done to my father." Oren stood between Hahnen'En and the cell door as the prison master descended the long stair. "Blood calls for blood, Hahnen'En. The law demands it."

Prisoners reached out to the prison master, begging for release, but he ignored them.

"No. I won't let you take my place." Hahnen'En lunged for Oren, shoving him away from the cell door. "I know I'm guilty." His gut wrenched at the admission, but he couldn't run from the truth anymore. "I'll pay the price."

"You are not able."

"Yes, I am."

"Once, all lauded you as a hero. Now you've murdered, stolen, lied. Your blood is guilty. To shed it in the name of redemption would be futile."

At the base of the stair, the prison master stopped.

Hahnen'En didn't move out of the way. "I can't—won't—let you do this."

"You refuse my gift?"

The thought of a sword through his chest made Hahnen'En's heart pound. His time was up, and he knew it. "I must."

Oren nodded solemnly. "If that is your choice."

The prison master opened the cell door and escorted Hahnen'En up the stairs. Oren followed.

When they stepped outside the prison, six guards ushered them to the top of the torchlit wall. In the courtyard below, an entourage, including the king himself and all men stationed at the prison, gathered.

Hahnen'En and Oren stood side by side before two armed men.

"I said I wouldn't let you take my place," said Hahnen'En.

"But I have already done it, whether or not you accept it."

"This is insane!" Hahnen'En tried to shove Oren away from the swordsmen, but a soldier grabbed him before he took two steps. The other man secured Hahnen'En's wrists in manacles attached to a chain that stretched up from the brick beneath his boots. There was barely enough slack to allow him to stand straight, much less move.

Oren remained unshackled.

The prison master spoke. "Oren, son of the Great King Haim, you are sentenced—at yours and your father's own bidding—to die by the sword to atone for the crimes of Hahnen'En the Traitor."

The swordsman standing before Oren brandished his blade.

"We will carry out your sentence at the baying of fourth watch," said the prison master.

Thick, dreadful silence filled the air, broken only by the crackle of torches and the heavy pound of his own heart.

The hounds bayed.

Below, the king wept silently.

"Stop!" Hahnen'En cried as the armed man rammed his blade through Oren's heart.

The king's son fell to the stone, his life's blood seeping from the wound in his chest.

He was dead.

A guard unchained Hahnen'En.

"You are free to go," said the prison master.

"But—but I have to pay my debt." Desperation clung to him. This couldn't be true. He had to be imagining it. No innocent man died for someone they knew was guilty.

"He has paid it."

"But—"

"Do you not accept his blood?" said the prison master.

"No," Hahnen'En whispered harshly. "I can't."

"Then go." The prison master pointed to the stairs leading to the courtyard and out of the prison. "He has given you a few hours' start on the hounds. Blood is shed. It is yours to decide whether you will honor his sacrifice."

Hahnen'En descended the stairs in a daze and stumbled from the prison. Every hundred steps, he stopped and watched for a moment as the guards and prison master reverently took Oren's body from the wall.

91

Simmer Lounge

Sunday, April 21st

Another cough punctuated Vic's recounting. She covered it with her napkin.

"You remember that word for word?"

"It's one of my favorite parts of the book," she said.

"Why?" He took another long drag of coffee. "It's awful. The man's own father wouldn't intervene. His men killed him—because he told them to. And for a stranger. Who does that?"

Vic's only answer was a quiet smile.

Two more cups of coffee later, Lane had finished the pot. He still felt horrible.

"Let's go." Vic got up slowly.

"Where?"

"To the van."

"If you're taking me to the ER for the cut, you don't have to."

"No, Lane. We're going to my parents'."

"You don't have to babysit me."

"You still need somewhere to stay. With the owner gone, this place won't be an option soon." She held out a hand. "Are you refusing help?"

He mulled his choices. "No..." He took her hand, and they made it to the front door.

"Dad?" Vic said. "All his stuff's in the back room."

"I'll help you." Even as Lane said it, he knew he wouldn't be able to make good on his offer. His vision was more stable than before, but he didn't trust his ability to walk a straight line, much less carry something all the way from the back of the bar to the parking lot.

"It's no trouble. I'll get everything." Bert left the van and ferried Lane's possessions to the vehicle.

Two hours later, they arrived in front of a ranch-style house in the Los Angeles suburbs. In the dark it was hard to tell most details of the yard, but a wide, kept driveway spanned the distance from house to sidewalk. Groomed plants and flowers occupied a row of planters in front of a bay window.

A red door opened, and Gabby Ellis beckoned them all inside. "Hello, Lane," she said. "Welcome to our home."

If his arrival surprised her, she hid it well. Bert whispered something to his wife.

"The guest room is just down the hall on the right." Gabby ushered Lane to the open door, keeping him steady as he walked not quite straight.

Conservative décor gave the bedroom an understated, distinguished air, but dark burgundy paint with white trim made it feel cozy. The matching bedspread and sheets were soft, and it took everything Lane had not to collapse into them.

Gabby patted his hand before letting go. "The bathroom's next door. Clean towels are in the linen closet inside. Bert will bring you some clothes and help wrap that hand so you can get a shower."

"Thank you."

Gabby smiled. "You're welcome."

Instead of going straight to sleep, like he ached to do, Lane took Mrs. Ellis' advice and grabbed clean underwear. Bert gave him a borrowed pair of pajamas. He would have worn his own, but digging through boxes at ten o'clock at night while trying to keep from either falling on his face or hurling all over his stuff didn't appeal to him.

Bert covered Lane's bandaged wrist in an electrical-taped grocery bag before he ventured into the guest bathroom.

When the water temperature was just under a scald, he stepped into the shower. Clouds of steam surrounded him as the warm air and pounding water afforded a sliver of peace. The shower at the public restrooms couldn't compare to this. Instead of keeping an eye out for pickpockets, he could relax and just take in the moment.

Once, he almost fell asleep but jerked awake.

The alcohol still made him sluggish, but thanks to the coffee, he could at least process thoughts, though the night was still hazy. He vaguely remembered calling people, though he'd have to check his phone to find out who.

He hoped he hadn't said anything too outrageous.

His wrist stung. A vague recollection of his sharpened credit card came to mind.

The conversation with Vic, however, was the clearest part of the ordeal. He remembered every word, though the drive to the Ellises was foggy. He would have to get Vic to tell him the rest of her story—and finish *Hahnen'En*. The passage she'd recounted had carried no personal significance when he'd read it, although pieces of it had invaded his dreams. After seeing Vic's face when she talked about it, he had to find out what happened afterward. If it could mean so much to someone, it had to be at least a little bit interesting.

He finished his shower and got into clean clothes. They smelled of orange blossoms—a refreshing change from the fake tropical-smelling stuff he'd used on his laundromat run.

By the time he left the bathroom, everyone else had gone to bed.

As he peeled the plastic bag off his hand and wrist, he wondered if Vic was still here, or if she'd driven home with the rest of his stuff in her minivan. It didn't matter. He was in no state to go through anything tonight.

He slipped under welcoming covers. Just before he drifted off, he discovered his copy of *Hahnen'En* on the nightstand. He briefly wondered who put it there.

Didn't matter.

He was too exhausted to read tonight.

92

102 Maple Leaf Lane, Los Angeles
Monday, April 22nd

Lane drank a third glass of water as he sat at the breakfast table with the Ellises, Vic, and Sophie. His head ached but, without him asking, Mrs. Ellis offered two aspirin. He gladly took them.

Any other morning, free breakfast would be amazing. Today, nothing on the table looked appetizing, but he ate anyway. The food would help ease the hangover.

"Sorry you don't feel good, Mr. Lane," said Sophie from her seat between him and Vic.

"It's okay. I'll be better soon. It's my own fault."

"Mommy, can I stay with Papa and Nana and Mr. Lane today?"

"Sure, sweetie. I've got a doctor's appointment soon anyway." Vic set a sliced banana on her daughter's plate.

"Are you gonna see Dr. Gordon? She's nice."

Vic nodded. "And I'll bring back a page for you to color."

"Horsies?"

"If she has any."

"Yay!" Sophie stuffed a chunk of biscuit in her mouth, chased by a banana slice.

"How're things on set?" Lane forced another bite of scrambled eggs.

"Jack's got his hands full trying to recast you. I didn't know you were gone until I came to the studio one day and you weren't there." Vic sipped water and braved a bite of toast. There was no edge to her voice, no anger.

He wanted to tell her the whole sordid story, but not with Sophie or the Ellises here. "I'm sorry you had to find out that way." He rubbed his aching head and took a break from eating as he pushed back hangover-prompted nausea.

Vic met his eyes. She didn't ask questions, but he wanted to offer something by way of explanation.

He bit his tongue. Maybe now was as good a time as any to tell someone pieces of the truth. At least he was less likely to be judged here. "Monica and I weren't together."

Vic picked up her water glass. "I never thought you were. So why were you living out of the back of a bar?"

If it had been anyone else asking, he'd have told them it was none of their business.

"Just after Valentine's Day, someone broke into my apartment. They took everything of value and stole my bank information. I had to freeze my account and open a new one. They're still sorting out all the fake charges. Being in the hospital with a dead phone the past few days kept me from checking to see what has and hasn't been returned. While I was sorting that out, I..." He fastened his gaze on his plate. "...Was evicted." Though it was humbling to admit, telling someone what happened eased the burden of carrying it alone for so long.

Bert took a long sip of coffee and exchanged glances with his wife. "If you'd like to stay with us, we'd be glad to have you."

Lane opened his mouth to say yes. He had nowhere else to go, and from what he knew of the Ellises, no one would bother him here.

"Before you accept," Bert continued. "There are conditions. If you can't live with them, we'll help you find someplace else."

Lane already knew what they would say.

"One church service a week—your choice of which one. No dating. No drugs, alcohol, or tobacco. And you'll need to get a job."

The dating he could live without. He wasn't ready to even think about that right now. A job, he understood. He'd been ready to find one last night. Alcohol shouldn't be an issue. After the last twelve hours, he wasn't interested in another hangover anytime soon. He couldn't smoke because of his acting anyway. Plus, getting high had never been for him—especially not after Stephen's accident. But the church services? "I haven't been to church since I was a kid. I wouldn't know what to do—how to act." He didn't add that church was the last place he wanted to be. God had done nothing for him. Why should he pretend to do something for God? According to Christians, there wasn't room for someone like him. If God couldn't support how Lane loved, he had no desire to support Him.

"That's all right. We don't expect you to. All we ask is that you go. You won't even have to pay for gas."

The thought of stepping foot inside a church made him want to leave right now. But finding another low-rent—or no-rent in this case—option in a decent neighborhood wasn't likely. He could stomach a few weeks, then find a place and move out. "Okay."

"I'll get the rest of your things from Vic's van before she leaves for her appointment," Bert said.

93

Seven Years Ago

Clear Creek Resort, Cabin 25, Rio Nido, CA
Sunday, December 2nd

Leigh shut her laptop and shoved it away. Her heart pounded. Tears fell in wide streams, dripping onto her hands, jeans, and comforter. A choked sob shoved through her tight throat. She hid her face in her hands as she told herself over and over that this didn't make sense. No one died for guilty people. It was idiotic—wasteful—completely unrealistic.

But even as she tried to reason through erasing the awful scene she'd just written, something in her heart told her this was how it had to be.

There was no other answer. Hahnen'En's life had to be bought back.

And Oren had paid for it in blood.

She curled into a ball atop the comforter and used a pillow to smother her tears. There was no use crying over someone who didn't exist.

Monday, December 3rd

Silence filled the pre-dawn darkness.

Leigh sat up in bed. Fatigue sagged under her eyes. At least once every hour, she'd woken to escape dreams. She couldn't call them nightmares. There was no bloodthirsty monster on her heels. She hadn't plummeted off a cliff, or drowned, or been trapped in a closet. Instead, all she could see were Oren's patient eyes just before the executioner stepped forward to take his life. The dream always cut off before the fatal blow. Every time she saw him, he seemed to recognize her. A spark of knowing always lit his face.

It made her uneasy.

As first light seeped through the trees and shadows retreated into corners, the Bible, propped atop the bedside table, stared at her, almost as if it, too, had literal eyes. She shifted to keep the book out of her peripheral vision.

It had been a few days since she'd picked up her old Bible. Reading it through had reminded her of what she'd heard growing up in Sunday School. A dozen stories had been constantly rehashed until she could recite them word for word. As a teen, the pool of stories had grown, but she'd stopped paying attention sometime after she'd turned twelve. At sixteen, she'd stopped playing the part of dutiful churchgoer. Despite her sordid history with Christianity, the time she'd spent reading the Bible these past two weeks had been...all right.

The longer she sat with her back to the Bible, the more she wanted to open it again. It might expunge the lingering echoes of last night's dreams.

She grabbed the book and laid it in her lap. The light blue cover was still pristine. As a child, she'd used it so seldomly. Before this getaway, she hadn't ever read it through. The rustling of pages filled the bedroom as she opened to the middle of the book, where her mother's folded note created a slight bulge. She flipped past the note without opening it. When she reached the section titled "John," she stopped. When she'd read through this, it hadn't made much sense. She'd scrunched crooked eyebrows at unfamiliar words before skipping ahead to a more straightforward section.

More browsing than reading, Leigh waded through the passage until she neared the end. Jesus stood at trial. Most of it was worded differently than she was used to reading, but she understood the essentials. Men lied about Him. The ones running the trial hated Him. It was obvious this was a sham, but enough people in power wanted it to happen, so it had.

As a little girl, Leigh had heard the story of Jesus' death—albeit, edited to exclude some of the more gruesome details. When she'd read it last week, this awful series of events had struck her. How could a man, especially an innocent one, endure so much torture? If Jesus was God, why hadn't he stopped this corrupt group from taking his life?

She rubbed tired eyes.

Flashes of last night's dream burned into her mind. Oren had let someone take his life, and he'd had the power to stop it too. But he'd allowed it to happen...so he could save someone else. Because he valued them. Because he cared about them.

Leigh's eyes shot open, and she flipped back to the beginning of Jesus' trial.

94

Lane took a plate from Gabby and wiped it dry. He would have done the washing, but drying kept his bandage from getting wet.

"You don't have to help with dishes," Gabby said. "I know hangovers can be nasty."

"It's okay. Keeps my mind off the headache." He stacked clean plates in the cupboard with the rest of the set.

"Did the aspirin help?" She handed him a fork.

"Some." He set the utensils on a clean towel to finish drying. "Vic didn't say how I got this, did she?" He held up his wrist.

Mrs. Ellis washed another fork before answering, "You cut yourself. Just before you called her."

That tracked with his hazy memory.

Mrs. Ellis handed him two forks this time. "Vic gave my husband your credit card to hold onto for a while."

"The sharpened one?"

Gabby nodded.

Considering his recent history with it, that was a good idea. It was maxed out anyway.

"So what made you decide to go into acting?" Gabby said as they finished the dishes.

"I fell in love with it in high school. First time I got up in front of people, I knew that was what I wanted to do."

"I was a teacher for thirty years before I retired."

"You miss it?"

"I do, but it's nice to have time with my granddaughter—and soon my grandson. And to have as much time with Vic as I can."

Sophie ran up, yellow playground ball in her arms. "Nana, will you come play catch?"

"I'll be right there. Get your shoes on."

"You wanna come, Mr. Lane?" Sophie looked up at him.

"Thanks, but I need to get some sleep."

"Did you stay up too late?"

"Something like that."

"Okay, bye." Sophie waved at him and scurried to the door, where she pulled on little pink and white sneakers over her socks.

"Vic said Sophie liked you," Gabby said. "She doesn't take to many adults. Always been particular—like Vic."

"She's a great kid. Vic's done well with her."

Gabby nodded. "Vic's had a lot going on the past few months. I only hope...I hope Sophie knows how much her mother loves her." She dabbed damp eyes. "You take however long you need to sleep. We'll let you know when it's time to eat, but we'll leave you alone as much as possible."

Lane waited until Mrs. Ellis and Sophie went outside before heading back to the guest room and falling into bed. He hoped his headache would be gone when he woke up.

He didn't rouse until Bert tapped his door. "Lunch is ready, if you're hungry."

Lane stirred and checked his phone. 12:23. He'd slept for four hours. His head still throbbed, but overall, he felt better.

He got up, brushed a few wrinkles out of his clothes, tamed his mild bedhead, and met the Ellises and Sophie in the humble dining room. He was about to ask if Vic was there when she emerged from the hall opposite his guest room. She looked tired but otherwise all right—at least, as all right as she typically looked these past few months.

"Let's pray." Bert bowed his head.

Sophie took Lane's hand and her mother's, just as she'd done at breakfast when Mr. Ellis had prayed over the meal. It had startled Lane this morning, and it still startled him now, but at least he didn't jump this time. His hand dwarfed hers, but she never let him go.

When Bert finished praying, Sophie released Lane and Vic. "Beans, please?" Sophie announced.

Lane hid a chuckle as Vic took a small helping of green beans for herself and doled out almost as much for Sophie. The little girl chomped them happily as her mother gave her a piece of pre-cut baked chicken, mashed potatoes, and cooked carrots. Sophie didn't complain about the vegetables. He remembered hating carrots as a kid. He didn't mind them now, but it used to be an ordeal to eat them.

Unlike this morning, he ate well, thankful to have something decent instead of the random fare he'd had back at the bar.

95

102 Maple Leaf Lane

Monday, April 22nd

During lunch, the Ellises chatted with Vic.

"How was your appointment?" Gabby said.

"Fran's keeping a positive attitude about everything," said Vic as she poked her food before taking a couple of bites. "Said nothing's changed."

"No change isn't the worst news," Gabby said. "The whole church is praying for you."

"I know. Thanks, Mom. This is going to be a big transition for me. For everyone..." She kissed Sophie's head as the girl ate a few carrots slathered in mashed potatoes.

"Still June?" Bert swallowed hard and took a long drink of water, as if he had something stuck in his throat.

"Yeah."

Gabby took Vic's hand. "Lots of people are going to love that little boy. Have you picked a name?"

"Almost." Vic slipped on a sweater hanging over the back of her chair, even though it wasn't cold in the house. "Not set on one yet."

She turned away from the table and covered a cough.

Gabby stirred potatoes, carrots, and beans together, eyes on her plate. "Will Sophie be staying with us this week?"

"I think it's time to bring more of her things over, don't you?"

Gabby sucked in a hard breath. "Yes. We've got her room ready for after the baby comes."

Lane was sure Gabby held back tears.

Vic smiled, but her eyes misted. "Good. She already loves staying with you. I just hope this change doesn't make her doubt God."

Gabby left her seat and went to Sophie. "If there's one thing I know, it's that this little girl right here," she hugged her granddaughter in between the girl eating, "loves two people very much: her Mommy, and her Jesus."

Sophie stopped eating at this. "I love you too, Nana." She hugged Mrs. Ellis back. "And Papa. And Mr. Lane." She grinned at all seated.

He didn't know what to say. To any of it.

Lane spent the afternoon searching job boards on his phone. Lots of places hiring, but few needed someone with his skill set. He found a listing for a call center agent. Not his preferred job, but right now, a paycheck was a paycheck. He could find a better job later or quit when—if—he found an acting gig. Right now, the important thing was to pay off debts.

As he filled out the online application, a text came in.

The credit card people. Wanting money again. He still needed to try talking them down from the impossible sum he'd been saddled with, but every time he found their number, he couldn't dredge up enough motivation to dial it.

He ignored the text as he finished the job application and submitted it.

By now he'd expected Tina to call or text again, but she'd been quiet since he'd gotten out of the hospital.

Before his eyes threatened to scream from reading tiny print on a bright screen, he filled out six more applications. He set the phone on the pillow, relieved to have a moment of rest from the monotony.

Vic still seemed unusually thin for a pregnant woman. What was the doctor's name she'd mentioned? Gordon? Fran Gordon?

He gave his eyes a hard rub and reopened his phone browser. He typed in the doctor's name, expecting to see a listing for some specialist OB, or—based on the way the family had acted at lunch—someone who worked with special-needs children.

When he found Dr. Francis M. Gordon, he wasn't expecting her title to be "Head of Oncology."

96

102 Maple Leaf Lane
Monday, April 22nd

Lane stared hard at the phone screen. Surely he'd misspelled the doctor's name. There had to be another Francis Gordon who practiced around here. He Googled obstetricians in the LA area, only to find none of them with a name anywhere near Francis Gordon. Then he searched for developmental doctors.

Nothing.

The only Francis Gordon was Jenkins Rawling's lead oncologist.

His stomach did a somersault, and he wanted to return lunch. It all made sense now—Vic's odd words about Sophie coming to live with her grandparents, the strange eating habits, the way she seemed sad when she looked at Sophie sometimes, the weight loss and pale skin. It all fit.

Vic was dying.

A knock on the door. "We're heading to the park for a walk," said Bert as he peeked in. "You want to come along?"

"No. Thank you." He hid the phone screen, though it was impossible for Vic's father to see it from the doorway.

"All right. We'll be back in an hour or two. How's the job search?"

"Filled out seven applications so far. Nothing exciting, but it'll help knock down some bills."

Bert nodded. "That's a good start. If you're hungry, dinner's around 6 or 6:30."

"Thank you."

Bert left.

The doctor's profile on his phone demanded his attention again. How long did Vic have?

She'd mentioned being due in June, but nothing else.

Why wasn't she terrified?

When dinnertime came, Vic wasn't at the table. Lane glanced at her empty chair at least five times.

"Vic's not feeling well tonight," Gabby said. "Had to get to bed early." She handled serving and supervising Sophie as the little girl ate her food without protest. "Any news from the police? You mentioned a break-in at lunch."

"Not yet. But I hope to know something soon. Not likely I'll ever see any of my stuff again, though."

"I'm so sorry," said Gabby. "Someone once broke into the house we used to live in near Boyle Heights. For seven years afterward, I locked the door every time I shut it."

"I did the same." He left out that the break-in wasn't the only contributing factor to that particular habit.

Gabby nodded. "It makes you feel you have to keep your guard up every second. I had to learn to trust God to keep us safe after that. Not an easy lesson."

He didn't want to talk about that. "Did you have any more break-ins?"

"No, just the one. We moved into this house after Vic got married. It was a pleasant change. Our neighborhood is worlds better, and I get to see my granddaughter every day, since we're closer to Vic."

Sophie giggled as Gabby tapped the little girl's nose.

"God's blessed us," she said. "We might have to go through some hard times, but He always sees us through."

But her daughter was dying. How could she say that?

He gave a noncommittal nod before turning his attention back to his food. He'd heard the platitudes before. His father was an expert at doling those out by the truckload. These people were nice, and he appreciated their hospitality, but staying here might prove challenging.

"Nana, can we go back to the park tomorrow?" Sophie said. "There were so many nice doggies who let me pet them."

"Papa and I are shopping for baby things tomorrow, but after that, we can go."

"Yay!" Sophie celebrated by popping a big bite of meatloaf in her mouth.

Lane wondered if Sophie realized her mother would be gone soon. How cruel to take both a child's parents before their fifth birthday. One more transgression on God's long list of crimes against the innocent.

97

102 Maple Leaf Lane
Monday, April 22nd

For four hours after dinner, Lane scrolled through job listings again, filling out two more applications and one online survey.

There wasn't a TV in the guest room, and he didn't feel like listening to anything on his phone after a long day of staring at it, so he showered and changed for bed. This time, he covered his forearm in plastic wrap so as not to have to ask for help.

When he came out of the bathroom, he jumped and held back a startled curse.

Sophie stood in the hall in a long, blue nightgown decorated with galloping ponies. The bathroom light cast a long shadow behind her, and she held a stuffed horse. It covered half her face, but she hugged the plush toy tight and hid her eyes in its fluffy, white coat.

"Did you need to use the bathroom?" Lane stepped into the hall, leaving the light on in case she said yes.

"No." Sophie's little voice was higher than usual.

"Did you have a bad dream? I think your grandparents' room is down the other hall."

"No." Now her voice strained.

"Is your mom here?"

Sophie nodded, face still hidden.

"You didn't want to go see her?"

This time, Sophie shook her head.

Lane crouched beside her. "Is something wrong?"

Sophie threw her arms around his neck and cried, "Nana and Papa are sad about Mommy."

If she'd been concerned about this at dinner, she hadn't let on. "I'm sorry."

Sophie sobbed quietly for a few minutes before letting him go when the hiccups started.

"Do you...want to talk about it?" Lane's legs ached from holding a crouch, so he sat cross-legged on the carpeted floor. His bare feet were still warm from the shower.

Sophie sat across from him, horse in her lap as she rubbed tears from her eyes and held her breath to staunch the hiccups. Wet streaks traced her face.

Lane grabbed two squares of Cottonelle from the bathroom and offered them to her.

Sophie took them with muffled thanks. "Mommy told me she's going to Heaven soon and my little brother and me are gonna live here with Nana and Papa."

What a conversation to have with an almost-five-year-old. When had Vic broken the news? "You must be sad."

Sophie shook her head. "Mommy hurts a lot now. She won't when she goes to Heaven. And Daddy's there, so she won't cry anymore."

Sophie leaned forward as if sharing a secret. "I know she cries sometimes because she misses Daddy. So do I. Are you sad your daddy's not here anymore?"

She remembered him mentioning his father's death. He couldn't feel anything but relief over that man dying. All he'd ever done was condemn and paste on a fake smile for his church friends. When they'd gone out to Sunday lunch at local restaurants, he'd left those little pamphlets at the table—What were they called?—and commented on the way home that the waitress worked on Sundays so she "must not know the Lord." Never mind that he was part of the reason she had to work the weekend to begin with. "No. I'm not sad."

"Did your mommy die too, or is she here?"

"She lives in Ohio."

"That's far." Sophie tapped her chin. "But I don't think it's as far as Heaven. I asked Mommy once how far it was, and she said she didn't know. Not even Papa knows, and he knows lots of things. Do you see your mommy a lot?"

Lane remembered vividly the last time he'd seen his mother. It had been ten years ago. She'd come to LA without his father's knowledge. Her face when she'd seen him...it still hurt to remember the disappointment. He had been with his ex, Mitch, then. "No. I don't."

"I'm sorry." Sophie patted his knee. "I'll miss Mommy when she goes to Heaven, but I'm gonna be happy when I get to go see her again. I get to help my little brother learn about Jesus when Mommy leaves. She said I can tell him about all the people in the Bible. Did you talk to Mommy about Jesus?"

The girl's bluntness still astounded him. He couldn't remember the last time an adult was this transparent—or direct—with him, aside from Vic. "Sort of."

"Mommy loves to tell about Jesus and Lazarus. She talks about it more now that she's going to Heaven soon." Sophie didn't have trouble pronouncing the name, as Lane had expected. Vic must have said it often.

"She told me about Lazarus. Stories help lots of people when they're worried or upset."

Sophie frowned and said very seriously, "Mr. Lane, Lazarus isn't a story. It happened. For real."

Vic had been insistent about this same point. She'd clearly gone through a very personal experience that had changed her life, but he wasn't ready to say the Bible was true just based on that. "How do you know?"

It was a hard question for an adult, much less a child, and he regretted posing it the instant it slipped out. He'd asked Vic the same question.

"Because Jesus loves me. People who aren't real can't love me."

Her mother's impassioned response had rocked Lane, but Sophie's lanced his heart like molten rebar. God had ripped away her father, and He was taking her mother. God had uprooted her from her home and would soon force her into a new reality she didn't fully understand yet.

And she maintained God loved her.

It didn't make sense. How could God love someone and commit such atrocities against them?

Sophie didn't deserve this.

No one did.

98

102 Maple Leaf Lane
Monday, April 22nd

Sophie's assertion still hung in the air.

Lane wanted to ask her how God could love her and do such awful things, but he kept the question to himself. He understood what it was to lose someone you loved. If thinking the Bible was real helped her right now, he wouldn't begrudge the girl that crutch. Time would help her understand she was wrong.

"Thanks for talking." Sophie stood.

"Are you still worried about your grandparents?"

"No. Jesus helps me not be sad. He can help Nana and Papa. And He can help you too, Mr. Lane."

"But I'm not sad."

Sophie stood just a hint taller than Lane now. "Yes, you are."

He expected a mild scolding to follow.

"It's okay to be sad. Just don't stay sad. Okay?" She hugged him again before scurrying back to her door, leaving Lane sitting in the empty hall.

His feet were cold now.

Tuesday, April 23rd

At breakfast, Sophie didn't mention their talk the night before. He didn't want to revive the conversation anyway.

Vic looked about the same as she had the day before—tired. No, weary. She'd applied enough makeup to hide the worst evidence, but her maternity top was too big and looked like someone had taken it in at least twice. She wore her hair up, but it didn't appear to be thinning, which didn't make sense if she was doing chemo—

He paused, whole grain toast halfway to his mouth.

She wasn't getting treatment.

He'd assumed she was, based on the nausea and vomiting. But why not take treatment? There were ways to work around a pregnancy without terminating. Unless it was already too late when she'd found out about the cancer.

His appetite vanished.

To be polite, he finished his toast and hoped no one noticed his half serving of uneaten eggs.

After breakfast, Vic left for the set, but she didn't take Sophie with her.

"We're heading out," said Bert. "Since you'll be staying, here's a key."

Lane slipped it into his pocket. He'd put it with his other keys when he returned to the guest room.

"We'll be back before lunchtime. Gabby's making squash casserole. You've got to try it. Even if you hate squash, you'll love this." Bert shepherded Sophie to the door, where she put her shoes on.

He'd eaten things he hated to maintain conditioning, but squash he liked. "Looking forward to it."

When Sophie and the Ellises left, the house stilled, but it wasn't the same chilling silence as the bar's or the deep, crushing void of his apartment. This quiet wasn't lonely. It was peaceful.

Instead of going back to his room, he cleaned and put away breakfast dishes, careful to keep his bandage dry. He found the vacuum tucked in the laundry nook opposite the guest bathroom and tidied up the entryway.

He wondered if Vic and Sophie would sleep here all week or go back to their house.

Would Vic stay here until...?

He shook away the thought of finding her dead one morning. Shouldn't they call in hospice to make her comfortable? It wasn't a good idea to let her drive to and from the set. She had to be on medication, but maybe not with the pregnancy. Sophie had said Vic was in pain a lot.

Tires skidded down the street. Lane rushed to the door and ran to the sidewalk. A delivery van had just missed a cyclist.

No Vic in sight.

He didn't know why he'd hurried outside. Vic had left over an hour ago. She'd be at the studio by now.

More relieved than he wanted to admit, he went back inside the house.

Gabby's squash casserole was everything Bert had promised.

Vic didn't come home for lunch, but being on set meant she might be gone all day, especially if the shooting schedule was still messed up.

He wondered if Gibson had replaced him yet.

As Lane polished off his second serving of casserole, Sophie finished her plate and declared, "Nana makes the bestest food ever."

Mrs. Ellis' mood lightened. "Thank you, sweetie."

"I've got to agree. Gibson was a fool not to let you cook for the cast and crew." Lane surreptitiously reached for the casserole dish again.

Gabby smiled. "Do you like salmon?"

"Love it."

"Then we'll have that for dinner," Gabby said.

"You don't have to cater to me."

"I'm not. I've got some in the fridge that needs cooking. Bert's never been much for salmon, and Vic and Sophie don't eat much, so it's hard to find an excuse to make it." Gabby rubbed her husband's arm. "I'll cook you a nice, lean steak instead."

Relief crossed Bert's face.

"Thank you for putting everything away this morning. I didn't expect you to do any of that," Gabby said. "We were in such a rush to get out and get back, I just decided to do everything when we got home."

"It's no trouble. You've been nice enough to take me in. A few chores are the least I can do."

"Nana, you said we could go to the park." Sophie's feet dangled from her chair.

"We'll go as soon as everyone's done eating."

Lane had just scooped more casserole onto his plate. He was the only one who still had food. "You don't have to wait for me."

"That's all right. It never hurt us to spend a little more time sitting down together."

As Lane finished eating, Sophie chattered about the dogs she'd seen at the park yesterday.

He wondered if he could brave going out in public this soon after being discharged from the hospital. Maybe world might had forgotten about him again. He hoped so, but he wasn't willing to find out yet.

99

102 Maple Leaf Lane

Tuesday, April 23rd

Before the Ellises left for the park, Lane realized he'd forgotten about his car.

"Mr. Ellis?" Lane caught him just as the man snagged keys from the rack by the door.

"Call me Bert."

"Bert." Though Lane had been on a first-name basis with countless people older than him, it felt strange to call Vic's dad Bert. "My car's still at the bar. In my...previous state, I'd forgotten about it."

"Gabby?" Bert called out the front door. "I'm gonna take the truck. Be there in forty-five."

"Okay." Gabby waved as she secured Sophie in the back of a white RAV-4.

"You don't have to interrupt your plans. It's not that important."

"It's all right. One perk of being retired: schedules don't mean much."

"You don't mind?" If he'd asked his father to do this, the man would have railed at Lane for forgetting something so important—for getting drunk in the first place—and for living out of a spare room at a bar, getting steeped in debt, and almost everything else.

"'Course not. Always love driving the truck, but I don't get to do it as often since it's not car-seat friendly." Bert led Lane into the garage, where a blue '67 Chevy C10 sat.

"Restore this yourself?" Lane strapped into the passenger's seat, careful not to touch the immaculate paint job as he got in.

"Me and a friend finished it a couple years ago, right before he went on to Glory. Got to take him on a couple drives before his homegoing."

More death.

"Robert McDempsey. We were friends for sixty years. Knew him before I met Gabby." Bert opened the garage door with a clicker on his keys. "I miss him every time I come out here and see this old truck." Without taking his eyes off the opening door, he patted the dash. "But he's having the time of his life, and I wouldn't bring him back." Bert laughed. "He'd be cross with me if I did. I can hear him now: 'Bert, I finally made it outta there, and you brought me back? I told you how much I was lookin' forward to this!'"

Lane had anticipated death twice in the past week, but he'd just wanted to end the nightmare—to find peace. If he could bring someone back from death...

Stephen's face—as he'd last seen him, pale, dying on that hospital bed in St. Philip—came to mind. Lane would give anything to have his husband with him again.

Lester hadn't deserved to die either. And Vic certainly didn't deserve to.

Regardless of how good or evil people were, what point was there in believing in something purposeful beyond this life? There was no proof anything else existed. The only surety was right now.

But Sophie had been sure of life after death. As had Vic. "How can you believe that?"

"Heaven?" Bert backed out of the garage, down the driveway, and into the street as his wife and granddaughter left for the park in the RAV-4. "I suppose there comes a time in a man's life where he has to decide what he believes about a lot of things. Eternal destination is one of them. Haven't you ever felt that tug in your soul? That little voice that says there's something more than this?" Bert gestured to the street and surrounding houses as they rolled to a stop sign.

"I don't know." It was strange to admit to someone who was still a virtual stranger, but there was no point in lying now. He'd given Vic the same answer when she'd asked him if he believed in life after death.

"You sure?" Bert turned right. "Lotta people don't think they know one way or the other, but they're usually not being honest with themselves."

The statement hit him like an oncoming train. When his father had first discovered his dating habits—during summer break after his first year of college—he'd thrown open the door to Lane's room and shouted, "You're going straight to Hell!" before hauling out a suitcase and stuffing it full of Lane's possessions.

He hadn't spent another night in that house.

His phone rescued him from having to answer Bert, but he didn't look at the caller ID—didn't really care who it was if it kept him from having to continue the conversation. "Hello?"

"Lane!" Stacey's excitement flooded through the receiver. "They agreed to a settlement. I'm meeting with everyone in a couple weeks!

Sorry to call you during work. Wait. Why does it sound like you're in a car?"

"Gibson has us starting late today." Since she didn't seem to already know, he wasn't about to tell her the truth.

"Okay. Well, have a good time, and don't work too hard. Stephen used to tell me all about how crazy those filming schedules are. Got any idea when the movie's coming out yet?"

"Not sure."

"Okay. Well, let me know."

Someone in the background spoke.

"Aunt Sherry says she saw your picture in a magazine and on one of those talk shows she likes to watch. Something about you and Monica Henderson?"

Lane's stomach dropped. He'd rather pick up his conversation with Bert now. "Monica's big on drama. I wouldn't pay any attention to that."

"See, I told you it wasn't true," Stacey said to her aunt. "Okay. Huddles says bye."

"'K. Later."

Stacey hung up first.

Lane held the phone to his ear five seconds longer than necessary to avoid talking to Bert, but as soon as he put his cell away, the other man spoke.

"Sister?"

"In-law." Maybe he could stop this topic right here. "I married her brother."

But Bert didn't flinch. Vic must have already told him. "She doesn't know you're not in the cast anymore?"

"Didn't see a reason to tell her. She's got enough to deal with."

"Truth can be hard, but in my experience, it's worth it."

They made it to the highway.

Lane pretended to read something on his phone.

100

They arrived at the bar.

Lane had escaped additional conversation by checking job boards the entire trip down the highway. A queasy stomach was a small price to pay for not having to discuss anything deeper than who'd gotten back with him about applications.

Bert parked in front of the bar.

"It's around back." Lane hopped out of the truck. "Thanks for the ride."

Bert nodded. "No problem."

But instead of immediately pulling out, the other man stayed where he'd parked as Lane rounded the building.

His Versa sat right where he'd left it, beside the dumpster. He circled the car. A six-inch dent in the back bumper and a wide, black scrape along the back passenger door glared at him.

He hurled an obscenity at whoever had hit him. Had to be the dump truck. Space was tight back here, and trash pickup was Monday night. Why hadn't he thought to get the car before now? His insurance wouldn't cover this. If he wanted it fixed, he'd have to scrape together the money himself.

He tried the marred door.

The reek of mold escaped in a putrid whoosh. The baking soda boxes were probably toast.

At least the door opened, but he had to slam it to get it to close.

With a growl, he slipped into the driver's seat, holding his breath until he got the car started and rolled down all the windows except the back right—which wouldn't go down at all now.

At least he still had gas.

He turned on the A/C and cranked it up to flush out more of the reek. As he pulled around the building, Bert gave him a nod. Lane turned onto the highway. Bert followed.

As he breezed down the road, he turned on the radio, skipping through daytime talk shows and public broadcasting stations until he found a stream of mindless pop music. Half the songs bemoaned breakups or cheating partners, and the other half insisted the singer was on top of the world. He normally couldn't stomach either, but it was better than thinking about his car or anything Bert had said on the way here.

102 Maple Leaf Lane

He wasn't sure where to park. Bert's truck went in the garage, and the RAV-4 and Vic's van stayed in the driveway. Parking on the pristine, well-maintained grass felt wrong, so he stationed his car as far to one side of the driveway as possible without crumpling the lawn.

Inside, he looked for something to do, but Gabby had already put away lunch dishes, and nothing needed cleaning, not even the bathrooms. He didn't have enough laundry to warrant a load. As he searched for something to do, he wandered down the hall containing the master bedroom, Sophie's room, and the room Vic appeared to be staying in.

All doors stood open, and everything was neat except Vic's room. Clothes lay on the end of the bed and draped two chairs, and the bed was unmade. A line of crumpled papers trailed from the trash can under a small writing desk.

He walked in to pick up the trash.

On the desk sat a closed laptop plugged into the charger, a journal and pen, and a Bible—the same light blue one Vic had mentioned before. In the cover's corner sat her name, embossed in silver: Victoria Leigh Ellis.

He ran a finger along the spine. It was even more wrinkled than the copy of *Hahnen'En* she'd given him. He would have left then, but something poking from the center of the book stopped him.

If it had been the journal, he'd have resisted his curiosity, but the people in his parents' church had left their Bibles anywhere and everywhere. They hadn't cared if others moved or read them. He was pretty sure Vic wouldn't mind him looking either.

He cracked open the Bible's worn cover.

Inside the front flap was a brief address from the Ellises: "Happy tenth birthday, Victoria. From Mom & Dad." Beneath it, in a different color pen was a date: December 3, 2012.

He turned to the note. It was a three-by-five sheet of stationery addressed to Vic. The signature at the bottom belonged to Mrs. Ellis.

This was too personal. He shouldn't read it.

At the bar, Vic had said she'd found a note her mother had left in her Bible—one event preceding the writing of *Hahnen'En*.

If this was that note, it might help him understand what prompted Vic writing something so odd—what had shaped her perception of God.

Since Mrs. Ellis' slanted script only filled the front of the paper, he didn't have to disturb the note to read it.

My dear Victoria Leigh,

I know you didn't want to bring this, but I packed it anyway. Your father and I agreed this trip would be good for you because it would let you be alone with God. As difficult as it is to not intervene, we know that's what He wants from us for now.

When you declared you didn't want God, we were sad, but we were angry too—with you and Him. We'd raised you in church, Christian school, a Biblical home life. We didn't understand why you chose not to accept the things we taught you—why you still don't. It especially hurt us when we learned you'd decided to start a relationship with another woman, something we thought you knew was wrong.

We've asked God to forgive us for being angry with you, and we hope you'll forgive us too.

Please know we're praying for you.

Psalm 139 says God loves you whether you run to Hell or fly to the middle of the ocean. Running from God is impossible. It doesn't matter where you go. He is there with you, and I'm praying He brings you someone special, someone who can help you in a way we can't. God can still reach you, no matter how far you go into that pit of bitterness and sorrow you're drowning in. I know He will find a way to send you just the person you need.

With all my heart,

Mom

He shut the Bible and left, first the room, then the house. He grabbed house keys and locked the door behind him as he headed for the sidewalk, hands in the pockets of old jeans.

Gabby's words to Vic echoed through him. Unlike his and Stephen's parents, she had still cared about her daughter despite the rift between them. She'd never stopped loving Vic.

A breeze sifted through oak boughs in a loud whisper that reminded him of coming rain. An SUV rolled by. The driver waved. Lane raised a hand in acknowledgement.

Three houses down, kids too young to be in school played outside under a sitter's supervision. None of them knew what it was to have a parent refuse them love. At least, he hoped they didn't.

He ached to run, to fly past each house, leaving behind snippets of anger-filled conversations from his past. If only he still had his running shoes. But whoever had broken into his apartment had taken them.

The day Ian Parker had said he didn't want anything to do with Stephen or Lane was still all too clear. The storm of words his husband and father-in-law had exchanged was cemented in his memory.

The famed Ian Parker had been set on Stephen learning to manage his investment empire. But Stephen had wanted a simpler life, one where he had time for family and friends. When Stephen had married Lane, Ian had voiced disapproval, threatened to write his son and son-in-law out of the will. To end the exchange, Ian had said he never wanted to see his son again.

And he never had, because Stephen's life had ended only a week later. Not that it had taken that long for Ian to revoke access to the trust fund.

Lane's husband had died knowing his father hated him.

Lane had watched his own father's funeral knowing they would never reconcile.

He tried in vain to hold back memories of harsh words and cold stares. Each one made his chest just a little tighter. In all their cases, the withdrawal of love had come partly because of relationships their parents didn't approve of. But with Vic, that love had been restored—multiplied, even. He wanted to know why.

101

102 Maple Leaf Lane
Tuesday, April 23rd

Two hours after Lane returned from picking up his car, he sat on the couch, staring at a magazine piece about bathroom remodels as thoughts about Vic and her parents crashed through his mind. Bits of Stephen and Ian's last argument kept interrupting his thoughts too.

Sophie bounced in the door ahead of the Ellises.

"Hi, Mr. Lane!" Sophie tossed her shoes by the door and hopped onto the couch beside him. She sat on her knees. "There were lots of nice doggies, and a nice kitty at the park, and Nana and Papa pushed me on the swings and even let me go down the big slide." She stretched her arms out as wide as they would go to depict the length of the slide.

"Sounds like you had fun." Lane set the magazine on the coffee table.

Sophie gave him an animated nod and held up a green pinecone. "See what I found?" She plopped it into his hand. "Why's it all closed up?"

"I suppose it's not ready to open yet."

"But why? Doesn't it want to be pretty and have somebody make it into something nice? Or turn into a big tree?"

She must not realize you didn't have to plant the entire cone.

Its rough ridges dug into his palm. "It might open someday, but it's not the right time." He didn't want to tell her it might never open.

"I hope it opens soon, and I can plant it, and a tree will grow."

"That'll take a long time."

"It's okay. I can wait." Sophie hopped off the couch.

Lane handed her pinecone back, and she scurried to her room as the Ellises put away shoes and keys.

"Is where I parked all right?" said Lane. "I can move if it's not."

"That's just fine," said Gabby. "Bert got his truck back in the garage without a problem, and Vic can park behind the RAV-4. We'll move her van if we need to."

"Any job prospects?" said Bert.

"Nothing yet. Haven't found anything else I can apply for. Everyone's looking for experience I don't have." He supposed he could lie on the applications, but voicing that possibility felt unwise.

"There're a few people at church needing part-time help. It's not much, but it would be something to bridge the gap."

He could stomach the Ellises—even liked them to a degree—but he didn't want to work for a religious person. "Thanks, but I wouldn't know how to contact them."

"Not a problem," said Bert. "We'll introduce you tomorrow night at church."

He'd forgotten he had to attend mid-week service this time. "Oh. All right." If someone wanted to hire him and things didn't go well, he could always make up an excuse for why it wasn't working. None of them would want to hire him anyway, once they found out who he was.

"Up to some yard work?" Bert picked out a pair of grass-coated shoes and lugged them toward the door connecting the house to the garage.

Anything to get out of this conversation. And forget that note. "Sure."

Lane showered before dinner to rinse off the grass and dirt from his excursion in the yard that afternoon. As he walked out of the bathroom in fresh clothes, Vic came through the front door.

"Lane!" She hurriedly hung keys on the rack by the door and kicked off her flats before stepping onto the carpet.

Her outburst pulled him into the living room quickly.

"What is it, dear?" said Mrs. Ellis from the kitchen. "Is everything all right?"

"I found something on the way home." Vic's closed palm concealed her prize.

Lane crossed the living area to see what she was holding.

"Sometimes I go by pawnshops when I'm out. Gives me someplace to just look around and think. I've gotten great book ideas at pawnshops." She took a couple of deep breaths and muffled a cough on her shoulder. "I was at Green's down the road from the studio and was looking at their jewelry selection when I spotted this." She opened her hand. In it sat a tungsten ring identical to the one Lane still wore.

He'd left that ring at Monica's after...what happened there.

"Here." She placed the ring in his hand. "Is it your other one?"

On the outside, it certainly looked like Stephen's ring, but the proof would be on the inside. He picked up the ring and tilted it, so the overhead light shone on the band's interior wall. Engraved there was

"4/30/18"—their wedding date. Beside it was written "Lane Thomas Harris & Stephen Jacob Parker."

Lane thought he might never breathe again. What were the chances of Vic finding this in the pawnshop she'd walked into today, of all days? "Thank you," he whispered.

"I remembered you said you lost it. Somebody must have found it."

Not somebody. Monica.

"Oh, and these were there too." She held up a pair of running shoes—almost new. "They looked like your size, so I picked them up. If they don't fit, or you don't want them, I can give them to the thrift store or take them to church."

Those shoes looked like the same ones he'd had before the break-in.

"You didn't have to do that." He took the shoes and flipped them over. They were his size.

"I know, but why not?"

"Well, I'm sure I'll use them once I can get an exercise routine going." He didn't mention how desperately he'd wanted these a few hours ago.

"Dinner's ready," Gabby said from the kitchen.

Lane dropped the shoes in his room. Before he returned to the dining area, he slipped Stephen's ring onto his right hand. The band was loose, as was the one on his left hand, but when he got back in shape, they would fit again. To make sure it didn't fall off, he moved Stephen's ring to his right, middle finger.

He'd been without it too long. Just looking at it gave him some small measure of comfort.

When he got back to the dining room, Gabby's promised dinner of salmon and vegetables waited for him.

"Vic, would you say the blessing tonight?" said Bert as Lane sat across from Vic and her daughter.

Sophie, now seated between Gabby and Vic, took her mother's and grandmother's hands, and Vic held out hers to Lane. It still felt strange, but he took it.

"Lord," said Vic, "thank You for all Your blessings. Help us love as You loved, and give of ourselves as You gave of Yourself. We love You, and we know You love us."

The rest of Vic's prayer turned to static as Lane tried to reconcile how someone in Vic's situation could say something like that. She was dying. If God existed and He could heal, why leave her in this condition? And above all, why would she think He loved her if He wouldn't intervene?

It didn't make sense.

102

Seven Years Ago

Clear Creek Resort, Cabin 25, Rio Nido, CA
Monday, December 3rd

This time, as Leigh reviewed the story of Jesus' crucifixion, she saw things she hadn't previously noticed. Not once had He tried to talk His way out of what was coming. Even when His enemies dragged Him before local authorities, He hadn't offered a defense.

She reread the horrible scenes leading up to Jesus' bloody death, when He was nailed to a cross, on display for the world to see. Last time she read this, it had struck her as revolting. Why would something so dirty be included in a book that was supposedly about all things holy and righteous? Not that there hadn't been plenty of gross and gruesome things earlier in the book, but none of them had happened to the Son of God.

As she followed Jesus through everything—being beaten, whipped, his face ripped to pieces, forced to carry a heavy wooden beam across his mutilated back, and finally being nailed to that beam—instead of wrinkling her nose in disgust, she read it all with wide, damp eyes.

Leigh had heard it before. Jesus died and rose from the dead three days later. She'd never grasped the horror of it before. Now, it gripped her.

When Jesus said, "It is finished," Leigh shut the Bible. A few tears pattered onto the blue cover. She shut her eyes, wiped them clear.

She needed to write.

In numb silence, she slid the Bible off her lap and let it sit beside her as she reached for her laptop with one shaky hand. She unplugged it and set it atop crossed legs. The small computer's underside was warm from charging all night.

With an unsteady breath, she opened the lid. Her unfinished manuscript was still open. Near the middle of the half-empty page, the cursor blinked at her.

She couldn't put this off any longer.

Unwilling to accept Oren's sacrifice on his behalf, Hahnen'En had run from the keep. With the hunting hounds soon to be on his trail, he headed for the desert to the East. Just before sunrise, he stopped beneath a withered oak and set his face toward the keep. Its high parapets were just visible above the tree line. The sun's warm glow would soon outline everything in orange and gold.

The weight of what Oren had done settled on his sagging shoulders.

With an angry shout, he fell to his knees beside the worn, battered tree. "I didn't ask you to do this," he said. "I deserve to die for what I've done. But because of you, now I'm back where I started—hunted like an animal." He ground his fingers into the dirt, raking up handfuls of it before letting the soft earth fall from his blackened hands. "You shouldn't have died for me." His voice softened as he remembered the prince's face just before the sword had pierced his heart. "How can I accept what you did?" Hahnen'En's knees dug into the disturbed earth, marking his clothes with wide, damp stains. "It isn't right that you paid what I owed."

The bay of a hound rose through the trees. Hunters would find him before the sun rose.

There would be no escape this time.

He shut his eyes and bowed his face to the ground. Last night's awful scene returned. The flash of metal, spreading blood, the look of peace on Oren's face.

"Do you not accept his blood?" the prison master had said.

How could he? Oren had owed him nothing. And yet he'd given Hahnen'En everything he had.

"Everything..." He breathed the single word. It whispered across the earth, so quietly Hahnen'En barely heard it. But though it didn't echo in his ears, the force of it reverberated through his heart.

These past hours, he'd been asking the wrong question.

It wasn't a matter of how he could accept what Oren had done. How could he not? How selfish was he to reject a gift so dearly bought?

"I'm a fool." The words seeped from Leigh as Hahnen'En said them. "I accept the blood shed on my behalf."

She stopped typing.

Silence enveloped the cabin as shafts of beautifully new light broke through the old windowpane and pooled at Leigh's feet. She reached for it, the golden rays bathing her fingertips in warmth.

If the story of Jesus was true, how could she push away a sacrifice so complete? How could she turn her back on it?

"I'm a fool..." she repeated Hahnen'En's words, choking on the last one. "Please forgive me."

It was a simple prayer—not the ritual "pray with me" liturgy so popular with previous pastors of her parents' church. Most Christians she knew would frown on it. But as the light of morning fell over her, she didn't care what they would have thought. It didn't matter anymore.

Believing something she'd long ago dismissed was the last thing she'd expected of this retreat. And when she got home, who would believe how it happened? She dared a little smile. Those stuff-shirts would be horrified if they knew she'd prayed alongside a fictional character. But he'd been more of a friend to her this week than any of them ever had.

Maybe God had brought Hahnen'En to her. Just like her mother had said in her note.

The thought sent tears to her eyes.

She smoothed the front of her old Bible. Its blue cover shone more brilliantly than she remembered. Even the flowers on the worn comforter popped with color.

Instead of loneliness, the stillness around her was a blanket of peace.

The hole left in her heart by her son's death was still there, and it ached horribly. Both wrists throbbed from a week and a half of constant typing, and the scars from that night in the shower stall two years ago itched.

Once, she hadn't had any desire to picture her future. There was no reason to. What value did her life have since she'd lost the one person she loved most in this world? But now she dared think there might be something worth living for.

She would pursue it until her last breath.

103

102 Maple Leaf Lane
Wednesday, April 24ᵗʰ

1:11 a.m. Lane lay awake.

He should have been tired from the yard work earlier, but though his body wanted to sleep, his mind wouldn't stop. It didn't matter what he did, how he tried not to think.

Events continually surfaced.

He fingered Stephen's ring, relieved at its miraculous presence. He would have to pay Vic back for the ring and shoes as soon as he could.

He checked his old bank account.

A couple small transactions had been reversed since he'd last checked, but the bulk of the money was tied up in three large checks, all made out to illegible names. The memo field was blank on all three. Not that he expected thieves to leave a note saying how they'd spent his money. There was no knowing how long it would take to get even part of it back.

He closed the browser tab and tossed his phone onto the blanket with a muffled thwump. His predicament would only get worse since, tonight, he had to attend his first required church service to fulfill his terms of residency in the Ellises' house.

If he recalled correctly, mid-week services were smaller. That might be good. Fewer people to stare at and judge him. Or it might be bad. Fewer people meant more would have opportunity to pry.

The church his parents had taken him to as a kid had boasted its share of gossipmongers. This one wouldn't be any different. Before next Sunday, he'd be the talk of the congregation.

He hoped the Ellises were prepared for the consequences if someone posted online about his presence at their church. That was the last thing he needed—more social media attention.

Sunglasses and hair dye were means of camouflage he'd used for a couple months after he'd married Stephen. But that was only a temporary solution. Attending services was what he had to do to get by now. People would find out sometime, be it now or ten years from now. Hiding behind tinted lenses and colored hair wouldn't help. Better to blend in. Act as if he belonged. That prospect wasn't any more palatable than hiding, but it might be more effective. At the very least, he needed to remain inconspicuous.

He tried again to get to sleep. Unfortunately, sheep counting and mindless carpet commercial jingles failed to lull him.

At 3 a.m., he considered reading more of Vic's book, despite his earlier thoughts about it, but he opted to spend time at a job board instead. Maybe he could find something before the service. Avoid conversations he desperately didn't want to have with people who would never accept him.

His eyes burned, but he spent the next hour staring at the screen, looking for anything that might save him.

104

Lane spent the morning avoiding Vic, who grabbed a late breakfast and rested a few hours in her room before heading to the studio around 10 with the promise of being home by 4:30 for dinner.

"That girl's always been a doer," said Gabby as she admired a picture Sophie was coloring. "Even when she was little, she hated leaving things unfinished."

And yet, she was going to be forced to leave a lot unfinished soon.

A truck pulled up outside.

"Mail's here. I'll be right back." Gabby grabbed slip-ons and headed for the end of the driveway.

"Mr. Lane, look." Sophie held up her coloring page. It was the picture of horses Vic promised to bring from Dr. Gordon.

"They're blue?"

Sophie giggled and put the paper down. "Horsies can be any color they want to be, and these ones wanted to be blue." She filled in the first horse's withers and flank with a sky-blue crayon before trading for navy to finish the second one. "Blue's the bestest color. Mommy said so."

"You like blue?"

Sophie nodded as she colored. "The sky is blue, and Heaven's up higher than the sky. Mommy said she wants her house in Heaven to be blue with a red door—like Papa and Nana's house. What color do you like most?"

Lane hadn't thought about it. "Green, maybe."

"Green is nice too. The grass is green, and trees, and Papa and Nana's mailbox."

He hadn't noticed the color of the mailbox, but now that he thought about it, Sophie was right.

Mrs. Ellis returned with a stack of envelopes. She set two in a rack by the door—probably bills—tossed a few into a small recycling bin, and brought the other five to the table. "These are all for Vic." She laid the envelopes beside Sophie's coloring station. "The people from church have been wonderful through this whole thing. They've sent cards and letters almost every week since—" She must have realized she'd almost mentioned Vic's illness because she switched subjects with startling speed. "I'll clean up and get lunch ready."

As Vic had promised, she was home for dinner. She opened her mail in her room, and when she emerged again, her eyes were glassed and red, but she was smiling. "Got another letter from Mrs. Holloway. I wish she could be at the service tonight. I'd love to see her."

"Her son will bring her Sunday," said Gabby as she finished setting the table. She hugged Vic quickly before taking a seat. "Before you know it, it'll be time to leave for church."

Mrs. Ellis' words proved too true.

As Lane stuffed shirttails into newly cleaned jeans, he couldn't help but feel out of place. The Ellises were dressed nicely; Bert in a clean polo and khakis, Gabby in a short-sleeved, flowery dress. Vic looked about the same as she always did in her too-big maternity shirt and dark skirt. Sophie wore a plain dress and slip-ons.

"Your dad can drive the van," Gabby said to Vic. "It fits five."

"Thanks, Mom, but I'd like to take some time with just Sophie and me. Fran says, unless I suddenly get worse, I'm still fine to drive."

"All right. We'll meet you at church." Mrs. Ellis sat in the back of the RAV-4, leaving the passenger's seat open for Lane.

"I can sit in the back," he said.

"No. I insist." Gabby tapped the headrest in front of her as Bert got in the driver's side.

Hesitantly, he got in.

New Bethany Baptist Church, Los Angeles

Lane sat in the vehicle a full five count after the Ellises got out.

Two trucks, one station wagon, three large vans, a compact car, an SUV, Vic's van, the Ellises' crossover, and another handful of cars filled the small parking lot.

He didn't want to leave the car. Stepping out of this vehicle meant he'd crossed a line—one he'd never intended to cross again. Not even if forced.

He'd sat in his parents' church's parking lot on multiple occasions, having sneaked out of the service to play football in the nearby field with the neighborhood kids or hang out with a couple of the less reputable older guys while his oh-so-pious dad sat in a pew and raised amens to a shouting preacher's sermon about humility.

Lane wrapped the door handle in one hand, pulling enough to get his fingers around it but not enough to click the door open.

They'd said he had to come, not that he had to go inside. But he knew what they meant.

He wondered how many would recognize him—or if he'd go unnoticed, like at the ER when he'd followed Lester's ambulance to Jenkins Rawling.

Lester. Another casualty in God's cruel reality.

The air inside the RAV-4 warmed as the last hints of A/C died.

The Ellises waited beside the vehicle. They didn't look at him, didn't tap the window in impatience or talk loudly about how long he was taking, as were his father's favorite strategies to expel him from the car.

He wasn't a child anymore. No one could make him do this if he chose not to. Not even the Ellises.

His phone read 5:45. In the late evening light, the little church building looked like something out of a small-town magazine. Its white steeple, with a thin cross atop it, reached toward the sun-drenched sky. The building could have fit on the Ellises' property.

People waved to Bert and Gabby as they crossed the parking lot. Vic helped Sophie from the van, and three other little girls—dark-headed triplets—ran up to Sophie, their parents not far behind. Muffled laughter leaked in from the parking lot.

Instead of the dutiful march of parishioners he was used to, these people stopped to talk with one another on their way inside.

A middle-aged man, probably six or seven years older than Lane, got out of a work truck. He wore jeans too, though his were battered, and he tossed a hard hat into the passenger's seat before cleaning his face and hands with a wet wipe and grabbing a well-used Bible out of the console.

These weren't the same people Lane had attended church with as a kid or teenager.

Before he realized what he'd done, he popped the door. The cab light flicked on. Before he lost his nerve, he stepped onto the faintly lined pavement.

A man in an untucked shirt, battered khakis, and work boots herded four kids—all under ten. "Hey, Bert, Gabby," he said.

"Hey, Kyle." Bert nodded.

Before Kyle could greet Lane, one of his kids smacked her brother, and he had to defuse the situation.

Lane concentrated on taking deep breaths. It was just a gathering. Nothing special.

He shut the vehicle door too hard and winced.

No one seemed to notice. Mrs. Ellis patted his arm. He jumped at her unexpected touch. Crickets chirped as the sun sank lower, and he took his first step toward the building.

Two-second pause.

Another step.

Pause.

The third step seemed to break an invisible chain, and he crossed the rest of the parking lot without stopping, even when he reached the front steps.

Numb, he ascended the stairs and stepped inside a church for the first time in twenty years.

105

New Bethany Baptist Church
Wednesday, April 24ᵗʰ

When he entered the church's tiny foyer, he expected something much grander than the simple table decorated with a single flower arrangement and a stack of pamphlets—bulletins, he remembered they were called. Also on the table sat a large, open Bible. Gold edged its pages. It wasn't actual gold, though it made the book seem somehow more important.

But he didn't touch anything on the table and followed the Ellises inside.

To his chagrin, they ushered him to a pew toward the front. People chatted around him and shook Bert's and Gabby's hands in greeting. Then the words he hoped not to hear came.

"This is Lane." Bert directed an older man wearing a collared shirt and dress pants to him. "Lane, this is Pastor Silas Hendrick."

It would be the pastor. But surprisingly, the man wore no tie. Weren't preachers supposed to always wear ties?

"Good to meet you." Hendrick held out a hand in greeting.

Lane took it more out of duty than genuine interest. "Nice to meet you too."

"Bert tells me you're a friend of Vic's?"

"You might say that."

"In my years here, I've never met anyone quite like Vic." Hendrick's smile seemed genuine, and there was something in his eyes that was different from any pastor he'd met before.

"Me neither," Lane said.

"So, are you visiting the area?"

He wished that were true. "No. I'm...staying with the Ellises for a while."

"Do you have a home church?"

This was getting painful, but lying to a preacher—especially in front of the Ellises—seemed inadvisable. "No."

"Well, maybe you'll like it here. We're a family, but we love new people just as much as old ones."

Someone walked up to Hendrick, mercifully ending the conversation when the pastor excused himself.

Vic sat beside Lane, only for Sophie to squeeze between them.

When the before-service chatter quieted, the pastor brought a humble wooden podium to the front instead of using the nice one on the platform.

His parents' pastor would never have stooped to such a thing. He always preached from the platform, whether the audience was two or two thousand.

"Let's sing a couple songs before we get to tonight's message."

Hendrick picked up a blue, hardback hymnal and flipped to the middle. "I know how much this group likes to sing."

Sophie grabbed a hymnal from the rack mounted on the back of the pew in front of them. Her little arms drooped under the book's weight. "Here," she whispered, holding the book out to Lane.

"We'll stay seated tonight. I know it's been a long week for most here." Pastor Hendrick's eyes flitted to Vic but didn't linger.

A young man in his mid-twenties took a seat at the piano.

"Jon," Hendrick looked over one shoulder at the pianist, "let's do 412."

The pianist turned to the song and played a brief introduction while everyone found their place.

Lane couldn't remember the last time he'd used a hymnal. His parents' church had them but never used them—they sang little at all, if he recalled correctly. Searching took a while until Sophie grabbed a handful of pages and brought him much closer to his goal. He made it to 412 just as the small congregation began singing.

The song was old, and he didn't recognize it. He wasn't even sure his parents would know this one. There was no chorus, only four verses that led right into one another. Then, instead of singing the first and last verses as he expected, the people moved from verse one into verse two.

Even Sophie sang, and she seemed to know the words, though her version of some of them made him hide a chuckle.

As they sang, Lane read the first verse.

Here is love, vast as the ocean, loving kindness as the flood,
When the Prince of Life, our Ransom, shed for us His precious blood.

Who His love will not remember? Who can cease to sing His praise?
He can never be forgotten throughout heav'n's eternal days.

The verbiage was thick in places, and he didn't understand most of it, but these people sang nothing like his parents' friends and fellow church members. They seemed to mean what they sang—understand it. Even the teenagers.

The congregation finished the third verse and rolled into the last:

In Thy truth, Thou dost direct me by Thy Spirit, through Thy word,
And Thy grace my need is meeting as I trust in Thee, my Lord.
Of Thy fullness, Thou art pouring Thy great love and pow'r on me,
Without measure, full and boundless, drawing out my heart to Thee.[1]

As the last words echoed through the small church, Vic covered her face with a tissue, from a box tucked into the pew.

"That's Mommy's favorite," Sophie whispered.

Hendrick paged to another song. "And we'll do 178."

The piano started up a song Lane knew: "It Is Well with My Soul." This time, getting to the page went smoother, and again they sang every verse. No one seemed upset about it, either.

Sophie sang clearly, as did Vic, though she wasn't very loud. In his shock of before, he hadn't realized she sang in a soft soprano. Her voice was thin now, but it still held traces of when it had been full and beautiful.

Just one more thing cancer had taken.

---

1 https://hymnary.org/text/here_is_love_vast_as_the_ocean

The group sang without the piano on the last verse, and their voices chilled him as they finished the final chorus.

"Great singing as always," said Hendrick as the pianist took a seat with a young woman, probably his wife. "Let's turn to John 11."

Vic's tired eyes lit as she opened her light blue Bible, and the pastor began reading.

"Let's start in verse 14. 'Then said Jesus unto them plainly, Lazarus is dead.'"

Lane didn't have a Bible, nor did he want one, but Gabby held hers open so he could follow along if he chose.

Sophie sat up and listened as Hendrick read through the rest of the chapter. Lane listened intermittently as he heard again the account of Lazarus' death and resurrection by Jesus. How could Sophie listen with such rapt attention?

Vic rubbed away tears as she followed along, and the Ellises both listened intently. Everyone in attendance appeared to be invested too, so Lane listened with them, for the most part, even though that hadn't been his intention.

106

New Bethany Baptist Church
Wednesday, April 24ᵗʰ

When the service ended, he expected everyone to leave. Instead, people congregated in groups to talk or hand out cards or birthday gifts.

Sophie waved to the triplets she'd walked in with, and they clustered into the pew behind Lane. The girls sat on their knees on the padded bench to talk to Sophie. She mentioned Lane's name at least twice, but he didn't turn around.

Mrs. Ellis sat with Vic, talking quietly as Bert made rounds with several men in the church.

"Hello." Kyle, the man from the parking lot, sat sideways in the pew in front of Lane, elbow propped on the pew's lip. "Sorry I didn't get to say hello before. My four whirlwinds wait for no one." He offered a hand in greeting. "Kyle Whitman."

Glad he'd worn long sleeves to cover his bandaged wrist, he took the man's hand and considered giving a fake name, but that would only delay the inevitable. "Lane Harris."

Kyle froze for a half second, and surprise flickered in his eyes, but he hid it quickly. "Good to have you. You live close?"

"Sort of." He didn't want to explain the situation again.

A girl who looked to be about eight slid into the pew, her younger brother right behind her, hands waving in the air as he growled monster noises. "Daddy!" She tugged Kyle's sleeve. "Daddy, Daniel's chasing me. Please make him stop!"

"Daniel, leave your sister alone."

"But Daddy, Lauren's no fun." Daniel scowled at his sister and crossed his arms in a pout.

"Why don't you go play with Sam and Franklin?" Kyle pointed to two boys from the largest family in the room as they headed for a corner door with two siblings. "They're probably going to the game room."

"Okay..." Daniel sounded disappointed, but that didn't keep him from running after the four other kids, calling for them to wait for him.

"Where are Heidi and Chrissa?" Kyle said to Lauren.

The girl pointed to the pew behind Lane. Both kids, a little younger than Sophie, sat with the triplet girls and talked.

Kyle looked relieved. "Why don't you talk with Mrs. Garrison and Mrs. Ellis for a while?" He nodded toward Vic and her mother.

Lauren looked at Vic nervously. "Do I have to?"

"No, but it would be nice of you."

Lauren muttered attrition and went to sit in front of the two women, who seemed glad to see her.

Kyle let out a sigh.

"She's not quite comfortable with Vic," Lane noted, glad to turn the conversation to someone else.

"Ever since the...diagnosis just after Gav's accident, Lauren's been standoffish around her. Can't say I wouldn't have done the same if I were her." Kyle's eyes darted to Sophie. "I don't know how that little girl has the fortitude to not just sit and cry all the time. It's hard enough for an adult to process losing a parent, much less an almost-five-year-old. But God gives grace. When I lost my wife three years ago, I didn't know what I was going to do. The twins had just turned one, and money was tight. We had to move across town to a smaller house." His eyes misted, but he acted as if they hadn't. "Lauren was about Sophie's age when it happened. She took it hardest. Still hasn't gotten over it. When God led us to this church a year later, I was afraid I would lose my daughter. She was already so angry and bitter. Back then, Vic and Gav taught the younger kids' class, and Lauren got attached to Vic. That's when my little girl gave her heart to Jesus." This time, Kyle didn't hide a quick swipe of his eyes. "Because God sent Vic, my daughter's gonna be okay. Maybe not now, or when Vic leaves us, but I know He'll bring Lauren through."

More death. More hardship. Yet another instance where God—if He was as powerful as so many Christians claimed—could have intervened but didn't. The first song they'd sung tonight was titled "Here Is Love." But this wasn't love. "That's...cruel."

Kyle didn't get upset, didn't look shocked, didn't chastise him for the assertion. "I once thought that too. When God took my Katie, I didn't know why He'd done it—how He could be so unloving? That was my mantra for months: 'Why do you hate me, God? What did I do that made my family and me deserve something so horrible?'" Kyle looked up at the LED-lit ceiling. "But God doesn't operate the way we do, Mr. Harris."

"Lane, please," he insisted.

"All right. Lane. God sees so much more than we can imagine. He has a plan for all of us. No coincidences."

Lane almost cringed. That had been one of his father's favorite phrases: "coincidence isn't real." But Kyle hadn't said it the way his father did. "How can you be so sure?"

Kyle nodded to Lauren, who had rounded the pew and now hugged Vic. Then he crooked a thumb toward his four-year-old twins, who chattered excitedly with Sophie and the triplets.

Just then, Daniel burst through the door, grinning. "Daddy! Can I go to Sam and Franklin's house on Friday after school? They're gonna play board games and they asked me to come. Franklin said his mom can get me and bring me home before eight o'clock. Please, Daddy?"

Kyle glanced at who Lane assumed were Sam and Franklin's parents and gave them a grateful nod. "You can go."

"Thank you, Daddy." Daniel rushed back to his friends.

"At the church we were at, my kids were four of six in the entire congregation. Now, they're four of many. I don't know what I'd do without this place, these people. I loved my wife, but when God took her, he worked in my family in ways that never could have otherwise happened. Have you ever gone through something that changed you?"

That awful day at St. Philip replayed. Lane folded his hands, and Stephen's ring touched his. "Yeah." He said it more harshly than he intended.

"That's how I felt when Katie died. What's your relationship with God, Lane?"

How was he supposed to answer that? You couldn't have a relationship with someone you couldn't see or hear or touch. He opted for honesty in the hope he might end the conversation. "Can't say I have one."

Kyle didn't seem surprised. "That's where we all start. Key is not to stay there."

Lane braced for the inevitable "salvation talk."

But Kyle checked his watch instead. "Gotta get the kids to bed." From his wallet, he produced a business card. "If you ever want to talk, my cell's on here. Call any time."

To be polite, Lane took the card, though he didn't intend to use it.

Kyle said goodbye to those around him and gathered his kids. "See you Sunday?" Kyle said as he passed Lane on the way out.

"Maybe." He might try a Sunday service, but not the morning one. Too many people. Sunday evening should be small. He would try that—fulfill his weekly quota and avoid a mid-week trip.

"See you." Kyle shepherded his children out the door.

107

Lane read Kyle's business card. Whitman Construction and Remodel. Self-employed. That explained the work clothes, and how he could navigate four children's schedules by himself. Kyle's number sat in one bottom corner.

Lane would never use it, but just in case, he added a new contact. Just as he tucked away his phone and Kyle's card, Bert approached. "Couple of our regulars are out tonight, so I'm afraid we can't make the introductions we were hoping for. I saw you met Kyle, though."

"Yeah."

"Guess we should get home. This group likes to talk. If we stayed till everyone left, we'd be here past 9." Bert chuckled. "An old man needs his sleep."

Lane stood and crowded out of the pew with Bert, Gabby, Vic, and Sophie.

Pastor Hendrick stopped Vic on the way out and talked with her a minute before she joined them again. She seemed encouraged by whatever he'd said.

"Nice to meet you, Lane," said Hendrick. "Hope to see you back soon."

To be polite, he nodded. Coming back wasn't on his list of things to look forward to, but it also didn't seem the worst fate in the world anymore. The only one who'd recognized him was Kyle, and he hadn't commented.

Gabby helped Vic down the front steps as Sophie sped to the bottom and waited patiently for her mother to make the descent.

When they reached the vehicles, Mrs. Ellis didn't let go of Vic. "Bert, can you help Sophie into her car seat?"

"I can do it by myself." Sophie got the back passenger van door open and hopped into her seat before buckling each strap correctly.

Vic sagged, and Mrs. Ellis yelped as her daughter's weight pulled them both toward the pavement.

Lane caught Vic before either woman landed, and it took everything to keep her up. Even with her slight frame, his lack of conditioning made the task much harder than it'd been when he'd caught her when she'd fainted at the studio.

"Let's get her on the backseat floorboard in the van." Bert helped Lane move Vic.

It wasn't a full minute before she came to. "Another one?" She rubbed tired eyes. "It's been two weeks since last time."

"Sweetie, I don't think you should drive home," said Gabby. "I'd take you, but you know I can't see at night."

Bert pulled out his phone. "I'll call Ann and her daughter to come get you. We'll stay until they get here."

"I'll take her," Lane said even before the other man could unlock his phone.

Bert and Gabby both seemed surprised by the offer.

Vic laughed, but it quickly spiraled into a cough. "It's okay. He had to drive me home from the studio once."

"Seems God was looking out for us tonight, having Lane with us," said Bert. "We'll meet you back at the house."

Pastor Hendrick approached just as Vic sat up and stood with Gabby's and Lane's assistance. "Everything okay?"

"We're fine," Vic said. "Thanks for stopping."

"You have someone to drive you home?" Hendrick reached for his cell.

"Lane's going to take me." She gave the pastor a weary, reassuring smile. "He's staying with my parents."

Lane opened the passenger door as Gabby helped Vic into the seat.

"Goodnight, Pastor," said Vic. "See you Sunday."

"Lord willing," said Hendrick quietly as Lane eased into the driver's seat. The pastor stepped a few feet from the van but didn't get in his car—or go back inside—until they pulled out of the parking lot.

Lane's parents' pastor would never have stopped to offer help in the middle of the parking lot, much less call someone on behalf of a parishioner.

As Lane followed the Ellises back to their house, Vic leaned against the door. Two streets past the church, he thought she'd fainted again and was about to nudge her when she sat up.

"How was your talk with Kyle?" she said.

"Fine." Another conversation he didn't want. But he supposed he could tolerate it until they got back to the house. Being rude to a dying woman wouldn't win him any points. "He seems nice."

"Did he tell you about his wife?"

"Briefly."

"Brain aneurism. Nothing anyone could have done."

At least it had been quick. Stephen had suffered for over an hour before they'd dragged him out of the wreck and taken him to the hospital.

"Gotten to read any more of *Hahnen'En?*"

"Not yet. Job hunting."

"Sorry Dad couldn't introduce you to his friends tonight."

"It's all right. I'm sure I'll hear something back soon. Lots of places hiring right now."

"I'm sure God will send you where He wants you." She slanted the A/C vent away from her and pulled her thin sweater close. "He has so far."

Lane didn't even know where to begin answering that assertion, so he didn't. Instead, he turned the air off.

Vic let go of her sweater and stopped shivering.

108

102 Maple Leaf Lane
Wednesday, April 24th

When they got back to the Ellises', Lane helped Vic from the car.

Gabby took Sophie inside to get ready for bed, and Bert ferried their things in. Sophie watched her mother over her shoulder until the closed front door obstructed her view.

"How long do you have?" Lane said as he supported Vic.

Crickets chirped during the slow journey from the van to the house.

"You figured it out," she said with a smirk. "Guess I was right about you being smart. Doctor says about two more months." They stopped for Vic to catch her breath. "Should be enough time to get this little one on his way before I go." She rubbed her baby bump. "I've got twice weekly appointments to make sure the cancer stays confined to my lungs, and that this kid doesn't decide to do anything he's not supposed to before his due date. Don't know how long I'll be able to drive myself to appointments, though. Might have to get Ann to take me next time."

"I'll do it." He owed her for finding his ring, after all.

"I couldn't ask you to—"

"You didn't. I offered."

"What about your job?"

"When I get one, I'll work it out. Do you have another visit this week?"

"Friday at 10." She stopped again, about ten feet from the door. "Thank you for getting Sophie and me home tonight. If I'd known I was this bad, I would have taken Dad up on his offer to drive everyone."

"It's not a problem."

"Still. Thank you."

That night, what Kyle had said about God using circumstances to shape people's lives kept coming back. After the service, he'd exchanged his bandage for something less obtrusive—a wide Band-Aid—but the cut beneath it still seemed to glare at him. He curled his fingers together, and both rings clinked.

Stephen's death wasn't the only thing that had changed his life.

Lester's had too.

So had meeting Vic.

How unjust was it that she would only be part of his life for four short months? And leave behind a little girl and a newborn? The Ellises would care for them, but grandparents and parents were two different things.

"You're nothing but a ringmaster who never lowers the whip," Lane whispered to the ceiling.

He hadn't meant to verbalize it.

It was the first time he'd spoken to God. Ever. Even as a child, he hadn't bought into prayer or speaking to an invisible someone. He told himself he still didn't.

The lamp on the bedside table remained on, and *Hahnen'En* sat beneath it, unfinished. He put his phone on to charge, and his fingers brushed Vic's book. If he didn't finish it soon, she'd be gone before he understood why she was so attached to it.

He picked up the book.

It was 2 a.m. when he set *Hahnen'En* down. Only one hundred more pages, and it would be over. He still felt animosity toward Oren's father, who'd let his son die, but it was just a story. The plot had followed Hahnen'En as he tried to atone for his misdeeds while staying out of more bounty hunters' traps.

So far it wasn't going well, and if events continued unhindered, Hahnen'En would end up exactly where he'd been before—awaiting execution. But this time, there would be no Oren to save him.

Lane sympathized with the man. He wouldn't have let someone else pay his debts either, no matter what that meant. He had his pride to consider. But something about Oren's death still nagged Lane, and his hand itched again at the memory of the man's touch in his dream.

How could someone he'd never met leave such an impression? There was no real reason to feel anything for someone who didn't exist. He reminded himself none of it mattered as he clicked off the lamp, but as he drifted to sleep, Vic's words from weeks ago came back.

"How much of it is fantasy, you'd have to decide for yourself."

109

102 Maple Leaf Lane
Thursday, April 25ᵗʰ

Another vivid dream plagued Lane.

He stood atop the prison keep wall. No chains bound him. Only steps away, Oren faced the end of a sword.

Hounds bayed. The blade poised to ram through Oren's heart.

"No!" Lane lunged for the weapon.

Too late.

Instead of knocking aside the sword, he skewed the blade's entry point. Too low. Instead of dying instantly, Oren slid off the blade and toppled with a groan as his gut wound seeped.

"Why did you do this?" Lane kneeled beside Oren.

Guards moved to take Lane away, but a wave from Oren pushed them back.

The man's hand touched his, covering Stephen's ring. It was steady and held no hints of the horror crippling Lane. "Because I value your soul above my life."

"You don't even know me." His head pounded. How could this be happening? "You can't do this. I won't let you." He tried to pack the wound, stop the bleeding. Blood oozed between his fingers and pooled around his knees, soaking both pantlegs.

Oren stopped him from staunching the blood. "I have already done it. Will you not accept that?"

He couldn't answer.

There *was* no answer.

Not one he was willing to give.

Just after 4 a.m., Lane woke. The sour stink of death threatened to smother him.

He grabbed his phone, tapped on the flashlight, and threw back the covers. No blood on his legs. His hands were clean too.

But they didn't feel clean.

Blood's sticky matte seemed to coat them—to taunt him. Beneath the guilty wash of blood, Oren's touch lingered.

Lane stole one breath at a time.

This wasn't real.

Four times he reminded himself of that before the smell of blood vanished, his heart stopped pounding, and he wiped the sheen of sweat from his face and neck without fear it would return.

No matter what his dreams asserted, Oren wasn't real. No one had bled and died for Lane's crimes.

He clicked off his phone's flashlight and set the device on the bedside table, beside Vic's book. As he lay in bed, eyes shut, a single line of the song from Vic's church looped in his head: "When the Prince of Life, our Ransom shed for us His precious blood."

All hope of sleep abandoned, he got up and paced.

He turned on something on his phone—anything to drown the repeated words. Sports videos on YouTube droned, and after an hour of endless walking, his feet ached, despite the plush carpet.

He switched to a channel that played nature sounds, but the words stuck.

Demolition videos. A woman singing grating versions of popular kids' songs. And yet...the words remained.

Not even a constant stream of howling coyotes could cut them off.

"Leave me alone!" Lane barked to the ceiling.

The song faded.

Bleary, he trekked to the bathroom for a morning shower before breakfast, hoping no one in the house had heard him.

110

102 Maple Leaf Lane
Thursday, April 25ᵗʰ

Still hazy, Lane sat down to breakfast with the Ellises, Vic, and Sophie.

Gabby handed Vic a small cup. In it rattled a handful of pills, but they looked more like vitamins than drugs—probably to help counteract her lack of eating. Vic downed the pills with water before sharing the morning prayer—which Sophie said today.

"Everything all right, Lane?" Bert grabbed a stack of three pancakes from the serving plate. "Heard some bizarre noises this morning when I got up around 5."

How could he explain this? "Phone's been acting strange since the screen broke. Got stuck playing random videos this morning, and the volume was on. Sorry to disturb you."

"No problem. Made me chuckle a little, reading Leviticus, drinking my coffee, and being serenaded by coyotes."

Vic seemed amused at this too as she cut a small piece off her single pancake—no syrup.

"Papa, what's a keye-oh-tee?" Sophie said as she sliced two pancakes with a child's plastic knife and fork.

"Coyotes are a kind of dog. They like to howl and make all sorts of noise at night."

"Can I pet one?" Sophie said.

"No. They might not like that," said Bert. "Coyotes don't care for people too much, and they can be mean if they get scared or don't feel safe."

"Maybe they just haven't met anybody they like. They'd like me."

"I'm sure if they ever liked anyone, it would be you," said Gabby. "But let's not find out."

"Okay..." Sophie seemed disappointed until she took a bite of her breakfast. "Yay! Chocolate chips!"

Lane served himself three pancakes.

"Papa, would coyotes listen to Jesus if He told them not to be afraid? Jesus told the water to calm down, and the wind to stop blowing, and they listened."

Sophie's question made Lane hesitate an instant as he cut through the pancake stack.

"Yes, sweetie. They would listen to Jesus." Bert grabbed two breakfast sausages from another plate and set them with his pancakes.

"Would He talk to them like you talk to me?" Sophie said.

"I don't know," said Bert. "He could if He wanted. Jesus speaks to people in different ways sometimes. What might not mean much to me would mean a lot to you."

"Like blue horsies remind me about Heaven?"

Bert nodded. "Just like that."

Lane rubbed the back of his hand, and Stephen's ring tinged against his fork.

Between breakfast and another round of yardwork with Bert, Lane checked his email. Nothing new on when the bank might get his money back.

He expected to have more unread texts from his debtors, but they'd been silent for two weeks. They'd figured out he couldn't pay them. Or they'd handed off the bills to collection agencies. Soon, calls would bombard him. But at least they would go to the voicemail graveyard where he could delete them, unheard.

No one else had texted. Not even Stacey or Tina.

Fewer people to avoid.

He unpacked two boxes of clothes but hesitated to arrange them in the room's single, five-drawer dresser. Putting things away meant staying more than a few days, but it was easier to fish out clothes if he knew where they were instead of hunting in boxes all the time. Lane changed into work clothes and carried shoes to the connecting garage door.

Bert was already there, holding two rakes. He handed Lane a pair of work gloves. "Ready to re-mulch the back flowerbeds?"

He took the gloves. Gardening wasn't his favorite activity, but it was something to do—keep his mind off the night's dreams. "Where's the mulch?"

"Got it out back already. Wheelbarrow too. Just gotta pour the mulch in it, and we're ready to go."

They circled the house.

"Bert? Do you ever think about what will happen after...Vic's gone?" It was hard to say.

Bert put his hands in the pockets of his work jeans. "Sometimes I do, but I know God's in control."

Another platitude.

"My father used to say that." He hadn't meant to sound harsh, but he couldn't curb his disgust. "What does that even mean?"

Bert didn't miss a step. "It means God knows what He's doing, and I trust Him to do the right thing for us."

"But He's taking your daughter away."

This time, Bert stopped. "Yes, He is. But that parting won't last forever. We'll be together again one day soon."

"And that's okay with you?"

"It is." His voice was thick, but firm.

"What about Sophie—and that baby? They're never going to know their parents."

"They'll have a Father in Heaven who loves them even more than Vic, or Gav, or Gabby, or I ever could."

Lane cursed. "That's garbage! My parents turned me out when I was twenty. They didn't lift a finger to help me after that. Didn't call or visit except to say they were disappointed or didn't approve of my choices. What's the difference between that and a supposedly all-powerful, invisible God who won't even keep a kid's mom from dying? He's never done anything for me, and He certainly won't do anything for Sophie!" It hurt more than he thought to imagine the little girl bereft of both parents. And what would happen if Bert and his wife died? Who would take care of Sophie and her brother then? DSS? They had enough on their plate. The kids would get lost in the system—no doubt separated too.

"Are you sure He hasn't done anything for you?" said Bert.

"Quite."

"Yet you're standing here, alive." Bert clapped Lane's shoulder and trotted to the back yard without another word.

Death had taken so many in his life, and yet death hadn't taken him, no matter how he'd invited it. The cut on his wrist ached, even though it was healed enough that it shouldn't have hurt. The night he took the sleeping pills. The night he'd almost cut his wrists in the hospital.

Both times he'd fled the agony of a single memory—Stephen's accident.

They'd driven separate vehicles that day. He'd been three cars behind Stephen when the other driver had plowed into him.

If he'd left the parking lot first, he would have been the one hit.

But his car didn't start until the third turnover, and Stephen had beaten him out of the lot. They'd been on their way to the office to set up a friend's birthday party. Stephen was supposed to pick up wings and drinks.

The light had been red.

The other driver had mowed through another car before he'd smashed into Stephen.

Yes, Lane was alive. But emptiness, deep and encompassing, threatened to pull him in—like it had that night at the bar when he'd held those pills in his hand.

The misery had to end.

But he didn't know how to stop it.

111

102 Maple Leaf Lane
Thursday, April 25th

Mulching with Bert lasted until lunchtime. Neither man spoke as they spread treated red cedar chips over the flowerbeds and around shrubs. All that remained of the old mulch was disintegrating clumps.

When they finished, Bert carted in the wheelbarrow and put away the last partial bag of unused chips. Lane grabbed both rakes and followed him.

"Rack's on the wall." Bert pointed to one side of the garage where a shovel hung. "Thanks for the help. Always easier with two people."

Lane said nothing as he put the tools away.

Inside, he cleaned up and changed.

After the meal, Gabby left for a women's Bible study group, and Bert took Sophie to the backyard to learn to toss a frisbee. Lane sat alone on the living room couch, and Vic slept in her room.

Set against the opposite wall was a six-foot-high wooden cabinet, closed. It could have housed anything, but he assumed it held china or other dinnerware.

He was glad the couch didn't face Vic's room. It was almost too much to sit here, knowing she lay only a couple of rooms away, awaiting death. How could she just let this happen? She wasn't fighting, wasn't talking like she might have a chance.

She was resigned. Content to die.

Lane got off the couch and went to the guest room, where he shut the door and leaned against it.

His heart pounded again, like it had early this morning after rousing from his dream. He still remembered it. And the previous one.

He had to get out of here—just for a little while. Clear his head.

But where would he go? Most bars weren't open this early, not that he knew where any were around here. He didn't have the money to spend anyway.

Shopping wasn't for him. Again, no money.

He'd just eaten.

He could buy a bus ticket and ride to the end of the line. But then what?

The running shoes Vic gave him peeked from under the bed. A run usually helped. He hadn't run outside since February, but now was as good a time as any. No one in the neighborhood seemed to recognize him, so circling the block a few times wouldn't hurt.

After donning fresh socks, he took the running shoes to the front door and sat on the bench beside it to put them on. He pried open the tongue to slip one foot in.

Markered on the inside of the shoe were the letters *LTH*. There was a reason these shoes looked like the ones he'd had.

Because they were his.

Lane grabbed both shoes and hurried to Vic's room. He hated to wake her, but he had to.

When he thudded down the hall, she sat up, hair mussed from her nap. She ran fingers through tangled locks to smooth them. Her eyes were bleary, probably both from illness and exhaustion. "Lane. Everything all right?"

He held up the shoes. "Where'd you get these again?"

"Are they the wrong size?" She shook her head. "I knew I'd guessed wrong."

"Wrong? No. They fit perfectly because they're mine." He pulled the tongue back and showed her the letters. "Those are my initials. I put them there the day I got them. My ring and shoes were at the same pawnshop, right?"

"Yeah. Green's. Couple blocks from the studio." She seemed more alert now. "The break-in. Whoever it was could have held onto your stuff until recently and unloaded it at Green's. The owner wouldn't have known. It would just be a pile of junk to him." She got up, unsteady.

Lane reached out to balance her before she fell.

"Let's get over there." Vic bent to get a pair of flats and almost fell again but adjusted her trajectory, so she plunked onto the bed.

"I can go alone. Besides, you should be resting."

Vic laughed. "I don't think so. Get me those, please." She pointed to the shoes she'd attempted to grab.

Lane set them in front of her. "You're not letting this go, are you?"

Vic shook her head and gave him a tired, but intrigued smile. "I wrote detective novels, remember? We can take the van." She shot off a text before getting up again. "Told Dad we'd be back by dinner." She made it to her feet, this time without toppling. "I just have to go slow."

He tucked under her arm. "You don't have to do this. I can ask the owner a few questions without you. See if it was coincidence both things ended up at the same pawnshop. They could have circulated through multiple places by now. It's not likely any more of my stuff's there."

"I'm going." Her voice was firm.

It took three minutes to get Vic to the door, and another two to get her to the van. She surrendered her keys, and Lane revved up the minivan. He pulled out of the Ellises' driveway and headed for Hollywood.

112

Green's Diamond and Pawn, Hollywood
Thursday, April 25th

The shop owner, a man in his early sixties, dusted tempered glass cases filled with pocket watches, necklaces, and rings. Racks of DVDs, CDs, and even vinyl records filled one section of the store, while clothes, shoes, hats, purses, and other accessories hung in another. Anything from boom boxes to drum sets was here.

The owner greeted them as soon as they entered. "Afternoon, folks. Can I help you find anything?"

Vic, now standing under her own power, gave the old man a smile. "Hi. I came in here a few days ago and bought a ring and a pair of shoes."

"Sorry. No refunds." He pointed to a sign prominently displayed on the register. "If you wanna sell them back, I'll have to give you a third less for it. Restocking fee and all."

"Oh, no, it isn't that. I told my friend about this place." She nodded to Lane. "And we're here to look around."

He caught what she was doing. "You don't have any good suits, do you? Mine aren't the best fitting anymore."

"Just put some more out the other day. Sell to the Hollywood crowd mostly, so it's hard to keep them in stock here. Sometimes I get the same suit back three, four times. Cheaper than renting, and long as they come back clean, I don't care." He directed them to a rack near the window opposite the door they'd come in. "See anything you like, I can hold items for three days."

"Thank you," said Vic as the owner returned to his cleaning. To Lane, she whispered, "They took your suits?"

"No. Stephen's." He pretended to check the length of a jacket sleeve. "I only kept two suits, and they weren't anything to speak of. Stephen's tastes ran more exotic than mine."

Lane pulled out his phone and swiped through old photos, careful to steer clear of the cracks in the screen. Each swipe was war as he passed images of him and Stephen he hadn't looked at since the funeral. He came to the one he was searching for—a wrap party for Renfrow's film, the one he'd been cast in a couple years ago. In the picture, Stephen wore a dark gray suit, tailored. It outclassed Lane's attire by leaps and outmatched most others' clothes except Renfrow's. "He knew how to dress. When he...died...I—"

Vic pulled out Gavin's ring. It clinked on its chain. He didn't have to explain. She understood.

He finished looking through the rack. "They're not here."

"What else did they take?"

"My laptop. Among other things."

They went to the used electronics section, and he quickly checked the laptops. None of them were his. Then they moved on to TVs.

This time, he found what he was looking for.

He pointed to a 55-inch Smart TV. "That's from my apartment." He kept his voice low. "See the chip in the bottom left corner? I ran into it with the coffee table when we first bought it. Still worked fine, though."

"Can you hold this TV for us?" Vic said to the owner.

"Sure." In a feat of surprising strength, the old man hauled the TV behind the counter. "Name?"

"Garrison," said Vic.

"Or Harris."

The old man markered both names on a notepad and taped the paper to the TV. "Find anything else, and I'll add it on."

"Thank you," said Vic.

Lane browsed the movies and came across a title he recognized. He pulled out the opened Blu-Ray case. From it slipped a note in Stephen's handwriting: "Happy three months." It was addressed to him. "This was my favorite movie as a kid. I can't believe I never saw this note before." He wanted to take the paper, but leaving it would help prove it was his. It took everything he had not to keep the note in hand as he browsed through the rest of the movies and picked the ones he knew were his. Inside, behind each disk, were his and Stephen's initials in black Sharpie. They'd labeled each one only a few days after the wedding. It was more to see their names together than to mark ownership.

When they got back in the van, he pulled up a copy of the police report from his apartment break-in. On it was listed everything he'd reported stolen, including the shoes Vic had bought, and the TV, and assorted movies he'd asked the shop owner to hold.

Lane called the number on the report.

113

When he hung up, Vic looked at him expectantly. "What'd they say?"

"They'll come by in the next day or two. Since it's not an emergency, it isn't a priority, but they're interested because it's part of a line of crimes from the past two years. Come to think of it, the officers who took my statement mentioned that. They didn't seem optimistic about finding leads." He fingered Stephen's ring.

"This could be the breakthrough they've been looking for," said Vic, seeming excited. "I'd love to use this in a book."

Lane looked away just as Vic seemed to realize what she'd said.

"I'm not upset. Plus, I'm not sure what I'll be writing after June, but it'll be great, whatever it is."

"How can you say that?" Lane put his phone away. "You, your dad, even Sophie. You talk like this isn't the end of the world for you."

"Because it isn't. It's only the beginning. I just get to start forever sooner than most. Am I sad I won't get to be here for my kids' special moments?" Vic teared up. "Yes. I am. But they're in excellent hands with their grandparents, and I know God has them too. He won't let them go, Lane Harris." She took his hand. It was smaller than his, weaker, paler. But the strength in its grip reminded him of Oren's hand. "He hasn't let you go, either."

He didn't pull away from her. "You of all people should be furious about this! But you—you aren't."

"It doesn't make sense to you, does it?" She gave him a lopsided smile.

"No. It doesn't. And neither does that book of yours. It's awful! A man died to pay for the crimes of someone he didn't even know. I don't dream much, but I keep having nightmares about it."

"So did I."

"You...did?"

Vic nodded. "After I wrote that scene. I kept seeing him die...over and over. It wouldn't leave me alone. I was rereading the Bible and came to the book of John—the same book Pastor Hendrick preached from last night. Chapter 3 says God loved us so much He gave His only Son for us. A little later in the book, we find out just what that means, when Jesus is crucified for the sins of the whole world."

"I've heard the story," said Lane.

"It's an account, not a story. It happened. Jesus died, yes, but it wasn't just another death. He was beaten, mocked, whipped, nailed to a cross. The Bible says His face was unrecognizable. He died a criminal's death, shedding Divine blood and raising Himself from death three days later. If we accept this, it covers our sin, our wrongs, and grants us a place in eternal fellowship with God."

"My parents believed that." A bitter edge clung to his words.

"They may not have done everything right," said Vic. "My parents didn't—no one's perfect—but they're right about this. They're right to believe."

"All my life I've been told I'm going to Hell because I was attracted to other men." Stephen's ring seemed colder than usual. "And people like you are the ones who said it." The words bit harder than he'd intended.

"People like me?" Vic pointed to herself, and anger flashed in her voice. "People who once lived however they pleased—who realized that wasn't fulfilling and tried to end their life? People who found their lowest point, only to look up and find God's open hand waiting for them to take it? People who've learned there's only one love that lasts?" Her grip on his hand strengthened. "The only difference between us is belief."

"I'm sorry. I didn't mean to throw you in with my father. You're nothing like him."

"It doesn't matter if I am. Your father was harsh—really, really harsh. It isn't any one specific sin that sends people to Hell, and if more people remembered that, we'd be better off. But your father wasn't wrong about Jesus Christ. People like us, who find love with others of the same sex, we're no different from those who lie, or harbor pride and bitterness. Jesus had strong words for all those sins.

"The Bible lists seven things God especially hates. And do you know what the first is? Pride. Christians love to point at Sodom and Gomorrah in the Old Testament and condemn homosexuality, but they forget about the religious leaders Jesus called out for pride in the New Testament. If they stopped and really looked at the two, they'd find pride was the root cause of both groups' sin. That pride simply manifested in different ways."

"So why is it supposedly sinful to love someone of the same sex? According to Christians, didn't God make all of us? If that's true, isn't He the one who made me this way? I loved Stephen more than I've ever loved anyone else. I would have traded my life for his—even wished I'd been the one in that car the day he—" Memories of that moment in the hospital last fall hit him. "How can love like that be wrong?"

His words hung in the charged air. He'd asked other Christians this same question. Most hid panic and changed the subject. Others fired back hot retorts. Some backpedaled until they'd fumbled their way into the answer they thought he was looking for.

He wanted—needed something else. Something that didn't feel hollow, disingenuous, or cruel. He needed to know what Vic had to say. She'd never claimed the bisexual label, even though she clearly could have. He needed to hear why she'd abandoned diverse love.

Vic gave him a soft smile. "You really want to know?"

He nodded.

"Are you sure you're ready for the answer?"

The way she said it gave him pause, but not for long. "No. But I want to be."

114

Six Years Ago

716 Olin's Mesa Blvd., Huntington Park
Wednesday, April 10th

Leigh knocked twice.

The temptation to get back in her car and drive home almost won. But before she could turn her back to the small Craftsman-style house, the front door opened.

"Leigh, so good to have you here." Mrs. Elanor Hendrick motioned her into the entryway. "Dinner's on the table. We're so happy you decided to join us tonight. You go ahead and sit down. I'll bring in a fresh pitcher of limeade."

The table sat four, and Pastor Hendrick had already taken the chair farthest from the kitchen. Sitting next to him didn't feel like the right choice, so she left an empty chair between them. The older man's quiet calm both reassured and unnerved her at times. Since she'd started attending church more than once a week, it shocked her how often this man's sermons seemed to be speaking directly to her.

Mrs. Hendrick entered with the promised limeade and set it in the middle of the table, beside a half-filled water pitcher. Once everything was in place, she sat between her husband and Leigh.

Pastor Hendrick bowed his head. "Father, thank You for giving us this time together to talk about what You've said in Your Word. We're thankful for Leigh and everything You've done in her life, and we ask that You use all of us to build up one another in Christ. Thank You for Elanor and all she did to make this meal special for us. Bless our time at this table. In Jesus' name, Amen."

To keep from having to start the conversation, Leigh grabbed the flower-patterned bowl of string beans and scooped some onto her plate before handing the dish to Elanor.

"Bert said you wanted to talk about the sermon from a few weeks ago." Pastor Hendrick snagged a dinner roll from the basket and passed it to Leigh. "Your parents told us what happened while you were away these past few years. I'm sorry for your loss."

Leigh pried open a roll and used the tines of her fork to spread softening butter. She layered a crosshatch pattern into both halves of the mangled bread. Tim still came to mind often, but since she'd gotten back from Rio Nido, she'd moved his urn from the fireplace mantel to a small shelf at the end of the hall.

"And I'm sorry about the abuse you experienced," Hendrick continued. "There is never a reason for domestic violence."

She still wore scars from several of her old boyfriend's bouts of anger, but many of them had faded so much even she didn't remember where they were.

"When you felt the need to take your own life, I'm glad God prevented you from succeeding."

Her wrists still ached sometimes—usually after long sessions of typing or working with her dad out in the garden.

"But none of those things is why you're here." The pastor cut a portion of his sirloin.

He was right. She should just say it. Get it over with.

She liked Hendrick. He wasn't anything like the pastor they'd had when she was a kid, and offending him three minutes into dinner wasn't on her to-do list tonight. But, like her, he appreciated honesty.

"If God didn't want me to be attracted to other women, why did He make me this way? You said a few weeks ago that any sexual relationship other than in a marriage between a man and a woman is sin. So, if what I had with Nakasha a few years ago was wrong, why would God make me do it?" Leigh waited for startled sputters or the clatter of dropped forks.

Instead, both the pastor and his wife nodded.

"Those are some big questions," said Hendrick. "But are you sure they're sound?"

Leigh stabbed a bean. "Why wouldn't they be?"

"God is not the author of evil."

"I know *that*." It came out condescending. "Sorry. I just...that doesn't answer my questions. I've heard all my life that God doesn't make us sin. We choose that ourselves. But are people who live outside the whole Biblical marriage thing really so bad? Love is good, so why do Christians draw a line and call some love right and some wrong? No one says anything about it when men are physically attracted to women. Everyone calls it normal and turns a blind eye when some guy gets his girlfriend pregnant and then leaves her for the next girl he sees. But as soon as men even hint at looking at other men the same way they might look at a woman, Christians lose their minds and start spouting stuff about Sodom and Gomorrah and a couple other passages in the Bible. And don't get me started on how much hate women in same-sex relationships get from religious people."

Pastor Hendrick set a bowl of roasted carrots near Leigh, but she didn't reach for it, instead pouring half a glass of limeade. "When I was with Nakasha, she was the only person who ever treated me like I was valuable. When I was pregnant and had no place to go except a crowded dorm, she asked me to live with her. She worked twelve-hour shifts so she could be there for me and my...my son. She held my hand while I was in labor and made sure I was okay while I recovered. Everything she did was for me. And, yeah, I was attracted to her. What's so wrong about that?"

Hendrick left his seat. "Excuse me a moment."

It had only been five minutes since they sat down, and already the pastor was making a quick exit. She should have expected this. Alternate sexuality wasn't something Christians talked about in polite company. New Bethany's previous pastor hadn't brought it up at all.

Coming here for answers had been a mistake.

Maybe she would just have to wrestle with who she was in secret and hope God either took away her attraction to women or let her know it was okay.

But since she'd accepted Jesus as Saviour, something in her was different. Every time her eyes lingered too long on another woman, a quiet prompting came to look away, to think about something else— usually work or other practical things. But lately she'd also started humming to herself. Songs she'd heard in church, or ones her parents liked to play on those ancient cassettes in the living room. They took the edge off, but the desire to look never fully went away.

"I'm sorry," Leigh said to Elanor. "I didn't want to upset anyone." A few months ago, she wouldn't have meant that.

Elanor drizzled steak sauce over her carrots. "You don't have to apologize for anything. No one's upset. Silas just needed to get something. He'll be right back."

True to Elanor's word, the pastor reappeared, carrying a leather-bound Bible.

Hendrick moved his nearly untouched plate aside and opened his Bible. "Loving someone unconditionally isn't wrong. If it were, God wouldn't have sent His Son to the cross. But that kind of love isn't the only one you experienced with Nakasha. There was intimate physical and emotional union too. And that union with someone of the same sex is what God forbids. He doesn't call everyone to marry, but those He does call, He lays out His specific plan for in His Word. One man and one woman. For life. That's what He asks of us. For those He's called to singleness, He asks abstinence, in both body and mind—not because sexual union is shameful or wrong, but because God hasn't called them to be that kind of example to others. When we, in pride, decide we know better than God, go against His mandates, and paint over His specially designed illustration of Christ and the Church, that's sin."

Leigh propped her fork on the edge of her plate. A bean wedged uncomfortably between the tines. "Sounds pretty cut-and-dry." She flipped the fork over. The bean stayed in place. "But life's not like that."

"It's true life doesn't always seem straightforward. But that's why God gave us His Word." Hendrick laid an open hand on his Bible.

"And it's why we have to spend time in it, so we can get to know God and what He says and thinks. When we're in tune with His heart, life doesn't always get easier, but it makes a lot more sense."

"So what does that mean for people like me?" Leigh said.

Hendrick flipped to a passage near the end of the Bible. "What do you know about spiritual gifts?"

"Not much, but what does that have to do with anything?"

Hendrick started reading. "I beseech you therefore, brethren, by the mercies of God, that ye present your bodies a living sacrifice, holy, acceptable unto God, which is your reasonable service." He didn't stop until he'd read almost half the chapter. "God created all of us as individuals, and every person is born with a gift—sometimes more than one. That gift isn't something we magically obtain when we become Christians. It's part of our basic makeup, something that defines our lives in ways we can't always see. It drives us to think, to feel, to act. God gave us these gifts to help each other and build His church. Before we become Christians, because of sin, our natural inclination is to use our God-given gifts for ourselves. We take those gifts and twist them into things God never intended them to be. In pride, we believe we know better than God, so we use our bodies in ways that don't glorify Him."

The pastor Leigh remembered from her years in junior high talked about how horrible sin was, the greatness of God's love, and giving the Gospel, but not much else. Sundays had become repetitive and boring very quickly. This was different from anything she'd heard before.

As if he'd sensed her unspoken questions, Hendrick continued. "God gifted me with the natural tendency toward teaching. I love seeing people's eyes light up when they understand something, and those hours I spend studying for a sermon are a highlight of my week. Getting to know this Book and all the nuances of what God has to say and then sharing them with others...that is what warms my heart and prompts me to thank and praise God.

"But what if, instead of keeping to the point, I started rambling about minutia and set myself up as someone who had all the answers? Or if I decided to hide away in my office for months on end and abandon the church God called me to lead? That would be a perversion of the gift God gave me, and it would be sin."

"So you're saying God *did* make me this way."

"No. I'm saying God gave you an incredibly powerful gift. One that lets you feel deeply and intensely. You see the world with Mercy's eyes. But because of sin and without the Holy Spirit to help you properly cultivate that gift, it became damaging to you. It directed you toward feelings and experiences God forbids because they contradict who He is and His plan for us. That intense, emotional drive made itself king of your life. No one is created same-sex attracted, even though it may feel very much like some are, because many experience those feelings early in life. People can be born with keen emotional insight, the need to be understood, and the desire to establish deep, meaningful relationships. If left unchecked, sin takes that need to find and forge connections and perverts it, pushing people to ignore God's Word and find their own ways to create satisfying human connection.

"God is the standard by which we judge all things, including what motivates us. His Word is 'a discerner of the thoughts and intents of the heart,' and because God loves us, He shows us where we've gone wrong. Sometimes that revelation is hard to receive, but it doesn't make it any less necessary." Hendrick quietly shut his Bible and laid it in front of the empty chair, bridging the gap between him and Leigh. "You might be surprised just how much this Book says about situations like yours."

Leigh used her steak knife to shove the stuck bean free of her fork. "Some of that makes sense, but...I'm not sure I get everything you said."

"Spend time in God's Word, Leigh. He'll help you understand truth. Your parents would love to help you too, as would Elanor and I."

Leigh remembered her mother's bewildered, hope-filled face just before she'd left the house to come over here tonight. "I don't know if my parents are ready for that."

Pastor Hendrick took his wife's hand. "You might be surprised what God can do."

115

Green's Diamond and Pawn
Thursday, April 25th

Lane had never heard anyone speak this way. Preachers, his parents, their friends. All they ever did was speak in generalities and hushed whispers when it came to topics like alternate sexuality. As if this one thing was wholly different from every other soapbox and sticking point in Christianity. As if anyone who dared even think of participating in it was now contagious and had earned a special place in Hell.

But while pieces of what she'd said made sense in a way, a lot of it still didn't. "So you're saying my attraction to Stephen was just a symptom." He couldn't reconcile how something that felt so right and wonderful could be wrong—or even destructive. It made no sense.

"That's a rather blunt way of putting it, and it's only one aspect, but yes. It also paints an inaccurate picture of who God is and how He designed us. Same-sex relationships are a manifestation of pride and an arrow pointing to the heart of everything—to the need for God and His ability to save us from our own destructive selves.

"Sin is grievous to God, whether that sin is physical or spiritual. When I rejected God as a teenager. When I chose to ignore God's ordained order for marriage. When I slept with my boyfriend. When I chose to act on my physical attraction to Nakasha. When I tried to end my own life. All of it, whether or not it had to do with my tendency to desire a physical connection with both men and other women, was sin.

"One wrong merits Hell. It doesn't matter what that wrong is. Jesus bled and died on that cross so long ago, but the day I accepted that as Truth was the day God helped me start over."

"You said some of this is about pride and contradicting God's design. What if I know better than some tyrannical being in the sky? Why should I care anything about what God thinks if He cares nothing about me?"

"Why do you think God doesn't care about you?"

"Why do you think He does?"

Vic's eyes lit. "Even before I believed—when I hated Him—He loved me. When I decided my way was better than His, He loved me. When I tried to end the life He gave me, still, He loved me. And when I sat alone in a cabin, writing a story I didn't understand until I'd finished it...He. Loved. Me. When He took my baby boy, He loved me. When he took my husband, He loved me. When He takes my life, He will still love me. Because the truest love is not how we feel—it never has been. That's just how the world around us defines it. Love is so much more. It's a bloodied cross, an empty tomb, a gift of eternal life and hope. It's deeper than we can fathom, without measure, full, and boundless. God has shown me over and over that He loves me. God cares about you too, Lane. He cares more than you'll ever know."

His parents had never discussed faith like Vic—or Sophie. A not-quite-five-year-old had shown more concern for him than they did.

How could such totally different people follow the same God?

"Are you sure you believe what my parents do?" He tried to laugh, to cut the tension. It came out strained.

"Well, I don't know them, but from what little you've said, yes. At least, on the point of claiming Jesus Christ as Saviour. Christians aren't superhuman. Some want you to think they are, but we're like everybody else. We make mistakes. We just handle mistakes differently—at least, we should. That's what's so amazing about God. He takes people on their own journeys. Each one, He leads. That might look different for you than it does for me, but His goal is always the same—to make us more like His Son, like Him. For me, that journey began with a book, with a man most people would say doesn't exist. But God brought him when I needed him, and he's real for me." Tears brimmed her eyes. "For my father, that journey began in a Sunday School classroom. For my mother, a piano lesson. God finds us, no matter how far we try to run from Him. We can still reject Him if we choose. He gives us that choice. But why turn away the one Person who can save us from ourselves? Who can change our lives so much we don't even recognize the people we used to be? Who can give us joy, peace, love, hope, and a place in Heaven with Him?"

Silence fell between them.

Vic's eyes—hazel—pleaded with him.

But Lane came back to the same question he'd asked Bert hours before. What had God ever done for him? All this—everything Vic had said—it was either long in the past, written by people he didn't know, or it was so incredibly different from anything he'd ever heard that he needed time to think about it.

If he accepted Vic's claims that his sexual attraction to other men was wrong, he wasn't sure he wanted to consider what that meant for him. So far, God had only shown him hardship and heartbreak. Vic claimed God loved him, but there was too much evidence to the contrary. He couldn't accept a God who treated people with disregard.

Lane wanted to dismiss everything Vic had said. He wanted to get out of the van and start walking. But her hand in his anchored him to the seat.

He didn't want to think about this right now—didn't want to do anything but get his life back to normal. It was all too much.

"I'm sorry, Vic. I can't do this." He withdrew his hand from her grip.

She looked ready to cry, but she sat back in her seat and breathed a quiet, "Okay."

He started the minivan and pulled out of the parking lot.

Neither said anything on the return drive to the Ellises'.

116

102 Maple Leaf Lane
Thursday, April 25th

That evening, after a dinner involving little conversation on his part, Lane went straight to his room. Nothing back from his applications. He was about to gather clothes for a shower when his phone rang. "Alisha. Hey."

"Lane? Are you okay? You sounded drunk when you called after the funeral. I've been so busy with my new job I haven't had time to return your message."

Lane froze. He'd forgotten to check his call log to see who he'd talked to that night at the bar. Had he really drunk-called Alisha? "Sorry about that. It was...a rough night."

"You talked about some things in your message—God, death. It was pretty long, but I listened to the whole thing. Do you really believe all that?"

"I don't exactly remember what I said."

"You mentioned Vic."

His gut clenched. She was in his head even when he was out of it.

"I didn't know she'd lost her husband."

What should he say?

"Her little girl sounds really sweet. Can we get together and talk sometime soon? How about when I take a night off?" Alisha paused. Voices in the background said she was probably on a break. "I'm really worried about you. You're living at the bar, aren't you?"

"No." It was true at the moment. He wasn't living there. Anymore.

"So where are you?"

"I'm at a friend's house."

"Oh. Okay." Her hesitance said she didn't quite believe him, but couldn't prove he was lying. Stephen used to use that tone. So did Stacey. "I drove by the bar a couple nights ago. All the lights were off, but there was a chair lying by the door. I hope nobody broke in."

He vaguely remembered toppling the chair. "I'm sure everything's fine. We'll talk later, okay?" It was the politest way he could find to force an end to the conversation. Her break was probably over anyway.

"All right. But we're going to talk. As soon as the manager schedules me off, I'm calling you."

"Sure." He hung up before she did.

With dread, he opened his call history. He found Sunday night's entries quickly. Vic's number was closest to the top, followed by Alisha's, but before he'd called either of them, he'd called...Monica.

117

102 Maple Leaf Lane
Thursday, April 25th

Monica's number burned into the screen.

He didn't remember a single thing he'd said to her. Didn't even recall dialing her number, much less holding a conversation.

His talk with Alisha was missing from his memory too. The only conversation he recalled was with Vic, and vodka haze shrouded that. His memory from that night wasn't clear until his encounter with that obnoxious coffee.

He put his phone on charge and headed for the bathroom. It wasn't even 7 yet, but he had to end this day.

Despite a long, hot shower, Lane wasn't tired when he got into bed. He turned off the lamp and shut his eyes, hoping sleep would find him, but events circled in his head until he felt like he was stuck in a washing machine. At least he'd found a few of his things today. Not much, but better than nothing.

He hadn't seen Stephen's baseball collectibles at the pawnshop. Likely, they'd sold already. If they were ever there. Unless the thief had the sense to find a collector who would pay decent money for them.

Vic's words from several hours ago burst into his thoughts. He wanted to be angry with her for what she'd said. What right did she have to declare how he loved to be wrong? If anyone else had told him the things she had today, he'd have labeled them a bigot and their words hate speech.

But the memory of her pleading eyes wouldn't go away. There was no hate in those eyes. Only concern and genuine compassion. She had loved the same way he had. Then she'd turned her back on it—because the God she loved asked her to.

But the question remained: Did God care about Lane Thomas Harris? He was still quite sure the answer was a resounding "no."

He put his phone aside only to bump Vic's book. The paperback toppled from the table and lay open on the floor. He clicked the lamp back on and leaned out of bed to pick *Hahnen'En* up. His bookmark— the metal one Vic had given him—hung dangerously near the edge of the pages, at risk of falling out. He scooped up the book and adjusted the marker. His folded Post-it still stuck to the cold metal. Vic's note was still there, waiting for him. Every time he opened *Hahnen'En*, he saw it.

"1 John 4:9-21."

Another John. He pulled up the browser on his phone and discovered there were four Johns. One long section of the Bible, and three short. This reference was part of a short passage.

Curiosity sent him to a search engine. It wasn't like he was opening an actual Bible.

The first result was from a site that provided the full book in a host of different versions. He scrolled through the listed options until he found something familiar.

The first part of the section from Vic's note both intrigued and irritated him: "In this was manifested the love of God toward us, because that God sent his only begotten Son into the world, that we might live through him. Herein is love, not that we loved God, but that he loved us, and sent his Son to be the propitiation for our sins. Beloved, if God so loved us, we ought also to love one another."

He'd intended to skim the first line or two and close the tab.

But he kept reading.

118

102 Maple Leaf Lane
Thursday, April 25ᵗʰ

Lane had heard sections of this before, a long time ago, but it hadn't meant anything to him. He still didn't understand it, and he'd had to find a definition for at least one word he'd never seen before, but when he reached the section's end, he found something he remembered— not from childhood but from his conversation with Vic in the Green's parking lot: "We love him, because he first loved us."

She'd said this almost verbatim earlier.

But again, what proof did he have that God loved him? His husband was dead. His father had hated him, and his mother wouldn't speak to him. The man who'd tried to help him was gone. Stacey was over a hundred miles away. He'd lost his home, his valuables...even his money was gone. He couldn't afford groceries, much less a security deposit. His car was still running, but who knew how long that would be true? Monica had violated him, stolen his dignity, and smeared his name. And on top of it all, he looked like an extra in an apocalypse movie.

He shook his head and put his phone away.

Hahnen'En sat on the bedside table. He had less than a quarter of the book left, and he might not have opportunity to read after he got a job. He needed to finish it before Vic...

No.

Later.

He set the book on the table beside his phone and tried again to sleep.

Friday, April 26th

Just after breakfast, his phone rang.

The police.

Lane quietly left the living room as the Ellises readied Sophie for a day at the zoo.

"Is this Lane Harris?" said the woman on the other end of the line.

"Yes."

"Detective Lancaster, LAPD. We sent a unit out to the establishment you reported yesterday. Looks like we'll need to keep your things for a while, as they appear to be part of an ongoing investigation."

"It's that burglary ring, isn't it?"

"I'm afraid I can't comment on that, sir. All I can say is we aren't able to release your possessions to you at this time. How did you come across these items?"

"A friend bought some things for me at that pawn shop, and when I looked at what she'd given me, I discovered it was mine."

"Do you still have the items in question?"

"Yes."

"Please bring anything of yours purchased there to the station at

Hyacinth and Courtney as soon as possible. I'll put a note in the file."

Stephen's ring was still loose on his finger. He didn't want to part with it again. If he gave it up now, there was no way of telling when—or if—he'd get it back. But he couldn't withhold evidence from a police case. That would get him in more trouble. "I will."

He hung up.

"Ready to ferry me around town?" Vic's voice behind him made him jump. "Sorry. I thought you heard me."

"It's all right. I just got a call from the police." He didn't look at her as he spoke. "They visited the pawnshop yesterday after I called, and they took my stuff to the station. They want me to drop off the running shoes and...the ring...over there as soon as I can."

"Then we'd better get going if we want to make the hospital on time." She smiled.

He couldn't bring himself to be glad about this. Yes, it meant he might be one step closer to learning who'd stolen his life, but it also meant he was losing another piece of himself he desperately wanted to keep.

And he had to go back to Jenkins Rawling.

Why had he agreed to this? He had to back out of it, get someone else to take her. That neighbor of hers—Ann? She would take Vic.

But one look at her, and he couldn't refuse. She seemed even more tired now than before they'd left for Green's yesterday. The trip had drained her.

"Let me get those shoes." He went into his room, snagged the running shoes, and walked with Vic to the door.

LAPD Hyacinth St. Community Police Station, Los Angeles

Lane sat across from Detective Lancaster. With gloved hands, she took his running shoes and the reluctantly-surrendered ring and sealed them in evidence bags.

"Was there anything else at the establishment in question?" said Lancaster.

"Not that I know of."

Lancaster checked an on-screen document, probably a copy of the police report from the burglary. "Says here you're still missing a laptop, assorted clothes, jewelry, and collectibles. That sound right?"

He nodded.

"Are you and your friend in the waiting area the only people—other than the business owner—who you're aware of having touched these objects barehanded?"

"My late husband, Stephen Parker, did. Months ago." Saying Stephen's name again was surreal.

She tapped her keyboard. "Looks like we already have your husband's prints, so no problem there. With your consent, we'll need to fingerprint you and your friend, just to rule you out."

"Sure." Anything to get pieces of his life back.

Lancaster directed him to a fingerprinting station on the other side of the room before getting Vic.

The process took less than two minutes, and when he swiped the ink from his fingers with a wet wipe, he felt as if he'd lost himself. His right hand was empty again. But giving up the ring one more time was necessary.

Vic wiped the ink off her hands too and thanked the man at the fingerprinting station.

"We'll be in touch," said Lancaster.

"I hope you find whoever this is."

"Me too. We've waited a long time to get these guys," Lancaster said as she saw them out.

119

Lane sat in the oncology waiting room.

Vic had gone in ten minutes ago. She'd said she wouldn't be more than twenty but, in his experience, appointments often stretched.

Other patients sat in the waiting room. Three women, two men, one girl who looked no more than twenty. Most wore hats or scarves over thinning and non-existent hair, and their faces displayed varying shades of green.

The girl bolted to the in-office bathroom, holding one hand over her mouth. Lane's stomach turned. The others seemed unfazed.

One tall, thin woman, the most recent arrival, grabbed a magazine and sat beside him. "Just diagnosed?"

"Uh. No. Waiting for someone."

"Ah. The nice friend who takes you places when you can't drive and your family's busy." She opened the magazine—something about island vacation spots.

"Yeah." Lane didn't want to have this conversation.

"It's okay." She flipped to a page with scattered photos from Jamaica.

"Cancer's not contagious." She gave him a wry smile and adjusted her canary-yellow beret, accented by the deep ebony of her skin. Her ankle-length skirt matched her headwear and brightened the room. "This actually isn't from the radiation." She patted her covered head. "I ditched the hair in college. Too much hassle. So, who'd you bring?"

He wasn't sure he should tell this woman anything, much less something like that.

"I'm not a stalker. We're a pretty close group here. Dr. Gordon's the best thing that's happened to most of us. Today's pretty quiet." Her face fell. "We lost somebody yesterday."

"I brought Victoria Garr—"

"Vic's here? Oh! I was hoping I'd see her this time. I got here later than usual, and she must have already gone back by the time I made it up. What kind of sadist puts oncology on the third floor?"

"Did you want to talk to her?"

"Yes!" The woman closed her magazine. "Jazzmin. Call me Jazz." She offered a hand.

"Lane." He shook her hand, though her grip was much weaker than his, and he was reticent to clasp her hand too hard, lest he hurt her.

"That's a great name. Not too old-fashioned, but not too modern to be common. I've never met anyone named Lane before."

"And I've never met a Jazzmin."

"We're even then. Hey, you said you brought Vic. You met her Sophie?"

Lane nodded.

"Sweetest child I've ever seen. I wish Vic brought her more often, but I understand why she doesn't. I don't bring my son with me, and my treatments are going great. Something about bringing a kid into a cancer ward doesn't seem right, ya know? But that little girl of hers is the sunshine we need in here. Vic talks about God a lot. You believe in Him too?"

He didn't want to answer Jazz, but saying nothing was rude, and he wasn't sure how long Vic would be gone. Better to answer and ease out of the conversation as soon as possible. "Sure." It was the answer she wanted.

"That's good." Jazz put the magazine on a side table between sections of chairs. "I don't know what I'd do without having God in my life right now. And I can't imagine going through what Vic is without Him. God's used this cancer to bring me to the end of myself—make me realize just how much I need Him. Never would have learned trust like this if I hadn't gotten that diagnosis last year. Talk about something that changes your life. Cancer will do it. Know what I mean?"

Lane checked the waiting room door and wondered how much longer Vic would be.

"What am I saying? Of course, you know. If you've been Vic's friend any time at all, you know that. I'm sure you've got a story too— something God's used to point you to Him. I think we all do. Just takes some of us longer to see it than others. Has Vic told you her story?"

"Yeah." Would this woman never shut up?

"She was a stubborn one, that girl, but when God got hold of her heart, she changed. Some of us have to lose everything to find out what we really need isn't something we can find ourselves. It's something God gives us, but we've gotta accept it. That's the hard part for folks—

accepting. We want to be self-sufficient, but we're just not." She sat back in her chair. "Not even those movie stars and all their popularity and glamor can save themselves from an eternity of suffering without God. When I was little, I wanted to be a movie star so bad."

"It's not all it's made out to be."

Jazz chuckled. "I'm sure of that. If there's one thing I know now, it's that only God can satisfy."

Lane nodded to keep her from asking more questions.

A nurse stepped into the waiting room. "Jazzmin Paris?"

"That's my cue." She got up. "Good to meet you, Lane. Sorry I missed Vic. Will you tell her I said hey?"

"Sure."

Jazz chatted with the nurse as she left the waiting room.

Lane sat alone with Jazz's magazine, which still lay closed on the nearby table.

120

Jenkins Rawling Memorial Hospital
Friday, April 26ᵗʰ

Five minutes after Jazz left, Vic returned. "Ready?" She adjusted her purse strap.

"Yeah." He set Jazz's magazine on the table in the middle of the room.

As they left, everyone waved or said goodbye to Vic.

Lane waited to pull into traffic. "Jazz asked me to say hey."

"Oh, I missed her..." Vic seemed disappointed. "I was hoping to see her today. She's almost done with her treatments, and hopefully she won't be coming back after they're over, except for routine visits."

"You want to go back in?"

"No. It's all right. I've got her number. It's just different sitting with someone. Plus, I need to go home and take a nap before I fall asleep sitting up."

An opening in traffic. Lane took it. "Appointment go okay?"

"I told Fran about my episode Wednesday. She agreed it's best I stop driving. Neither of us were sure when this point would come, but it's here now. Thank you again for taking me to my appointments. At least this won't last forever." She offered a wan smile.

He couldn't return it.

Vic's momentary silence felt like the instant before Stephen's accident. "I have less time than we thought."

He steeled himself for the worsening prognosis.

"Probably going to be the beginning of June instead of the end." She laid a hand over her unborn son. "He'll come early, but he'll be all right. Fran talked to my OB, and she knows what's going on. They'll have a team ready when the time comes."

He wanted to be angry with her, to demand to know why she wasn't trying to stop this. But how could he make that judgment? He wasn't the one with terminal cancer, the one with constant pain, the one who had to worry about one young child and another about to be born. "I'm sorry."

"It's all right."

Stephen's face, frozen in terror, flashed to mind.

When the truck had plowed into Stephen's Camry, he'd sprinted to the scene, leaving his car parked in the turn lane. He hadn't pulled Stephen from the wreckage—hadn't even been able to try. The vehicle had been too twisted.

EMS had gotten Stephen out, but the damage had already been done. On the outside, Stephen wasn't badly hurt, but broken bones shoved into vital organs had caused too much internal bleeding.

The EMTs hadn't even let Lane ride with them to the hospital.

He would never forget the panic in Stephen's eyes—the understanding that he was about to die. He'd known his husband wouldn't make it, but he'd clung to hope until the very end, when the doctor had walked into that waiting room.

"You really are fine with this..."

"I wouldn't say that exactly." Vic's expression turned bittersweet. "I'm looking forward to Heaven—to not having this pain anymore, to seeing my Timothy and my Gav, and everyone else who's gone on before me. I'm looking forward to taking Jesus' hand and seeing so many other people I love and who've been there for me when I needed them. But like I said yesterday at Green's, I'm sad I won't get to be there for Sophie's and my son's firsts. I won't get to come to their first day of kindergarten, or their sports games, concerts, recitals, exhibits—whatever they choose to do—or their graduations, or their weddings, or get to hold my grandkids. At least for Sophie, I know she and I will meet again someday, and my greatest prayer is that I'll meet my son too."

Though Lane had never put stock in an afterlife, Vic had, and she was sure of it. No matter how he challenged her belief, how he questioned her, what she went through, she maintained that faith. "I don't understand." Part of him wanted to, and part of him couldn't bear to hear any more, but he didn't stop her when she continued.

"It was God's peace that kept me from ending my life after Gav died, from terminating this pregnancy, from curling up in a corner and waiting to die. I might not know what will happen here after I'm gone, but I know where I'll be—Who I'll be with—and that is such a comfort. I'm going home soon, Lane. And I'll never have to leave."

They passed the exit that would take them to Simmer. It had been a brief haven for him, but he'd never considered it home. Every time he'd walked in, the urge to return to his old apartment had always nagged him, told him he didn't belong.

Since he'd come to the Ellises', that sense, while still there, wasn't as loud.

Something else in Vic's voice lingered after her words, and he only realized it after they'd passed the exit.

"You want to go."

Tears welled in Vic's eyes. She nodded.

Every time he pulled something from a box of his things, that pang—that longing to go home—returned. Once, he'd even walked to the front door, ready to put on his shoes, get in his Versa, and drive to Huntington Park. But he couldn't go back. The apartment wasn't his anymore. If he found somewhere that felt like home again—he would go without hesitation. How could he blame her for feeling the same?

"I understand," he said.

And, to his surprise, he meant it.

121

102 Maple Leaf Lane
Friday, April 26th

After dinner, Lane retreated to his room and dug through job boards. Before he realized, it was 11 p.m.

A quick shower, and he was ready for bed.

The events of the day had drained him more than he thought— especially the time at the hospital. The cancer patients in the waiting room had all looked worn out, like Vic. But there was a spark in her that wasn't in most of the people he'd seen today. Jazz shared it, and despite her constant chatter, she seemed good-hearted.

Slowly his thoughts quieted, and he fell asleep.

Saturday, April 27th

No dreams.

But Lane had woken to a knock on his door and Bert's announcement of breakfast. He'd forgotten to set his alarm. He threw on clothes and ran fingers through bedhead before hurrying to the table.

Sophie giggled when he arrived. "Mr. Lane, you've got lines on your face."

Vic, who looked a bit more tired than yesterday, hid a smile.

He turned on his phone camera. Even with the cracked screen, deep creases from his pillowcase clearly crisscrossed his cheek and forehead. He must have slept hard.

"Let's pray," said Bert.

Sophie, who sat between him and Vic again this morning, snagged his hand immediately.

"Father, we thank You for Your blessings, including another day with our Vic."

Lane didn't listen to the rest of the prayer. Did Bert know his daughter's time was shorter than expected?

When everyone had served themselves, Bert took a sip of his coffee. "You coming tomorrow?"

Lane's heart sank.

Sunday. He'd forgotten. Might as well get it over with. He'd planned on trying the evening service this week anyway, to see if it was less well-attended than mid-week.

"Yes," he answered, "but not in the morning."

"All right. We'll expect you for the evening service. We can introduce you to a few more people who might help you find work. You've already met Kyle. He's been trying to find someone to help him for a couple months, so—"

Lane almost spit his coffee. "Kyle's looking for help?"

"He didn't mention it?" Bert said.

"No. He gave me his card, though. He does contracting, right?"

Bert nodded. "He mentioned last Sunday he was looking for someone to work with him a few days a week so he can be home with his kids a little more often. He's finally got enough work to afford to pay somebody. It might be seasonal, and not much to start, but it would be something."

"I'll text him after breakfast." This was a possibility he could live with. As long as Kyle would take him.

The other man talked a bit much for Lane's tastes, but he might converse less if they were working, or at least bring up fewer non-work-related subjects. He would have to learn on the job, but if Kyle didn't care, it could work. And he didn't mind a low starting wage. The guy seemed fair, and he needed time with his kids.

He texted Kyle as soon as he'd helped Gabby put away breakfast dishes.

Kyle responded within ten minutes. I'd be glad to talk with you. You coming Sunday?

Evening.

See you there.

New Bethany Baptist Church
Sunday, April 28th

This time, Lane got out of the back of Vic's minivan.

Bert had driven, and Vic had taken the passenger's seat to avoid motion sickness. Gabby sat with Sophie in the middle seat, which left him in the back.

He expected it to be like the back of most minivans, cramped and a little sticky, but though he struggled for leg room and his hair brushed the headlining, he didn't find so much as a juice stain.

Though it was the evening service, a few more vehicles than Wednesday filled the lot. People crossed the parking lot with greetings and waves as Lane accompanied the Ellises inside.

They went to the same pew they'd sat in a few days before, and Lane found a place beside Vic. Sophie sat between them this time too, but she grinned as she did it.

"Good to see you again, Lane," said Pastor Hendrick as he passed their pew. Someone else snagged the pastor before he could start a longer conversation. "Hope to see you back often."

The congregation sang just as heartily today as before, and Pastor Hendrick's message held the same note of genuineness, though Lane didn't listen to most of it. He was busy finding Kyle.

Near the end of the service, someone in the next pew back dropped a handful of colored pencils. Several rolled under the pew and ticked against Lane's shoes.

As clandestinely as possible, he scooped them up and handed them over one shoulder.

"Sorry," came the whisper.

It was Kyle. One of his kids was picking up the rest of their dropped pencils.

As the message concluded, everyone stood, but not to leave. While a few slipped out quickly, most stayed, including Kyle and his kids.

"You wanted to know about that job?" Kyle said.

"I do. I'll warn you, though, I've never done construction work."

"Can you use a hammer and a paint roller?"

"Sure."

"Then, long as you're willing to learn the rest, I'm willing to give you a chance. How about Tuesday?" He held out a hand.

Lane took it. "Sure. Just one thing...I'm taking Vic to her appointments at the hospital."

"That's all right. Part of the beauty of being self-employed. If you've gotta leave for an hour, most of the time you can work it out."

"You're not going to interview me?"

"Kind of already did—on Wednesday."

"What about...?" Lane pointed to his face.

"If someone recognizes you, then they do. Hollywood's next door. It isn't like people around here have never met actors."

His experiences at the bar implied otherwise. "I've had a complicated relationship with social media lately."

"What actor hasn't? You're a public figure, and people are going to take advantage of that. Never mind that they wouldn't know what to do with the attention you put up with all the time. Plus, I know better than to believe everything I read online."

"Thanks." This time, the word came easier. "What time Tuesday?"

"7:30. I'll text you the address. I pay gas and meals, so keep track of your mileage and receipts. If you go a bit over your daily allowance, I'll pay the difference."

Kyle's son, Daniel, tapped his arm. "Daddy, I'm hungry."

"We ate before church."

"But I'm hungry again."

His daughter, Lauren, joined in. "I'm hungry too, Daddy."

"Then you can help Daniel eat those leftovers from earlier. There's plenty to go around." To Lane he said, "They're vacuums. I don't know where they put it. If I ate as much as they do, I'd be thirty pounds heavier. I'll just be glad when I have a little more time to plan meals instead of throwing something together last minute. Anyway, gotta get everyone home. See you Tuesday."

"Bye," Lane said as Kyle guided his kids to the door.

No more staring at his phone screen for hours hunting work. At least for now, he would enjoy the respite.

122

102 Maple Leaf Lane
Sunday, April 28th

Not an hour after they got back to the Ellises' house, everyone was asleep except Lane.

A few minutes after 11, instead of sitting in his room, he took a spot on the living room couch. He'd finally gotten out his own pajamas and returned Bert's. The black pair he wore now were the oldest and plainest, but the most comfortable. He'd had them since before he'd met Stephen. They were baggy now, but he would fill them out again with proper diet and exercise.

He tucked his feet under a blanket the Ellises kept on the couch.

One door was open on the wooden cabinet across from him. He got up to close it. Inside sat a 32-inch flatscreen TV, remotes, and a small collection of movies and TV shows, mostly classics and children's content. He shut the door and returned to the couch.

Someone went into the bathroom down the hall behind him—the one between Vic's room and Sophie's. Just as he was about to settle into the magazine article he'd started last week, the rattle of vomiting made him pause.

Vic.

He tapped the closed bathroom door, hoping he wouldn't wake the Ellises. Or Sophie, assuming they were still asleep.

Inside, Vic groaned.

Lane tapped the door again. "You okay?"

Another groan.

He tried the knob. Unlocked.

He shut the door behind him to keep in as much sound as possible. The stench of dinner and stomach acid almost made him regret that choice.

Vic leaned over the sink.

"Your doctor didn't give you nausea meds?" Lane ran the sink to clear it and wet a washrag before handing it to Vic.

"The nausea's from pain."

"The cancer?"

Vic gave the slightest nod, as if expecting another wave of vomiting if she gave any more effort.

He swept her hair out of her face and found a tie in the cabinet hanging above the toilet.

"Thanks," she managed before throwing up again.

"You can't take the pain meds?"

"I have, but what I can take doesn't touch this." She wilted onto the toilet seat, shaking. The robe she wore covered all but the hem of her dark blue nightgown. "I have low-dose Fentanyl patches, but I've been trying not to use them since there's not a lot of research about the risks to an unborn baby. Fran said I should be able to use one every couple weeks without problems, but to avoid more than that." She pulled up one robe sleeve to reveal a clear patch on her upper arm. It glinted in the harsh yellow of the bathroom light.

If Vic was in enough pain to use a patch and was still this nauseous, he couldn't imagine how bad it was. "I'm sorry."

"It's all right." She whispered it.

He was about to protest that it wasn't all right, but everything she'd said to him in the parking lot at Green's stopped him. It might not be all right. But it was something she had to go through right now—something that was just another step to her. It was like when he had to do scenes he hated to audition for a part he really wanted. To her, this was no different.

He both admired and doubted her. She wouldn't be around to raise this baby, but she had given him the chance to live instead of terminating to seek aggressive treatment. He didn't know a lot of women who would make that choice.

Monica certainly wouldn't have thought twice about terminating a pregnancy if she discovered she had terminal cancer. She'd have thrown herself into a treatment regimen immediately, without consideration for a potential child.

"Something...wrong?" Vic whispered as she struggled to rise.

"Just thinking." He took her elbow and helped her reach the sink just before she threw up again.

"It's good to think," Vic said just before Lane clicked on the fan and ran the sink again, holding his breath against the smell.

Nothing was keeping him here, but he stayed anyway.

She'd done the same for him.

123

102 Maple Leaf Lane

Monday, April 29th

Just before dinner, Stacey texted.

It's official. I'm getting a settlement and Gunther and Louis are toast. This is amazing! I can move out of Aunt Sherry's and get a new car. Huddles can eat that expensive food he likes.

She followed the text with a GIF of a cartoon cat running back and forth across the screen.

That's great news, Lane replied. When are you signing the papers?

Later today! I'm on my way to L.A. now. They're paying for me to drive down there, something about it being a more convenient location than Bakersfield. We should meet up afterward to celebrate. As long as you're done shooting for the day.

She still didn't know he was off *Evident*.

He'd let her stay in the dark for a little longer. At least until this settlement business was over and she'd gotten back on her feet.

Sure, he sent back.

He checked his frozen bank account. A few more charges returned, but the large ones remained unresolved. This time, though, there was a note attached to them. He tapped the little red icon. "On indefinite hold."

He groaned.

Hopefully Stacey didn't want to go anywhere too pricey tonight. His money would be hung up for months.

At least that meant whoever did this to him might face consequences.

He logged out of his bank account.

Who was he kidding? If this was part of an investigation, his life might never look the way it used to. The police had said the burglar's MO matched something they'd been chasing for over a year. They wouldn't solve it in a few weeks with leads from a single case.

Bert knocked on his door. "Lunch is ready if you're hungry."

"Thanks."

Since Lane had taken Vic to her appointment Friday, it had gotten harder to look at her. Especially last night. Knowing how close she was to death brought back too many memories of losing Stephen. But as awful as that had been, in some ways, this was worse. Stephen's death took hours, not months. This slow torture was the closest thing to Hell he'd witnessed. He couldn't imagine going through it.

It was 7:45, and Stacey still hadn't texted. Her meeting must have started later than she'd thought.

He was halfway to the living room when his phone buzzed. "Hello?"

"Mr. Harris?"

"Yes."

"Detective Lancaster. We met Friday at the station."

The woman who'd asked for his and Vic's fingerprints.

"There's been a...development in your case, and we need you and Ms. Garrison to come to the station. Tonight."

Stacey might have to wait.

"We'll be there in half an hour."

"Thank you."

Lancaster hung up.

"I've gotta get to the police station," Lane said to Gabby and Vic, who sat on the couch, reading. "They asked for you too," he said without looking at Vic.

"I'll get my purse." She started for her room. Once on her feet, she wobbled.

"Dear, you can't go out this late." The concern in Gabby's voice made Lane regret committing to meet the detective tonight.

"But I need to, Mom." Vic grabbed the sofa arm for support as she almost collapsed. "If I can help solve this case, I want to do it."

"I know, sweetie, but can't they do this without you?" Mrs. Ellis glanced at Lane with pleading in her eyes.

"I think they'll understand if you don't come by tonight." He slipped on his shoes and took his keys from the rack by the door.

"I'm sorry." Vic seemed upset she couldn't go with him.

"It's okay."

Gabby patted Vic's arm. "I'll take you tomorrow, after you've had some rest."

"All right." Vic deflated.

Sophie thudded across the living room in bare feet and threw her little arms around him. "Don't go, Mr. Lane." She looked up at him with pleading eyes. "I want you to stay."

He had to go, whether or not she understood why. "It's really important that I talk to the police tonight." He mussed her hair.

"But—but—" Her lower lip quivered, and tears pooled in her eyes. "But it's dark outside."

"I didn't think you were afraid of the dark."

"I'm not." She buried her face in his pant leg, muffling her next words: "But you might get lost."

Lane chuckled at this. "It's okay." He held up his phone. "This will tell me where I am."

Sophie eyed the phone suspiciously. "Mommy's phone does the same thing." She wiped wet eyes. "But what if it stops working?"

"It won't. I promise. I charged it this morning."

Slowly Sophie let him go. "Okay." Her hazel eyes still begged him not to leave the house. "Bye."

"I'll see you later."

He stepped outside into the gathering darkness, keys in hand.

124

Wavy Palms Way, Los Angeles
Monday, April 29th

Lane turned onto the same street for the third time.

His GPS had him going in circles. This wasn't the route he'd taken to the Hyacinth Street station a few days ago. He double checked the address. It was right.

He should have waited until morning. It was already past 8, and nothing looked the same in the dark under the harsh glare of streetlights.

He pulled into a vacant lot and checked the map. Despite the glitchy GPS on his phone, he manually plotted a course that would get him to the station. Just before he pulled out of the lot, he got a text.

Stacey's number: Meet me at the studio.

That was the last place he'd expected her to go.

I thought you wanted to celebrate.

While Lane was typing a reply, his phone rang. Stacey was video calling him. She never did that.

He picked up.

The phone screen cast light on too-familiar crimson lips, and crazed eyes rimmed with smudged makeup.

"Monica," he said the word with all the civility of a curse. "What did you do to Stacey?"

"Wouldn't you like to know?" she taunted. "Come to the studio. No police. Or the next time you see your sister-in-law, she'll be in a body bag."

If he'd had the luxury of acting on his anger, he'd have smashed his phone. Monica had destroyed too much already. He refused to let her hurt Stacey.

Lancaster would wait.

"Be there in twenty." He ignored the map and headed for Hollywood, heedless of the speed limit.

Studio 73-C

He parked outside the dark studio.

The well-lit parking lot was empty except for his car and Monica's tan Suburban. People drove by, leaving other studios. Some were just arriving for late call times on other sets, heedless of Monica and her twisted plans.

He tried the studio's front door. Unlocked.

He fumbled through the small entryway, phone in hand, assistive lighting on to combat the enveloping darkness. A sharp reek hung in the lobby air, as if someone had just burnt out a fan. Inside the studio, one light pointed at the floor in a pool of blinding brilliance surrounded by a sea of black.

Lane waded through the darkness and adjusted the light so it pointed straight up, casting a thin veil of visibility over the empty studio.

It was past 8:30 now.

The same chemical stink from the lobby wafted from behind him.

"Looking for me?" Monica stepped out from behind a set wall. A disheveled ponytail trailed across one shoulder, and smeared, dark makeup highlighted her wide, too-dilated eyes. She tracked his every twitch.

"You're disgusting, coercing me here by threatening someone I care about," he spat. "But then again, all you've ever done is force me." He imagined his hands crushing her throat, cutting off any excuses or attempts to manipulate. "Where's Stacey?"

Her grin shifted from pleased to predatory.

Lane took a ready stance.

Even in this dim light, dark shadows lingered beneath Monica's nose, mouth, and eyes. "I'll tell you. But only after you give me everything your pathetic, rich husband left you." The rage in her voice swelled with every word. "I've looked for it everywhere. Where is it?" She hurled Stacey's phone at him.

He dodged. The pink rhinestone case flew past his shoulder and clattered across the concrete floor.

Monica's fist followed, catching him squarely in the chest. "Tell me where the money is!" she shrieked.

It was her. She'd wiped out his bank account.

"There isn't any," he roared back. "You took everything I had!"

She lunged at him, throwing punches with inhuman fury. This wasn't like their on-camera fight. Her blows carried enough force to send him reeling backward.

Two men slinked out of the shadows. The gate guard who'd

watched him leave countless times. And one of the lighting guys.

He'd seen them at that bar the night Monica assaulted him, then outside her apartment when he went home afterward. But he remembered them from somewhere else too—at least one of them had rented the apartment a few doors down from him.

It was all connected. The rape, the burglary, the check fraud, and now kidnapping Stacey...every bit of it. Monica had been after a fortune Lane had never possessed.

"You're hiding it somewhere. Your idiot husband was heir to billions. You're his beneficiary." Monica struck again, connecting with Lane's jaw before ramming another hit to the middle of his chest. "Give it to me!"

The two men advanced.

Lane fought to breathe in the wake of Monica's blow.

It was three against one. He had to find Stacey and get out of here.

At least she hadn't hit him hard enough to knock him out, and he was still on his feet. Under normal circumstances, he could easily best Monica. But this crazed version of her would take every ounce of strength he had. And if those two guys got ahold of him, this fight would be over. Both had a couple inches on him and at least forty pounds apiece.

He threw up hands to protect his face. "Leave me alone," he bellowed before throwing a counter punch just below Monica's throat.

She took the hit. Unfazed, she targeted his ribs.

He sidestepped in time.

Barely.

How was she so fast? She'd never been this quick or strong in their choreography sessions. She had to be high out of her mind.

Sweat beaded his forehead, from the stuffy studio and thoughts of Stacey but also his struggle to breathe, his need to escape.

He'd taken hits before. The panic of not being able to fill his lungs would pass soon, and he'd draw regular breaths again. Until then, he couldn't wait for his fate.

There was a terrifying wildness in Monica's swings now. She charged him with a bone-rattling screech. "Tell me where it is!"

Both men were within fifteen feet of them now. He wasn't sure why they hadn't immediately descended on him. With every second, Monica grew bolder and more frenzied. He had to end this, get out of here now. If he didn't...he wouldn't live to regret it.

He swung at her again—too high. The blow connected with her arm. No time for a second hit. He hauled in one unrestricted breath before the two of them crashed to the floor in a savage tangle.

Monica scrambled behind Lane, and her arm snaked around his neck. Both legs wrapped his chest, and her red heels scraped his stomach and sides.

The two men stalked closer. Only five feet separated him from them.

With impossible strength, Monica tightened her grip.

Lane had seconds before he would black out. He grabbed Monica's foot, planted an elbow inside her leg, and twisted the foot up toward his chest.

Her knee gave.

She screamed, and her grip loosened enough to let him twist free and scramble away, barely escaping as one of the men lunged.

He put ten feet between himself and them, then fifteen. Where was the emergency exit sign? It should have glowed bright red. "I don't—have any—money. We never accepted—a single dollar—from Ian Parker. Stacey—would have told—you the same thing."

Monica staggered upright, favoring her injured knee. She lurched toward him, followed by the tech guys. She spewed a few less-than-savory labels for Stacey. "She lied for you, like a good sister."

"Where—is she?" Lane put the studio light between himself and his assailants. He just missed tripping over the coiled cord at the base of the light, but Monica caught it with one heel and crashed into the stand, sending it toward him. The two men skirted her, heading Lane's way with increasing speed.

He darted for the entrance. Before he reached the door, the downed light flashed, blinding him for two short seconds.

But it was two seconds too long.

Monica, somehow back on her feet, slammed into him, driving him to his knees. "You don't answer me, then I don't answer you." She flipped Lane onto his back and pinned him to the cold concrete. Her thumb slipped into the back of his collar, restricting his head and neck. Her other hand immobilized his hip. One knee buried in Lane's gut while the other pressed against his throat. "Couldn't just hand over the money. Wanted to keep it for yourself."

Hot spittle showered his face. The stink of burnt plastic clouded Monica. Her hand on his hip was too warm, almost hot. Still-dilated eyes locked on him.

He wanted—needed—to throw her off, take away the crushing pain that kept him from fighting back. She'd had too much power over him these past two months.

The knee in his gut, the weakened one, was within reach.

He balled a fist and swung.

Monica roared curses as Lane connected with the injured joint.

The instant pressure on Lane's neck let up, he grabbed for the hand pinning his hip. He cranked one of her fingers backward until Monica's scream accompanied a sick snap.

He ripped free of her as she staggered to her feet with another enraged shriek. She was between him and the front door, and the two men moved to box him in. If the main entrance was ahead, the emergency exit had to be to his left.

He bolted for it, hoping panic hadn't disoriented him.

Lane hit the crash bar at full speed. The impact rattled through him, but the door didn't open.

125

Lane hit the door again.

It remained stubbornly closed.

He wheeled, but Monica had recovered and was coming toward him. The two men had blocked all other avenues of escape.

Lane cursed more thoroughly than he had in his entire life.

"You can't get out of this, Laney." With her good hand, Monica pulled something from a pocket. Light glinted off a razor blade, which she gripped in iron fingers. "I'm not letting you go until you give me that money."

She advanced.

Even if he got the razor blade out of her hand, he'd have to contend with her and the two men, and if Monica was high, it was likely her accomplices were too.

He didn't have a chance.

For the second time in his life, Lane prayed.

If God cared anything about him, He'd get him out of this and save Stacey.

Monica's twisted knee kept her from running, and somewhere in the scuffle, she'd lost a heel, which gave him valuable time.

Lane pumped the crash bar again. The only person who could ever get this thing open was—Vic! She'd told him how to open this once.

He reached for the memory. Instead of beating the door, Lane gave the crash bar one more try, this time, an angled push, which sent him reeling outside.

He slammed the door just as Monica reached it.

The next instant, he sprinted for his Versa, got in, and flew out of the parking lot. When he reached for his phone, it was gone. Probably still in the studio.

No GPS or map to follow, no option to call 9-1-1 for him or Stacey, and no hints as to how to get to the Hyacinth Street police station from here. He didn't dare stop someone and ask to borrow a phone. There wasn't time for that. It would only be a minute or two before his attackers were on his tail. At least if they were following him, they couldn't do anything to Stacey. Assuming all three came after him.

But he needed to get his bearings. He would have to backtrack, but he couldn't lose his pursuers. They had to stay with him. He needed to keep them away from Stacey, wherever she was. Once he reached an area he recognized, he could get to the station.

He kept a respectable lead on Monica, but not so much as to lose sight of her and her cohorts as they piled into the Suburban.

No one was at the guard shack, so he rammed through the flimsy, red-and-white-striped barrier. The *crack-snap-thunk* of broken metal and plastic against his grill made him wince.

He rolled the stop sign as fast as he dared and tucked into traffic.

The Suburban pulled in several cars back and kept weaving in and out of its lane. Traffic was starting to thin, but there were still enough cars between Lane and his pursuers to maintain a protective barrier. At least for now.

The clock on the dash said it was 8:53, but it was always wrong. He couldn't remember if it was fast or slow.

Wavy Palms Way, Los Angeles, CA

Lane didn't look at the clock again until he sped past the In-and-Out a couple miles from the Ellises'. It still had the same advertisement on the sign.

He had to get to Hyacinth Street, or at least get a squad car's attention.

Monica and her accomplices were only two cars back now, and they'd run every light and stop sign since leaving the studio.

The SUV's brights switched on, blinding Lane.

He flicked his rear-view mirror up and angled down his side mirrors.

Traffic was thinning too fast.

The SUV careened around a truck and cut in right behind Lane. To his left sat a former grocery store, now an empty building. Weeds forced through cracks in the parking lot. The SUV's engine revved just before it whipped beside Lane's battered Versa and swerved toward him.

He veered left to keep from getting sideswiped, then gunned it and sped past. His Versa jerked, almost taking him into a spin as the other vehicle smacked into the rear, driver-side door and sent the back half of his car jinking toward the empty parking lot.

They were close enough now that Monica's face was unmistakable behind the wheel. She'd caught him. And the rage she wore said she had no intention of letting him get away again.

126

Lane gripped the wheel as the Suburban rammed into him, sending his car off the road, over the curb, and into the open lot, where he clunked over a low parking stop. If it had been any taller, he wouldn't have had the ground clearance to make it over.

The SUV sped his way, blinding lights trained on him in the driver seat.

He was about to get T-boned. If the Suburban hit him, he wouldn't survive.

Flashes of Stephen's accident. Blood. Broken glass. A twisted body.

There were only two exits from the parking lot. One was at the other end, too far to reach in time.

But the other was close.

Lane hit the gas. The Versa's back tires clunked over the parking stop just as the SUV whizzed past, clipping the bumper. His car spun. He prayed he wouldn't roll.

The car leaned to one side, tipped up on two wheels. Lane threw his weight in the opposite direction, trying to right the vehicle, and finally the car settled onto all four tires.

Monica was still recovering from the hit, which had sent her spinning too—thankfully in a different direction.

Lane gunned the engine and headed for the nearer exit. He bounced onto the road without stopping and drove as fast as he dared. A few streetlights weren't working, so all he had to depend on in places were his headlights. At least Monica hadn't bashed either of them out.

If he could just get to the police station.

He glanced in his mirror every few seconds.

Headlights closed. The Suburban sped toward him. He shoved the gas pedal to the floor.

The little Versa shot forward, but with everything it had gone through tonight and these past few weeks, it wasn't capable of matching the SUV's speed.

Monica caught him again and tried to shove him off the road. Instead of speeding up, which he couldn't do anyway, Lane braked just as the SUV swerved into his lane. The Suburban careened off the road and sailed into the ditch.

He didn't stop to find out if Monica and the two men with her were in any state to follow him.

LAPD Hyacinth St. Community Police Station

Lane staggered into the station, heart still pounding. "I—I need to speak to Detective Lancaster," he managed to the officer at the front desk. "Lane Harris. She's expecting me."

"Are you okay?" said the young man—who looked fresh out of the police academy with his long sleeves and perfectly straight tie.

"No. They have my sister-in-law. And they tried to kill me. Twice." Saying it somehow made it real, and with each word, his jaw ached a little more from where Monica had punched him.

Everything hurt, and any second, he expected that SUV to crash through the front of the station.

"Mr. Harris?" Lancaster stepped out. "What happened?"

He told her everything.

Jenkins Rawling Memorial Hospital, Los Angeles

Lane sat on a bed in the ER. He wasn't seriously hurt, but Lancaster had insisted he get to the hospital. He had whiplash, lots of bruises, and a hairline jaw fracture. An ice pack helped numb his face and bring down the swelling. Thankfully the fracture wasn't bad. His only symptom was jaw pain, which blended with every other ache, twinge, and throb.

He was more worried about Stacey.

Lancaster had sent multiple units to the crash site and the studio and had an ambulance dispatched. He hadn't heard anything else.

He flexed his jaw. A mistake. The painkillers they'd given him were good, but a move like that still hurt.

His doctor returned. "Looks like you're okay to go home tonight. No internal injuries as far as I can tell, but keep a watch out for anything unusual and come straight back if you think something's wrong. I've seen plenty of people who ended up on the wrong end of a fight, and most of them fared much worse. Some didn't even make it here. You were lucky."

"What about my sister-in-law? Have they found her yet?"

The man typed something on a tablet. "Haven't heard. You have a pharmacy I can send your pain prescription to?"

"I need to know if Stacey's okay."

The doctor looked up. "Mr. Harris, I can't tell you anything because I don't know. You'll have to contact the police. Now, what pharmacy do you use?"

"The Walgreens on Pine Bough's fine," Lane said.

"Rest that jaw as much as possible. You can go whenever you're ready." The doctor moved on to his next patient.

Lane slipped off the bed. The instant his shoes touched the floor, he realized a new set of aches that weren't there when he'd been admitted. His legs screamed at him, but they were just sore from the tension. That would go away in a day or two, and the pain meds helped a lot as he shuffled into the lobby.

He needed to get back to the station.

The ER door was only a hundred feet away, just across the waiting room. He headed for it. Every step hurt.

"Excuse me?" The nurse at the intake desk waved him down as he passed. "Do you have someone coming to get you?"

"I need to get to the Hyacinth Street police station. Which way is it?"

The nurse eyed him. "I know that look. If I tell you, you're gonna walk there."

Lane didn't answer.

"Hyacinth is over two miles away. At that pace, you won't make it."

"I have to get back. Someone I care about is missing."

"You got a phone?"

"Lost it."

The woman appraised him for several quiet seconds then held up a finger. "Give me a minute." She unlocked her cell and selected a contact from a sea of names. "Dequan. I need a favor." She paused. "No, you won't have to go to that all-night sushi bar again." Another pause. "I have a patient who needs a ride to the Hyacinth Station." She glanced at Lane. "Nah. He really needs to get over there. Seems the decent sort. Can you take him? Okay. Five minutes. Bye." She stowed the phone in a pocket. "My son will be here soon. He'll get you where you need to go."

"You didn't have to—"

The woman held up a hand. "Sometimes you just know you need to do somethin'. This is one of those things. You need a hand getting to the door?"

Lane shook his head.

"All right. I'll be praying you find whoever it is you're looking for."

He wasn't sure what to say to that, so he nodded and headed for the ER entrance. By the time he stepped outside, a twenty-something young man was waiting beside a squad car. "Lieutenant Williams, LAPD." He nodded to Lane. "Guess you're the one needing a ride?"

"Thanks for the pickup. I'd have gotten there myself, but..."

"No problem. Hop in. You can have the front. Unless you intend to cause trouble, then I'm gonna have to ask you to get in the back." Williams grinned and got behind the wheel.

Lane took the offered passenger seat. Shutting the door sent a jolt of discomfort up his arm. Stacey had to be terrified right now. He hoped the police had found her and that she was okay.

The ride to the station took less than ten minutes. When he shuffled into the waiting room, Detective Lancaster and a circle of four officers clustered around someone in a chair.

As Lane approached, the group parted.

There sat Stacey. Her mascara ran down her cheeks in jagged lines, and her hair was mussed. Tear stains spattered her yellow blouse, and one of her matching heels was missing.

The moment she saw Lane, she flew out of her chair and ran to him, her gait thrown off by her missing shoe. She threw her arms around his neck and squeezed him hard enough to hurt.

He didn't care.

Stacey held on until Detective Lancaster approached. "We found her tied up in Henderson's apartment. She's okay, just really shaken up." Lancaster put a comforting hand on Stacey's arm. "We don't need to ask any more questions right now. Henderson and her friends, on the other hand, are in for some very long, very uncomfortable conversations tonight.

"Unfortunately, your car is out of commission. We can't even get it to crank. Do you have another way home? If not, I can get someone to drop you off."

"Will it take someone off Monica's case?"

"Yes. Temporarily."

"Then I'll find another way."

"All right." Lancaster headed for the door separating the waiting room from the rest of the station. "Let me know if you change your mind."

Lane approached reception. Stacey, still quiet, clung to his arm.

"Is there a phone I can use?" he said through the growing pain in his jaw. "Neither of us have ours."

"Sure." The guy at the desk slid a landline phone toward him. "Just dial 9 to call out."

"Thanks."

His finger paused over the 9. He didn't remember Bert's number. Or Vic's.

He would have cursed, but he didn't have the energy.

There was only one number he had written down. Lane dug out his wallet—which he'd miraculously hung onto—and found Kyle's card.

127

102 Maple Leaf Lane

Monday, April 29th

He braced for the brief jolt as Kyle's truck tires hit the dip at the end of the Ellises' driveway.

"Either of you need help inside?" Kyle shut off the engine.

"No. Thanks." Lane slid out of the work truck, careful not to land too hard. "I'm sorry to take you away from your kids this late." He opened the back passenger door and helped a still-silent Stacey out of the truck. She'd taken off her single heel, leaving her in foot socks. At least the Ellises' driveway was smooth concrete.

"Don't worry about it. My mother-in-law loves any excuse to spend time with her grandkids." He got out of the truck and walked Lane and Stacey to the door. Kyle never asked if they needed help, but he stayed within reach.

Inside, the living room light was still on, and before Lane unlocked the front door, Bert opened it. Gabby and Vic stood behind him in the entryway.

"Bert read us Kyle's text twenty minutes ago," said Gabby. She put an arm around Stacey and took Lane by his least-bruised arm, then ushered them inside. "Sophie just got to sleep. She's been up since you left. Insisted we pray for you, so we did."

"Thanks for your help," Bert said to Kyle. "You want some coffee or water, or something for the ride home?"

Gabby led Stacey into the kitchen and coaxed her into a chair.

"Nah, I'm good. Glad to help." Kyle turned to go. "Guess we'll need to push back your start date."

"If you need to hire somebody else, I'll understand," Lane said through the pain in his jaw.

Kyle shook his head. "It's no problem. I'll wait." His eyes darted to Vic, who looked ready to collapse. "I suppose I'll see most of you Wednesday."

In a few weeks, Vic would be...

It was too hard to think about, and Stacey's soft sobs didn't make it easier.

But tonight, he could have been dead himself if it weren't for Vic and that tip she'd given him about the studio door. It had saved his life, and probably Stacey's.

"Thank you," Lane said.

"No trouble." Kyle hopped into his truck and backed out of the driveway.

Lane started toward the kitchen, but Bert stopped him. "Gabby will take care of her. You sit down."

Lane sank onto the couch and, despite his discomfort, leaned into the cushions.

Vic sat beside him.

The clock on the kitchen wall read 11:15.

Time crept toward midnight.

Stacey was safely tucked in Sophie's bed, having exchanged her blouse and slacks for an old pair of Vic's pajamas. Sophie had been moved to an air mattress in her grandparents' room.

For a while, Lane thought Vic had fallen asleep, but when silence filled the house, she tucked her feet under her and faced him.

"You should get to bed," said Lane around his aching jaw.

"So should you. It's been a long day."

"I can't sleep right now." To distract himself, Lane reached for his phone, but he'd forgotten it wasn't in his pocket.

"We haven't heard the whole story yet, have we?" Vic folded her hands in her lap expectantly.

Lane shook his head. He pulled over a blanket and twisted the fringed edge between two fingers. "When...I thought Monica was going to kill me...twice, I asked God not to let me die. And to save Stacey."

Vic pulled a second blanket from the other end of the couch and spread it over her, both hands tucked into its warm folds. "And now you're sitting here. And she's asleep down the hall."

"I suppose so."

The house was so still it was as if they were the only people who existed. All the lights were off, except one lamp sitting atop a side table. Its glow warmed the couch and touched the coffee table, letting the rest of the room fade into vague twilight. It was nothing like the harsh LEDs in the studio.

In this light, Vic didn't look as haggard. The dimness restored years to her face, though she was still thin. Her skin gathered up the lamp's warmth and had turned from pasty white to pleasant orange-pink.

Soon, she'd be gone.

And he'd still be here.

"I know you don't think God's done anything for you." Vic's weary eyes locked with his. "But He has. Tonight proves that."

"Your dad told you what I said a few days ago."

"You thought he wouldn't?"

"My father and I didn't talk much."

"I know, and I can't speak for your relationship with him, but I can tell you God doesn't leave His children. Though I walk through the valley of the shadow of death." She whispered the last part.

Lane recognized it as being from the Bible, and before he realized, memories from Sunday school kicked in, and he was finishing the quote: "I will fear no evil, for Thou art with me."

"Yes, He is with you. He was tonight. He spared your life. And Stacey's. And this isn't the first time."

Lane wanted so badly to block out the memories of Stephen's crushed car, of how it could have been him—of how he wished it had been him. Then other memories came—these of the night he'd downed the bottle of sleeping pills. When he'd almost cut his wrists in the hospital, and a muddled memory of almost doing it again when he'd faded into that vodka haze.

Other memories came now, from childhood, his teenage years, college.

"No. It's not."

"And do you know why He's spared you so many times?" Vic

seemed to pull strength from the question. "Because He loves you. Not the way you loved your husband, or the way I loved Gav, or Nakasha, or even my kids. God's love is perfect, holy, complete, and vast as the ocean. No human's love can ever match God's, no matter how much we think it can.

"Your dad might not have wanted you in his family, but God wants you in His, and He keeps proving it to you, if you'll set aside the lies you've told yourself about Him—about love—over the years and just stop and listen."

Her words speared deeper than his bruises, scrapes, and the dull pain in his jaw.

Every time he'd thought he didn't want to live, God had intervened in the person of Vic Garrison. Even when someone else had tried to kill him, Vic's words had helped save his life and the life of someone he cared about. She had held out a hand to him when even her own parents were initially hesitant. She understood him like no one else he'd met. Her life mirrored his. It couldn't be coincidence they'd met—that she'd chosen him that day at the studio.

Kyle's words: "No coincidences."

Then there was Sophie. The little girl had taken to him, showing him little bits of compassion when those around her hadn't bothered to notice his struggle.

Over the past five days, he'd prayed three times. The first had been in anger, the other two in desperation. He hadn't thought he believed in God. But he'd called to Him when he had no other recourse.

And God had answered.

He rolled his blanket's fringe until a clump of strands, wrapped into one long swirl. The house cooled, and the clock ticked just past 12:15.

People who didn't exist didn't answer.

People who didn't exist didn't love.

128

102 Maple Leaf Lane
Tuesday, April 30th

He'd heard the story—account—repeatedly as a kid. Sunday school teachers relayed it often, how Jesus died a bloody death to rescue everyone who'd ever lived from all the horrific things they'd done.

Lane had experienced plenty of horror, plenty of wrong done to him and by him. He knew the consequences of living with it, how it devoured pieces of who he was until he didn't recognize himself.

The men who'd written the Bible might not be alive to recount what had happened to them, but Vic sat beside him, and she had told him what God had done for her. He'd seen firsthand who she was now, and he'd seen evidence of who she'd once been.

The change was undeniable.

If God could take away this awful emptiness, the pain he'd tried so hard to stop, his anger, and the heavy loneliness that smothered him every day, Lane would let Him.

For the first time in thirty-eight years, he believed.

"It's true—what you said at Green's. About Jesus. And...I'm ready to accept that."

Vic sat straight, eyes open wide enough to raise both eyebrows. "You—you are?"

"Yeah. I am." The corner of his mouth tipped upward. His jaw still hurt, but the pain seemed a faint memory, and a quiet knowing filled him.

He wasn't alone anymore.

Vic buried her face in her blanket as she burst into tears.

"Isn't this supposed to be a happy moment?" He grabbed the Kleenex box on the coffee table and nudged her with it.

She revealed tear-glazed eyes, but instead of sadness, joy filled them. "It is," she choked out as she accepted the Kleenex, then did the last thing Lane expected. "Mom! Dad! Sophie!"

The little girl was first to thunder down the hall, and she hopped onto the couch between Lane and Vic. "What is it, Mommy? Are you okay?"

Vic hugged her daughter tightly. "I'm more than okay, sweetie."

Bert and Gabby arrived a moment later, both wearing housecoats.

"Do you need to go to the hospital?" said Bert.

"What are you still doing up? You need your rest," said Gabby, concerned.

Vic sidestepped her parents' questions. "Lane—he—he believes."

Bert's groggy expression vanished. "You finally listened?"

Lane nodded, careful not to irritate his jaw.

Gabby came around the couch. "I would hug you but considering"—she gestured to his bruises and scrapes—"everything, I'll skip it for now." She patted his shoulder instead.

"Did you ask Jesus into your heart, Mr. Lane?" Sophie moved to sit between Lane and her mother.

"I don't know. Isn't there supposed to be a prayer or something to go with this?"

"If you want to pray, you can," said Vic. "But a prayer is just a prayer. You already have what matters, and that's faith."

"That's good because I have no idea how to pray. I saw people do it when I was younger, and my father loved to make a show of it, but I never did it myself. Unless you count today."

"Praying's easy, Mr. Lane," Sophie said. "I did it when I asked Jesus into my heart." She took his hands, laced his fingers together, and bent them into place.

He felt like a kid in church, only this time he focused on what he was doing.

"Okay, close your eyes and bow your head," Sophie said.

This was a far humbler position than his father had employed. When called on to pray in services, the man stood tall, raised his face to the roof, and shouted loud enough for the guy in the back sound booth to hear through the tinted plastic walls.

"Do you wanna make up what you wanna say? Or do you wanna say what I say?" Sophie's little hands covered barely half of his.

He wasn't confident he could pray coherently. "I'll just follow you."

"Okay." Sophie seemed unconcerned about praying out loud in front of her family. "Jesus, this is for Mr. Lane. He doesn't know how to talk to You yet, so I'm gonna help him." From that preface, she went straight into a simple prayer. "Dear Jesus." She gave him time to say it too. "I'm sorry for the bad things I've done. Thank You for dying on the cross to take away my sin, and for coming into my heart today and saving me. In Jesus' name, Amen." She released his hands after the last word of the prayer.

Before Lane opened his eyes, Sophie threw her arms around his chest. "I'm so happy!"

Though her grip was far from strong, the embrace hurt, but he hugged her back without complaint.

"Sweetie, Mr. Lane's got a few bruises right now," Vic said.

"Oh. Sorry." Sophie pulled away from him, but her grin didn't dim. "But I'm still happy."

The girl's joy prompted something in Lane he'd never experienced.

"Thank you, Sophie. I'm glad too." He smiled this time, though he wasn't sure where the sentiment came from. It sprang up inside him, like water from a new well.

He expected to feel some kind of deep, instant change, but there was only the sense that he was home now—this knowledge that God was with him here, in this humble place, with these caring people.

The terror of earlier that night evaporated.

He was at peace for the first time.

129

102 Maple Leaf Lane
Tuesday, April 30th

After everyone else had gone to sleep, Lane, still dressed, sat on the guest bed. He hadn't even pulled back the comforter. The Ellises kept the house a bit warmer at night than he was used to, so whispers of air from the ceiling vent only washed over him every so often. In the quiet darkness, the joy from two hours before still enveloped him. But with it came something else.

An ineffable sadness. A knowing that though God had saved him, there was someone else who had never accepted the truth.

Stephen.

His husband had been clear about many things, including his rejection of the possibility of a higher power. Stephen said the best person to believe in was yourself, and he'd encouraged Lane to embrace that belief too.

Lane clasped his hands. His wedding band still hugged his ring finger, but Stephen's missing ring tore a hole in his heart. He would never again see the person he'd loved most in all the world.

That knowledge seeped into him. It was a dull, thick ache that pulled him in, threatening to consume him. If only he could hand over this soul-crushing grief. But he didn't know how.

He uttered a single word: "Help."

It didn't erase his sadness. Didn't make him shed any fewer tears for Stephen. But it did ease the pain.

And for tonight, that was enough.

130

Six Years Ago

2785 Wanderer's Way, Los Angeles
Thursday, May 16th

Leigh hung her mother's favorite purple blouse and kept sorting the load of still-warm clothes in the dryer. One of her father's staticky socks stuck to her hand. She shook it off only to have another grab her arm.

"You don't have to do that." Her mother scooped the last armful of clothes out of the dryer and laid everything on top of the washer.

"I know." Leigh shut the dryer and kept sorting.

"Sweetie, what is it? You have that look on your face."

Leigh paused, a plain green tee half-folded. "It's so weird..." She finished folding the shirt and set it aside. "I've been thinking a lot about that conversation I had with Pastor and Mrs. Hendrick a few weeks ago."

"You said it went okay."

"It did." Leigh pulled a floral skirt free of the pile. "They said a lot of things I hadn't really thought about before. Stuff I never heard in church."

Her mother looked away. "I'm sorry we couldn't help you more."

Leigh laid a hand on her mother's arm. "None of what I did was you or Dad's fault. I chose to do it, and neither of you could've stopped me."

"It still hurts to know there wasn't anything I could do. As a parent, that's always been one of my biggest fears. That something would happen, and I wouldn't be able to help you."

Leigh put an arm around her mother. "It's okay. If there's anything I'm learning, it's that God is bigger than us and our limitations. And..." She separated a pair of dress pants from a clingy polo. "God changes us into the people He wants us to be."

Two brightly colored socks dropped out of the polo as she hung it up.

"You and Dad always called me Victoria when I was little. I liked it because it sounded so important and refined. Then, when I left home...I wanted nothing to do with you or God, so I made everyone call me Leigh. It was so different from Victoria. Short. More modern. It made me feel a little rebellious, like I'd made a clean break from a stifling past." She arranged the dress pants on their hanger and adjusted them until the seams hung correctly. "I'm not either of those people anymore—the innocent little girl or the angry rebel. But God used both those phases of life to make me into who I am."

Her mother grabbed the last two shirts and folded them with care. "You thought about all that in the last fifteen minutes?"

"Not really. It's been more of a gradual thing. You know, something that keeps coming to mind and doesn't fully make sense for a while. But I think I get it now." Leigh draped a pile of freshly hung clothes over one arm. "Mom, I want you to start calling me Vic." The words tumbled out with barely a pause between them.

She'd thought long and hard about this. Going back to Victoria wasn't right. Her innocent view of life was long gone. But Leigh, the angry, sad young woman, wasn't who she was either.

A dozen versions of her first and middle names decorated a sheet of notebook paper in her room. She'd listed everything she could think of until the simplest answer of all came to mind. Short, but a callback to a time she hadn't been tainted by the world's darkness. It was the perfect reflection of how God was working in her life.

"Vic," her mother tested the name. "It's...different."

"So am I."

Her mother smiled. "Yes. I suppose you are."

131

102 Maple Leaf Lane

Tuesday, April 30th

Lane slept until noon, and no one bothered him, not even for breakfast. When he roused, an all-encompassing ache covered him, but it was skin deep. Instead of debating whether he should get out of bed, he dragged himself to the shower. The hot water beat away some discomfort and lent a sense of well-being he'd never noticed before.

Bert was coming down the hall when Lane left the bathroom. "You're up. Feeling any better?"

He groaned, but the hopelessness that once tinged the sentiment was absent. "Just really sore." He touched his jaw. "And this doesn't feel the greatest."

"Gabby picked up your prescription. It's in the kitchen if you need it."

"I should take that." He followed Bert. "How's Stacey?"

"Gabby brought her breakfast this morning. She's talking now. Still withdrawn. What happened really hit her hard."

"I'll go see her after I take those pain pills."

"I think she'd like that."

In the living room, Vic sat on the couch, watching news on the TV.

The weather droned, followed by a piece about local politics.

Days on the calendar in the dining room were crossed off. Today was the 30th.

His and Stephen's first anniversary.

Grief knifed his heart again, and he stopped in front of the calendar. With one index finger, he touched the unmarked date. There would always be something in him that mourned for Stephen, though it might fade over time. He couldn't bring back the dead, no matter how much he wanted to. Stephen's time was over, his choice made.

"It's right here." Bert opened a high cupboard containing household medication, Vic's dietary supplements, and other vitamins.

"Thanks." Lane's finger slid from the calendar page, but he stayed two more seconds before moving on.

He checked the directions on the medication before taking out a single pill. It was the same shape as the sleeping pills he'd taken only a couple of weeks ago, but instead of the dull beige pink, these were plain white. He downed the single pill with water and carefully locked the bottle's cap before putting it away.

Gabby reentered the kitchen.

"Thanks for taking Stacey in last night," Lane said.

"We're glad to have her," she replied. "Poor dear's been through quite enough. I'm about to take her some soup."

"I can do that." Lane held out open hands until Gabby gave him the steaming bowl. He shuffled down the hall. Yesterday's ordeal was quickly catching up to him. Hopefully, the pain killers would kick in soon.

Stacey's door was half-open.

"Hungry?" He sat on the edge of the bed and held out the soup.

"Not really." Stacey's voice had an edge to it.

He set the bowl on the bedside table. "Are you all right?"

"No! No, I'm not! How can you even ask that? And how are you not falling apart too? People tried to kill us, and you're acting like nothing happened." Anger fueled her words.

"You're okay, and that's what matters to me. The rest of it, I can deal with."

"Nuh-uh. What's really going on?"

He hadn't considered how she might react to last night's decision. "Stace, there's something I need to tell you, but I don't think—"

"Lane!" Vic called from the living room. "You've got to hear this!"

"I'll be back." He squeezed Stacey's hand and, with some difficulty, stood.

He made it to the living room just as the "Breaking News" announcement flickered to a shot of a chaotic movie studio. A reporter stepped over a broken light. "Early reports say Lane Harris, former member of the cast of the upcoming film *Evident*, is alive and was seen at Jenkins Rawling Memorial Hospital's emergency room late last night. Police found his phone inside the studio after what appears to be an altercation between him and his former co-cast member Monica Henderson."

The reporter stepped out the open side door. The crash bar looked like a gorilla had beaten it. "Police arrested Henderson near the Hyacinth Street police station around 9 p.m. last night after they found her and two accomplices in a ditch. All three presented symptoms of drug use. Back to you, Macy."

Macy McConahan, the Channel 12 news anchor, picked up. "We received this exclusive clip from an anonymous source."

The view switched to a grainy cell phone video of Monica's attempt to T-bone him in the empty parking lot. Vic covered her mouth as Lane clunked three feet forward, and Monica hit him, spinning both vehicles in opposite directions. Whoever shot the video uttered a string of expletives the news channel bleeped out.

Macy hid shock as her fellow anchor passed her a piece of paper. "This just in. This morning, police also apprehended *Evident* co-star Monica Henderson and two others in relation to a burglary ring the LAPD has been investigating for over a year. Police won't give details, but Henderson appears to be responsible for multiple burglaries in the Hollywood, Huntington Park, and greater Los Angeles areas. It remains to be seen whether this is connected to the incident last night concerning Lane Harris. We'll keep you updated."

Vic turned the TV volume down.

She held up her phone, displaying a wall of text. "Jack says the police contacted him a couple hours ago, confirming Monica was the prime suspect in those burglaries. Including yours. They found her prints all over the stuff from the pawnshop. If it weren't for you, the police never would have caught her." Vic's face was serious. "Lane, I'm so sorry. I had no idea she was—"

"I know." He stopped her. Everything that happened after the break-in—it all led him here, and he was a different person because of it. Now he understood far better how Vic viewed her past. "You couldn't have stopped her. And you did more for me than anyone else ever has. For that, I can't ever thank you enough."

132

102 Maple Leaf Lane

Tuesday, April 30th

After a late lunch, Bert handed Lane a cased phone and wall charger. "It's a few years old, but it works. We can hold you on our plan until you get your own phone back or buy a new one."

"I won't impose on you like that."

Bert held up a hand. "You're family now. Besides, you can't go around with no way to contact people."

It was true. He needed to call Tina. And Alisha. Not to mention everyone else who would try to call him.

"Turns out we have the same carrier. Phone company says you can keep your old number, but you'll have to go to the store and have them do the transfer since you can't access your old phone. And they won't be able to pull over any content that isn't backed up. That'll have to wait until the police give back your old phone."

"I don't know what to say."

"Don't have to say anything. Now, I've gotta get Vic to an appointment. See you later." Bert helped his daughter into the living room.

Before she stepped out the door, Vic looked back at him. She was so thin and pale. Soon she wouldn't even be able to go to the hospital for appointments. Would they call in hospice? Or would her parents care for her until she passed? Sorrow rose in his throat, but he packed it down. She was ready for this—ready for death.

This time, thinking about it still hurt, but it wasn't raw. Instead, it was more of a dull ache. And in place of the empty darkness that once awaited him at the end of that awful word, now there was a promise there. He would see Vic again. This would not truly be goodbye. He'd heard others say it. Now he believed it.

Once Bert and Vic left, Lane went down the hall to Stacey's room. The soup he'd brought earlier was gone, and Stacey was bundled under the covers, back to the door. When he knocked, she didn't stir.

"Stace? It's me."

She still didn't respond.

"I said I'd come back." He sat in the same spot as before. The bed sagged a little under his weight.

Stacey shifted away from him.

"So you are awake."

"Yes," she said quietly. "Why won't you tell me what's going on? Why are you at Vic Garrison's parents' house and not your apartment?"

He'd forgotten. His new faith wasn't the only thing she didn't know about. He hadn't told her about the eviction, getting kicked off *Evident*, living at the bar, his attempts at taking his own life.

"It's...a long story."

She kept her back to him, but after a minute she said, "I've got some time."

"You're not going to like most of it."

"Will it help me understand what happened last night?"

"Yes."

She rolled over and took Lane's hand. "Then tell me."

When he'd finished recounting everything that had happened since Stacey left for Bakersfield, the room went silent.

Stacey sat up and held a ragged Kleenex to her nose. "How could you?" she whispered, though the force of each word shook her. "How could you not tell me? All those times I called or texted, and you didn't answer. And when you were in the hospital. You lied through your teeth about why you were there."

"I'm sorry. I didn't want to worry you."

"I don't care. I'm just happy you're okay." Her frown deepened. "There's still something you're not saying."

"You always could tell when me or Stephen was lying." His heart rate rose. Of everything he'd told Stacey, this was the one thing he was most worried about. "Last night, I..." He didn't know how to say this. The truth stuck to his tongue, begging to be said. But fear kept whispering to him, saying he should keep this to himself. "I'm a Christian."

She slapped him. The sting lingered.

"You swore you'd never believe what your father did." Anger sharpened her words.

"This has nothing to do with my father, I promise. I'm sorry it upsets you."

"Get out." Stacey pointed to the door.

"Let me explain—"

"I don't want to hear it!" She crossed her arms and wouldn't look at him. "I'll leave in the morning. I can catch a bus back to Bakersfield."

Reluctantly, Lane left Stacey alone. He went back to the guest room. Even though it was still early, he changed and tried to sleep.

But sleep wouldn't come. Thoughts of Stacey and their conversation plagued him as he wondered if he might have handled things better. Both of them had just survived incredible trauma, and then he'd given her even more difficult news. He should have known better.

He needed something to get his mind off the last hour and a half.

Hahnen'En sat on the bedside table. He picked it up and returned to the story that once made no sense to him.

His phone read 1:06 when he reached the last couple pages of the final chapter. His eyes drooped, but he had to know how this ended. Oren's death still hit hard, even though he understood why it had to happen.

Hahnen'En seemed to share Lane's sentiments as he attended the prince's memorial, three days after his death.

People filled the woods surrounding the prince's funeral bier. The king's personal guard circled Oren's body. Common people clustered in family groups or with friends. Nobles waited in solemn silence, and sadness filled every face as the king stood beside his only son.

Hahnen'En didn't dare approach the gathering. This was happening because of him. Even if the common people didn't recognize him, the king's guard would. They'd been there when Oren had died in his place, and he was sure they wouldn't be overly happy to see him again.

If nothing else, Hahnen'En needed to show his gratitude for Oren's selflessness. It was only right he give respect to the man who had taken a sword for him and paid an impossible debt.

Men, women, even young children filed past the prince's body, leaving flowers, ribbons, jewelry, and handmade ornaments on and around his still form.

Hahnen'En waited until everyone, including the king, was gone. He didn't have long. The men tasked with burying Oren would arrive shortly.

A breeze whispered through the trees, brushing a handful of wildflowers off the prince's bier. The bright pink and purple blooms fluttered to the ground, steps from Hahnen'En's boots. For the second time in three days, he kneeled. The soft, damp earth wasn't as pebble-ridden as the ground surrounding the prison keep.

"They love you," he said to Oren's still form. "All of them. Even the littlest ones." He scooped a purple flower from the grass. All eight petals were still perfect. "I don't understand why you died for me—someone who had no love for you." He set the flower with the multitude of others piled within arm's reach. "I don't know why your father stopped hunting me when I accepted your blood as my ransom. But as long as I live, I will remember. And I will tell others what you did." He bowed his head and wished he could talk with Oren again, this time as a friend instead of a stranger.

A hand on Hahnen'En's shoulder brought him instantly to his feet. He turned, expecting the gravediggers. But it was only one man, dressed in white. Even his boots were cleaner than fresh snow, and though he stood on damp earth, not a speck of it clung to him.

"What is your business here?" Hahnen'En's hand crept to the hilt of his dagger.

"Don't you know me?" He extended a hand.

"I've never seen you before." Hahnen'En scanned the surrounding forest, just in case this intruder wasn't alone.

Not a single leaf was out of place.

"If you mean to take the prince's body, you'll have to get through me." He brandished his blade. He'd have preferred to use his sword, but there was no room, not with his opponent already so close. The dagger would have to do.

"Peace, Hahnen'En."

At the sound of his name, he lost his grip on the dagger hilt. The blade thunked into the grass.

The bier was empty. Except for the dark clothes the prince was wearing during his funeral and the settled blanket of flowers and gifts left by the attendees, there was no sign of the body.

"Oren?" Hope thickened Hahnen'En's voice.

The prince nodded, hand still extended.

Hahnen'En took it and pulled the other man into an embrace. "This can't be. I saw you die."

Oren pulled back, holding Hahnen'En at arm's length. "And so, I did. But Death couldn't hold me, my friend. It wasn't strong enough."

"I don't understand."

The prince smiled. "I must go to my father. Walk with me, and I'll tell you things you never knew were possible."

133

102 Maple Leaf Lane

Thursday, May 2nd

True to her word, Stacey left that morning. She thanked the Ellises for their kindness and walked out of the house, wearing a pair of black flats Gabby had given her.

Lane walked her to the end of the driveway, where an Uber picked her up.

Stacey muttered a quiet "goodbye" before shutting the door.

Franklin Park

Friday, May 10th

Lane sat across from Alisha at a picnic table in the shade of an oak as the afternoon sun crept around them. "I'm sorry it's taken so long to sit down and talk." He took another bite of one of Gabby's chicken salad sandwiches, which she'd insisted on making when she found out he was going to see Alisha. The Ellises had let him borrow the RAV-4 too, since his car was junked and he couldn't afford a new one. Not with what little his insurance was willing to give him.

Grayson had long since polished off two sandwiches and a bag of chips and was running around the nearby playground with three other boys.

Alisha wiped her fingers on a napkin. "Don't apologize. I've been following the news over the past week and a half. How did you manage—losing everything?"

"I didn't." He set his sandwich on a paper plate. His jaw was much better now, but he still had to be careful how fast he ate or how long he talked. "Thus, the drunk call in the middle of the night last month. I'm really sorry about that, by the way. Lester's death hit me hard, and I spiraled out of control when I got back to the bar afterward. If it hadn't been for Vic, I'd probably be dead." He nudged a stray oak leaf off the table. Saying Lester's name still hit hard.

"Well, I'm glad she got to you in time," Alisha said. "How'd she find you, anyway?"

"I called her."

"You drunk called Vic Garrison?"

He nodded. "She came to the bar, made me a pot of nightmare coffee, and told me her story." Lane related the things Vic said to him that night. "It was...the first real conversation I'd had with anybody about God."

Alisha sipped a tumbler of ice water. "You mentioned God when you called me that night too. I didn't know what to make of it."

"He's part of my life now," Lane said.

Alisha threw her trash in a nearby garbage can. "I don't really understand, but I'm glad you've found something that works for you." She smiled. "You're a lot less down now. I can tell you've been through stuff, but you don't have that defeated look anymore. I still can't believe Monica Henderson tried to kill you."

"She had every advantage. But God got me out."

"This is the most you've mentioned God any time I've talked to you."

"It's the first time we've talked since I realized He wasn't the enemy."

"What do you mean?"

Lane told her everything.

When he finished, Alisha said, "That's quite the story. I'm so sorry about everything and, like I said, I'm glad you found something that works for you."

"But you don't buy it."

Alisha's polite smile confirmed it. "It's a nice thing to believe. I think it's good to help people and do what you can when you can, but to believe someone died to save me—whatever that means—a couple thousand years ago? That's not something I'm willing to step into. You've gotta admit, it's pretty shaky."

"I don't think so. Not anymore."

Alisha checked her phone. "Well, thanks for this. It was great, but I've got to get Grayson home so he can finish his homework before the weekend."

"See you later?"

"Sure. I'll text you when I have another day off. And thanks for including Grayson. It means a lot to me. What few friends I have don't usually like me bringing him along."

"No problem. He's welcome anytime."

Alisha herded her son to the car. Grayson waved as they pulled out of the parking lot.

Lane stayed at the weathered picnic table a while longer.

His phone buzzed. He pulled it out, hoping it might be Stacey. He hadn't heard from her since she'd gone back to Bakersfield.

Just an email ad.

He tucked the phone away and headed for the parking lot.

LAPD Hyacinth St. Community Police Station
Monday, May 13th

Lane approached the reception desk. "I'm here to see Detective Lancaster."

"If you'll wait right over there, she'll be with you soon." The young woman at the desk pointed to the same row of chairs he'd bypassed two weeks ago, after Monica had tried to kill him.

This time, the overwhelming urge to fight or run was gone, though he was a bit anxious. Lancaster had called half an hour ago, saying she needed to talk with him.

Almost forty minutes later, she retrieved him from the waiting area. "Have a seat, Mr. Harris." She pointed to the chair on the other side of her desk. "I suppose you've seen the news about Ms. Henderson?"

"I heard she was arrested two weeks ago."

"Once she sobered up and found out all the potential charges, she talked fast. Attempted murder was the clincher, though. Seems Henderson was in heavy debt to a local cocaine dealer. She'd already cleaned out a few others' accounts over the past couple years, and you were her next target."

"But I'm broke."

Lancaster tapped her phone. "You were married to the late Stephen Parker."

He twisted his wedding band. Its cool, textured surface was like fine grains of sand against his fingers. He'd chosen this band. When Stephen had seen it, he'd loved it so much he'd insisted on getting a matching one.

"Mr. Harris?"

"Sorry." The word came out strained. "Go on."

"Seems Ms. Henderson thought your husband might have made arrangements for you to have access to his family's money. She had accomplices watching you for a while. They lost track of you about four weeks ago."

"I moved in with some friends."

"Good thing. Henderson and her goons were going to confront you, but she says you weren't where you should have been, and she couldn't find you."

Thus, the kidnapping. She didn't know where he was, so she had to make him come to her. "How did she find Stacey?"

"According to her, luck. She was on her way to a meeting with her dealer when she saw your sister-in-law coming out of one of the buildings downtown. Sent her cronies in and they ferried their prize— Stacey—back to Henderson's place.

"When we picked her and her friends up that night at the crash site, they were all out of their minds on cocaine. It took three officers and two tasers just to bring her down. The other two were equally uncooperative. Didn't you say you went hand-to-hand with them? It's a miracle you got out of that fight alive."

Memories of the scrape of new denim as Monica's knee dug into his throat brought Lane's hand to his neck. He wouldn't soon forget her wide, crazed eyes and the deadly edge in her voice. He'd stared into a few shadows a bit too long on the way here, making sure no one was lurking in them.

"Yeah. It was."

"It'll be a while before we return your property—red tape and all that—but you'll get it back. Unfortunately, other than what you and Ms. Garrison found at the pawnshop, I'm afraid we may never track down the rest of your valuables. They've been gone too long."

A pang of loss hit Lane. A lot of those things were Stephen's. "I understand," he said. "Thank you for everything you've already done."

"It's my job, Mr. Harris. Unlike some, I'm glad to do it."

134

Six Years Ago

New Bethany Baptist Church
Sunday, June 16th

In the fellowship hall, Vic stood in line behind a woman twice her age. She couldn't recall the lady's name, but remembered seeing her in every service she'd ever attended, including the ones from childhood.

Ten to fifteen people separated Vic from her parents. She'd intended to stick close to them, but a well-meaning church member had stopped her, wanting to talk about some ladies' get-together in a couple weeks. Vic had listened politely and gotten out of the conversation as quickly as she could, but by then, most of the church had already gotten in line for the potluck.

She reached for a Styrofoam plate and plastic fork just as the person behind her did. A hand several shades darker than hers pulled back to let her go first.

"Sorry," they both said at the same time.

The hand belonged to a young man, maybe a year or two older than Vic. His tightly curled hair and rounded nose reminded her of Nakasha, but the resemblance ended there. Mirth filled his dark eyes, and he smiled brighter than Nakasha ever had.

"Didn't mean to try to get ahead of you. I was checking something on my phone and didn't see you." He stepped back. His phone jutted from a wide breast pocket.

"You're good." Vic grabbed her plate and cutlery and started down the line. Potlucks had always been fun when she was a kid. All the different foods she got to eat that she normally wouldn't have. Now, as an adult who'd seen and experienced far too much of the world, she eyed everything with a bit of suspicion before reaching for a serving spoon.

Halfway through the line, the man behind her dropped his fork, which skittered under the table. He sighed. "This just isn't my day."

"Maybe it'll get better," Vic offered as she spooned Crock-Pot macaroni onto her plate, then offered him the serving spoon.

He took it and scraped the rim of the dish. "I can't believe nobody's taken this yet."

"The burnt stuff?" Vic laughed.

"Not burnt. Caramelized."

"Whatever you say." She grabbed tongs and put a large helping of salad on her plate before dishing up cut melon and strawberries.

He did the same, but also fished a piece of baked chicken from an Anchor dish.

Vic reached the end of the line and searched the room for her parents. They'd taken seats at a middle table, with several friends.

"Where you sitting?" said the man behind her.

"Don't know yet. You?"

"Here's fine." He pointed to a couple of empty chairs at the end of a table. "You want to join me?"

Vic glanced toward her parents. They were absorbed in conversation. Probably something about retirement funds and shuffleboard. "Sure."

She set her plate down across from his and sat.

"You want something to drink? I need to get another fork anyway."

"Sure. Water's good."

He was back a moment later with two cups of water and one replacement fork. "Gavin Garrison. Call me Gav." He held out a hand.

When she stared at it, he awkwardly withdrew. "Sorry. Habit. Too many corporate meetings."

"No, no. I just didn't expect a handshake as part of an introduction. I'm Victoria Ellis. Vic. Nice to meet you, Gav. I haven't seen you here before."

"Just moved from Georgia. Work stuff. My dad knows Pastor Hendrick, so I thought I'd come visit. Didn't know there was gonna be food until I got here."

"Something about special meetings," Vic replied. "So, what do you do?"

"Software engineer. Out of one of the big Silicon Valley companies."

"I thought that was up near San Francisco."

"It is. I get to telecommute. Company's trying to cut overhead, so lots of us are working from home now. And how about you, Vic? What do you do?"

"I'm a writer. Have you heard of *Hannah Stanton*?"

"Wait, you wrote those?"

Vic smiled and nodded.

"I have got to tell my parents I met you. They aren't going to believe me." He pulled out his phone and sent a quick text. "So have you written anything else, or was *Hannah Stanton* your Magnum Opus?"

A slow smile spread across Vic's face.

"I take it that means there's another story I need to hear." He propped an elbow on the table, fork poised over his "caramelized" mac and cheese. "Tell me all about it."

135

New Bethany Baptist Church
Sunday, May 19th

Lane sat between Sophie and Bert as the morning service started.

Vic had wanted so badly to come today, but she couldn't get out of bed. Not even with the help of both her parents. Gabby had stayed home with Vic.

Lane tried to pay attention, but thoughts of Vic's coming death and Stacey's continued silence wouldn't let him.

102 Maple Leaf Lane

When they got home, Vic was still in bed.

He knocked lightly on the open door. "Hey."

"Lane. Come in." Vic set her Bible on the nightstand, propped up against her pillows, and staunched a sick cough with two folded Kleenexes. "How was the service?"

"I didn't pay much attention, to be honest."

Vic gestured to the chair beside her bed. "You can sit."

Lane took the chair. "This is a twist. Me here and you there." Had it only been a month since he'd tried to end his life? He rubbed his scarred wrist and recalled the sour taste of the Ambien's quick-dissolve coating.

Vic laughed but ended up coughing again. She sipped from a water glass before resting both hands atop her unborn son. "Heard anything else about getting your stuff back?"

"Detective Lancaster says it's probably a lost cause. What we found is likely to be all I ever get back." He stared at his folded hands. "I finished *Hahnen'En* a couple weeks ago. Then I reread it. It was a little like looking in a mirror."

"The same happened for me," said Vic. "While I wrote that book, it changed the way I saw myself. When I accepted the truth, it was like God had raised me from the dead—like Lazarus. That was when I realized I didn't need to fear death anymore. Ironic, isn't it? I was afraid of death but threw myself toward it. When I didn't fear death, I stopped pursuing it."

"Same." Lane perched an ankle atop the opposite knee. "I wanted the emptiness to go away, so I tried to force it. I'm glad I failed."

Vic's smile brightened. "God gives purpose every day. Before I knew Him, I did what made me feel better. But once God gave me new life, I found real purpose. I lived knowing death would come one day, but not being afraid of it, because God is more powerful than death." She shifted as if uncomfortable.

"You okay?"

"He's moving." She tracked her baby bump with one hand. "He's all over the place today. Maybe he knows it's almost time for him to make his entrance." She patted her middle.

"Have a name yet?"

"Still deciding."

"Any candidates?"

"A few."

"But you're not going to spill, are you?"

"Nope. Not yet."

Silence separated them.

Vic only had a couple weeks left. She'd quickly become the best friend he'd ever had.

He wasn't ready to let her go.

Bert had told him he could pray anywhere even without speaking aloud. As Lane sat beside Vic's bed, he silently prayed, *God, I don't want to lose her. Not now. Not yet. I'm not ready. Please...*

He swallowed hard.

Vic's time was almost here. He couldn't change that, and He knew in his heart God wasn't going to either, but somehow giving that grief to Him made it bearable.

136

Warm water filled the kitchen sink.

Lane turned off the faucet and started washing the morning's dishes.

Gabby was in Vic's room, and Sophie colored at the coffee table in the living room. A curious quiet had gripped the house these past two days. As if they were all waiting for what they knew would come any day now.

Bert stepped into the kitchen, grabbed a clean glass, and poured water from the Brita pitcher on the counter. "'Bout to head out back. Garden needs weeding again. Feel free to join me if you like."

Lane propped a plate in the dish drainer. "I might stay in today. Keep Sophie company."

Bert nodded.

Lane thought he'd leave it at that and head outside, but the older man leaned against the counter and slowly sipped his water.

"Having you around's been good for Vic. I'm sorry about the circumstances that brought you here, but I'm glad to have you." Bert finished his water. His glassed eyes fixed on his granddaughter, who was just visible through the entryway into the living room. "Gav would have been glad to know you." He set his empty glass on the counter. "I'm sure Vic'll tell him all about you."

Lane stopped mid-scrub. The back of his throat ached as he nodded.

Bert's hand rested on Lane's shoulder. "I'm gonna miss her too." His voice was thick. "But I'm so glad 'goodbye' isn't forever."

As Bert left, Lane leaned over the sink, the faint *pop, pop* of soap bubbles filling the hard silence.

Wednesday, May 22nd

Stacey's text arrived after 8 p.m. Lane hadn't expected to hear from her at all, much less three weeks after she'd walked out of the Ellises' house with scarcely a word.

Started back to work last week.

He replied, Doing okay?

A long pause.

Three bouncing dots in the corner of the screen said she was typing. The dots disappeared. Ten seconds later, they were back, then gone again.

Finally, Stacey's reply popped up. I guess I just don't get why you did it. You were against this for so long. I mean seriously, these are the people who would sooner send guys like you and Stephen to Hell than look at you.

Not these people.

Stacey typed for a few seconds before her reply appeared. Well, kudos to you for finding the only Christians on earth who don't think that.

Even without hearing her voice, he could feel the sarcasm dripping from her words. *I don't want to fight about this*, he sent back.

Whatever. Her code for "drop the subject."

I'd love to talk about it with you sometime.

Pause.

Got a busy few weeks. Weekends are packed too.

How about after the first of the month?

She didn't reply.

Lane stared at the screen for several minutes, waiting. When nine o'clock rolled around, he set the phone on the bedside table and headed for the shower.

Half an hour later, he climbed into bed, more than ready for sleep.

His phone buzzed. He'd forgotten to turn on "Do Not Disturb." If he didn't do it now, he'd be listening to notification sounds all night. He reached for the phone.

On the screen sat a text from Stacey. Only one word: *Maybe.*

All right, he sent back. Talk later.

137

102 Maple Leaf Lane

Thursday, May 23rd

Lane stepped into Vic's room.

Gabby had done her best to keep everything pleasant, with an open window, clean sheets, and room spray, but the scent of coming death lingered.

He hung back. Watching Vic slowly edge toward death, especially this past week, was crushing. Frequent memories of Stephen's passing bombarded him. But with Vic, it was different. Grief still brought heaviness, but it wasn't all-consuming. "You wanted to see me?"

Vic gave him a weak nod and pointed to the chair beside her bed. "I'm sorry to leave you—just starting your journey with God." She held out an open hand.

Lane took it.

These past four days, she'd lost what little vibrance she'd had left. Her skin was pale, her fingers thin, cold. Life might slip from her at any moment.

He forced a smile. "Don't apologize." It was harder to talk with her than he'd expected. Grief stopped his throat as he recalled moments spent with her over the past few months.

Had so little time passed since that first audition? In those few months, she'd shown him unimaginable truth.

"I wish I had more time to see you on your way," she said in a whisper. "But you'll have to go ahead without me."

Lane had told himself he wouldn't cry about this. It wasn't all sad. He would see her again someday, and she wouldn't be this hollow shell anymore. She'd be beautiful, whole, and standing with Jesus Himself when he met her again. And she would sing with more than the echo of a voice he'd heard at church. She would rival the angels.

"Lane…" Vic let go of his hand and touched his face. "It's all right. Really." Her smile lit her eyes. "I'm ready for this."

"I don't want you to go." His voice thickened, making speaking a feat he didn't dare attempt again.

Vic snagged a Kleenex and dried his face. "I know." Tears tracked her cheeks. "But that's not why I wanted to talk to you."

He didn't have the fortitude to ask.

"I decided his name." She laid her other hand atop her unborn son. "I wanted him to remember his dad, but I also wanted a name that would remind him how God persists and reaches people who think they're too far removed from Him." Vic took both of Lane's hands in hers. "He's going to be Dylan Lane Garrison. Gav's middle name was Dylan. It's Welsh. It means 'great tide.'"

"Like your song," he managed.

"So it is."

"I don't know what to say."

She squeezed his hand. "You don't have to say anything. But

Lane...if something happens to my parents, will you watch out for Sophie and Dylan?"

No one had ever asked this of him. None of his friends had kids. Even if they did, they weren't thinking about their eventual deaths. "You mean be their guardian until they're adults?"

"If they need you to be. And even if they don't, my parents are almost seventy. There will be things they can't help with. Would you be there when my kids need you?"

"I once said children wouldn't be part of my life, and you told me, 'You never know.'"

"Well, I wasn't wrong, was I?"

"No. You weren't. I'd be honored to watch out for them."

"That's good, because I already amended my will."

"You knew I'd say yes?"

"Snubbing a dying woman isn't your style."

Lane wanted to laugh, but he couldn't around the lump in his throat.

Saturday, May 25th

Another dream came, different from all the others.

Lane sat beneath a tree. Its towering boughs spread over him, covering a section of flower-rich meadow. Guarding him on all sides were low mountains and, in the distance, a woman climbed the slopes.

As if she sensed his gaze, she raised a hand to him before vanishing over the horizon.

An insistent knock woke Lane. He blinked hard and rubbed bleary eyes.

"It's time." Bert's voice. "Pastor Hendrick is meeting us at the hospital."

Lane swung out of bed, threw on clothes, and hurried to the living room.

It was still dark outside. The kitchen clock read 3:12.

Vic sat in a wheelchair, face so ashen he feared she was already gone, but she offered a wan smile as her father pushed her to the van and helped her inside before stowing the chair.

Sophie, very much awake, sat in her car seat beside Vic. "Mommy?" She took Vic's hand. "Are you going to be with Jesus?"

"Yes, sweetie, but first, we're going to meet your brother, Dylan."

Sophie seemed to contemplate this before she answered. "I know you wanna go see Jesus, and Daddy, and lots of other people, but...I don't want you to go right now."

Vic's eyes flooded with tears. "I know, but Jesus wants me to."

"Don't cry, Mommy. I understand."

This only made Vic cry more. "Thank you, sweetie."

As Lane climbed into the back, Vic's hand brushed his—a feeble attempt to get his attention. He sat and leaned forward.

Vic turned just enough to look at him sideways over the back of the bench, and he shifted further down the seat to make it easier for her.

"That day at the studio. When I first saw you." She smiled weakly. "I saw myself in you. I knew God wanted me to reach out to you. I'm so glad I did." Tears slipped down her pale cheeks. "Spend time with God. Learn who He is. Let Him guide you. He'll never leave you," she whispered. "He'll even walk through Death with you." The words seemed to take the last of her strength, and she said nothing else as her mother got into the passenger's seat, and her father started the van.

Jenkins Rawling Memorial Hospital

Three hours later, Lane sat on a couch in a maternity ward family room. Pastor Hendrick stood silently with Bert. Vic was still in recovery after her Cesarean.

Gabby offered Lane the sleeping newborn.

"I've never held a baby. I don't think this is a good—"

"You won't break him," Gabby said as she settled Dylan in Lane's arms.

The little boy carried no signs of the ordeal his mother had gone through to get him here.

Sophie sat on her knees beside Lane and rose high enough to see her brother. "He looks happy."

"Why are you whispering?" Lane said.

"Cuz I don't wanna wake him up. I'm his big sister, and I'm supposed to look out for him. Mommy told me so."

"I'm sure you'll do a fine job."

"We're glad you came," said Bert. "Vic considered you a good friend these past couple months."

"Yeah..." Lane kept his eyes on Dylan. "I thought the same of her."

His borrowed phone buzzed. A text.

He would get it later.

The door opened, and Dr. Gordon walked in. She took in the group before speaking, but by her stiff walk and the slow, deliberate way she opened and shut the door, Lane knew what she was going to say. "Vic left peacefully before she woke up from sedation."

The Ellises reached for the Kleenex box on the nearest table.

Sophie hugged Lane's arm and whispered, "Jesus, tell Mommy I love my new brother."

Lane held onto Dylan a little tighter.

138

Green Hill Memorial Gardens, Los Angeles
Tuesday, May 28ᵗʰ

Lane sang with the crowd at Vic's graveside. "Here Is Love."

This time, it meant something.

His father's funeral had been stiff and cold, Stephen's had been filled with unutterable despair, but this one was...hopeful. Though all mourned Vic's passing, this wasn't a true goodbye.

Pastor Hendrick had officiated both the funeral and graveside. The whole church was in attendance, along with most of *Evident*'s cast and crew, and a host of strangers.

He mingled with Vic's friends and acquaintances until he spied a bright yellow beret. "Jazzmin?"

"Lane!" The woman immediately hugged him. "Vic told me you became a brother. She was so excited when she called that night. Didn't even apologize for the hour, not that I minded." She grinned. "And call me Jazz."

"How're you doing?"

"Doc says I'm in remission. Feelin' better than I have in a long time. Brought my son today. He only met Vic a few times, but he loved her and Sophie." She pointed to a little boy in a suit and clip-on tie talking with Sophie. Vic's daughter looked sad, but not despondent. "My husband had to work, but he sends his prayers." Jazz found the Ellises standing nearby. "Good to see you. Hopefully we'll meet up again sometime." With one eye on her son, she crossed the crowd and gave Gabby a hug.

Lane slipped both hands into the pockets of a borrowed gray suit. He loosened his tie and stood alone as the attendees mingled. There was a reception at the church, but nobody seemed in a hurry to get there.

His borrowed phone buzzed.

Multiple unread emails.

Only weeks ago, he would have cursed when Kennedy Funeral Home popped up as one sender and St. Philip and various credit card companies as the others. He considered reading them later but decided it was better to get bad news over with.

Two sets of the same email, the first sent Saturday morning. The day Vic died. The next set arrived seconds ago.

When he opened the first email, from Kennedy, he did a double take.

A receipt. Paid in full.

Same with St. Philip. And the credit cards.

He hadn't paid, and Stacey couldn't even if she'd wanted to. Stephen's parents were out. The Ellises weren't aware of his bills, and none of his old friends would care enough to pay his debts.

He still wanted to find a way to repay what he'd stolen from Lester. With these monster payments gone...

"Harris." Jack Gibson sauntered up to Lane.

He stowed his phone.

"I wanted to apologize."

"You don't need to—"

"Yeah, I do. I should have known something was going on with Henderson. Both previous casts she was part of had issues with her drumming up fake relationships, not to mention a rash of unexplained burglaries. Mostly wealthy targets, though, not—" He stopped.

"Not guys like me?" Lane finished. "It's okay. I know I'm not in high demand."

Gibson chuckled. "You might be soon with all the effort Tina's taking right now to leverage the press explosion from all this."

"Sorry about *Evident*."

"Why? We got great footage. The scenes we didn't get to, we can shoot without much hassle. And consider yourself rehired, by the way. I never replaced you."

"But weren't you running over budget? All this extra time will cost you—"

"We had someone else provide the needed funds."

"Who?"

Gibson glanced at the closed casket. "Vic. She and Gavin didn't advertise it, but they were well off. With her outlandish sales from multiple bestselling books, Gavin's job, and solid investments, their net worth's into seven figures."

The emails.

Vic had paid his debts.

"I suppose I'll see you at the premiere in November, but before I go," he fished an envelope from his inside jacket pocket, "Vic wanted you to have this."

Lane accepted the envelope, but he waited until Gibson ambled away to open it. Inside was a folded piece of paper.

A property deed. To Vic's house.

A note tucked inside the deed was in her handwriting.

Dear Lane,

You'll protest, but you can't argue with a dead woman. Sophie doesn't need the house, and it's just going to sit there unused unless someone moves in. I know you'll take care of it, so I'm giving it to you. We transferred all of Sophie's things to Mom and Dad's, but there's still lots of my junk in there. Mom, Dad, and Sophie might want some of it, but feel free to do what you want with the rest. I'm sorry I'm not around anymore, but I'll see you again one day, and you can tell me all the crazy stories about my kids. Thank you for looking out for them.

With Gav and me gone, it's a relief to know they have someone besides my parents.

Being part of a kid's life can be terrifying, but God's with you. He always will be, and fear doesn't have a place in our hearts because of that. Remember Lazarus? After Jesus raised him from the dead, he knew there was nothing to fear, because if God could conquer death, He could give strength for anything in life.

So live, Lane. Live like Lazarus.

See you later,
Vic

Discussion Guide

The Matter of Spiritual Gifts

Different circles of Christianity have varying views on spiritual gifts, so to give clarity, I'm providing a brief look at my view on the subject and why I believe that view is vital to the discussion of homosexuality.

Scripture gives us three lists of gifts: Romans 12, Ephesians 4, and 1 Corinthians 12. The specific gifts I'm referring to here are the ones in Romans 12. I've seen multiple sources describe these seven gifts as "motivational," or "the reason behind what we do." Whichever of these seven motivational gifts God has given you lays the foundation for who you are and how you experience and respond to life.

Motivational Spiritual Gifts: (Def) – inborn characteristics God has woven into the fabric of every person.

The list of motivational spiritual gifts:

1. Prophecy: A concern for truth
2. Ministry/Serving: A concern for physical needs
3. Teaching: A concern for education
4. Exhortation: A concern for spiritual needs
5. Giving: A concern for providing
6. Ruling: A concern for order
7. Mercy: A concern for emotional needs

Source: Romans 11:33–12:8 (KJV) (<u>emphasis mine</u>)

O the depth of the riches both of the wisdom and knowledge of God! how unsearchable are his judgments, and his ways past finding out! For who hath known the mind of the Lord? or who hath been his counsellor? Or who hath first given to him, and it shall be recompensed unto him again? For of him, and through him, and to him, are all things: to whom be glory for ever. Amen. I beseech you therefore, brethren, by the mercies of God, that ye present your bodies a living sacrifice, holy, acceptable unto God, which is your reasonable service. And be not conformed to this world: but be ye transformed by the renewing of your mind, that ye may prove what is that good, and acceptable, and perfect, will of God. For I say, through the grace given unto me, to every man that is among you, not to think of himself more highly than he ought to think; but to think soberly, according as God hath dealt to every man the measure of faith. For as we have many members in one body, and all members have not the same office: So we, being many, are one body in Christ, and every one members one of another. Having then gifts differing according to the grace that is given to us, whether <u>prophecy</u>, let us prophesy according to the proportion of faith; Or <u>ministry</u>, let us wait on our ministering: or he that <u>teacheth</u>, on teaching; Or he that <u>exhorteth</u>, on exhortation: he that <u>giveth</u>, let him do it with simplicity; he that <u>ruleth</u>, with diligence; he that sheweth <u>mercy</u>, with cheerfulness.

A few years after I wrote the first draft of *With Mercy's Eyes,* my pastor did an in-depth study of spiritual gifts. At the time, I had no idea what mine was or how to use it. Over the next year or two, my pastor went through spiritual gifts three times, and I came to terms with the gift(s) God had given me. Mercy (tempered a bit by Ruling). One result of this combination is that I notice emotion-related patterns and micro-cues (little things people do/say when they experience specific emotions). Something as small as the way someone pronounces certain words can tell me how they're feeling or what they might be thinking in that moment. It allows me to respond to that person in a way that can relieve emotional distress, bolster feelings of happiness, or otherwise undergird them emotionally.

As I did research for this book, I got to read five autobiographical accounts from people who lived in homosexuality, became Christians, and left their previous lives. As I read the first two books, a pattern emerged. Like me, the people I was reading about evidenced key characteristics inherent to the gift of Mercy, and, like me, they had been tempted to go down the path of same-sex attraction. Although they chose to act on their temptation and I didn't, it was still a curious similarity. That was when I started to wonder if there was a correlation between a tendency toward same-sex attraction and the gift of Mercy. When I finished the third book, I was almost 100 percent certain there was a connection. By the time I finished book four and then book five, I was sure of it.

The thing about spiritual gifts is, before salvation, we have no reason to use them for anyone except ourselves. If we care about something or someone, they may benefit from our gift(s), but we will naturally be prone to using them selfishly. When sin perverts our motivational gifts and pushes us toward something God forbids, we have no qualms about doing what we want instead of what God wants.

Our sin nature takes our God-given motivational gifts and twists them into something God never intended. For someone with the gift of Giving, that might be evidenced by miserly behavior (e.g., not paying employees or refusing to provide for their family). For someone like me, who has the gift of Mercy, that might mean forming unbiblical relationships, including sexual relationships outside of a biblical marriage (e.g., homosexuality).

After salvation, God calls us to use our gifts not for ourselves, but for others. Specifically for other Christians, but also for non-Christians. If we've misused our spiritual gifts, there are consequences, and the life we might have had may no longer be possible. But God is good. He "knows our frame" (Psalm 103:14 NKJV), our frailty, and He uses us despite ourselves.

When we know our spiritual gift(s) and take time to learn how to use it/them on purpose, it's an incredible blessing and encouragement, not only to us, but to the people God has for us to help.

This book shows us two people who have the gift of Mercy. Both fell into the trap of forming unbiblical sexual relationships, but when they stopped defining themselves by their sin and became more concerned with what God asked of them than how they felt, their thoughts and actions changed. God redeemed them for Himself and gave them new life.

Practical Interaction Tips & Information

I cannot and do not claim to have all the answers when it comes to interacting with people who are same-sex attracted or living homosexual or other LGBTQ lifestyles, but here are a few principles and Scriptures I've found helpful and comforting.

What God Says:

1. The foundational problem with sexual sin of all kinds is that it presents a perverted image of God. Ephesians 5:31–32 tells us the marriage covenant represents Christ's relationship with the Church. When we try to change the illustration God personally gave us, we declare that we know better than our omniscient God, and that's a dangerous place to be.

2. God calls some people to singleness and some to marriage. We see this in 1 Corinthians 7:7. If someone is called to singleness and refuses that calling, it's just as damaging as someone called to marriage refusing to marry.

3. The Bible tells us that, with God's help, we can escape sexual sin. 1 Corinthians 6:9–11 says there were Christians in the Corinthian church who engaged in (among other things) sexual sin. But when they became Christians, they put away that sin and chose to do what God asked of them.

4. The Bible says in 1 Corinthians 10:13 that God will not allow us to be tempted without making a way for us to escape that temptation. Experiencing SSA thoughts and feelings is not a sin. Choosing to entertain those thoughts and feelings or act on them is. Escaping temptation may not be easy, but it will always be possible with God's help.

*Personal note: When we go through temptation, if we focus on the all-consuming thoughts, sensations, and urges assaulting us, we will fall. But when we choose to fix our eyes on God and His peace and blessing, He will help us through those moments. And we will find our relationship with Him is all the stronger because we endured.

What We Can Do:

1. View others as valuable.

People aren't less valuable to God because of the types of sin they've committed. Otherwise, God would have given us a list of sins Christ's blood doesn't cover, and He most certainly didn't do that. Every soul is unfathomably valuable in the sight of God, and when we interact with people living LGBTQ lifestyles, it's vital we remember that.

We shouldn't discriminate whom we share the gospel with based on their stated sexual orientation. Those in homosexual relationships are just as precious to God as those in heterosexual relationships. We may be tempted to shy away from interactions with anyone living in unbiblical sexual relationships, but we can't give in to that temptation.

2. Exercise God's love and compassion.

1 John 4:10 (KJV) says, "Herein is love, not that we loved God, but that he loved us, and sent his Son to be the propitiation for our sins." God extended holy, sacrificial love to people who didn't love Him.

Many people living unbiblical sexual lifestyles don't have a good history with Christians and Christianity. That history may negatively influence how they treat you, and it may not. Whatever happens, we are called to show others God's truth and character.

If a non-Christian chooses to confide in us that they're experiencing same-sex attraction, that is an amazing show of trust. Being present for that person is a way we can show that we care about them. We can ask questions, take time to learn more about them and their situation, and give God's truth as God leads. Salvation and a relationship with God are the priority. When someone accepts Christ as Saviour and makes God their priority, accepting what God says about their sexuality will be a natural consequence.

*Personal note: If a fellow Christian confides experiencing same-sex attraction, that is also an incredible demonstration of trust. Encouraging and building up fellow Christians who experience SSA is a privilege. Just as some people are more prone to addiction, some are more prone to experience SSA than others. Through study and personal experience, I'm inclined to believe this tendency is due to our sin nature twisting God-given gifts and talents. Chances are, your fellow Christian already knows acting on SSA is sin, so berating them is not helpful. Learning more about them and their situation, giving them an accountability structure, and encouraging them in God's word is.

3. Speak timely truth.

Interacting with people living in same-sex relationships can be incredibly hard, especially for those who have never experienced same-sex attraction.

Those who have the deep need to speak truth may be tempted to confront sin in ways that hurt rather than help the people they're trying to win to Christ. Christians who speak untimely truth rarely do so intentionally.

Those who are disposed toward considering someone's feelings may be tempted to withhold truth when they ought to speak out. If God wants us to speak and we remain silent, we're just as wrong as people who speak when they ought to remain silent. Actually, we bear even more blame, because we knew what we were supposed to do, and we didn't do it.

Knowing when to speak truth means listening to God. Listening to God necessitates recognizing God's leading. Recognizing God's leading comes from spending time with God. If we spend time with God and intentionally and consistently seek His leading, He will help us navigate even the most challenging interactions with grace and strength.

Our identity is in Christ, not our sexual orientation. Choosing to define ourselves by our sin is rebellion against God. But God doesn't withhold salvation from rebels.

If someone you know is living in an unbiblical relationship, bringing up their sin in every conversation won't help. That constant prodding of an open wound will only drive them away—both from you and from God. When God prompts you to speak, do it. When He impresses you to listen, listen.

Discussion Questions

Chapters 1–9

1. How did you respond to Lane losing his husband? What did you think about his relationship? Did those thoughts influence your response to his loss? How would you respond to someone who had just lost a spouse?

2. What did you think about Vic's initial interactions with Lane? Do you think she knows about his sexual orientation? Why or why not? Would knowing a stranger's sexual orientation change how you treat them?

3. What do you think about Stacey's and Lane's views about life in Chapter 3? Do you agree that everyone needs to be happy? Why or why not?

4. How did you respond to Lane's reluctance to kiss Monica? How would you respond if you were in his place? Do you think Lane's sexual orientation played a part in his response? Why or why not?

5. How was Leigh's relationship with Trev different from Lane's relationship with Stephen? Was either relationship biblical? Why or why not?

6. How did you respond to the events of Chapter 7? Would you have kept the truth from your family?

7. What did you think of Leigh's reaction when she found out she was pregnant? What would you have done in her situation? Why?

Chapters 10–18

1. How does Lane show love to Stacey? How does she respond to his efforts on her behalf?

2. Why do you think Lane responds the way he does to the talk show and magazines? How would you respond if you were in his place?

3. What did you think about Leigh's decision regarding her pregnancy? What challenges might she face now that she's made that decision?

4. What was your first impression of Lester? How did his profession and sexual orientation influence your thoughts about him?

5. How did you respond to Leigh's relationship with Nakasha? How is it different from her relationship with Trev? What does the Bible say about these relationships?

Chapters 19–34

1. What do you think of Gibson's response to the situation with Lane and Monica? Would you have handled it differently? Why or why not?

2. Why do you think Monica told Lane about his mother's comment on social media? How did you respond when Lane found the link on his mother's social media page? What did his response to the funeral reveal about his previous interactions with Christians? What practical steps can we, as Christians, take to be genuine to those around us?

3. What does Vic's behavior tell us about her book, *Hahnen'En*? Do you think Lane's curiosity will prompt him to read Vic's book? What did you think about Vic's comment to her mother at the zoo?

4. What does Monica's behavior say about her as a person? Why do you think people believe her?

5. How did you respond to Leigh's sudden loss? Did her sexual orientation and living situation factor into your response? Why or why not?

6. Going forward, how do you think Lane will handle so many significant losses in his life? How has he handled his losses so far?

7. How does Leigh handle loss? How is her response different from Lane's? How are their responses similar? How did you respond to Lane's and Leigh's situations?

Chapters 35–45

1. How does Lester show love to Lane? How does Lane respond to Lester's kindness? Would you have helped Lane? Why or why not?

2. How do Leigh's parents show love to her? Do you think Leigh appreciates her parents' actions? Why or why not?

3. How does Lane respond when he learns about Vic's loss? Is his response to her loss different than Vic's response to his loss? Why or why not?

4. What does Leigh's anger say about her state of mind? Do you think time away from home will help? Why or why not?

5. Why do you think Lane is becoming more comfortable around Vic? What do Vic's words and actions say about how she views Lane as a person?

Chapters 46–54

1. How do you think Leigh's childhood was different from or similar to Lane's? Why?

2. How does Sophie show love to Lane? What do her actions say about how she views Lane as a person? How does Sophie reflect God's heart toward those in difficult situations?

3. How does Lane respond to losing yet another piece of his life?

4. How does God use Leigh's circumstances to direct her to Himself?

5. What do you think about Lane's decision in Chapter 51? What led to that decision? How else could he have handled his situation? How will his decision affect his relationship with Lester?

6. Why do you think Monica refuses to leave Lane alone? How are her words and actions toward Lane different from Vic's words and actions toward him? Why?

Chapters 55–62

1. Why does Leigh start writing a new story? How do you think her experiences and thoughts will influence this new story?

2. How did you respond to what Lane did in Chapter 56? Do you think he was justified? Why or why not? How would you have responded if you were in his place? What do you think about Gibson's response to the situation?

3. How much has Lane lost? How have those losses influenced his thoughts and behavior?

Chapters 63–71

1. Why is Lane content to remain anonymous while he's at the hospital? What do you think has contributed to this thought process? How does his mother's message influence his thoughts and actions?

2. What thoughts and emotions do Lester's situation bring up for Lane? Why?

3. How does Lane respond to the panhandler? Why? How does the first call about Lester influence Lane's actions?

4. How does the scene Leigh writes mirror her life?

5. How does the second call about Lester influence Lane's thoughts and actions? What other factors have contributed to bringing Lane to this point? Would you help Lane? Why or why not? If you would, how? What do Vic's actions in this situation tell us about her as a person?

6. Why does Leigh give her main character a name? How do you think this will influence her as she continues writing her new story?

Chapters 72–81

1. How did you respond to Vic showing Lane her scars? How do you think this will influence Lane's future interactions with her? How would you help someone who was in Lane's place?

2. How does God show Lane mercy in Chapters 74–79? What does this tell us about how God views Lane?

3. Why is Lane surprised to learn about Vic's past? How has God used difficulties in your life to change you?

4. In Chapter 81, how does God use Leigh's writing to point her to Himself? Has God ever used a story to help you better understand something?

5. Why do you think Leigh is reluctant to write this scene?

Chapters 82–93

1. What do Monica's actions say about her priorities? How are her priorities different than Vic's?

2. Why does Lane remain distant during the funeral? What does his behavior before, during, and after the funeral tell us about his state of mind?

3. How does Vic respond to Lane? What does her response reveal about her view of Lane? How would you have responded if someone in Lane's state called you for help? What does the Bible say about Christians helping those in need?

4. How does God work in Leigh's life in Chapters 90 & 93? In what ways has God directed Leigh to this point in her life?

5. In what ways are Leigh's and Lane's lives alike? How are they different?

Chapters 94–101

1. How do the Ellises respond to Vic bringing Lane home? What do you think contributes to this response?

2. In Chapter 95, how did you respond to what Lane discovers about Vic? Why? Does it change the way you think about her? Why or why not?

3. How do Lane's interactions with Vic change after he makes his discovery? How do his thoughts about God change? Why? How does his conversation with Sophie influence him?

4. What do Bert's interactions with Lane tell us about his beliefs and priorities? How might Vic's past have prepared Bert for helping Lane?

5. Why do you think Lane responds the way he does to finding the note in Vic's Bible? How is Vic's relationship with her parents different from Lane's relationship with his parents? How is it similar?

6. How does Lane view God? What are some things that have contributed to that view?

7. Why do you think Lane responds the way he does to Sophie bringing him the pine cone? What does his response tell us about his thoughts and beliefs?

8. Do you think Vic's pawnshop find is a good thing? How might it help or hurt Lane?

Chapters 102–110

1. How did you respond to Leigh's choice in Chapter 102? How do you think this will affect her life going forward?

2. What do Lane's memories tell us about how he views church? How do his memories differ from what he experiences at the Ellises' church?

3. Why do you think Kyle took time to talk with Lane? What do Kyle's words and actions tell us about him?

4. How does God get Lane's attention? What has God used in your life to turn your thoughts to Him?

Chapters 111–118

1. How has God used Lane's circumstances to bring him to this point? Where do you think he would be if he'd never met Vic?

2. What does the Bible say about spiritual gifts? What have you been taught about spiritual gifts? Do you know your spiritual gift? Did you know spiritual gifts are part of our inherent makeup and are ingrained in us from conception? Does this change the way you think about spiritual gifts?

3. Do you agree with Pastor Hendrick's explanation in Chapter 114? Why or why not? How is it different from other explanations of same-sex attraction (SSA) you've heard/read?

4. How does this explanation of same-sex attraction influence your view of Christians who struggle with SSA or have given in to temptation regarding SSA? Does it change how you think about non-Christians living an LGBTQ lifestyle?

5. Why do you think Vic hasn't brought up the subject of Lane's sexual orientation until now? How has Lane's relationship with Vic changed since he first met her? How does Lane respond to what Vic says about SSA and sexual orientation?

Chapters 119–130

1. How does Lane respond to Jazz? How are Jazz and Vic alike? How are they different?

2. Why do you think Lane struggles with what he knows about Vic?

3. Why do you think Lane is all right with working for Kyle? How did their previous interactions contribute to that?

4. How does Lane respond to Monica's call? What does this call tell us about Monica's values and beliefs? What does it tell us about Lane's state of mind concerning Monica?

5. How does God intervene during Lane's interactions with Monica? In what quiet ways has God been working on Lane's behalf all along? What does this series of events tell us about how God views Lane?

6. What do the events of Chapters 123–127 tell us about how Lane views Stacey? How does Stacey view Lane? Has their relationship changed since Stacey moved? Why or why not?

7. What do Vic's actions in Chapters 127 & 128 say about how she views Lane? What do Sophie's actions say about how she views Lane? How do both Vic and Sophie show God's love to Lane?

8. How do you think Lane's decision will affect his life going forward? Why? How do Lane's thoughts in Chapter 129 reflect his beliefs and values?

9. What do you think of Leigh's decision in Chapter 130? How does this decision reflect who she is and how she views God?

Chapters 131–137

1. Why do you think Stacey responds to Lane the way she does? How will her response affect their relationship?

2. Why do you think Lane was initially hesitant to finish reading Vic's novel? How has Vic's book influenced Lane? How did it influence Vic?

3. How does Alisha respond to Lane's story? Why?

4. What does Lane's conversation with the police tell us about his state of mind?

5. How is Leigh's experience with church different from or similar to Lane's?

6. How has Lane's relationship with Vic changed since their conversation at the pawnshop? How has God used Vic and Lane in each other's lives? How has Lane's relationship with Bert and Gabby changed since Lane came to live with them?

7. What does Gibson's conversation with Lane tell us about who he is as a person?

8. What do Vic's words to Lane say about how she views life and eternity?

Print-friendly discussion questions and reader resources can

be found at: www.withmercyseyes.com

Acknowledgements

Through every step of the publication process for this book, God's hand has been undeniably present. Despite all my efforts to either put it off or to force it onto the scene too early, He brought this book to be in His time. Every milestone is stamped with His purposeful presence. From editing dates to the cover reveal and beyond, all of it is indelibly marked by my personal, loving Saviour, Jesus Christ. No one is beyond His reach, and nothing is too hard for Him.

To my email team: you supported this book in prayer for nearly sixteen months before publication day. I got to have so many conversations with you, both about this book and the topics it addresses. Thank you for reading my emails and keeping both me and this story in prayer.

To my editors: Angela, Brianna, Emma, and Michaela, God brought your names to mind well before I contacted any of you, and His choices are always perfect.

To my betas: M, B, and Y. M, I know that, due to things beyond your control, you never got the chance to read this book in its early form, but the fact that you were willing to meant everything to me. B & Y, your incredible insight, hard-hitting questions, and thorough feedback are one of the reasons this book became what it is. God brought your names to mind specifically some time before the beta reading phase began, and His way is always best.

To my formatter: Elizabeth, yours was another name God brought to mind long before I booked you. Thank you for all the amazing work you've done to make the interior of this book as wonderful as it is.

To my early readers: you are a special breed of champion, one I am constantly grateful for.

To my family, who saw this book years before anyone else did: thank you for supporting it and me throughout the entire process.

To my pastor: God used you to help me understand this book in ways I otherwise never would have.

To the crew at MiBlart: thank you for an incredible cover.

And to you, the reader: thank you for spending your time in this book. The biggest prayer I and my publishing team had for *With Mercy's Eyes* was that God would bring it to the people who need it. And that prayer is now answered in you.

About The Author

D. T. Powell has loved stories since before she can remember, and it was one of those stories that God used to change her life and prompt her to start writing. In addition to writing book reviews for a magazine as well as original contemporary and speculative fiction, she has actively contributed to the fanfiction community since 2013. Her original work has been published by Writers Digest, Clean Fiction Magazine, Twenty Hills Publishing, The Order of the Pen Press, Wolrdsmyths, and Cadence Writing. She enjoys reading, playing pickleball, and playing an occasional video game. You can find her online as dtill359.

Her favorite verse is Psalm 126:5, "They that sow in tears shall reap in joy."

You can sign up for D.T.'s newsletter via her website: www.dtpowellwrites.com. Join her mailing list for access to two subscriber exclusive short stories, a nonfiction essay, and several social media themed author resources. She expands her Newsletter Exclusives archive every year.

Follow D. T. on Instagram @dtill359, Facebook @D. T. Powell, Author, Goodreads @D. T. Powell, and Amazon.com.

Made in the USA
Middletown, DE
18 April 2025

74330318R00333